Nexus

Hanna Ross

Published by Hanna Ross, 2024.

This is a work of fiction. Similarities to real people, places, or events are entirely coincidental.

NEXUS

First edition. November 7, 2024.

Copyright © 2024 Hanna Ross.

ISBN: 979-8227900562

Written by Hanna Ross.

Chapter 1: Collision of Fate

The pungent aroma of sizzling street food mingled with the distant echoes of laughter and shouting, creating a symphony that was uniquely Neo Crescent. I pushed through the throngs of people, my senses heightened in this electric atmosphere. The low hum of synth beats vibrated through the air, underscoring the vibrant chaos around me. Every corner was a canvas splashed with color and life, yet beneath this vibrant façade lay an undercurrent of danger, a hidden darkness that often left a bitter taste in my mouth.

As I rounded a corner, a deafening crash pierced through the night, causing me to stumble. Instinctively, I turned, heart racing, to find a sleek, black vehicle crumpled against a lamppost, shards of glass sparkling like shattered stars against the asphalt. The driver stumbled out, a figure I recognized immediately—Darian Cross, the enigmatic heir to a powerful tech empire, with a reputation as dangerous as the streets I traversed.

His eyes locked onto mine, a piercing blue that seemed to see through the bustling chaos around us. There was an unspoken understanding in that moment, a collision of our fates that sent a jolt through the air. I hadn't expected to see him here, of all places, but then again, Neo Crescent had a way of pulling people together in the most unpredictable ways.

"Need a hand?" I called out, feigning nonchalance, though the pulse of adrenaline surged beneath my skin. My heart thudded not just from the shock of the crash but from the undeniable magnetism that seemed to draw me to him. He was trouble wrapped in charisma, a tempest that promised both chaos and excitement.

Darian flashed a grin, one that could easily charm the hardest of hearts. "You're just in time to rescue me from a terrible fate," he quipped, brushing off his coat as if the whole ordeal were merely an inconvenience. I couldn't help but roll my eyes, a smirk breaking through my initial concern.

"Right, because getting hit by a car is the highlight of your evening," I shot back, stepping closer to inspect the damage. The car's front end was a mangled mess, but the real wreckage was the palpable tension hanging between us, a tightrope walk that felt both exhilarating and dangerous.

"What's your plan now, Cross? Call for backup or simply hope no one notices?" I asked, raising an eyebrow as I surveyed the scene. There was something undeniably magnetic about him, and I hated that it pulled me in against my better judgment.

"Depends. Are you volunteering to be my accomplice?" he replied, his tone playful yet edged with sincerity. The world around us faded into a blur, and for a moment, I was acutely aware of just how close we stood, the warmth radiating from his body nearly enveloping me in a cocoon of reckless thrill.

"Only if it involves less vehicular mayhem," I retorted, stepping back slightly, trying to regain some composure. But the banter came easily, like an old dance, and I could see the glint of challenge in his eyes.

"Can't promise anything," he replied, a hint of mischief in his voice. "But I'm not the only one causing chaos tonight. You were practically a magnet for trouble before I even made my grand entrance."

I shot him a glare, though I felt the corners of my lips twitching upward. "Let's not pretend you're not just as much of a magnet. It's not every day you end up in a heap of wreckage on a Tuesday night."

"Touché," he conceded, his gaze flickering momentarily to the distant glow of emergency lights weaving through the crowd. "But the question remains—are you in or out?"

The invitation hung in the air, and I weighed my options. My instincts screamed at me to walk away, to distance myself from the tangled web that was Darian Cross, but curiosity gnawed at me, and beneath it all was a thrill I couldn't deny. The city was alive with possibilities, and what better way to explore them than with the one person who made my heart race for reasons both exhilarating and maddening?

"Fine," I declared, steeling myself. "But I'm not responsible for any more crashes." The words came out more boldly than I felt, and I could see a spark of surprise in his eyes.

With that, I felt an unorthodox alliance form between us, a partnership destined to ignite the night with chaos and adventure. We turned from the wreckage, leaving the scattered remnants of the crash behind us. The streets pulsated with energy, the sounds of laughter and music inviting us deeper into the heart of Neo Crescent.

As we walked side by side, I stole glances at him, trying to decipher the layers beneath his charming facade. Was he merely a thrill-seeker or something much more complicated? The flicker of uncertainty danced in my mind, but I found myself drawn to him, intrigued by the enigma he embodied.

The nightlife of Neo Crescent unfolded around us, bright and alluring, filled with secrets and laughter. But I knew one thing for certain: this night would mark the beginning of something entirely unexpected, a twist in our destinies that neither of us could foresee. With every step, I felt the electric charge of fate wrapping around us, a collision that promised to unravel the very fabric of our lives.

We slipped into a nearby alley, a narrow passageway illuminated by the flickering glow of neon signs. The air was thick with the mingled scents of street food—spicy skewers and sweet pastries—and the distant sound of laughter echoed like a siren call, drawing us deeper into the heart of Neo Crescent. Darian led the way, his confidence palpable, as if he thrived in the murky depths of this city while I floundered, caught between awe and apprehension.

"Where are we headed?" I asked, the thrill of our spontaneous escape washing over me, yet tinged with a hint of concern. The way Darian moved, with a purposeful grace, made me acutely aware of how out of place I felt. My heart raced, not just from the prospect of adventure but from the reality of walking beside him, the man whose reputation had preceded him like an urban legend.

"Just a little place I know," he replied, glancing back with a sly smile. "Trust me, you'll love it."

"I don't know if I can trust you," I shot back, feigning seriousness but unable to hide my amusement. "After all, you just wrecked your car. What other brilliant decisions are you capable of?"

He chuckled, the sound rich and warm, reverberating through the alley. "Oh, you have no idea. I'm a veritable fountain of questionable choices. But if you want to keep your heart rate up, you'll stick around."

I matched his stride, trying to suppress the fluttering in my stomach. We turned another corner, and the alley opened up into a small courtyard, vibrant with life. A hidden gem tucked away from the bustling streets, it was lined with colorful murals that danced across brick walls, each telling a story of love, loss, and rebellion. The soft glow of fairy lights hung above, casting a warm, inviting ambiance that was almost intoxicating.

In the center stood a bar, its wooden counter polished to a shine, and the air filled with the sound of clinking glasses and cheerful conversations. It was the kind of place that promised anonymity amid a crowd, a sanctuary where one could shed the weight of the world, if only for a night.

"Welcome to The Lantern," Darian proclaimed with a flourish, his eyes sparkling with mischief. "Best cocktails in the city, and the only place where the bartender knows your name—even if you don't."

"Do you come here often?" I asked, unable to resist a playful tone as we approached the bar.

"Only when I need a reminder that life doesn't always require a plan." His expression softened for a moment, a flicker of something deeper lurking beneath his charming exterior.

We settled onto barstools, and I couldn't help but admire how effortlessly he slipped into conversation with the bartender, a cheerful woman with bright pink hair and tattoos that snaked up her arms. He ordered us both a drink, something fruity and colorful, a concoction that promised to be as reckless as our evening had begun.

"So, what's the story here?" I gestured around the lively courtyard, taking in the laughter and the chatter, the ease with which people seemed to connect in this little enclave. "You seem to know everyone."

"Maybe I just have a face that inspires trust," he joked, raising an eyebrow. "Or maybe it's the money. Either way, it's nice to be in a place where I'm not just Darian Cross, the corporate shark."

"Ah, yes, the feared corporate shark," I teased, leaning in conspiratorially. "What do you do when you're not crashing cars or charming bartenders?"

He smirked, a playful glint in his eye. "I save the world, one cocktail at a time. Or at least try to keep my sanity intact in a city like this."

"I can relate to that," I replied, savoring the moment, the camaraderie that had sprung up between us. "But I'm more of a daydreamer than a corporate savior. I wander through the chaos and hope I don't get swept away."

"Daydreaming is a dangerous hobby," he said, his tone shifting slightly. "But it can lead to unexpected adventures, like this one."

Our drinks arrived, bright and cheerful, topped with little umbrellas that seemed almost absurd in their cuteness. I took a sip, the sweet and tangy flavors exploding on my palate, and looked at him, genuinely curious. "So, what's the real reason you crashed your car?"

Darian hesitated, his smile fading just slightly. "Let's just say my night had already been complicated before I met you. But I'm not one to dwell on the past. It's all about the now."

"Complicated how?" I pressed, unable to resist peeling back the layers that surrounded him.

"Let's just say there are things in my life that are less glamorous than they appear," he said, his tone casual but his eyes revealing an intensity that suggested deeper waters.

"Welcome to my life," I replied, finding a sense of kinship in his admission. "Every day feels like a balancing act between dreams and reality, and I never quite know which side I'll land on."

As we spoke, I felt the energy around us shift. The noise of the bar faded into the background, the vibrant colors of the courtyard blurring into a soft wash of light. In that moment, it was just us—a young woman and a man with an enigmatic past, finding solace in shared experiences and the promise of something new.

But then, from the edge of the courtyard, I caught sight of a figure watching us intently, their presence chilling my blood. A shiver crept down my spine as I turned away, trying to shake off the sudden wave of unease. Who were they, and what did they want? In a city like Neo Crescent, nothing was ever quite as it seemed, and the shadows had a way of creeping closer when you least expected it.

"Hey, are you okay?" Darian's voice cut through the fog of my thoughts, pulling me back to him. The concern in his gaze sent another thrill through me, one that both comforted and terrified me.

"Yeah, just thought I saw someone I knew," I replied, my voice steady despite the unease curling in my stomach. "But I must have been mistaken."

"Want to get out of here?" he suggested, a hint of urgency in his tone. "I'm not ready to deal with complications, and I have a feeling this place might be about to get a lot more crowded."

The unspoken words hung between us, the promise of an adventure flickering like the lights above. I nodded, a newfound resolve filling me. Whatever awaited us in the shadows could wait just a little longer. Tonight was ours to seize, and I intended to embrace every chaotic moment.

We slipped out of the courtyard, leaving behind the fading laughter and shimmering lights, the warmth of The Lantern fading into the chill of the night. The streets felt alive, the pulse of Neo Crescent echoing in our footsteps. As we walked, I tried to shake off the lingering unease from the figure I'd spotted earlier, reminding myself that shadows were just shadows in a city that thrived on secrets and stories.

"Where to now, fearless leader?" I asked, trying to keep the atmosphere light despite the thrill of uncertainty swirling in my gut.

Darian smirked, his expression that of a man relishing the chaos of the night. "There's a rooftop I like to visit. It has the best view of the skyline and absolutely zero distractions." He winked, a playful glint in his eyes. "Plus, we can get away from any lurking figures you might be worried about."

"Is that your way of saying you don't want to deal with my past?" I shot back, a teasing edge to my tone. "Because let me tell you, I'm pretty sure I'm the one with the chaotic baggage here."

"Everyone's got their baggage. It's how we carry it that matters," he replied, his voice smooth yet tinged with something deeper, a sincerity that made me pause.

The city unfolded before us as we navigated through the dimly lit streets, the neon signs flickering above like fireflies caught in a dance. I marveled at how Darian seemed to fit right into the night, moving through the maze with an effortless grace that made me feel both excited and slightly envious.

We reached a narrow staircase tucked away between two buildings, barely noticeable to the untrained eye. Darian glanced back at me, a hint of mischief in his smile. "Up for a little adventure?"

"Always," I said, trying to match his bravado even as my heart raced with the thrill of the climb. The stairs creaked under our weight, and I couldn't help but think of how many lives had passed through this hidden passage, each with their own secrets and stories.

When we finally emerged onto the rooftop, the city sprawled out before us, a canvas of lights and shadows. The view was breathtaking—Neo Crescent glittered like a jewel against the inky sky, the skyline punctuated by towering buildings that seemed to touch the stars. I felt a sense of exhilaration wash over me, the height adding a layer of freedom I hadn't expected.

"See? No distractions," Darian said, leaning against the ledge, his gaze fixed on the horizon. "Just us and the city."

I joined him, leaning on the railing as the cool breeze tousled my hair. "This is amazing," I breathed, taking in the sheer beauty of it all. "It's like we're on top of the world."

"Better than the chaos below, right?" He turned to me, and for a moment, the world around us faded into a soft blur, his intense gaze pulling me in. "Sometimes you need to escape to see things clearly."

"I can't argue with that," I replied, feeling the weight of the night's events slip away, replaced by an exhilarating sense of possibility. "But are you sure you're not just trying to escape your own chaos?"

"Touché," he said, laughter bubbling in his throat. "But isn't that what makes us human? Running from our own disasters?"

I chuckled, feeling the connection between us strengthen, an invisible thread weaving our fates tighter. "If running from chaos is human, then I'm practically a marathon runner."

"Then let's keep running," he said, a spark igniting in his eyes as he straightened up, ready for whatever lay ahead.

We stood in comfortable silence for a moment, taking in the vastness of the city below us, a million stories unfolding in the darkness. I felt a sense of calm wash over me, yet the nagging feeling from earlier crept back in, something in the pit of my stomach warning me that the night wasn't finished with us yet.

"Hey," I said, breaking the silence as I turned to him. "What's really going on with you? I mean, aside from the whole car crash debacle. There's more to you than this carefree façade."

He hesitated, a flicker of vulnerability crossing his features before he masked it with a playful smirk. "You really want to dig into my emotional baggage? I thought we were having a good time."

"Come on, you can't tease me with that and then not give me something," I prodded, nudging him lightly with my shoulder. "I promise I won't tell anyone. Just two friends on a rooftop."

"Friends?" He echoed, his voice teasing yet serious, and I felt the shift between us, a sudden tension hanging in the air.

"Isn't that what we are?" I shot back, but I could feel the heat creeping up my cheeks as the weight of the word settled between us.

"Maybe," he replied, a sly grin on his lips that made my heart race. "But friends don't usually share rooftops at midnight."

"Okay, fair point," I conceded, looking away to hide my embarrassment. The tension was palpable, the air thick with unspoken words as we stood there, two souls caught in a moment of uncertainty.

Just then, a noise shattered the tranquility of the night—a sudden crash followed by a guttural shout echoed from below. My heart dropped, instinctively pulling me back to reality.

"What was that?" I gasped, scanning the street below, my senses heightened.

Darian's expression shifted, his playful demeanor replaced by a sharp focus. "We should check it out," he said, his voice steady but with an edge of urgency that sent adrenaline racing through my veins.

I nodded, feeling the thrill of danger spike within me. We rushed to the edge of the rooftop, peering down at the scene unfolding below.

A group of shadowy figures was gathered around a car that had skidded to a halt at the curb. The headlights illuminated their faces, and I felt a chill run down my spine as I recognized one of them—a familiar face that had haunted my past.

"What the hell?" I whispered, my breath hitching in my throat.

"Do you know them?" Darian asked, his tone now serious as he leaned closer, his body taut beside me.

I didn't respond, my heart pounding as I watched the confrontation unfold. Words were exchanged, harsh and urgent, and suddenly, one of the figures pulled something from their jacket—a glint of metal that caught the light, causing my heart to race faster.

"Run!" I shouted, grabbing Darian's arm just as the chaos erupted below us. The shadows surged forward, and I turned, instinctively pulling him back towards the stairwell.

But as we made our way back, I caught a glimpse of the glinting object again, realization dawning on me as the weight of my past collided with the chaos of the present. My heart raced, knowing that whatever lay ahead would not only test our resolve but threaten to unravel everything we had just begun to build.

The night was far from over, and as we descended, I couldn't shake the feeling that we were about to be caught in a storm of secrets and danger—a storm that could change everything.

Chapter 2: A Web of Deception

The cold wind sliced through the alleyways of Neo Crescent like a blade, stirring the refuse that littered the cobblestone streets, carrying with it the echoes of a city that had long since lost its way. I tightened the collar of my jacket, feeling the coarse fabric rub against my skin, a reminder of my own unyielding resolve. Each step brought me deeper into the darkness, where flickering neon signs cast ghostly shadows that danced and swirled, morphing the ordinary into the extraordinary.

Darian was a specter in this world, an enigma wrapped in layers of complexity. He had the ability to make the very air around him crackle with tension, each interaction a high-stakes game where the rules shifted like sand beneath our feet. We had been thrust together by circumstances neither of us had chosen, an uneasy alliance born of necessity. Yet, the way his dark eyes pierced through me, tracing every line of my resolve, ignited something primal within. It was infuriating—this mix of attraction and animosity. I could practically feel the heat radiating off him, a palpable force that pulled me closer, even as my instincts screamed to keep my distance.

"Trust is a luxury we can't afford," he said, his voice low and gravelly, reverberating off the walls like a warning. The way he leaned against the crumbling brick, arms crossed, gave him an air of casual dominance that both thrilled and unnerved me.

"And yet here we are, hand in hand in this wretched affair," I shot back, trying to mask the way my heart raced at his proximity.

The Shadow Syndicate was the malignant tumor festering at the city's core, its influence weaving through every stratum of society. I had stumbled onto their trail while digging into the recent string of disappearances that had gripped Neo Crescent in a vice of fear. Little did I know that unraveling the mystery would lead me to Darian, and by extension, to the ominous figure known only as the Shadow Man.

The nights spent poring over records and whispering secrets in the dim light of backroom bars had opened my eyes to a world I had only glimpsed in half-remembered nightmares. The Syndicate operated under a veil of silence, pulling strings in the shadows while the city above them continued its dance of oblivion. With Darian by my side, I felt as though I was plunging headfirst into a maelstrom of secrets and lies, each revelation a slippery step toward a truth that could just as easily shatter me.

"Do you ever wonder what lies beneath this façade?" I mused aloud, the question more for myself than him. The neon lights shimmered like broken promises, casting an eerie glow on the faces of passersby, their expressions etched with worry and resignation. "What makes a man choose this life?"

"Desperation breeds darkness," he replied, his gaze piercing through the smoke-laden air. "Most people don't choose this life; it chooses them. They think they have a say, but in the end, it's survival that dictates the path."

I considered his words, a knot of tension tightening in my stomach. There was truth in his cynicism, but it felt like a bitter pill to swallow. I had spent years believing in the possibility of redemption, of finding light even in the darkest corners of existence. Yet, standing beside him, I wondered if that light was simply a trick of the mind—a fleeting illusion in a city that thrived on chaos.

Our footsteps echoed in the narrow alley as we approached a nondescript door, the entryway to a den of iniquity where secrets were bartered like currency. I glanced up at Darian, my heart thundering as we prepared to step inside. He was the wild card in this game, unpredictable and volatile. I couldn't decide if he was my savior or my downfall.

"Ready?" he asked, a wicked grin breaking through his otherwise stoic demeanor.

"Ready as I'll ever be," I replied, masking my uncertainty with bravado.

The door creaked open, revealing a dimly lit room filled with the scent of smoke and something else—something more intoxicating, tinged with danger. I stepped over the threshold, the atmosphere shifting instantly, as if the walls themselves breathed in the secrets of those who had come before.

The room was alive with muted conversations, laughter tinged with desperation, and the unmistakable undercurrent of tension. A group huddled in a corner, eyes darting furtively, while a man at the bar counted stacks of cash with a practiced ease. My heart raced as I scanned the room, the shadows flickering like specters eager to whisper their secrets to anyone willing to listen.

Darian leaned close, his breath warm against my ear, sending a shiver down my spine. "Stick close to me. You never know who's watching."

His words hung heavy between us, and I nodded, trying to quell the flutter of nerves that had taken root in my chest. As we moved deeper into the chaos, I couldn't shake the feeling that the Shadow Syndicate was always two steps ahead, lurking in the shadows, orchestrating events in ways I had yet to comprehend.

And yet, in the heart of the unknown, a spark ignited between us, a tension that was both electric and terrifying. It was as if the very air crackled with unspoken words, weaving a web of deception that ensnared us both. The deeper we ventured into this underworld, the more I felt the boundaries of trust and desire blurring, intertwining in a dance as perilous as the shadows themselves.

The laughter in the dimly lit bar wrapped around me like a shroud, muffling the world outside as I took my first steps into this subterranean realm of secrets and lies. Neon lights flickered overhead, casting a kaleidoscope of colors across the crowd, illuminating faces that were often too weary or wary to bear the weight of their own stories. I could feel the pulse of the city thrum beneath my feet, an unyielding heartbeat of chaos and longing. In this place, the air was thick with possibility and danger—a potent mix that sent a thrill racing through my veins.

Darian's presence was magnetic, his dark aura drawing me in like a moth to flame. He wove through the crowd with the ease of someone who belonged here, his confidence both exhilarating and unnerving. I followed close behind, doing my best to match his nonchalance, though my heart drummed a nervous beat that echoed in my ears. He was the spark in this tinderbox of deceit, and I was a fuse waiting to be lit.

"Have you ever wondered why we're the only ones not losing our minds over this crowd?" I quipped, attempting to break the tension that crackled between us. "Everyone else looks like they just stepped out of a horror film, but we're here like it's just another Tuesday night."

Darian smirked, the corners of his mouth curling up in that infuriatingly charming way that made my stomach flip. "Maybe it's because we know how to play the game," he replied, glancing around with a mix of amusement and wariness. "Or maybe we're just two fools wandering into the lion's den."

"Good to know I'm a fool," I shot back, rolling my eyes even as a laugh escaped me. "But at least I'm a fool with a plan."

"Plans are overrated. It's the unexpected that keeps life interesting." His gaze locked onto mine, a challenge dancing in the depths of those dark eyes. The air thickened around us, charged with the unspoken truths hovering just out of reach.

Our banter was a fragile shield against the unease that gnawed at the edges of my consciousness. I could feel the eyes of strangers on us, shadows lingering a moment too long, as if the very walls were listening. This was not just a bar; it was a hive of intrigue, a nexus of whispered deals and unbreakable loyalties.

As we approached the bar, I caught sight of a woman seated alone, her fingers drumming rhythmically against the polished surface, lost in her thoughts. Her presence was magnetic, drawing people in with a subtle allure that belied her sharp gaze. She wore a crimson dress that hugged her figure, her hair cascading in waves that framed her face like a halo. I could sense that she was no mere patron; she belonged to this world, perhaps even to the Shadow Syndicate.

"Watch your back," Darian murmured, the gravity of his words grounding me. "She's not just another pretty face."

"Who is she?" I asked, my curiosity piqued.

"Celia," he said, his voice low. "She's the Syndicate's information broker. If anyone has the answers we need, it's her."

Celia looked up, her piercing gaze locking onto mine. A flicker of recognition passed between us, a spark that ignited an undercurrent of tension. I felt as if she could see straight through my facade, peeling back the layers of uncertainty that I tried so desperately to conceal.

"Darian," she drawled, her tone playful yet laced with an edge. "I didn't expect to see you here. What brings you to my corner of the world?"

"Just a little business," he replied, his voice smooth as silk. "Thought I'd pay a visit and see what secrets you're hoarding these days."

"And here I thought you only came to steal my charm," she shot back, her smile both warm and razor-sharp.

"Only if you're willing to share it," he quipped, leaning casually against the bar. I stood beside him, acutely aware of the energy crackling in the air. It was a game they both played with practiced ease, and I felt like a spectator in a performance I wasn't prepared for.

"Let's get down to it, shall we?" Celia said, her demeanor shifting as she leaned closer, her voice dropping to a conspiratorial whisper. "What you're looking for is more dangerous than you realize. The

Shadow Man doesn't take kindly to uninvited guests poking around in his affairs."

"Danger is what we thrive on," I interjected, surprising myself with the boldness of my words. "We're not here to play it safe."

Celia studied me for a moment, her expression unreadable. "And who might you be?"

"A partner in crime," I replied, feeling Darian's glance shift toward me, an eyebrow raised in amused surprise.

"A bold move. I like that." She smirked, taking a sip of her drink as if savoring a fine wine. "But know this: there are depths to this world that even the bravest of hearts fear to tread. The Syndicate is not a game; it's a labyrinth of lies."

"Then we'll navigate it together," I declared, surprising even myself with the conviction in my voice.

Celia leaned back, crossing her arms as a calculating smile played on her lips. "You really think you can handle the truth?"

Darian chuckled softly, the sound rich with admiration. "She's tougher than she looks. Trust me."

"Then let's see what you're made of." Celia's eyes sparkled with mischief, as if she was enjoying a secret only she knew. "Meet me here tomorrow night. I might have something for you. But be warned, I expect a show of good faith."

"Good faith?" I echoed, glancing sideways at Darian, who looked just as intrigued as I felt.

"Bring me something of value—information, a favor, a little chaos. Just make sure it's something the Syndicate would want to keep under wraps."

"Sounds simple enough," I replied, my pulse quickening with the thrill of the challenge.

"Simple is often deceptive," she retorted, her expression turning serious. "Choose wisely. The stakes are high, and the consequences? Even higher."

As we turned to leave, I couldn't shake the feeling that we had just stepped into a game far beyond our understanding. The weight of Celia's warning clung to me, mingling with the unspoken bond that tethered me to Darian. We were on a precarious edge, dancing along the brink of a dark abyss. And yet, as our shoulders brushed together, I felt a flicker of hope that perhaps, just perhaps, we would emerge from this tangled web of deception unscathed, ready to face whatever shadows awaited us in the depths of Neo Crescent.

The neon haze of the bar faded behind us as we stepped out into the clammy embrace of the night, the air thick with the scents of damp pavement and distant smoke. My heart raced—not just from the encounter with Celia but from the thrill of the unknown that loomed ahead. Darian fell into step beside me, the weight of his presence both a comfort and a challenge, like a tether to a reality I was still struggling to navigate.

"Do you really think we can trust her?" I asked, glancing sideways at him, the streetlights casting fleeting shadows across his face.

"Trust is a slippery thing in Neo Crescent," he replied, a hint of irony lacing his words. "But Celia has her own motives. If she gives us a lead, it could be worth the risk."

"Risk seems to be the theme of our little adventure," I muttered, shoving my hands into my pockets to shield them from the chill. "But what do we bring her? A packet of secrets? A slice of chaos?"

"Both, ideally," he shot back, the corners of his mouth quirking upward. "But knowing you, it'll be something dramatic."

I narrowed my eyes at him, resisting the urge to smile. "And what do you know about me?"

"I know that you're more than just a pretty face and a penchant for trouble," he said, his voice low and teasing. "You have a fire in you that's hard to ignore. It's intoxicating."

A flush crept up my cheeks at his compliment, the warmth flooding me in stark contrast to the cool night air. I couldn't deny the pull he had on me, a magnetic energy that crackled with unspoken tension. Yet, I couldn't let it distract me from the task at hand. The deeper we dug, the more I realized we were in over our heads.

As we navigated the labyrinth of streets that twisted through Neo Crescent, the city morphed into a character of its own—half shadow, half allure, forever dancing just out of reach. The flicker of headlights passed by like fleeting moments of clarity in the night, illuminating the faces of the lost and the damned. Each one a reminder of the stakes at play, a prelude to the chaos we were courting.

We arrived at a nondescript warehouse, its façade blending seamlessly into the desolation around it. I hesitated at the door, the atmosphere thick with anticipation. "Are you sure this is the right place?"

"Celia wouldn't lead us astray. Besides, it's the kind of place where people have their eyes wide shut," he replied, pushing the door open with a determined shove. The hinges creaked, and I braced myself for whatever awaited inside.

The interior was dimly lit, with scattered crates lining the walls and a handful of figures clustered in the far corner, their hushed tones wrapping around us like a shroud. I could sense the tension simmering beneath the surface, an undercurrent of fear mingling with desperation.

"Just like home," I whispered sarcastically, stepping inside.

Darian chuckled softly, the sound both soothing and dangerous. "This is just the beginning."

As we moved deeper into the warehouse, I noticed a young man pacing back and forth, his hands running through his disheveled hair. His eyes darted toward us, wide with anxiety. "You're here," he gasped, his voice trembling. "You're actually here."

"Who are you?" I asked, my curiosity piqued.

"Evan," he stammered, glancing around nervously as if expecting someone to jump out from the shadows. "I have information about the Shadow Man. You're in grave danger."

The room seemed to constrict around us, the air heavy with his revelation. "What do you know?" Darian demanded, stepping closer, his commanding presence demanding answers.

Evan gulped, his voice barely above a whisper. "He's planning something big, something that could change everything. I overheard him talking about a shipment that's arriving soon—a shipment that could secure his power over the city."

I exchanged a glance with Darian, our unspoken connection pulsing in the air. "What kind of shipment?" I pressed, my heart racing with the implications.

"Weapons," Evan replied, his voice shaking. "He's arming his followers, gathering strength. If he gets this shipment, it's over for all of us."

A chill ran down my spine. "We have to stop it. We can't let this happen."

"Are you insane?" Evan looked at me incredulously. "You're talking about going up against the Shadow Man himself. He has eyes everywhere."

"Then we'll just have to be cleverer than him," I replied, my mind racing. The weight of our mission settled heavily on my shoulders, but there was a flicker of resolve sparking to life. This was more than just a game; it was a fight for survival.

Darian's gaze turned sharp, scanning the room. "What's the plan, Evan? We can't just stand here."

Evan hesitated, looking between us as if weighing his options. "There's a meet scheduled for tomorrow night. That's when the shipment is supposed to arrive. If we can intercept it—"

"Then we'll do just that," I said, cutting him off. "We can't wait for the Syndicate to make their move. We need to take the initiative."

"Are you sure you want to dive headfirst into this?" Evan questioned, uncertainty creeping into his voice.

"I've never been one to sit on the sidelines," I replied, glancing at Darian. "And I suspect he feels the same way."

Darian nodded, his expression resolute. "Let's gather what we need. We'll infiltrate the meet, gather intel, and take down whatever operation the Shadow Man has planned."

The atmosphere crackled with energy, a charged anticipation that felt almost electric. As we strategized, I couldn't shake the feeling that we were setting ourselves up for something monumental—an act that would alter the course of our lives forever.

The hours slipped by in a blur of planning and preparation, our excitement mingling with the fear that gnawed at the edges of our resolve. We gathered weapons and supplies, careful to remain under the radar of prying eyes. With every moment that passed, the weight of the unknown pressed down on me like an impending storm, the air heavy with expectation.

Just as we finalized our plans, the sound of footsteps echoed in the distance, sharp and rapid. My heart seized, instinct kicking in as I turned to Darian, his expression mirroring my own apprehension.

"Someone's coming," he warned, urgency lacing his voice.

Before we could react, the warehouse door burst open, and a group of shadowy figures rushed inside. My breath caught in my throat as I recognized one of them—the unmistakable silhouette of Celia.

"You should have listened to my warning," she said, her voice dripping with a mix of mockery and menace. "The Shadow Man doesn't take kindly to intruders."

The atmosphere shifted, tension thick enough to slice. My instincts screamed at me, the air crackling with the weight of betrayal. I had stepped into a web of deception far deeper than I had anticipated, and the thread that held my fate was fraying with each passing second.

As the figures closed in, I felt the ground beneath me tremble, the chaos of Neo Crescent swirling around us, ready to consume everything in its path. The stakes were impossibly high, and as I locked eyes with Darian, I realized we were in a battle not just for our lives, but for the very soul of the city. The moment hung in the air, heavy with the weight of choices unmade, as the storm closed in around us, leaving no clear path to salvation.

Chapter 3: Threads of the Past

The ballroom was a riot of color and light, a swirling canvas of silk and laughter, where the glittering chandeliers cast a warm glow over the revelers. As I adjusted the faux diamond necklace that rested heavily on my collarbone, the weight of its fakeness matched the unease that sat deep in my gut. The music floated through the air, a symphony of strings and brass, punctuated by the occasional clink of champagne flutes. Here, among the elite, I was a carefully crafted illusion, a facade built to mask the reality of who I was—a thief infiltrating a world of opulence to steal back what was rightfully mine.

Darian stood beside me, his presence a paradox of familiarity and danger. Dressed in a tailored suit that accentuated his lean physique, he cut an impressive figure, his dark hair slicked back just so. But it wasn't his appearance that unsettled me; it was the way his eyes darted over the crowd, a predator assessing his prey. The years had sharpened his features, adding an edge that had once been softened by the innocence of our shared youth. Memories flickered through my mind—sunlit days and laughter shared, moments now tainted by betrayal and the sharpness of broken trust.

"Remember when we used to sneak in here as kids?" he murmured, his voice low, a velvet caress against the backdrop of laughter. "We thought we could charm our way into the rich and powerful with nothing but a smile."

"Charm? You mean you thought you could charm them," I retorted, my tone playful yet edged with an underlying tension. "I was merely trying to keep you out of trouble."

He chuckled, the sound rich and warm, and for a fleeting moment, the sharp barbs of resentment dulled. "And yet, here we are. All grown up and still playing the same game."

Game. That word hung between us like a specter, a reminder of everything that had happened. The mission we were on felt like a twisted version of our childhood escapades, where stakes were higher and the thrill of adventure was tainted by the knowledge of our history. I forced my mind back to the present, focusing on the task at hand. We had to locate the artifact, a rare gem hidden somewhere within the mansion. Its recovery was vital, not just for the money it would bring but for the way it symbolized a piece of my past that I needed to reclaim.

As we navigated through the crowd, I couldn't help but steal glances at him, searching for the remnants of the boy I once knew. There were moments, brief and fleeting, when I caught a glimpse of vulnerability behind his confident façade—when he smiled a little too wide or laughed a little too loudly, as if trying to convince himself that everything was alright. Yet, with every flicker of his true self, I felt the familiar sting of betrayal, raw and unyielding.

"Darian," I said suddenly, stopping in the midst of a swirling dance floor. "Why did you do it? Why did you betray me?"

He turned, surprise flickering across his features before his expression hardened. "That's not fair, Calla. You know why. I had no choice."

"No choice?" I echoed, incredulous. "You chose your ambition over our friendship. You chose power over loyalty."

"Don't you dare put this on me," he snapped, his voice low but intense enough to draw the attention of a few nearby guests. "You know as well as I do that the world we grew up in didn't leave room for sentimentality."

His words were like daggers, sharp and piercing, but there was something in his eyes—a flicker of regret, perhaps?—that made my heart ache. I took a step back, needing space to breathe. Around us, the music played on, but in that moment, it faded into an oppressive silence, thick with unspoken emotions.

"Then let's make this right," I said, forcing my voice to remain steady. "Let's finish this mission and get out of here. Together."

His gaze softened for a fraction of a second, and I swore I saw the boy who once believed in our dreams, the boy who used to spin tales of adventure beneath the stars. But just as quickly, the mask fell back into place, and he nodded, the walls he built around himself reinstated.

"Alright," he replied, his voice steady, though the tension between us was palpable. "We find the gem, and then we're done."

With a shared understanding, we moved through the throng of people, slipping into the shadows of the grand staircase that spiraled up to a second level. The world of wealth and excess continued below us, blissfully unaware of the thieves that lurked in their midst.

As we crept through the upper hallways, the air shifted; it was charged with secrets, history, and the echoes of our past. I could almost hear the whispers of old dreams curling in the corners, mingling with the scent of polished wood and the faint trace of lavender from the nearby blooms. My heart raced—not just from the thrill of the hunt, but from the anxiety that swirled like a storm inside me, clashing with the ghosts of trust that lingered in the air.

"Do you remember the night we stole that cake from Mrs. Worthington's party?" Darian asked, his voice breaking through my reverie.

"Of course," I laughed, the sound surprising even me. "You ate half of it before we even made it out of the garden."

"I was hungry!" he shot back, but the corners of his mouth twitched with a smile. "And it was the best cake I've ever had."

"In your defense," I replied, feigning seriousness, "it was an excellent cake."

Laughter danced between us, a brief moment of respite amid the tension, as we navigated the dimly lit corridor. But it wasn't long before our shared laughter faded, the weight of our unresolved past pressing down once more.

"Let's just finish this," I said, the lightness gone from my voice as we approached the door at the end of the hall. "And then we can figure out what we do next."

His expression turned serious, and the flicker of vulnerability I had seen earlier flashed again. "Yeah, I—"

Before he could finish, the door creaked open, and a figure stepped out, eyes glinting with a knowing look that sent a chill racing down my spine. Our dance of trust and betrayal was far from over, and the shadows that had haunted us both were about to collide in a way we never expected.

The figure that emerged from the shadows was a striking woman, her presence commanding and unapologetically magnetic. Clad in a gown of deep emerald that hugged her curves in all the right places, she exuded confidence, the kind that made the room shimmer with her arrival. Her hair cascaded in glossy waves, framing a face that bore an expression of mischief and intrigue, as if she knew secrets about the world that could unravel it. My heart sank. This was not a random gala-goer; this was Olivia Sinclair, the woman whose ambition had always outstripped her morals.

"Well, well, if it isn't the dynamic duo of disaster," she drawled, a wicked grin spreading across her lips. "I didn't realize I'd be blessed with such esteemed company tonight."

"Olivia," Darian said, his voice betraying none of the unease that gnawed at me. He had always been too good at maintaining his composure, a trait I both admired and envied. "What brings you here?"

"I could ask you the same, but I think we both know this soirée is just a cover for something a bit more... exciting." She took a step closer, her eyes glinting with amusement as she scrutinized us. "You're not here for the hors d'oeuvres, are you?"

I bristled at her insinuation but tried to hold my ground, even as my mind raced. Olivia had a talent for digging under my skin, much like a persistent splinter that refused to budge. "And you are?" I countered, matching her tone with one laced in ice. "The gracious hostess, or merely the gatekeeper to your next conquest?"

"Touché," she replied, unfazed. "I prefer to think of myself as an opportunist, and tonight, my dear Calla, the opportunities abound." Her gaze flickered to Darian, and I could sense the tension that crackled between them, remnants of a past I had never fully understood. "But I must admit, it's delightful to see you both again. Your reunion is practically a fairy tale, if fairy tales involved theft and deception."

"Charming," I shot back, my patience wearing thin. "What do you want, Olivia?"

"Oh, just a little chat about your charming little heist," she said, feigning innocence as she leaned casually against the door frame. "After all, a girl can't help but be curious when her former allies decide to take a trip down memory lane."

Darian's jaw tightened, and I could see the gears turning in his mind, calculating our next move. "You're not going to ruin this for us, Olivia. We don't want any trouble."

"Trouble? I'm merely a spectator in this tragic play," she quipped, her eyes sparkling with mischief. "But I do have a proposition. You see, I have my sights set on that lovely artifact you're after as well. Why don't we make this a little competition? Winner takes all."

My mind raced, caught between disbelief and the thrill of adrenaline. "You think we'd just hand over the prize to you?"

Olivia's laughter filled the corridor, echoing off the opulent walls. "Oh, Calla. You underestimate the allure of a little rivalry. Isn't that what brought you two together in the first place?"

Darian shifted beside me, his expression unreadable. "You know the stakes, Olivia. This isn't just a game."

"Isn't it?" she challenged, raising an eyebrow. "You've both danced with danger before, haven't you? Why stop now?"

I glanced at Darian, searching for a flicker of agreement in his eyes. A part of me wanted to throw caution to the wind and accept her challenge, to dive headfirst into this unpredictable game that was spinning out of control. But another part, the part that remembered betrayal and heartbreak, urged caution. "We'll think about it," I said coolly, hoping to buy time as I formulated a plan.

"Don't take too long, darling," Olivia cooed, winking before gliding back into the gala, leaving behind an atmosphere thick with tension and unspoken questions.

The moment she disappeared, I turned to Darian, a mix of frustration and uncertainty simmering in my chest. "This was supposed to be a straightforward job."

"Nothing is ever straightforward with Olivia involved," he replied, running a hand through his hair, a telltale sign of his mounting frustration. "We need to focus on the artifact. Let's stick to our plan."

"Right," I agreed, though my heart wasn't entirely in it. The thrill of competition, of outsmarting Olivia, tugged at me, a siren song promising excitement and danger in equal measure. "But what if we could turn this to our advantage?"

"Calla, this isn't a game. We have to be careful." His voice was firm, but I caught the flicker of challenge in his gaze. "Besides, she's not just after the gem. She's after us."

The weight of his words settled over me, a shroud of reality cloaked in shadows. If Olivia was aware of our mission, then the stakes were higher than I had imagined. "So what's the plan?" I asked, my pulse quickening at the thought of facing her again.

"We stick to the original mission," he said, his voice steady. "We gather intel, find the gem, and get out without drawing attention. If we can outmaneuver Olivia, we have a better shot."

I nodded, but my mind was already racing with possibilities. "And what if we find the artifact first? Maybe we can leverage it against her, force her hand."

Darian's expression softened, but the tension remained. "You're playing a dangerous game, Calla."

"And you know how much I love a bit of danger," I replied, letting a playful smirk slip onto my lips. "Let's just make sure we're not playing with our lives."

We exchanged a knowing look, a silent pact formed in the dim light of the hallway. Together, we would navigate this treacherous game, side by side, with old wounds and new tensions interwoven in the fabric of our partnership. The world below pulsed with laughter and music, oblivious to the storm brewing in the shadows.

As we moved deeper into the mansion, my senses heightened, the scent of polished wood and faint floral arrangements wrapped around me like a familiar embrace. Every footstep felt electric, each corner turned an invitation to danger. I could feel the rush of adrenaline coursing through my veins, a thrill that was both terrifying and intoxicating.

"Just keep your eyes open," Darian whispered as we entered a lavish sitting room adorned with exquisite art and decadent furnishings. "We have no idea how many eyes are on us."

"Let them watch," I replied, unable to suppress the spark of defiance igniting within me. "Let's give them a show."

With a quick glance at the extravagant decor, I spotted a door leading to a dimly lit corridor. The thrill of the unknown beckoned, a whispered promise of secrets waiting to be uncovered. "This way," I urged, stepping forward with purpose.

Darian followed, the weight of our shared past mingling with the thrill of the chase. Each step was a dance of tension and unresolved feelings, the ghosts of what we had been lingering just beneath the surface. There was no turning back now. The game had begun, and I was determined to play for keeps.

The corridor twisted like a snake, dimly lit by the flickering glow of sconces, the walls adorned with portraits of people who seemed to watch our every move. I led the way, driven by a mix of adrenaline and stubborn resolve. The tension between Darian and me hung thick in the air, punctuated only by the echo of our footsteps against the marble floor. My heart raced, not just from the thrill of our venture but from the fear of what might lie ahead.

"Do you think they're watching us?" I asked, keeping my voice low, glancing over my shoulder to catch Darian's expression.

"Who isn't?" he replied, a slight smile tugging at the corner of his lips. "We're the main attraction, remember? Just two star-crossed thieves at a high-society gala."

I laughed softly, grateful for the momentary levity. "Star-crossed? More like star-crossed rivals with a penchant for trouble."

He shrugged, his demeanor shifting as he stepped closer, the scent of his cologne mixing with the stale air of the corridor. "Trouble is what we do best."

We reached a heavy oak door, slightly ajar, and I hesitated, my heart pounding against my ribcage. "What if it's a trap?"

Darian raised an eyebrow, his expression one of challenge. "Then we'll deal with it together, just like old times."

Taking a breath, I pushed the door open, the creaking hinges punctuating the charged atmosphere. The room beyond was dimly lit, lined with bookshelves that seemed to groan under the weight of countless tomes. A large, mahogany desk dominated the space, littered with papers and a solitary lamp casting a warm pool of light.

As I stepped inside, my instincts screamed that something was off. The room was too quiet, the air too still. "Darian, stay alert," I whispered, scanning for any signs of life.

"I always am," he said, moving cautiously to the left, his eyes darting around the room like a hawk. "Let's find that gem and get out."

We began our search, rifling through drawers and glancing behind books, but the room was filled with nothing but mundane documents and a few dusty knickknacks. My frustration mounted as I unearthed nothing of value. Just as I was about to lose hope, a glint of light caught my eye from the corner of the desk.

"Over here," I called out, stepping closer. Beneath a stack of old ledgers, I uncovered a small, intricately carved box. Its surface gleamed even in the muted light, adorned with delicate filigree and a tiny lock that beckoned to be opened.

Darian leaned over my shoulder, his breath warm against my skin. "Now that looks promising."

I brushed my fingers over the cool wood, a shiver of anticipation racing up my spine. "What do you think is inside?"

"Only one way to find out," he replied, his voice low and enticing, making the air between us sizzle with unspoken possibilities.

I pulled out a hairpin from my hair, a relic of childhood mischief, and nudged it into the lock. The mechanism clicked, and I lifted the lid with bated breath. Inside lay a stunning gemstone, the color of midnight blue, sparkling like a star caught in a web of darkness. My breath hitched. This had to be it—the gem we sought.

"This is it," I whispered, unable to tear my gaze away. "We found it."

Darian's eyes widened, but before he could reach for it, a loud crash echoed through the room, making us both jump. The door swung open, revealing Olivia, flanked by two burly security guards. Her smile was triumphant, a wicked glint in her eyes that sent a chill down my spine.

"Well, well, looks like you two have found quite the treasure," she said, stepping into the room with an air of self-satisfaction. "But it seems you've been naughty little thieves."

I instinctively stepped in front of the box, my heart racing. "What do you want, Olivia?"

"Isn't it obvious?" she replied, crossing her arms over her chest. "The gem, of course. But more than that, I want a little revenge for the past."

Darian shifted beside me, his expression tense. "We're not playing your games, Olivia."

"Oh, but you already are," she purred, motioning to the guards who took a menacing step forward. "You see, it's not just the gem I want; it's the thrill of the chase. It's watching you squirm as I take what you've worked so hard for."

"You're delusional," I shot back, adrenaline flooding my veins. "You really think you can just waltz in here and take everything?"

"Why not?" she challenged, her grin widening. "This is a gala, darling, and I always win the prize. The real question is, how far are you willing to go to stop me?"

Before I could respond, the guards lunged, and I reacted on instinct, shoving the box toward Darian as I prepared to fight. "Get the gem out of here!"

In a split second, he grasped the box, but Olivia was quicker, her hand darting forward to snatch it back. "Not so fast!"

With a sharp twist, I grabbed her wrist, but she retaliated, pulling free and stepping back. "You really think you can take me on? You've always underestimated me, Calla. But I'm not the naive girl you once knew."

"I'm not the same girl either," I shot back, adrenaline surging through me. "I won't let you take this from us."

"Then let's make it interesting," Olivia said, her eyes gleaming with malice. "A game of wits. If you win, you keep the gem. If I win..."

She paused for dramatic effect, the air thick with tension. "I take everything."

"Like that's ever worked for you," Darian interjected, trying to assert control over the escalating situation.

But Olivia's gaze sharpened, and I felt the stakes rise exponentially. "Are you willing to gamble on it? Or shall I simply have my men throw you both out? The decision is yours."

I looked at Darian, his expression a mix of determination and uncertainty. "What do you think?"

"Let's play," he said, a fire igniting in his eyes. "We've come too far to back down now."

"Excellent choice," Olivia declared, her smile widening as if she had already won. "Let the games begin."

As she stepped back, gesturing for the guards to stand down, the tension crackled in the air, a mix of uncertainty and excitement that made my heart race. The room felt alive, charged with the electricity of impending confrontation. I could feel the stakes rising like a tide, swallowing us whole as we prepared for a showdown that would determine everything.

But as I glanced back at the gemstone, now sitting precariously on the desk, a sudden crash reverberated through the mansion, shaking the very foundations beneath our feet. The lights flickered and dimmed, casting eerie shadows across the room, and I couldn't shake the feeling that something—something much bigger than any of us—was about to change the game entirely.

In that moment, I realized the stakes were higher than a mere gem or rivalry; they encompassed everything we had fought for and everything we stood to lose. As the tremors subsided, a new noise echoed through the halls, a sound that felt like the harbinger of chaos, and I understood we were no longer just players in a game. We were part of something far more dangerous, and it was just beginning to unfold.

Chapter 4: Secrets and Shadows

The rain fell in sheets, a relentless percussion against the cobblestones of the narrow alley where I found myself cornered. The muted glow of the streetlamps struggled against the downpour, casting warped reflections in the puddles that gathered like small, murky lakes at my feet. Each drop that splashed against my skin sent a shiver through me, though not from the cold; it was the weight of the revelations I had just uncovered, pressing down like a leaden shroud.

I had pieced together fragments of whispers, shrouded meetings, and glances that lingered just a heartbeat too long. The Shadow Syndicate, a name that had danced on the fringes of my consciousness for weeks, now loomed large, revealing itself to be a spider at the center of a web I never knew I had stumbled into. But what chilled me deeper than the encroaching darkness of the storm was the truth I had unearthed about Darian. The man who had become an enigmatic force in my life, whose charm had pulled me closer even as I resisted. It turned out that he was not merely an ally in this tangled mess; he was, in fact, ensnared within it, a pawn in a game far more dangerous than I had ever imagined.

"Darian!" I shouted into the night, my voice slicing through the downpour like a blade. He appeared from the shadows, his silhouette sharp and defined against the dim light, a fierce intensity in his stormy eyes. My heart thundered, not from fear but from an all-consuming rage that begged to be unleashed. "You need to explain this to me. Now."

He stepped closer, his presence radiating heat that clashed with the cool night air, and the space between us crackled with unspoken words. "What have you found?" His voice was low, almost a growl, but there was a hint of something softer beneath it, a vulnerability that begged to be acknowledged.

"Found? Oh, just the fact that your cozy little life is built on a foundation of lies!" I took a step back, not wanting to be too close, too aware of the way his mere existence made my pulse race. "You're not just some charming rogue; you're tangled up in their schemes. You're a puppet, Darian, dancing to their tune. I trusted you!"

"Trust? Is that what this is about?" His laughter was bitter, a dark melody that danced around us like the storm clouds overhead. "You think I wanted this? That I chose to be part of their twisted game?" He ran a hand through his damp hair, water cascading down his forehead like a fallen star. "I didn't ask for any of this."

"You could have told me!" My frustration flared, each word like a spark igniting a fire. "Instead, you kept me in the dark, hiding behind your charming smile while I stumbled into danger, completely unaware of the stakes. How could you do that to me?"

The silence hung heavy between us, the rain drumming a furious beat against the stones. I could see the conflict in his eyes, the internal battle waging within him. He wanted to fight back, to defend himself, but the flicker of something more—fear, perhaps—kept him tethered to the ground. I should have felt vindicated, but the truth was that I was unraveling at the seams, emotions spilling over like the rain that soaked through my clothes.

"Maybe I thought it would keep you safe," he finally admitted, his voice raw, a whisper carried away by the wind. "Keeping you away from this world is all I ever wanted."

"Safe?" I scoffed, my heart racing faster than the storm. "You think lying to me would keep me safe? I'd rather know the truth, even if it shatters me."

He took a step forward, the tension between us palpable, thickening the air until it felt electric. "And what if the truth breaks us both?" he challenged, a spark igniting in his gaze. "What if knowing only leads to more pain?"

"Then let it break!" I exploded, the words tumbling out before I could catch them. "Let it break us if that's what it takes to get to the heart of this mess. I'm tired of hiding, tired of living in the shadows. If we're going to face this, we do it together—no more secrets, no more lies."

The challenge hung between us, both daunting and exhilarating. It was a moment suspended in time, the kind that could alter everything. His face softened, an inscrutable expression dancing across his features. I wanted to believe him, to trust that he would embrace this raw honesty as fiercely as I did. But the uncertainty clawed at my insides, a visceral reminder of all the broken promises that had led me to this precipice.

In that breathless stillness, anger morphed into something deeper, something undeniable that pulsed in the spaces between us. My heart raced with the kind of reckless abandon that only comes in moments of pure vulnerability. Before I could think, before I could question, I surged forward, closing the distance that felt like an eternity.

Our lips met in a collision of warmth and chaos, a breathless kiss that ignited the storm within me. It was passionate, a whirlwind of fury and longing, each breath mingling as if to erase the lines that had drawn us apart. In that electrifying moment, the tension, the secrets, the fears—they all faded away, leaving behind only the truth of our connection.

Darian pulled me closer, deepening the kiss, and I melted against him, feeling the heat radiating from his body as the rain drummed around us, a symphony of chaos. I could taste the salt of his emotions, feel the weight of his burdens pressing against me as he lifted me out of the shadows and into something that felt like hope, even as the darkness lingered just out of reach.

The world around us blurred, and for that fleeting instant, I allowed myself to forget everything but the fire igniting between us—a fire that could just as easily consume us both as it could light the way forward.

The kiss lingered like an echo in the night, a fragile spark in a tempest of emotions. As we pulled apart, breathless and wide-eyed, the rain continued its relentless assault, each droplet punctuating the tension that hung between us like a freshly spun web. My mind raced, torn between the exhilaration of our shared moment and the crushing weight of the truth I had uncovered.

"Darian," I whispered, my voice a thread in the downpour, "we can't just forget what's happening. You're caught in something far bigger than either of us, and I need to know how deep this goes."

He stepped back, his expression a mixture of defiance and vulnerability, like a lion caught between the instinct to fight and the need to protect. "You think I don't know that? Every day, I wake up to the knowledge that I'm playing a dangerous game." He ran a hand through his damp hair again, frustration radiating from him in waves. "I'm not just some plaything for the Syndicate. I made choices, stupid ones that brought me here."

"Choices?" I felt a scalding mix of anger and worry bubbling beneath my skin. "You could have chosen to be honest with me, to let me in instead of dragging me into this world without my consent."

He clenched his jaw, the tension in his shoulders coiling tightly. "And put you in danger? Do you think I'm that reckless?"

The fury bubbled over. "You already put me in danger! Keeping me in the dark doesn't protect me; it just leaves me vulnerable and confused."

"Confusion is the least of our worries." His voice was tight, but I saw a flicker of something deeper, a pain that transcended our argument. "The Syndicate is ruthless, and they won't stop until they get what they want. I was hoping to shield you from it, but—"

"But what?" I interrupted, my voice rising. "You thought I'd just sit back and let you handle this alone? You should have known me better than that."

"Maybe I did." He stepped forward again, the intensity in his gaze igniting a familiar warmth within me. "But I can't let you become a target. You're too important to me."

His words, raw and unfiltered, wrapped around my heart like a vice. "Too important? Or too much of a liability?" I shot back, the sting of his previous secrets hitting home. "You can't decide what's best for me, Darian. I deserve to know what I'm up against."

"Do you really want to know?" He challenged, and for a moment, I saw a flicker of fear behind his bravado. "What if the truth changes everything? What if it drives us apart?"

"Maybe it should," I retorted, the words spilling out before I could reign them in. "Maybe we shouldn't be together if we can't face this head-on."

His face darkened, a storm brewing behind his eyes. "You think I want this? You think I chose to bring you into my world? I didn't ask for this life, and I sure as hell didn't ask for the complications of falling for someone like you."

The admission hung heavy in the air, more powerful than the rain-soaked atmosphere around us. For a heartbeat, the world around us faded—the patter of the rain, the distant hum of the city—all drowned out by the weight of his confession. I felt my heart crack, a tiny fissure in the armor I had built around it, and yet, the vulnerability of the moment drew me closer.

"I didn't ask for this either," I said softly, my anger giving way to something tender yet fragile. "But here we are. Whatever this is between us, it's real. I want to fight for it, but I can't do it alone."

The storm raged on, but in that moment, the air shifted. There was a spark of understanding that flickered in his eyes, a mutual acknowledgment of the chaos swirling around us and the bond that had formed amid the turmoil. "You're right," he said, his voice a low rumble that matched the weather. "This isn't just about me anymore. It's about us, and I want to protect that—protect you."

The sincerity in his tone sent a ripple of warmth through me, breaking through the chill of the rain. But just as quickly, the uncertainty crept back in, like shadows flitting just beyond the edges of light. "Then let's figure this out together," I urged, my voice steadier now. "We need to confront the Syndicate head-on. We need to know what we're up against, and I won't let you face this alone."

He hesitated, his expression torn between hope and apprehension. "You don't know what you're asking for," he cautioned, the weight of his experience pressing against his words. "Once you step into this world, there's no turning back."

"And I won't look back," I replied, resolve hardening within me. "I'm tired of living in fear and shadows. It's time to take control of my life."

The corners of his mouth twitched, a flicker of admiration breaking through his earlier tension. "You're stubborn," he said, shaking his head with a hint of exasperation. "That's what I like about you."

I laughed, the sound slicing through the rain-soaked tension. "Stubbornness is a virtue in times like this, my dear Darian. It's what keeps me alive."

A smile danced in his eyes, and I felt a warmth bloom between us, a delicate thread weaving us closer amid the chaos. "All right," he said, voice firm with newfound determination. "If we're doing this together, we do it right. We gather what intel we can, figure out who we can trust, and strike first before they do."

"Sounds like a plan," I agreed, the adrenaline surging in my veins, chasing away the remnants of fear.

But just as the storm began to ebb, a new tension snaked its way into the air—a sense of impending danger, like a predator circling its prey. My instincts flared, and I turned to look down the alley, where shadows shifted in the dim light.

"What is it?" Darian asked, his voice dropping to a whisper, instinctively drawing closer.

"Someone's watching us," I murmured, scanning the shadows, the hair on my arms prickling as the reality of our situation closed in.

"Stay behind me," he ordered, his body instinctively positioning itself as a shield.

Before I could respond, a figure emerged from the darkness, tall and imposing, an unfamiliar aura radiating a chilling confidence. My heart raced as the stranger stepped into the light, their eyes glinting with a knowing gleam that sent a shiver down my spine.

"Did I interrupt something?" the figure drawled, a smirk playing on their lips.

I glanced at Darian, the tension between us sparking like kindling. The night had morphed from a tempest of emotions into a brewing storm of danger, and I realized with a jolt that we were now standing on the precipice of something far more treacherous than we had ever anticipated.

The figure stepped closer, the glow from the streetlamp casting an eerie halo around their head. A smirk played on their lips, an unsettling blend of amusement and malice that sent a chill racing down my spine. "Did I interrupt something?" they repeated, their tone dripping with mockery.

Darian's posture shifted, every muscle tensed as he shielded me instinctively, the air between us crackling with an urgency that felt palpable. "What do you want?" he growled, his voice a low rumble, barely containing the tempest of emotion swirling within him.

The stranger chuckled, a sound that felt like ice shards scraping against my skin. "I could ask you the same, but I think we both know you're in over your head. The Shadow Syndicate isn't a game, my friend." Their gaze flicked to me, assessing, calculating. "And neither am I."

"Then maybe you should tell us what you know," I shot back, surprising even myself with my boldness. This was not the time to cower in fear; Darian had made it clear that I was more than just a bystander in this twisted tale.

The stranger's eyes narrowed, a flicker of intrigue igniting within their depths. "Ah, so the little lamb has teeth after all." They leaned closer, the smell of rain-soaked asphalt and something sharp clinging to them. "I like that. But let me offer you a piece of advice: curiosity can be dangerous. It's a fool's errand to poke the bear."

Darian moved in closer, his body radiating heat and tension, an unspoken promise of protection. "You're in no position to threaten us," he said, his voice steady but simmering with intensity. "So either you explain yourself or you walk away—now."

The figure chuckled again, unfazed. "You think you have the upper hand, don't you? But the truth is, you're just two pawns in a much larger game. You want to know about the Syndicate? It's simple: they have eyes everywhere." They gestured grandly, as if encompassing the very shadows that cloaked the alley. "You're being watched, and they know everything you're up to."

My heart raced as the reality of their words sank in. "What do you mean, watched?" I demanded, my voice tinged with a mix of anger and fear. "Who are you? What do you want from us?"

"A delightful little mix of curiosity and desperation, I see," the stranger mused, their smirk deepening. "I'm merely an observer—a conduit of information, if you will. I want to help you... for a price."

"What kind of help?" Darian interjected, skepticism etched across his features. "And what's the catch?"

"Clever boy," they replied, their eyes glinting in the dim light. "You catch on fast. The catch is that the Syndicate will come for you soon. You need a plan, and I can provide that... for a favor in return."

"Favors don't come free," I warned, my instincts flaring. "What do you want?"

"Nothing that should concern you—yet," the stranger replied, their voice turning silky smooth. "But trust me, the Syndicate is closing in. They don't take kindly to loose ends, and you two are dangerously frayed."

Darian stepped forward, fire in his eyes. "What do you mean by 'loose ends'?"

"Oh, I think you know exactly what I mean." The figure stepped back, their smile widening, taking pleasure in the tension they'd stirred. "You'll need to make a decision quickly. The longer you wait, the tighter the noose around your neck grows."

The alley darkened further, shadows twisting as if alive, creeping closer as the weight of our predicament settled heavily upon us. I exchanged a glance with Darian, my heart pounding a frantic rhythm. "What do we do?" I whispered, the urgency of our situation settling over us like a dark cloak.

"We play along," he replied, his jaw clenched. "For now. We can't turn down an opportunity, especially not when we're on the edge of something catastrophic."

"Brave choice," the stranger said, clapping their hands together as if they were pleased. "You won't regret it. But I should warn you—betray me, and you'll wish you had taken the other path. The Syndicate has ears everywhere, and they won't hesitate to make you disappear."

"Just tell us what you need," I said, my resolve hardening. "We can't waste time."

The stranger tilted their head, regarding us with a mixture of respect and amusement. "Very well. Meet me tomorrow at the old clock tower—midnight. I'll give you what you need. But remember, trust is a luxury in this world. Don't let your guard down."

With that, they turned and melted into the shadows, their silhouette disappearing into the rain-soaked darkness. I felt a strange mix of relief and dread; we were now entangled in a web far more complex than I had imagined.

Darian turned to me, his expression unreadable. "Are you sure about this?"

"Do we have any other choice?" I shot back, frustration seeping into my tone. "We need information, and if this person has it, we take it. We can't fight what we don't understand."

He nodded slowly, and I could see the wheels turning in his mind, the weight of our choices heavy on his shoulders. "Then we prepare. Whatever happens, we face it together."

As the rain began to let up, revealing the glimmer of stars peeking through the dissipating clouds, a sense of determination surged within me. I wouldn't be a pawn anymore; I would carve my path through this darkness.

We walked out of the alley, stepping into the dim light of the street, the city pulsing around us, oblivious to the storm brewing just beneath the surface. But as we navigated the familiar streets, a prickle of unease crept into my thoughts.

"Darian," I said, breaking the silence. "What if this is a trap? What if they're leading us straight into the Syndicate's hands?"

He paused, turning to me, his expression shifting to one of grim resolve. "Then we turn the tables. If they want a fight, we'll give them one."

The determination in his voice was infectious, igniting a fire within me. "I'm with you," I vowed. "Whatever it takes."

But just as we rounded the corner, a chilling realization washed over me like a wave crashing against the shore. There, standing just beyond the glow of the streetlight, was a figure—dark, still, and unmistakably familiar. My breath hitched as recognition set in.

"Darian...," I murmured, my voice barely above a whisper.

The figure stepped forward, and my heart sank. "I see you've made new friends," came a voice, smooth and taunting, one I had hoped never to hear again.

The storm wasn't just brewing; it had arrived, and I was about to find out just how deep the rabbit hole truly went.

Chapter 5: The Edge of Trust

The air hung heavy with the scent of damp earth and moss, the kind that clung to your skin like an unwelcome embrace. The forest was alive, the rustling of leaves whispering secrets only the trees understood. I could feel the pulse of the ground beneath me, a rhythm quickening as I pressed forward, each step guided by a mix of trepidation and reluctant trust. Darian walked beside me, his presence both a comfort and a source of unease. Every so often, I'd catch a glimpse of him from the corner of my eye, his silhouette etched against the twilight, a shadow amongst shadows.

"What's wrong? You look like you've swallowed a lemon," he quipped, his voice a smooth blend of mockery and concern.

I forced a smile, though the knot in my stomach tightened. "Just contemplating my life choices," I replied, my voice tinged with irony. "Like why I'm relying on the Shadow Man's right hand to lead me into the belly of the beast."

Darian's laugh was low and rich, reverberating through the chilly evening air. "Ah, the sweet taste of irony. You could've been safe at home, curled up with a book, yet here you are, traipsing through the woods at dusk." His dark eyes glinted mischievously, but I sensed a deeper current beneath his teasing.

"Let's just say I've always preferred adventure over comfort," I shot back, determined to keep my tone light. But beneath the bravado, I felt the weight of uncertainty. The Shadow Man, a figure cloaked in mystery and menace, was more than just a name whispered in dark corners. He was a living nightmare, and here I was, stepping willingly into his domain.

The path narrowed, twisting through gnarled roots and thick underbrush that tugged at my clothing like greedy hands. Darian moved with an ease that betrayed his familiarity with the terrain, while I stumbled, caught between my determination to keep up and the instinct to flee. Each breath I took tasted of dampness and dread, and I fought against the urge to retreat into the safety of the familiar.

"Keep your eyes peeled," Darian murmured, his voice dropping to a hushed tone that sent a chill racing down my spine. "We're getting close."

The words hung in the air, heavy with foreboding. I glanced at him, his expression now serious, the playful facade slipping away like autumn leaves. "What do you know about him?" I asked, hoping to glean some insight into the man who had drawn me into this dangerous game.

Darian hesitated, and in that moment, I saw the flicker of vulnerability behind his hardened exterior. "More than I'd like. He's not just a monster; he's a man who thrives on chaos. He knows how to exploit weaknesses, and trust me, he'll try to exploit ours."

"Then why are we doing this?" I challenged, my heart pounding in my chest. "If he knows us, knows our fears, why would we risk it?"

"Because sometimes you have to play the game to win it." His gaze pierced through the gathering shadows, a mix of determination and something softer. "And sometimes, it takes a leap of faith."

Faith. The word hung in the air between us, a fragile thread stretching taut against the uncertainty of our path. I wanted to trust him, but trust felt like a currency I had long since spent, leaving me with only doubt as my companion. Yet, as we moved deeper into the labyrinth of the woods, I found myself drawn to him, not just as an ally but as something more—a flickering ember in the cold, dark night.

As we pressed on, the trees closed in around us, their branches arching overhead like the ribs of some ancient beast. The air thickened, pressing against my lungs as if warning me to turn back. But Darian's presence was a steady anchor amidst the swirling chaos of my thoughts. With each step, he seemed to absorb the darkness, becoming a living shield against the fears creeping up my spine.

"Do you ever wonder what you're capable of?" he asked suddenly, breaking the tense silence. "What lies beneath the surface?"

I glanced at him, surprised by the unexpected depth of his question. "I don't know," I admitted. "I've spent so much time trying to survive that I haven't thought about what I might actually be able to achieve."

"Survival is a skill in itself. But you might find you're more than you believe," he replied, his tone softening as he met my gaze. "You just have to be willing to confront the darkness within."

A rustle in the underbrush interrupted our moment, and I instinctively stepped closer to him, my heart racing. "What was that?" I whispered, scanning the shadows with wide eyes.

"Stay behind me," he commanded, his body instinctively shifting into a protective stance as he peered into the darkness. I felt a rush of adrenaline as the forest came alive with sound—the chirping of crickets, the distant call of an owl, and then, beneath it all, the faintest hint of footsteps.

My breath caught as a figure emerged from the thicket, cloaked in shadows and obscured by the twilight. It was a silhouette that seemed to meld with the forest itself, a sinister presence that sent a jolt of fear coursing through my veins.

"Darian," I breathed, a note of panic creeping into my voice.

He stepped forward, a low growl escaping his lips as he prepared for a confrontation. But in that instant, I caught a glimpse of the figure's face—a mask of familiarity tinged with betrayal.

"Do you trust him?" the figure asked, their voice smooth and taunting, reverberating through the night like a dark melody.

The question hung in the air, echoing the turmoil in my heart. Trust was a slippery concept, and as I stood between the shadows and the man I barely knew, I realized the edge of trust was far more precarious than I had ever imagined.

The figure before us stepped fully into the dim light filtering through the trees, revealing a face I had hoped never to see again. It was Lena, a ghost from my past, her eyes glinting with a mixture of mischief and menace. She hadn't changed much; the same fiery red hair framed her face, cascading like a waterfall of flame, but her smile was different—colder, sharper, as if it had been carved from ice.

"Didn't expect to find you here, darling," she said, her voice dripping with mock sweetness. "And with our dear Darian no less. How quaint."

Darian shifted slightly, placing himself between me and Lena, his posture tense and defensive. "What are you doing here, Lena?" he growled, his voice low, a warning simmering just beneath the surface.

"Isn't it obvious?" She took a step closer, her movements graceful yet predatory. "I'm here for the same reason you are. To find the Shadow Man."

I swallowed hard, my heart racing. Lena had always been unpredictable, a whirlwind of chaos that drew people in before leaving them battered in her wake. "And what's your plan?" I shot back, unable to hide the edge of skepticism in my voice. "You're not exactly known for your loyalty."

She laughed, a sound that sent shivers down my spine. "Oh, sweetie, loyalty is overrated. It's all about survival now, isn't it?" Her eyes flickered to me, and a smirk danced on her lips. "But don't worry; I'm sure we'll be on the same side for now. After all, the enemy of my enemy and all that."

"Trusting her is a mistake," Darian said, his tone urgent. "She's not to be trusted."

"I'm a walking disaster, but you've always loved a little chaos, haven't you?" Lena countered, her gaze flicking back to Darian, amusement playing on her features. "You should know by now that I thrive in it."

"Thriving in chaos doesn't make you trustworthy," I replied, crossing my arms defensively. My instincts screamed at me to turn and run, but I stood my ground, unwilling to let fear dictate my actions.

"Oh, but darling, we need each other," Lena insisted, her expression shifting to something more serious. "We're all looking for the same thing. The Shadow Man is a bigger threat than you know, and if we want to stop him, we'll have to work together."

The words hung in the air, laden with unspoken implications. I glanced at Darian, searching for a flicker of agreement, but his jaw was set tight, his eyes dark pools of skepticism.

"Let's say we consider your offer," he said finally, the words coming out slowly as if they were forged from iron. "What's your angle, Lena?"

She leaned in slightly, the shadows wrapping around her like a cloak. "Let's just say I've got information. Good information. I know where he's hiding, and I know his weaknesses."

I couldn't help but scoff. "And how do we know you're not just leading us into a trap?"

Lena's laughter was infectious, but it did little to ease the tension in my chest. "You don't, but then again, neither do I," she admitted with a shrug, her casualness unnerving. "But think about it—what other choice do you have?"

Darian sighed, rubbing the back of his neck, the weariness of a man who had been playing with fire far too long evident in his demeanor. "We don't have time to debate this. If we want to find the Shadow Man before he moves again, we have to act fast."

I took a deep breath, weighing my options. The forest felt like it was closing in, each shadow a reminder of the stakes at play. "Fine," I said, my voice steady despite the chaos swirling inside me. "But I'm watching you, Lena. One wrong move, and I won't hesitate to take you down."

"Delightful," she replied, a spark of mischief lighting her eyes. "I'd expect nothing less."

With a reluctant nod, we formed an uneasy alliance, each of us acutely aware of the fragile thread of trust binding us. As we moved deeper into the woods, the atmosphere shifted, tension thick enough to slice through. The path twisted and turned, leading us further from the world I knew and deeper into the unknown.

"Tell me more about what you know," I urged, glancing at Lena as we walked. "If we're going to pull this off, we need a solid plan."

She cast me a sideways glance, her expression shifting from playful to contemplative. "The Shadow Man has a network—people he trusts, people he can control. But there's one thing he underestimates: the element of surprise."

"What are you suggesting?" Darian asked, his tone cautious, but I could see the glimmer of intrigue beneath his skepticism.

"Simple," Lena replied, her eyes sparkling with a hint of mischief. "We draw him out. We create a distraction that'll have him scrambling. And when he's vulnerable, we strike."

"Sounds like a plan forged in fire," I said, raising an eyebrow. "And knowing him, he'll have contingencies."

"Exactly," she said, her tone turning serious once more. "He's always three steps ahead, but if we play our cards right, we can outmaneuver him. We need to find his weak spot—something he cares about."

"Care? The Shadow Man?" I echoed, my skepticism evident. "You make it sound like he has a heart."

"Everyone has something they care about," Lena insisted, a knowing glint in her eye. "Even monsters."

Darian's expression remained grave as he mulled over her words. "What if we use that to our advantage? Create a scenario that forces him to reveal himself?"

"Exactly," Lena said, a wicked smile curling her lips. "But we need to be ready to act quickly. The longer we wait, the more dangerous this becomes."

The plan began to take shape in the confines of our shared distrust, an unlikely camaraderie forged in the shadows of uncertainty. As we pressed deeper into the night, I couldn't shake the feeling that the true battle was not just against the Shadow Man but within ourselves, where trust battled suspicion and vulnerability danced with fear. Each step we took brought us closer to the heart of the storm, where secrets lay hidden, and the stakes grew ever higher.

As the trees thinned out, revealing a clearing illuminated by the silver glow of the moon, a sense of urgency prickled at the edges of my awareness. The night was alive with the hum of anticipation, and somewhere in the depths of that darkness, the Shadow Man awaited—just as I awaited the moment when the walls between trust and betrayal would finally shatter.

The clearing before us unfolded like a dark secret, a landscape drenched in moonlight that danced on the edges of shadows. The air felt charged, as if the forest itself held its breath, waiting for something momentous to happen. I exchanged a quick glance with Darian, whose expression was a mask of focus and determination. Beside him, Lena bounced on her toes, her eyes gleaming with mischief and anticipation.

"Welcome to the Shadow Man's playground," she said, her voice laced with a theatrical flair. "Or what's left of it. This is where he keeps his 'treasures.'"

I scanned the area, noticing the remnants of an old structure, crumbling stone walls that had once been grand but now resembled a tomb. Vines snaked their way through the cracks, reclaiming what had been lost to time, an eerie testament to the decay of power. "You mean the treasures of his victims?" I countered, my skepticism a shield against the rising tide of fear.

"Such a gloomy outlook!" Lena quipped, a smirk curling at the corners of her mouth. "But I suppose that's part of your charm."

"Charming or not, we need to keep our wits about us," Darian interjected, his voice steady, grounding me amidst the chaos of our situation. "Lena, where exactly is he keeping his 'treasures'?"

Lena waved her hand dismissively. "Relax! I've done my homework. There's a hidden chamber beneath the old ruins. If he has anything valuable—or dangerous—it'll be there. But getting in won't be as easy as a simple door knock."

"Of course not," I replied dryly. "Nothing worthwhile ever is." The chill of the night seeped into my bones, but beneath the apprehension lay an undeniable thrill. The adrenaline coursing through my veins urged me onward, drawing me deeper into this dark game we had all unwittingly entered.

As we approached the remnants of the structure, the ground beneath us shifted slightly, a reminder that we were stepping on ancient soil soaked in secrets. Darian moved ahead, his movements silent and fluid, as he surveyed the area for any hidden traps or lurking dangers. I followed closely, the weight of uncertainty pressing down on me, but I was not about to be left behind.

"Right through here," Lena said, pointing to a narrow gap in the crumbling wall. "If I remember correctly, it leads directly to the chamber."

"Wait." I hesitated, my instincts flaring. "What if there are guards? Or worse?"

Lena shrugged, her nonchalance infuriating yet oddly reassuring. "Then we deal with it. We've come this far, haven't we? Besides, I thought you liked a little danger."

I shot her a glare, crossing my arms. "I prefer danger with a side of caution."

With a resigned sigh, I stepped through the gap behind Darian, who was already scanning the interior of the chamber. The air shifted as we entered, laden with the scent of damp stone and something else—something metallic, sharp.

Inside, the chamber opened up, revealing walls adorned with ancient symbols and markings, remnants of a time long past. The flickering shadows cast by the meager light danced across the stones, whispering tales of those who had come before us, stories of power, betrayal, and ruin.

"This place gives me the creeps," I muttered, unable to shake the feeling that we were being watched, even as the silence enveloped us.

"Get used to it," Darian replied, his voice low as he moved closer to a stone pedestal in the center of the room. "This is where it all began, where the Shadow Man's true power lies."

"What do you mean?" I stepped closer, curiosity piquing despite the ominous atmosphere.

"This chamber is rumored to hold artifacts that amplify his influence. Items that can sway loyalties and manipulate thoughts," he explained, brushing dust off the pedestal to reveal intricate carvings. "He uses them to maintain control over his network."

Lena stepped forward, her eyes glinting with a mix of excitement and greed. "If we can find those artifacts, we could turn the tables on him. Make him vulnerable."

Darian's brow furrowed, but before he could respond, a low rumble echoed through the chamber, vibrating the very stones beneath our feet. I felt a jolt of panic rush through me. "What was that?"

"Earthquake?" Lena suggested, her voice dripping with sarcasm.

"Don't joke!" I snapped, looking around frantically. The ground trembled again, and a portion of the wall crumbled, sending a shower of debris cascading to the floor.

"Everyone, back!" Darian commanded, stepping protectively in front of me. As I stumbled backward, my heart raced, pounding a frantic rhythm against my ribcage.

The rumbling intensified, and I clutched the wall for support, eyes wide with fear. "This place is coming down! We have to get out!"

Just then, a section of the wall caved in completely, revealing a dark tunnel that seemed to lead deeper into the earth. A thick cloud of dust and debris filled the air, choking me with its acrid scent.

"Stay close!" Darian yelled over the chaos. "We need to find another exit!"

But as we moved toward the newly formed tunnel, a figure emerged from the shadows, silhouetted against the flickering light. It was the Shadow Man himself, cloaked in darkness, a sinister grin stretching across his face.

"Ah, my dear guests," he purred, his voice smooth as silk yet laced with malice. "I've been expecting you."

Lena cursed under her breath, and I felt my stomach drop. The plan had unraveled in an instant, replaced by the stark reality of our situation.

"Run!" Darian shouted, but as we turned, the entrance we had come through was now blocked by a cascade of stone, sealing us inside with our enemy.

"Did you really think you could infiltrate my sanctum without consequences?" the Shadow Man taunted, stepping closer, the shadows swirling around him like a living entity.

"Let's not keep him waiting," Lena muttered, her bravado cracking under the weight of impending doom.

Panic surged through me as I darted toward the dark tunnel, my mind racing. "What do we do?"

But before Darian could respond, the ground beneath us trembled again, and the chamber quaked, threatening to swallow us whole. Just as we reached the mouth of the tunnel, the Shadow Man's laughter echoed in my ears, a haunting melody that promised nothing but despair.

In that moment, I realized that trust was a fragile thing, and betrayal could come from the most unexpected places. With the walls closing in and the darkness closing ranks, I had to decide who to trust and how far I was willing to go to escape this nightmare. But as the shadows lunged forward, I felt a rush of determination surge within me.

"Together," I urged, my voice fierce. "We fight together!"

And with that, we plunged into the darkness, the weight of our choices pressing down like the very stones around us, and just beyond the reach of my grasp, a new danger lurked, waiting to spring its trap.

Chapter 6: Heart of Darkness

The shadows crept closer, thick and insistent, wrapping around us like a living shroud. The air was electric, charged with the low hum of tension as I pressed my back against the damp brick wall of the alley. My heart pounded in my chest, each beat a desperate call to action. Darian stood beside me, his presence both a comfort and a wildfire of confusion in my chest. I could feel the warmth radiating from him, the subtle tension in his shoulders as he scanned our surroundings.

"Do you see them?" I whispered, barely able to force the words past my dry throat. The night was dark, but the distant glow of streetlights illuminated patches of the alleyway, casting long shadows that danced like specters around us.

"Not yet," he replied, his voice a gravelly murmur, low enough to make the hairs on the back of my neck prickle. He turned to face me, his eyes gleaming with a feral intensity. "But they're close. We need to move."

A chill skittered down my spine, a whisper of fear that made me want to grip his arm and pull him closer. But I couldn't afford to show weakness—not now. The last encounter with the Shadow Syndicate had left me shaken, adrenaline coursing through my veins like poison. This was no longer just a game of hide and seek; it was a desperate battle for survival, and I felt it in my bones.

"Right," I said, drawing a shaky breath. "What's the plan?"

He hesitated, his jaw tightening as he glanced down the alley, assessing the risk. "We'll cut through the market. If we're lucky, we'll lose them in the crowd."

"Crowds and dark alleys—it's a recipe for disaster," I said, forcing a wry smile. "And here I thought my life couldn't get any more complicated."

He chuckled, the sound warm and reassuring, cutting through the dread that clung to me like cobwebs. "Just think of it as an adventure," he said, and his eyes sparkled with mischief. "Besides, you're the one who wanted to dive headfirst into danger."

"Maybe I was hoping for a less life-threatening version of adventure," I shot back, my heart fluttering as his grin widened.

With a shared glance, we took off, weaving through the narrow space between the buildings. The market lay ahead, its vibrant stalls a cacophony of colors and sounds that promised a momentary refuge. As we rushed forward, I felt the cool air whip around us, mingling with the warmth of Darian's body so close to mine. A curious thrill danced in my veins, igniting a longing I had kept firmly locked away, a sensation I wasn't ready to confront.

We burst into the market, a riot of life swirling around us. The scent of fried dough mingled with the tang of spices, a heady concoction that tugged at my senses. Laughter echoed off the cobblestones, and vendors shouted their wares, each cry a siren call to those wandering by. It was a vibrant chaos, one that offered a flicker of hope against the encroaching darkness.

"Stick close," Darian instructed, his tone serious now as he grabbed my wrist, guiding me through the throngs of people. I could feel the pulse of his energy, strong and magnetic, urging me forward.

We dodged through clusters of families and couples, my pulse quickening with each brush of our bodies. I marveled at how easily I trusted him, how his presence steadied me even as danger loomed on the edges of our reality. Each time our fingers brushed, a spark ignited—a heady, intoxicating connection that sent my heart racing for entirely different reasons.

"Over there!" he shouted suddenly, pointing toward a vendor selling brightly colored scarves. "We can blend in!"

With barely a moment to think, I followed him, diving behind the stall as I tucked myself against the wooden frame. The vendor's goods spilled over the table, silks and cottons draping like vivid rainbows in the twilight. I caught my breath, the fabric of a particularly deep crimson scarf brushing my cheek as I crouched low.

Darian joined me, his body brushing against mine, and I felt the warmth radiating from him again, igniting that unwelcome longing. The chaos of the market faded into the background as I focused on him, the way his brow furrowed in concentration, the slight sheen of sweat on his forehead that highlighted the rugged lines of his face.

"Do you think they saw us?" I whispered, my voice barely more than a breath, fear coiling tight in my chest.

"Not yet," he replied, his tone steady, but his eyes darted around, scanning for any signs of movement. "But we can't stay here for long. If they catch our scent..."

"Then we really will be in trouble." I bit my lip, a surge of adrenaline coursing through me. "What if we need to fight?"

He turned to me, his expression fierce and unyielding. "If it comes to that, I'll protect you."

A thrill shot through me at his words, a delicious mix of gratitude and something deeper that twisted my stomach. I wanted to believe him, to feel safe within the promise of his strength. But the lingering shadows of fear made it hard to trust that even he could shield us from the encroaching darkness.

"Okay," I said, my voice steadier than I felt. "What's our next move?"

"Just hold on," he said, gripping my hand tightly. "On three, we bolt for the other side of the market."

Before I could respond, he counted down, and on "three," we surged forward, weaving through the stalls. My heart raced not only from fear but from the thrill of the chase, an exhilaration that coursed through my veins as we dashed past startled shoppers.

Just as we approached the end of the market, a shout rang out behind us, chilling my blood. The Syndicate had found us.

The moment the shout rang out, a cold wave of panic surged through me. The world seemed to narrow, the bustling market fading into a blur as I felt the weight of our pursuers closing in. My instincts screamed for flight, yet my feet felt glued to the cobblestones, a heavy weight of dread anchoring me in place.

"Move!" Darian's voice sliced through the fog of fear, and in an instant, my body responded, propelling us forward. We ducked behind a stall filled with fragrant herbs, the sharp scent of basil and mint flooding my senses, grounding me just long enough to push through the panic.

As we navigated the narrow passageways between the stalls, I could hear the commotion behind us—the sound of boots pounding against the ground, shouts mingling with the laughter of unsuspecting shoppers. Adrenaline surged, making every nerve in my body come alive. It felt as though I was both in my body and outside it, observing the chaos unfold around us with a curious detachment.

"Right there!" Darian pointed toward a side street, its mouth gaping like an open wound. "We'll lose them in the back alleys!"

"Are you sure?" I hesitated, glancing over my shoulder just in time to see a figure break through the crowd—a hulking shadow with a menacing presence. "I'd rather not take a detour into a trap."

"Trust me!" His eyes locked onto mine, and in that moment, I saw the unwavering conviction beneath the chaos. It flickered like a beacon, urging me forward. "If we don't move now, we'll be cornered."

With a deep breath, I nodded, surrendering to the surge of adrenaline and the magnetic pull of his determination. Together, we dashed toward the alley, slipping into the darkness just as the figure from the market caught sight of us, its expression twisting into a snarl.

The alley was narrower than I'd anticipated, the walls closing in as we pressed onward. The air was cool, damp with the scent of earth and something faintly metallic that sent an unwelcome shiver down my spine. Shadows lurked in every corner, and I felt the weight of them pressing against my back, a reminder of how easily danger could close in.

"Keep moving," Darian urged, glancing back to gauge our distance from the Syndicate members. "They won't be far behind."

I picked up my pace, the pounding of my heart mingling with the echo of our footsteps on the cobblestones. "What's the plan once we lose them? We can't just run forever."

"I've got a place nearby," he said, determination lacing his words. "A safe house. It's not far, and it'll give us a chance to regroup."

"A safe house? Sounds like a bad plot twist in a terrible romance novel," I quipped, trying to inject humor into the mounting tension.

Darian chuckled, the sound low and soothing. "What can I say? I'm a sucker for a good trope."

A sudden turn led us deeper into the labyrinthine alleys, the sounds of the market fading into a haunting silence. The darkness enveloped us, thickening the air, and the only sound was our breathing, labored but steady.

"We can't stop yet," he said, his breath brushing against my ear as we paused for a moment in the shadows, the flickering light from a distant streetlamp barely illuminating his face. "Just a bit further."

"I don't know how much further I can go," I admitted, the exhaustion creeping in. "I've run enough for a lifetime, and it's not even noon yet."

"Just think of it as a workout," he replied, a teasing glint in his eye. "You'll thank me later when you're crushing it at the next charity 5K."

"Great, now I have to add 'running from assassins' to my list of workout goals," I shot back, but the levity was a welcome distraction from the dark reality surrounding us.

With renewed resolve, we pressed onward, navigating through twisting alleyways lined with brick and faded murals that told stories of a past long forgotten. The distant sounds of the city—a car horn blaring, the laughter of children—felt surreal against the backdrop of our frantic escape.

Finally, we reached a nondescript door nestled between two towering buildings, its surface unremarkable, nearly blending into the wall itself. Darian pulled a key from his pocket, a small, rusted thing that looked like it had seen better days.

"Here goes nothing," he muttered as he unlocked the door and pushed it open, revealing a dimly lit room filled with mismatched furniture and an old, worn-out couch that sagged in the middle.

"Welcome to my humble abode," he said with a flourish, stepping aside for me to enter. I hesitated on the threshold, taking in the clutter—crates stacked haphazardly in the corners, dusty shelves lined with books whose spines were cracked and worn.

"It's cozy," I replied, stepping inside and closing the door behind us. "A perfect hideout for a rogue. Just add a few more cushions and maybe some candles for ambiance."

"Ah, so you're an interior designer now?" he shot back, raising an eyebrow. "I'll keep that in mind for my next renovation project."

"Right after you finish your assassination career?" I quipped, but the weight of reality settled over me like a heavy blanket. We were safe for now, but the tension in the air was palpable, a reminder that our reprieve might be short-lived.

Darian stepped to the window, peering through the grime-streaked glass as if expecting to see the Syndicate storming through the door at any moment. "They'll be searching for us," he said, his voice tense. "We can't stay here too long."

"Then what's the plan?" I asked, moving to join him. "We can't just wait for them to find us."

His gaze remained fixed on the street below, deep in thought. "We need to gather information, find out what they want and why they're after us. If we can figure that out, we can turn the tables."

"Sounds simple enough," I said, though a pit of uncertainty settled in my stomach. "And if they find us first?"

"We won't let that happen," he assured me, turning to face me, his expression resolute. "We'll outsmart them."

"Right. Because that's always worked out so well for us," I replied, crossing my arms, but the determination in his eyes was infectious.

"Trust me," he said, stepping closer. The heat of his body radiated toward me, making the air feel thick with tension. "We're in this together."

In that moment, the world outside faded away, and all that existed was the palpable connection between us, forged in the fires of chaos. I felt that familiar warmth pooling in my chest, the thrill of something more blooming in the depths of my heart, even as the shadows loomed closer.

"Together," I echoed, a mix of fear and exhilaration swirling within me. Whatever awaited us outside these walls, I knew one thing for certain: I wasn't facing it alone.

The room was a peculiar blend of chaos and comfort, the air thick with the smell of dust and something faintly herbal. I paced in front of the window, peering through the grime-streaked glass. The street outside was deceptively calm, a stark contrast to the storm brewing within me. Darian stood a few steps away, his back to me as he scrutinized the street, his tension palpable, the weight of the world pressing down on his shoulders.

"Do you think they'll find us?" I asked, the question slipping out before I could catch it.

"They will if we're not careful," he replied without turning around, his voice steady. "But we've got the advantage for now. They're still looking for us in the market."

"Great, so we just have to sit here and hope they don't think to check the cozy little hideaway?" I leaned against the wall, crossing my arms, irritation bubbling beneath the surface. "Sounds like a solid plan."

He finally turned to face me, a wry smile playing on his lips. "I assure you, my hideaways are always a little more strategic than that. You just have to trust me."

"Trust is a tricky thing, Darian," I shot back, raising an eyebrow. "Especially when it's coming from someone who drags me into danger for a living."

"Fair point," he admitted, his smile fading slightly. "But right now, we need to focus on gathering information. They have a reason for hunting us down, and we need to figure out what it is."

I sighed, letting my arms drop to my sides, feeling the weight of my own thoughts. "You make it sound so simple, like we're just solving a puzzle over tea and biscuits."

"Ah, but isn't that the charm of it? High-stakes danger and intrigue over a cup of tea?" He stepped closer, his eyes sparkling with mischief, and for a fleeting moment, the tension between us shifted into something lighter.

"Maybe if the tea came with a side of scones, I could get on board," I replied, attempting to keep the banter alive even as my mind raced with possibilities. "But right now, we're stuck in this dusty room with shadows lurking around the corners. I'd prefer to not end up as a cautionary tale."

Darian's expression grew serious again as he surveyed the room. "We can't stay here long. I have a contact who might know why they're after us. If we can get to him before they find us, we'll have a chance."

"Great! A mystery contact with possibly dubious motives. What could go wrong?" I retorted, unable to keep the sarcasm out of my voice. "You have a knack for finding the most charming people."

"I like to think I'm a great judge of character," he replied with a half-smile. "Besides, this one owes me a favor. If he's still alive, he'll help us."

"Fingers crossed then," I said, trying to keep the lightness in my tone, but a knot of dread tightened in my stomach. "What's the plan?"

"First, we need to get to the other side of the city. It's a bit of a trek, but we can cut through the old industrial district. Fewer eyes, more shadows." He paused, glancing back out the window. "If they're already searching the market, they won't think to look there."

"Sounds like a lovely little field trip," I said, unable to suppress a wry grin. "Will there be snacks?"

"I can't promise snacks, but I can promise a bit of adrenaline," he quipped back, his voice laced with humor, and I felt a warmth unfurling in my chest, banishing some of the cold fear lurking in the corners of my mind.

"All right then, lead the way," I said, clenching my fists to suppress the nervous energy bubbling beneath my skin. "But if we get ambushed by more of your friends from the Syndicate, I'm holding you responsible."

Darian laughed softly, and it was a beautiful sound that momentarily chased the shadows away. "Deal. Just stick close to me."

We moved cautiously, slipping through the door and into the cool embrace of the night. The city felt different in the dark, the familiar streets warped by the veil of danger that cloaked us. I stayed close to Darian, our shoulders brushing occasionally, sending jolts of warmth through me that made it hard to concentrate on anything but the sound of my heartbeat echoing in my ears.

We navigated through winding streets, the buildings towering over us like silent guardians. I could hear the distant hum of the city, but it felt muted, as if the world was holding its breath in anticipation of our next move.

"What do you know about this contact?" I asked, hoping to distract myself from the growing tension that threatened to spill over.

"Not much, just that he's been in this game longer than most," Darian replied, his voice low as we ducked into a narrow alley. "He's got a reputation for being slippery but resourceful. If anyone knows what the Syndicate wants, it's him."

"Wonderful. So we're off to meet a slippery character in the dead of night. What a romantic evening." I shook my head, trying to keep the mood light despite the growing unease in my gut.

"I promise I'll make it worth your while," he said, his expression earnest as he shot me a sidelong glance.

"Is that a promise or a threat?" I teased, though a part of me felt the weight of truth behind his words. There was something about our circumstances that felt charged, electric, as if we were stepping into something far more dangerous than either of us anticipated.

Just as we reached the mouth of another alley, a sharp sound pierced the stillness—heavy footsteps, echoing off the brick walls, sending a chill racing up my spine. My heart leapt into my throat as I exchanged a frantic look with Darian.

"Hide!" he hissed, pushing me back into the shadows just as a group of men emerged from the darkness, their figures imposing and cloaked in black.

I pressed myself against the cool brick, barely breathing as they passed, their voices low but heated.

"He can't be far," one of them growled, his tone laced with menace. "He won't escape us again."

"We've tracked him through the market. He's bound to show up soon," another replied, their eyes scanning the area with unsettling intensity.

"Then we wait," the first one snapped, and my heart sank as I realized they were blocking our only escape route.

"What do we do now?" I whispered, panic tightening my chest.

"Stay quiet. We'll wait for them to pass," Darian replied, his voice barely above a whisper, his eyes fixed on the group. I could feel the tension radiating from him, an energy that made me acutely aware of our precarious situation.

But just as I opened my mouth to respond, a loud crash echoed from the other end of the alley, a sound like shattering glass that sent the group spinning around, their focus shifting from us to the noise.

"Let's go!" Darian urged, grabbing my wrist and yanking me back into motion as they turned their attention away. We sprinted down the alley, adrenaline surging through my veins, but just as we reached the next street, the familiar feeling of dread washed over me again.

In the distance, a figure emerged from the shadows, blocking our path—a tall silhouette, unmistakable and chillingly familiar. The world around me stopped, the sound of my heart thundering in my ears as I recognized the dark eyes gleaming with intent.

"Looks like we found you," the figure said, a smirk creeping across their face, and I felt the world tilt dangerously on its axis as everything around me spiraled into uncertainty.

Chapter 7: Betrayal's Whisper

The air was thick with the scent of damp earth, a lingering reminder of the storm that had just passed. I stood in the small clearing where the trees bent slightly, their leaves rustling in a playful breeze. The remnants of rain glistened on the vibrant green grass, each droplet sparkling as if nature itself conspired to distract me from the turmoil brewing in my heart. I clutched my cloak tighter around my shoulders, feeling both the chill of the evening and the even colder tendrils of betrayal creeping in.

Darian was at my side, his presence a warm comfort against the encroaching darkness. For weeks, we had forged a bond that felt unbreakable, one woven from shared glances and late-night whispers beneath the stars. His laughter had become a melody I longed to hear, and the strength of his hand in mine had kindled a flicker of hope in my chest. But hope, like a delicate flame, is easily snuffed out.

"I know you don't trust me completely," he said, his voice low, carrying a weight I hadn't heard before. "But I need you to believe that I would never—"

"Never what?" I interrupted, a sharpness creeping into my tone. "Never betray me? Or is it that you're just waiting for the right moment?"

He stiffened, the warmth between us dimming like the dying light of the day. I could see it in the way his jaw clenched, a muscle tightening with the pressure of unsaid words. There was something brewing beneath the surface, something that threatened to unravel the fragile alliance we had built. "What's going on, Darian?" I pressed, my heart racing as uncertainty gnawed at the edges of my resolve.

He took a step back, his eyes narrowing with a mix of frustration and something else—perhaps sadness. "You think you're the only one struggling here? You don't know the half of it."

The accusation hung between us, heavy and suffocating. I wanted to reach for him, to bridge the gap that had suddenly widened like a chasm. But the remnants of doubt were relentless, whispering that I would only be disappointed. "What do you mean?" I demanded, pushing back against the rising tide of fear.

"It's about the council," he said, his voice dropping to a conspiratorial whisper. "There's a rift, a faction that wants to undermine everything we've worked for. And they're closer than you think."

His words settled into my mind like stones in a pond, sending ripples of unease coursing through me. "What does that have to do with us?" I asked, trying to keep my voice steady. "Are you saying someone is—"

"Yes," he interrupted, his gaze unwavering. "Someone is planning to betray us. And I think… I think it might be someone from our own circle."

The revelation struck like a thunderclap, shocking the breath from my lungs. I could feel the edges of panic fray my composure, my thoughts swirling in a chaotic storm of disbelief. "How can you be sure?" I breathed, desperate for clarity in this muddied situation.

"I overheard a conversation," he confessed, his eyes darkening. "They were discussing a plan, a way to undermine the council's authority. They think they can take everything we've fought for and twist it to their advantage."

My mind raced with possibilities, each more insidious than the last. Trust was a fragile thing, and in this moment, it felt like glass beneath our feet, ready to shatter at the slightest misstep. "Who?" I asked, the word barely escaping my lips.

"I don't know," he admitted, frustration lacing his voice. "But I intend to find out. We need to be vigilant, but…" He hesitated, a storm brewing in his gaze. "I can't do this alone."

The gravity of his words sank deep, and I realized that the emotional tumult between us was just as threatening as the external danger. I had already pushed him away once, fearing the affection that grew like wild ivy in my heart. But now, with the world unraveling, I couldn't afford to isolate myself further. "Then let's figure it out together," I said, steeling my resolve.

His expression softened, a flicker of hope igniting in the depths of his eyes. "Together," he echoed, and for a fleeting moment, the darkness receded, allowing a sliver of light to seep through the cracks of our uncertainty.

Yet, as the words left my lips, I couldn't shake the gnawing dread that settled in my gut. The very thought of betrayal, especially from someone so close, twisted like a knife within me. I wanted to believe in the strength of our partnership, but each revelation felt like a stone added to a precarious tower.

"Just promise me one thing," I said, my voice steadier than I felt. "If we find out who it is, we confront them together. No secrets."

His nod was solemn, a pact sealed with an unspoken understanding. "Agreed. But we have to be careful. If they're as close as I fear, we can't afford to alert them to our suspicions."

The weight of his words settled heavily upon us as dusk encroached, shadows lengthening and whispering the secrets of the forest around us. A world once familiar was morphing into a labyrinth of uncertainty. With each rustle of leaves and distant hoot of an owl, I felt the walls of our reality closing in.

As we began to walk back towards the safety of the council's encampment, a sudden chill washed over me, like icy fingers brushing against my spine. A feeling I couldn't quite name settled in the pit of my stomach. The stakes had risen, and with it, so had the peril of our emotions. I could no longer distinguish between the danger lurking in the shadows and the growing affection I felt for Darian. In this twisted game of alliances, where hearts and intentions danced in the dark, I knew one thing with stark clarity: betrayal was a whisper away, and I had to be prepared for whatever came next.

The night air crackled with an electricity that had nothing to do with the stars twinkling overhead. As we walked back toward the council's encampment, a weight settled in my chest, a nagging sense that the foundation beneath us was eroding. I could see the flickering campfires casting dancing shadows, silhouettes of our comrades bustling about, unaware of the storm brewing just beyond our reach. I had to remind myself that trust, once broken, could rarely be stitched back together seamlessly.

"I don't know how to do this," I confessed, feeling the tension wrap around us like a thick fog. Darian walked beside me, his presence both comforting and disconcerting. "What if the traitor is someone we've fought alongside? Someone we trust?"

"Trust isn't something we can afford to give blindly," he replied, his voice steady. "We need to stay vigilant. Watch how people act, what they say. It's all in the details." He paused, glancing sideways at me. "You know that saying about keeping your friends close and your enemies closer?"

"Yeah, but how do you keep your friends from becoming enemies?" I shot back, the frustration bubbling to the surface. "It's like a twisted game of chess where the pieces are always moving, and I'm just trying to keep from getting checkmated."

Darian chuckled, a deep, resonant sound that warmed the chill of the evening air. "Sounds like you're not the queen in this game. More like a pawn trying to figure out how to become a knight."

I smirked despite myself. "Well, I don't mind being a pawn as long as I get to kick some serious butt along the way. But right now, I'm feeling more like a sacrificial piece. The last thing I want is to be a pawn in someone else's twisted plot."

"Then let's change the game," he said, his eyes narrowing with determination. "We'll play our own strategy. One where we're in control." His gaze met mine, and for a moment, the world around us faded. It was just us, standing on the precipice of something monumental. But that connection was a fragile thread, easily frayed by the shadow of doubt lurking between us.

As we approached the flickering light of the camp, the laughter of our companions drifted toward us, a stark contrast to the heaviness weighing on my heart. I longed to lose myself in their camaraderie, to forget the threat of betrayal that lingered like a specter in the air. But the moment was fleeting; the weight of our discussion followed me, shadowing every smile and every cheer.

I could see Ava, our fearless leader, animatedly discussing plans for the next mission, her arms gesturing as if she could physically mold our future with her hands. The confidence that radiated from her was infectious, yet as I watched her, a nagging thought tugged at the back of my mind. What if her confidence was a mask?

I turned to Darian, my voice barely above a whisper. "Do you think Ava could be involved? I mean, if someone on the council is conspiring, she would be a prime target for manipulation."

His brow furrowed, the flicker of doubt crossing his features. "I don't want to think that. But we can't rule anyone out just yet. Just keep an eye on her. And everyone else."

I nodded, feeling the weight of our unspoken fears settle heavily on my shoulders. "I'll try, but it's hard to look at people the same way once that seed of doubt has been planted."

The thought of being constantly on guard was exhausting, but I knew we had no choice. The campfire crackled as we joined the others, the warmth wrapping around us like a fragile blanket. Laughter erupted around us, an intoxicating melody that I wished could drown out the unease in my mind.

"Hey, where have you two been?" Ava asked, her eyes bright with curiosity. "We thought you were off planning a grand escape or something."

I exchanged a glance with Darian, a silent agreement passing between us. "Just... scouting the perimeter," I replied, forcing a smile. "You know, keeping our eyes peeled for any lurking dangers."

"Or maybe sharing secrets under the stars," Darian added, his tone light but a hint of something darker hovered in his words.

Ava raised an eyebrow, clearly unconvinced. "You two are a bit too secretive for my liking. Just don't forget who's in charge around here." Her teasing tone masked an underlying seriousness. I could sense the tension beneath her words, a subtle reminder that even in moments of levity, shadows loomed.

"Of course not," I assured her, forcing a laugh. "Your position as the supreme ruler is well-known and firmly respected."

"Ha! It better be!" she shot back, her laughter infectious. But as her gaze flickered to Darian, I couldn't shake the feeling that our lighthearted banter was merely a facade, a mask we all wore to shield ourselves from the growing uncertainty.

As the evening wore on, stories were shared and plans laid out, each moment drawing us deeper into a web of trust and camaraderie. But beneath the surface, I could feel the tension simmering. Whispers of distrust crept into my thoughts, mingling with my growing feelings for Darian. I watched him, noting the way his smile didn't quite reach his eyes, the furrow in his brow that suggested he was wrestling with his own demons.

"Hey," I said softly, catching his gaze. "Are you okay?"

He looked surprised, the tension easing from his shoulders for a brief moment. "Yeah, just thinking about the next move."

"Next move?" I echoed, feigning a lightness I didn't feel. "What are we, a chess match now?"

"Maybe. Just need to make sure we're not played." His gaze flicked to the group, his voice dropping lower. "We need to stay sharp. I don't trust anyone right now."

The weight of his words hung between us, a palpable reminder of the stakes we faced. I nodded, my heart racing at the thought of how quickly everything could spiral out of control. I longed to be vulnerable with him, to bridge the gap that had formed, but the specter of betrayal hung like a dark cloud over my heart.

As the fire crackled and the laughter echoed, a sense of dread settled within me. Trust was a tenuous thread, and the longer we danced around the truth, the more likely it seemed to snap. I resolved to keep my eyes open, but I couldn't shake the feeling that whatever lay ahead would demand more than mere vigilance. It would require a strength I wasn't sure I possessed—a strength to face not only the dangers lurking in the shadows but also the tumultuous emotions that threatened to consume me from within.

The flames flickered, casting elongated shadows that danced like specters around the camp. The laughter of my comrades became a distant echo, swallowed by the dread gnawing at my insides. I felt like an interloper at a celebration, while the world around me spun with joy I couldn't touch. As Darian's eyes flicked back to the group, a tinge of worry flickered in his expression, a shadow lurking just beneath the surface.

"I'm going to grab some water," I said, my voice shaking slightly. "Do you need anything?"

"Just keep your eyes open," he replied, his tone grave. The hint of warmth from before had been extinguished, replaced by an urgency that sent my pulse racing.

The short walk to the stream felt like crossing a tightrope strung high above a chasm of uncertainty. I glanced over my shoulder, where the flickering lights of the camp painted the faces of my friends in hues of gold and amber, unaware of the storm gathering just beyond their laughter. The gurgling of the stream was a welcome distraction, a reminder that nature continued its rhythm, indifferent to the chaos brewing within our hearts.

As I filled my cup with the cool, clear water, I heard the soft crunch of footsteps behind me. I turned, half-expecting it to be Darian, but instead, it was Ava, her expression earnest and concerned. "Hey, you okay?"

I forced a smile, hoping it looked more convincing than it felt. "Just needed a moment to breathe. Things are... intense."

She studied me, her eyes piercing through the façade I tried to maintain. "You and Darian seem different tonight. More... serious. Is everything all right between you two?"

"Just the usual tension, I guess. A lot riding on us," I replied, skirting the truth. I wanted to shield her from the darker shadows that crept into my thoughts, the unshakable feeling that betrayal was a whisper away.

Ava nodded, her gaze shifting toward the camp. "We've all got each other's backs, right? We're a team."

"Yeah," I murmured, though the weight of those words felt heavier than ever. "Just... make sure you watch your back too, okay?"

The moment lingered, and I could see the gears turning in her mind. "You think someone's out to get us?"

"Let's just say, I'm not taking any chances," I replied, trying to mask the fear that rippled beneath my words. I finished filling my cup and turned back toward the camp, the air between us thick with unspoken concerns.

As we approached, I felt a surge of warmth from the gathering, laughter erupting like fireworks against the dark sky. But beneath the surface of camaraderie, I sensed an undercurrent of tension, like the moment before a storm breaks.

I caught Darian's eye as I returned, and a flicker of relief washed over me. He was talking with a few of the others, his laughter bright against the shadows. I found myself smiling, the connection between us sparking again, but it was fleeting, like a candle flickering in a gust of wind.

"Where's my drink?" he called out teasingly as I approached, his eyes twinkling.

"Sorry, your highness. I had to make a detour to keep the royal court hydrated." I grinned, handing him the cup. "Don't get too comfortable. We still have a war to prepare for."

He took the cup, our fingers brushing just for a moment, igniting a spark that sent a rush of warmth through me. But the warmth was short-lived, snuffed out by the shadows that still loomed in the corners of my mind.

"Attention, everyone!" Ava's voice rose above the chatter, commanding immediate silence. I felt a shiver run through me as everyone turned to face her, the atmosphere shifting like the wind before a storm. "We need to discuss our next move."

I exchanged a quick glance with Darian, his brow furrowed, the lightness of the moment vanishing in an instant. The tension was palpable as we gathered closer, forming a semicircle around Ava. She paced slightly, the firelight illuminating her determined expression.

"There's been word of increased activity in the northern territory," she began, her voice steady. "Scouts report unusual gatherings, and we need to be prepared for anything."

The seriousness of her tone pierced through the jovial mood. "Do you think it's the faction you mentioned?" I ventured, my heart racing.

"It's possible," she replied, pausing to meet my gaze. "We need to stay one step ahead, which means gathering more intel. I want teams out at first light."

"I'll go," Darian offered, a hint of eagerness in his voice.

Ava nodded, her expression grave. "Good. But we'll need to strategize. We can't be reckless."

"What if the traitor tries to sabotage our efforts?" I couldn't keep the worry from creeping into my voice. "If they're aware we're onto them, they might strike first."

"Then we strike back harder," Darian said, his voice low but fierce.

The tension escalated, the air thick with unsaid fears. I could sense the doubts swirling among us, questions of loyalty lingering like a specter. Just as I was about to speak up, I felt a sudden chill brush against the back of my neck, a sensation that sent shivers down my spine.

"Something doesn't feel right," I muttered, looking around. The laughter that had once surrounded us now felt distant and hollow, replaced by an unsettling stillness that settled like fog.

"Let's just keep our guard up," Ava said, her brow furrowed. "Trust no one until we can figure out who's behind this."

But before we could gather our thoughts, a sharp rustle echoed through the trees, cutting through the tension like a knife. Every head turned in unison, hearts pounding as we strained to hear over the crackling of the fire.

"What was that?" someone whispered, the dread in their voice palpable.

Darian shifted closer to me, the warmth of his body a reminder of our shared resolve, but the fear in his eyes mirrored my own. "Stay alert," he warned softly. "We're not alone."

The forest held its breath, the night growing darker, more foreboding. And then, out of the shadows, a figure emerged—a silhouette breaking the boundaries of our gathering. It was a stranger, their features obscured, a cloak draped around their form like a shroud.

"Who goes there?" Ava shouted, stepping forward, her voice a mixture of authority and fear.

The figure paused, the tension thickening, their face hidden in the darkness. "I have a message for the council," they said, their voice muffled but clear, slicing through the anxiety like glass.

And as those words hung in the air, I felt the world tilt, the ground beneath me shifting as the truth loomed closer, shrouded in secrets and shadows. The night had just begun to reveal its true colors, and I had a sinking feeling that what lay ahead would change everything.

Chapter 8: Between Light and Dark

The pulsing lights of Neo Crescent flickered like restless fireflies, casting a kaleidoscope of colors against the slick pavement. I stepped into the thrumming chaos of the nightclub, the familiar scent of spilled whiskey and sweet, sticky perfumes wrapping around me like a welcoming embrace. The bass from the speakers vibrated through my chest, a steady heartbeat that drowned out the lingering echoes of my internal turmoil. I was searching for distraction, for a moment of clarity amidst the confusion swirling around Darian and the unpredictable shadows of our entangled lives.

I navigated through the sea of bodies, each one lost in their own revelry, laughter slicing through the air like shards of glass. It was a night made for forgetting, for losing oneself in the noise and heat. I ordered a drink—something fruity, something bright—hoping it would wash away the thoughts that clung to me like a heavy fog. As I leaned against the bar, my gaze drifted over the crowd, searching for any distraction that could fill the void in my heart.

And then I saw him. Darian stood across the room, framed by the swirling lights, a figure of magnetism and mystery. His dark hair tousled artfully, his leather jacket clinging to his shoulders like a second skin. He was a tempest in a world of calm, and I could feel the pull of his gravity from where I stood. My heart raced, a traitor beating louder than the music, and I turned away, desperate to shield myself from the magnetism of his presence.

Yet the night had other plans. As I sipped my drink, the air grew thick with tension, a palpable weight that felt like a storm brewing just out of sight. I caught snippets of conversation, hushed tones filled with fear and urgency—talk of the Shadow Syndicate tightening its grip on the city. Whispers fluttered through the air like ominous butterflies, each one a reminder of the darkness that lurked at the edges of our vibrant world.

"Did you hear about the raid last week?" A girl beside me said, her voice tinged with worry. "They took half the shipments from the docks. People are scared, and the Syndicate is making its presence known."

I shifted, my stomach knotting at the implications of her words. Neo Crescent had always danced on the edge of danger, but now it felt like we were teetering on the brink of an abyss. The city I loved was becoming a shadow of itself, and the realization gnawed at me. I needed to confront my feelings for Darian, to untangle the web of love and resentment that had formed between us.

But as the night unfolded, every time I attempted to dismiss him from my mind, every moment I tried to let the music wash away my confusion, there he was, lurking in the periphery, a specter I couldn't exorcise. I cursed under my breath, downing my drink in a single gulp. The fruity sweetness turned bitter on my tongue, the alcohol igniting a fire in my veins that was not entirely unwelcome.

The dance floor swirled with energy, bodies moving in a chaotic rhythm that mirrored the turmoil within me. I waded into the fray, the music wrapping around me like a shroud, pushing my thoughts of Darian to the background, if only for a moment. But as I swayed to the beat, I felt a presence beside me—a shadow that seemed to flicker and shift. I turned, and there he was, standing mere inches away, a dark smile playing on his lips.

"You're trying too hard to forget, you know," he said, his voice a low rumble that sent a shiver down my spine.

My heart thundered in my chest as I met his gaze, that intense, piercing gaze that seemed to see right through me. "I'm not trying to forget anything," I shot back, attempting to muster the bravado that always seemed to crumble in his presence. "I just needed a distraction."

"Is that all this is for you? Just a distraction?" he asked, stepping closer, the heat radiating from him almost overwhelming. The space between us crackled with an electric tension that was impossible to ignore.

"Yes!" I insisted, though my voice wavered. "This is about me. About enjoying my life without the shadows of...whatever this is between us."

He tilted his head, studying me with an intensity that felt like he was peeling back my layers, exposing the rawness underneath. "You're not fooling anyone," he replied, his tone a mixture of challenge and concern. "Not even yourself."

In that moment, I felt the world around us fade away—the pulsing lights, the frenetic energy of the dance floor, even the looming threat of the Syndicate. It was just us, caught in a web of unspoken words and shared history, and it terrified me. The boundaries between love and hate blurred, and I didn't know which side I was standing on anymore.

"What do you want, Darian?" I asked, frustration lacing my words. "Do you want me to pretend it doesn't hurt? That I don't feel anything when I see you?"

His expression softened, just for a heartbeat, revealing the vulnerability beneath his bravado. "I want you to be honest. With me and yourself. This city is changing, and we're both part of it. We can either face it together or let it tear us apart."

I swallowed hard, my heart thundering with the weight of his words. The stakes were higher than I had ever imagined, and yet, as I stood there, so close to him, I couldn't help but wonder if maybe, just maybe, the darkness wouldn't consume us if we stood side by side.

The music thumped like a heartbeat, a visceral rhythm that matched the confusion swirling in my mind. The moment stretched, hanging between us like an unresolved note, taut and electric. I could feel the heat radiating from Darian, each pulse of the music syncing with the rapid drumming of my heart, and every instinct screamed for me to step back, to retreat into the shadows that had become my refuge. But instead, I stood rooted in place, caught in the intensity of his gaze, as if he were the only light in the chaos that surrounded me.

"I don't want to pretend," I finally said, my voice steady despite the turmoil inside. "But what does that even mean for us? You're entangled in things that could get us both killed."

His eyes darkened, a flash of something unguarded crossing his features. "I know what I'm in, and I know what I'm risking. But I'm also willing to fight for what matters to me."

"Is that supposed to be me?" I shot back, my sarcasm a flimsy shield. "Because I'm not sure what I'm supposed to be fighting for anymore. We're in different worlds, Darian."

"You keep saying that," he replied, the corner of his mouth quirking up in a half-smile that didn't quite reach his eyes. "But maybe you're the one who's making it too simple. What if I'm not the monster you think I am?"

"Are you suggesting I give you a chance to prove you're not?" I crossed my arms, the action more defensive than defiant. "Because that sounds like a terrible idea."

Darian stepped closer, his voice dropping to a conspiratorial whisper that sent a jolt of electricity through me. "Maybe it's a great idea. Or maybe it's just what this city needs—a little chaos to shake up the status quo."

The challenge in his words resonated with me, igniting a spark of rebellion I hadn't felt in a long time. The city outside was cloaked in uncertainty, the air thick with the threat of the Syndicate's tightening grip, but standing here with him felt like standing on the edge of something exhilarating and terrifying all at once.

"Fine," I said, the word escaping my lips before I had a chance to think it through. "Let's say I'm willing to entertain the idea. What do you want from me?"

Darian's gaze intensified, the weight of his stare making me feel both vulnerable and empowered. "I want you to be part of this—part of the fight. Not just as a spectator, but as someone who understands what's at stake. You see the darkness; you have the strength to challenge it."

"And you think we can fight the Syndicate together?" My skepticism dripped from my words, but beneath it lay a thread of intrigue. "That's your big plan? We take them on like it's some kind of romantic comedy?"

"Maybe it is," he countered, a playful glint in his eyes. "Romantic comedies need a bit of chaos, right? You know, like the kind of chaos we're creating right now."

His grin was infectious, breaking through the tension like sunlight after a storm, and for a moment, I allowed myself to imagine the impossible: us against the world, partners in crime and camaraderie, battling shadows together. The thought sent a thrilling shiver through me, but reality swiftly crashed back in.

"We're not a team, Darian," I reminded him, my resolve hardening. "We can't just waltz into the Syndicate's lair and hope for the best. This is serious."

"That's exactly why I need you," he replied, his tone shifting to something more earnest. "You're smarter than anyone I know. You see the patterns where I see chaos. You can help me understand how to fight back without losing everything."

The sincerity in his voice stirred something deep within me, a longing that thrummed beneath the surface of my carefully built defenses. Maybe it was the thrill of the moment, the adrenaline coursing through me, or perhaps it was the unspoken connection that had always existed between us, now illuminated in the haze of the club. Whatever it was, it urged me to consider the possibilities.

"Alright," I said, the word tasting both sweet and terrifying on my tongue. "But we do this my way. No reckless plans. I won't lose myself in this madness."

"Deal," he said, extending a hand toward me, an unexpected truce forged in the heat of the moment. I hesitated, a flicker of doubt creeping in, but then I placed my palm against his. The contact sent a spark of warmth coursing through me, igniting the remnants of my resolve.

We stood there, locked in our makeshift alliance, the noise of the club fading into the background as a new kind of understanding began to form between us.

And just as I felt a tentative sense of hope budding within me, the lights flickered ominously, plunging the club into sudden darkness. A moment later, the room erupted in panicked whispers and shouts, a chaotic tide of fear that surged through the crowd like an electric shock. I felt Darian's grip tighten around my wrist as the chaos unfolded, a palpable reminder of our fragile alliance.

"What's happening?" I shouted, trying to make myself heard above the din.

He leaned in closer, his breath warm against my ear, the hint of danger sharpening the air between us. "I think they're here."

Before I could react, a group of men stormed in from the back, their faces obscured by the dim light and the shadows that clung to the corners of the room. They moved with purpose, their presence radiating an aura of intimidation that sent shivers racing down my spine. My instincts screamed at me to run, but I was anchored by Darian's side, our fates momentarily intertwined in a whirlwind of uncertainty.

"What do we do?" I asked, my heart pounding against my ribs as I scanned the room for a potential escape route.

"We stick together," he replied, his expression a blend of determination and concern. "And we find a way out of here. Now."

The words barely left his lips when the first shot rang out, shattering the air and plunging the nightclub into chaos. My pulse quickened, a wild drumbeat echoing the panic that gripped the crowd. I could feel the weight of the moment crashing down on us as we wove through the throng, the stakes higher than I had ever imagined. There was no time for fear; only the instinct to survive, to fight back, and to understand just how deeply I was intertwined in this tangled web of light and dark.

The chaos surged like a living creature, thrumming with an intensity that made the air electric. Bodies collided, screams echoed off the walls, and I felt the primal urge to flee rise within me, every instinct screaming for safety. But with Darian at my side, I was anchored, his presence a fierce shield against the storm erupting around us.

"Stay close!" he shouted over the cacophony, his voice cutting through the panic. We ducked behind the bar, its polished surface still sticky with spilled drinks and the remnants of last night's revelry. The bartender, wide-eyed and pale, was crouched low, hands trembling as he fumbled for his phone, desperately trying to call for help.

"This is insane!" I hissed, my pulse racing as I glanced over the bar's edge. I could see the men, clad in dark suits that blended into the shadows, moving with a precision that spoke of practiced violence. They swept through the crowd, eyes scanning for something—or someone. My breath quickened, the thrill of danger mingling with a darker fear that coiled in my stomach.

"Whatever happens, don't let go of me," Darian said, his grip tightening around my wrist. The heat of his hand seeped into me, offering a strange comfort amidst the chaos. "We need to find a way out, and fast."

"Great plan," I replied sarcastically, trying to mask the fear that bubbled beneath my bravado. "Shall we throw ourselves at their feet and beg for mercy?"

He smirked, that infuriatingly charming smile cutting through the panic. "No, but I might consider a dramatic escape if you're up for it."

With a deep breath, I nodded, steeling myself for whatever madness lay ahead. It was time to embrace the chaos instead of hiding from it. We edged along the bar, carefully peeking out at the scene unfolding. The men were methodical, their movements fluid and calculated as they pushed through the throngs of terrified patrons. My stomach churned with each shouted order, the atmosphere thick with tension.

As I focused on the closest man, my mind raced with possibilities. "What if we create a diversion?" I suggested, trying to quell the rising tide of panic. "Something to distract them long enough for us to slip out."

Darian raised an eyebrow, a spark of mischief flickering in his gaze. "I like the way you think. What do you have in mind?"

Before I could formulate a plan, a nearby table flipped over, sending glasses crashing to the floor. A group of revelers bolted, their fear propelling them into the dark corners of the club. The commotion drew the attention of one of the Syndicate men, his icy gaze landing on our hiding place.

"Now or never!" I urged, my heart racing as adrenaline surged through me. Darian nodded, determination etched on his face, and together we bolted from our refuge, weaving through the chaos, our movements synchronized like a well-rehearsed dance.

We sprinted toward the back exit, the flickering lights casting frantic shadows on the walls. The pounding of our feet echoed like a war drum, urging us onward. Just as we reached the door, a gunshot rang out, the sharp crack splitting the air, followed by a chorus of panicked screams.

"Go!" Darian shouted, pushing me ahead of him. The adrenaline fueled my limbs as I burst through the exit, the cool night air hitting me like a wave. But my relief was short-lived as I turned to find him still inside, his expression fierce with resolve.

"Darian, come on!" I screamed, panic clawing at my throat. "We can't leave you behind!"

"Just go!" he roared, and the raw desperation in his voice sliced through me, igniting a spark of fear that froze me in place.

Time seemed to stretch as I weighed my options. Behind me, chaos erupted, the sound of shattering glass and cries echoing against the darkened streets. I took a step back toward the entrance, my heart screaming at me to not abandon him, but before I could make another move, he stepped out, gunfire erupting behind him.

"Run!" he urged, eyes wild with intensity, and I took his hand, pulling him with me as we sprinted down the alleyway, my breath coming in sharp gasps. We dashed past the flickering streetlights, their glow casting an ethereal light on the damp pavement.

Darian led the way, his instincts guiding us through the maze of alleys that twisted like a web through Neo Crescent. Every corner we turned felt like a heartbeat, a moment of reprieve from the chaos we had just escaped. But the adrenaline coursing through me was laced with fear, the question lingering in my mind—how far would we have to run before we were safe?

"Where to now?" I panted, glancing over my shoulder as shadows danced in the periphery, every sound magnified by the stillness that followed our frantic escape.

"There's an old warehouse a few blocks away," Darian replied, his voice steady despite the chaos we'd just left behind. "It should be empty; we can regroup and figure out our next move."

My heart sank at the thought of another hiding place, but I nodded, the need for safety overriding my instincts. "Lead the way."

As we turned down another dimly lit street, I felt a pang of regret for the life I had been living. The vibrant nightlife of Neo Crescent, once a refuge, now seemed a distant memory, replaced by the harsh reality of the shadows closing in. Yet, in the midst of this turmoil, something inside me stirred—a fierce determination to confront the darkness, to reclaim my life.

But just as we approached the warehouse, the world around us shifted again. A sleek black car screeched to a halt beside us, tires squealing against the pavement. My stomach dropped as the door swung open, revealing a figure cloaked in shadow, a familiar face that sent a jolt of disbelief coursing through me.

"Get in!" the figure barked, urgency lacing their voice.

My heart raced, recognition dawning as I took a hesitant step forward. "Lila?"

Darian's grip on my arm tightened, his expression shifting to one of wariness. "We don't know if we can trust her."

"Trust me!" Lila insisted, her eyes darting nervously toward the alley. "There's no time to explain. They're coming for you!"

Before I could respond, Darian pulled me back, uncertainty flashing in his gaze. "This could be a trap."

But as the shadows loomed closer, a new wave of adrenaline surged through me. "We can't just stand here!" I exclaimed, glancing between them. The air crackled with tension, the choice weighing heavily on my shoulders. "We have to decide—now!"

Lila's voice pierced through the chaos, desperate and insistent. "Please! I'm trying to help you!"

With a final glance at the darkness creeping up behind us, I felt the weight of the decision settle in my gut. The path ahead was fraught with danger, and I had no idea where it would lead us. But in that moment, one thing was clear: I was done running, done hiding from the shadows that threatened to consume me.

"Let's go," I said, my voice firm as I stepped toward the open door of the car, my heart racing with the unknown that lay ahead. I was ready to confront the darkness, to fight for what mattered, even if it meant risking everything. As we climbed inside, I glanced at Darian, determination mirrored in his eyes.

But just as the door slammed shut, a deafening explosion erupted in the distance, shaking the ground beneath us and casting the night into chaos once more.

Chapter 9: A Fractured Alliance

The streets of Neo Crescent throbbed with a pulsating energy that felt almost alive, the kind of chaos that made the hairs on the back of my neck stand at attention. It was the kind of night where the moon hung low and luminous, casting its silver gaze over the city, illuminating the intricate labyrinth of alleys and forgotten corners where shadows mingled and whispered secrets. I ducked into one of those shadowy recesses, my heart racing, each thump a reminder of the urgency of the moment. The air was thick with the scent of rain-soaked asphalt and the faint smoke of something burning in the distance, a promise of impending danger.

Darian emerged from the darkness, his presence like a jolt of electricity that sent my pulse into overdrive. "You can't just run off like that," he said, his voice a low rumble, as if he were trying to anchor me against the swirling storm of panic that threatened to sweep us away. He stepped closer, the tension between us palpable, a coiled spring just waiting for a spark to unleash it.

"I wasn't running off," I shot back, my tone sharper than intended, betraying the tempest of emotions roiling inside me. "I was trying to get a sense of what the Shadow Man's up to. We need to know how to counter him." But beneath the bravado, I could feel the truth: I was terrified. We were standing on the precipice of something vast and unknowable, and I had no idea how to pull us back from the edge.

"Whatever he's planning, it's worse than we imagined," Darian said, his gaze piercing, as if he were trying to peel away my bravado to expose the raw vulnerability beneath. "We can't just rush in without a plan." His words hung in the air, heavy and charged, as we both stared into the darkness that loomed around us.

"Then what do you propose?" I challenged, crossing my arms defiantly, a futile attempt to shield myself from the truth. I knew he was right; strategy had always been my forte, yet in this moment, it felt as if we were drifting, the ground shifting beneath our feet. "Sit here and wait for the chaos to reach us?"

"No," he replied, frustration edging his voice, "but we can't act recklessly. This isn't just about us anymore." He stepped closer, the distance between us charged with unspoken words and feelings that simmered just beneath the surface. "We have the city's fate in our hands."

His intensity made my heart race. I wanted to scream, to break the tension with a laugh or a snarky comment, but the gravity of our situation held me hostage. Instead, I found myself lost in the depths of his stormy eyes, seeing the reflection of my own fears mirrored back at me. "I know," I finally admitted, the words barely a whisper. "But I can't just stand by and do nothing."

"We won't," he promised, and there was something in his voice—a steadiness that anchored me, made me feel like I could face whatever darkness lay ahead. "But we need to work together. We're stronger that way."

Together. The word hung between us, a fragile thread binding our fates. In that moment, it felt as if the world had narrowed to just the two of us, our desires, our fears, and the uncertainty that loomed over us like a storm cloud.

A low rumble echoed through the streets, the ground shaking slightly beneath our feet, breaking the spell that had woven us together. "What was that?" I gasped, glancing toward the source of the sound. The city was alive with shouts and the cacophony of sirens, the unmistakable signs of chaos erupting in the heart of Neo Crescent.

"The Shadow Man is making his move," Darian said, his voice low and fierce, igniting a fire in my chest. "We have to stop him."

With a nod, I turned to face the streets, the horizon of Neo Crescent sprawled before me, a tapestry of light and shadow, hope and despair. "Where do we start?" I asked, my voice steady now, fueled by a blend of determination and adrenaline.

"Follow me," he said, motioning for me to stay close. We navigated the alleyways, our footsteps silent against the pavement, the city vibrating with an undercurrent of panic. It felt as if we were threading through a nightmare, shadows stretching and curling like tendrils, eager to ensnare us in their grasp.

As we rounded a corner, the scene that unfolded before us sent a chill skittering down my spine. Flames licked the sides of a building, orange tongues flickering against the inky night, and people scrambled in every direction, fear painted across their faces. I could see the figures of the Shadow Man's minions—dark cloaked figures moving with a fluidity that betrayed their intent.

"Darian," I whispered, grabbing his arm, "what do we do?"

"Get to the source. If we can disrupt whatever he's planning, we can turn this tide," he replied, his expression fierce, a warrior poised for battle.

Together, we surged into the chaos, adrenaline pumping through our veins. The heat from the fire was fierce against my skin, and the acrid scent of smoke filled the air, but it only fueled my determination. Each step brought us closer to the heart of the fray, a clash of wills and power that felt like an echo of the tumult brewing within my own heart. As we navigated the chaos, our breaths synchronized in a rhythm of fear and courage, I knew that this night would shape our destinies, intertwining them in ways we could neither predict nor escape.

With a resolve that cut through the chaos, I reached for Darian's hand, and for a moment, the world around us faded away. Together, we would face whatever shadows awaited us, our hearts beating as one amidst the turmoil.

The air crackled with the energy of chaos, and as we darted through the fray, the world around us transformed into a riot of sound and fury. I could hear the panicked shouts of civilians mingling with the crackle of flames, the sound reverberating through the air like an ominous symphony. Each step felt heavy, like wading through molasses, the weight of the situation pressing down on me as we maneuvered past the terrified masses.

"Where do we even start?" I asked, my voice barely rising above the din, my heart pounding in my chest like a war drum. The streets were alive with a restless energy, and with every glance, I felt the creeping dread of what might come next. Darian's grip tightened around my hand, a steady reminder that I wasn't alone in this tempest.

"Over there," he pointed towards the center of the chaos, where a group of cloaked figures huddled together, their intentions shrouded in secrecy and malice. "That's where they're gathering. We need to break them up before they unleash whatever they're planning."

I nodded, but the doubt clawed at my insides. "What if we can't? What if they're too powerful?" The thought of confronting the Shadow Man's minions made my stomach churn, but I had come too far to let fear paralyze me now.

"Fear is what they thrive on," Darian replied, his tone fierce. "We can't give them the satisfaction."

With a collective breath, we surged forward, weaving through the remnants of overturned carts and debris, the city's heartbeat palpable beneath our feet. The heat from the fire was stifling, and the acrid smoke filled my lungs, but it was nothing compared to the adrenaline coursing through my veins.

As we approached, I could make out their forms more clearly—shadows cloaked in darkness, faces obscured by hoods. They moved with an unsettling grace, as if choreographed by an unseen conductor. One of them, taller than the rest, turned slightly, and I caught a glimpse of a glinting object in their hand—a dagger, sharp and glimmering, poised for action.

"Darian, we need a plan," I said, panic creeping back into my voice. "We can't just charge in there. They look ready for a fight."

"Agreed," he murmured, scanning the area. "We need a distraction."

"Do you have something up your sleeve, or are we just improvising at this point?" I shot back, trying to inject some levity into the gravity of our situation, but the truth was, I was terrified.

"Let's hope my charm can work its magic," he replied, a smirk tugging at the corner of his mouth, the tension easing just a fraction. "Wait for my signal."

With that, Darian slipped away into the shadows, his figure blending seamlessly with the darkness. I watched, my heart racing, as he approached the group of minions, a confident swagger in his step. If anyone could distract them, it was him. The seconds stretched into eternity, each tick of my heartbeat echoing in my ears.

And then it happened. With a flourish, he gestured dramatically, catching their attention, and the shadowy figures turned, momentarily caught off guard. "Hey there, gents!" he called, his voice ringing out with a casual bravado that made my stomach flutter. "What's a couple of villains like you doing in a lovely city like this? Planning a hostile takeover?"

I had to stifle a laugh, half-amazed at his audacity. Darian had a way of turning tension into comedy, even when everything was on the line.

The tallest figure stepped forward, voice low and menacing. "You should leave while you can, boy. This doesn't concern you."

"Oh, but it does now!" Darian replied, taking a step closer, unabashed. "You see, I've got a soft spot for cities that don't go up in flames."

I held my breath, heart in my throat, watching the scene unfold. It was working. The figures were distracted, shifting their attention from their nefarious plans to the audacious man in front of them. It was a small window, but it was all we needed.

I moved silently, positioning myself behind a stack of crates, peering out to see the commotion. As Darian continued to bait them, I caught a glimpse of the dagger—the one that had gleamed in the shadows—now dangling loosely from the figure's hand. The opportunity felt electric, pulsating with the promise of action.

With one last deep breath, I sprang into action, darting from my hiding place, my mind racing with possibilities. I tackled the closest figure, catching them off guard and sending both of us tumbling to the ground.

"Now that's what I call teamwork!" Darian shouted, grinning wide as he sidestepped an attack aimed at him. The moment felt surreal, like something out of a story where heroes were always a step ahead of the villains, but I couldn't afford to let that thought distract me. I had to stay sharp.

I grappled with my opponent, their cloak slipping, revealing a face contorted with rage. "You'll pay for this!" they spat, and I felt a surge of determination. I wasn't here to back down. With a swift move, I knocked the dagger from their grip, the clang echoing against the pavement as it skittered away.

Darian's laughter rang out like a beacon amidst the chaos, invigorating me. "Watch out, now! I hope you brought your dancing shoes!"

I could hardly suppress a smile at his antics, even as I struggled against my opponent. With a final shove, I managed to break free, scrambling back to Darian's side, breathless and exhilarated.

"Nice move," he said, his eyes glinting with pride. "Now let's finish this."

As we regrouped, I felt a strange kind of confidence bloom within me. We were in this together, our strengths intertwining like the very shadows we fought against. With renewed determination, we faced the remaining minions, our hearts synced in a rhythm of resilience and defiance.

But then, from the periphery of my vision, a darker shadow loomed, one that made my stomach drop. The Shadow Man himself emerged from the chaos, his presence suffocating, an aura of malevolence that sent a chill through the air.

"Fools," he hissed, his voice like ice. "You think you can stand against me?"

Darian and I exchanged a glance, our earlier bravado crumbling in the face of his undeniable power. "Well, we're not just going to roll over," I retorted, my voice steadier than I felt, fueled by the adrenaline coursing through my veins. "We've come too far to turn back now."

He laughed, a dark, menacing sound that sent a shiver down my spine. "You have no idea what you're up against. But I'll enjoy watching you fail."

As he advanced, the shadows around him seemed to shift and pulse, a living darkness eager to envelop us. In that moment, a surge of fear washed over me, mingling with the flicker of hope that had ignited in the fight. Darian and I stood side by side, hearts pounding, knowing that our survival depended not just on our strength but on the fragile alliance we had forged. It was time to face the shadows together, come what may.

The air thrummed with tension, a palpable energy that made the fine hairs on the back of my neck stand on end as the Shadow Man advanced. He was a dark figure, his presence like an all-consuming void that threatened to swallow us whole. My mind raced, seeking a strategy to confront the looming threat, yet the cold dread creeping in from the edges of my consciousness was hard to shake.

"Okay, we can't let him get the upper hand," I murmured, glancing at Darian, whose jaw was set in determination. The flickering flames illuminated his features, casting shadows that danced across his determined expression. "What do we do?"

"Stay focused," he replied, his voice steady despite the chaos surrounding us. "We can't show fear. He feeds on it."

I nodded, the knot of fear in my stomach twisting tighter. As the Shadow Man drew closer, I could see the unmistakable glint of malice in his eyes, a storm brewing that promised devastation. "You're so sure of your power," I called out, trying to buy time, my voice stronger than I felt. "What makes you think you can control all of this?"

His lips curled into a sinister smile. "Because I thrive in the darkness. You two are merely fleeting candles in the wind. Soon, all light will be extinguished."

"Sounds like a bad metaphor for a villain," Darian quipped, stepping forward, defiance etched across his face. "But guess what? Candles can burn brighter when pushed. And we're not going out without a fight."

The Shadow Man's amusement was chilling. "Fight? You think you have the strength to face me?" He extended his hand, and the shadows around him twisted, curling like living smoke, coiling toward us with a hunger that made my heart race.

"Darian, watch out!" I shouted, my instincts kicking in as I lunged forward, but it was too late. The shadows snaked around Darian, pulling him back, the darkness enveloping him like a vice.

"Let him go!" I screamed, panic surging through my veins as I struggled to comprehend the horror unfolding before me. The shadows constricted tighter, and Darian's expression twisted from confidence to one of grim realization.

"Get away, Alina! You can't help me!" he shouted, but my resolve only hardened. I would not abandon him.

With a burst of adrenaline, I charged at the encroaching darkness, summoning all the courage I could muster. "You want a fight? Then take it!" I hurled a piece of debris from the ground, aiming for the heart of the shadow. It hit with a satisfying thud, momentarily breaking the Shadow Man's focus. The dark tendrils receded just a fraction, enough for Darian to gasp for air, his features strained but fierce.

"Nice shot!" he exclaimed, hope flickering in his eyes. "But we need to do better than that."

"Any suggestions?" I shot back, my heart pounding as the shadows shifted ominously, threatening to pull Darian under once again.

"Distract him! I'll find a way to break free!" His voice was urgent, and for a fleeting moment, I saw the fierce determination in his eyes, a spark that ignited something deep within me. We were not done yet.

"Hey, Shadow Man!" I yelled, throwing my hands up in mock surrender. "Why don't you pick on someone your own size? I hear your ego is bigger than the entire city!"

His eyes narrowed, rage flashing across his face. "You think your jests will save you? You'll pay for this insolence!"

"Oh, I wouldn't count on it. You seem more like a 'runaway villain' than a 'take-on-the-world' type," I taunted, trying to keep his attention fixed on me. It worked—his focus shifted, and the shadows that had tightened around Darian slackened ever so slightly.

Darian seized the moment, using the loosened grip to his advantage. "Now, Alina!" he shouted, breaking free from the tendrils with a powerful surge of will.

As he lunged toward me, the darkness around him flared, a momentary battle of wills. I held my breath, the world narrowing to the space between us. "Together!" I called, extending my hand.

In that instant, everything felt charged, the air thick with potential as our fingers brushed, an electric jolt that surged through my body, linking us in that moment of peril. The shadows recoiled as if stung, and I felt a rush of strength, a connection that anchored us both.

Darian met my gaze, and the fire in his eyes ignited a fierce determination within me. "We can do this," he said, his voice steady despite the chaos. "On three, we fight back."

"Let's do it," I replied, my heart racing, anticipation flooding my veins.

"One... two... three!"

With a simultaneous shout, we turned toward the Shadow Man, channeling our combined energy into a surge of light and courage. The shadows around us shrieked in protest, and the very ground trembled beneath our feet. It felt as if the city itself rallied behind us, the vibrancy of Neo Crescent pulsating with life against the encroaching darkness.

But just as we were about to unleash our power, the Shadow Man laughed, a low, sinister sound that sent a chill down my spine. "Foolish children. You think your bond can overpower me? You are nothing but pawns in a game you cannot comprehend."

With a wave of his hand, the shadows writhed violently, shifting and coiling around us like a serpent ready to strike. My heart plummeted as I realized that he was no mere villain; he was a master of the dark arts, a force of nature that we had underestimated.

"Alina!" Darian shouted, but the shadows surged forward, engulfing him in an oppressive wave, his form swallowed by the darkness. "No!" I screamed, stretching my hand out in a desperate attempt to reach him, but it was too late. The shadows roared, a cacophony of anguish and triumph, and I felt the ground beneath me crackle with energy.

A vortex of darkness spiraled around us, and in that moment, the world turned upside down. The shadows tightened, constricting my breath, and I felt myself teetering on the edge of oblivion, the light flickering as it was drawn into the consuming darkness.

"Darian!" I cried, desperation clawing at my throat. I could see him, just out of reach, his eyes locked onto mine, a mixture of fear and determination reflected back. "We're not done! We can't let him win!"

The vortex howled, and I felt my strength wane, my connection to him fraying at the edges. "Fight it!" he shouted, his voice barely audible over the din, but it resonated deep within me, igniting a spark of defiance that refused to be extinguished.

With one last surge of will, I focused on the light within me, drawing on every ounce of courage, every moment of our shared bond. I reached deep into the shadows, searching for a thread of hope, a glimmer of connection that could bridge the abyss.

But as I did, the darkness pulsed, and the Shadow Man's laughter rang out like a death knell, echoing in my ears. "You cannot escape your fate!" he taunted, and I felt the pull of despair tighten around me.

As everything began to fade, the world spinning into chaos, I caught one last glimpse of Darian, his features a mask of resolve. "I believe in us!" he shouted, and with those words, everything snapped.

The shadows shuddered, the vortex spiraling tighter, and then—I fell.

Chapter 10: Echoes of Truth

The alley was a labyrinth of shadows, twisting and curling around us like the tendrils of smoke rising from the crumbling remains of a burnt-out café. My breath came in shallow gasps, the scent of damp concrete mingling with the lingering aroma of burnt coffee, a bitter reminder of the chaos that had brought us here. Darian's presence was both a comfort and a thorn in my side; he moved with a quiet confidence, his footsteps barely making a sound against the cracked pavement, but I could feel the weight of his secrets pressing down on my chest like a heavy shroud.

"What are we even looking for?" I asked, my voice barely above a whisper as we turned a corner. The flickering neon lights above us cast ghostly reflections, illuminating the graffiti that covered the walls—each spray-painted word a testament to lives lived in the margins of society. I brushed my fingers over the wet surface, feeling the coldness of the paint seeping into my skin, a reminder that this world was alive, vibrant, yet so desperately forgotten.

Darian paused, his dark eyes scanning the shadows as if he could coax forth the answers hidden within. "A way to find out who he really is," he replied, his voice low, laced with a gravelly tension that hinted at deeper currents swirling beneath the surface. The unspoken question hung between us: could we trust each other enough to unearth the truth, even if it meant digging into our own pasts?

With every step, I could feel the delicate fabric of our uneasy alliance fraying, as if the very act of moving forward was unraveling the strands of trust we had barely begun to weave. The shadows danced around us, swirling and flickering, blurring the line between ally and adversary. I could still feel the sharp sting of betrayal from our last encounter, the moment when he'd turned his back on me, leaving me exposed in the chaos.

"Right," I said, forcing a smirk as I stepped over a puddle, its surface reflecting the neon glow above. "And just how do you plan to do that? Knock on doors until someone spills their secrets over coffee?" The sarcasm dripped from my tone, a defense mechanism against the unease that settled in my gut.

Darian shot me a sideways glance, the corners of his mouth twitching in amusement. "As tempting as that sounds, I think we need to be a bit more...creative." He gestured toward a rusted metal door slightly ajar at the end of the alley, the dim light within beckoning us like a siren's call. "After you."

I hesitated, feeling the cool metal of the door handle against my palm as I pushed it open. The creak echoed through the silence, a warning we both ignored. Inside, the air was thick with the scent of stale beer and something else—something sharp and metallic that made my skin crawl. A flickering bulb swung from the ceiling, casting erratic shadows that danced along the walls, creating an eerie backdrop for the scene unfolding before us.

The room was cluttered with mismatched furniture and discarded remnants of lives left behind. An old jukebox sat in the corner, its glass cracked but still holding the promise of a melody long forgotten. I glanced at Darian, his silhouette framed by the doorway, his expression unreadable. "This place is...cozy," I said, the sarcasm slipping through my lips like a nervous laugh.

He stepped inside, his gaze sweeping over the room as if searching for hidden dangers. "Don't let the ambiance fool you. It's a hub for information. If anyone knows something about the Shadow Man, it'll be here."

I nodded, trying to suppress the flutter of apprehension that danced in my chest. "Great. So, what's the plan? We just ask people about him and hope for the best?"

He raised an eyebrow, a faint smirk playing at his lips. "You catch on quick. But, yes, we'll need to be more subtle than that."

Before I could respond, a figure emerged from the shadows—a tall, wiry man with an unkempt beard and eyes that glinted with the intensity of a predator. "What do you want?" he growled, his voice rough like gravel. I could feel the tension spike in the air, a taut line pulled between threat and curiosity.

Darian stepped forward, his posture relaxed but his gaze steely. "We're looking for information. About the Shadow Man."

The room fell silent, the air thick with an unspoken understanding. The man's expression shifted, suspicion etched across his features. "A lot of people are looking for him. Not many come back."

"Lucky for us, we're not afraid of shadows," I chimed in, injecting a note of bravado into my voice, even as my pulse quickened. The man's gaze flicked to me, calculating, as if assessing whether I was worth the trouble.

"What do you know?" Darian pressed, leaning against the bar that ran along one side of the room, a casual act that belied the urgency of our mission.

The man snorted, crossing his arms over his chest. "Know? I know he's got a past that would chill your bones. A ghost of sorts, leaving a trail of bodies in his wake. You sure you want to dig into that?"

I exchanged a glance with Darian, the unspoken weight of our quest pressing down on us. "We're already in too deep," I replied, my voice steadier than I felt. "We have to find out who he is—before he finds us."

"Then you'd better brace yourselves. The truth has a way of biting back."

The tension in the room thickened, wrapping around us like a shroud as the man began to speak, each word drawing us deeper into a web of secrets and lies. I felt the ground shift beneath my feet, the fragile threads of our alliance fraying even more as the echoes of truth began to surface.

The man leaned back against the bar, his eyes narrowing like a predator assessing its prey. "The Shadow Man is a ghost in these parts, haunting the alleys and leaving a wake of whispers in his path. No one knows his real name, but everyone knows to fear him." His voice was gravelly, edged with the weight of countless secrets. "People who dig too deep... well, they tend to vanish."

I exchanged a glance with Darian, whose expression had turned serious, every trace of humor evaporating in the face of danger. "What do you mean by vanish?" I pressed, my voice steady despite the knot forming in my stomach. "Are we talking about missing persons or something more sinister?"

"Let's just say it's hard to find a body when the river runs cold." The man's smirk was devoid of warmth, and I felt a chill skitter down my spine. "The last folks who tried asking questions about the Shadow Man ended up in the trunk of a car, last seen driving away from here."

"Sounds delightful," I muttered, my sarcasm failing to mask the unease creeping in. "But we're not here to become cautionary tales. We just want to know who he is and why he's targeted us."

He studied us for a moment, and I could see the wheels turning behind his eyes. "You two are a curious pair. But curiosity has a cost, you know." His voice dropped to a conspiratorial whisper. "I can tell you where to find a lead, but it won't come cheap."

"Of course," Darian replied, his tone deceptively calm. "What's the price?"

The man leaned in, a glimmer of mischief dancing across his features. "Information doesn't come free. I need a favor—something simple, but you'll have to go to the edge of town. There's a girl, a friend of mine. She's mixed up in something she can't handle. Get her out, and I'll give you everything you need."

A thousand alarms blared in my head. "And if we refuse?" I shot back, my instinct kicking in. "What's stopping you from sending your friends after us instead?"

He chuckled, an unsettling sound that echoed off the walls. "You think I'm here to play games? I'm offering you a choice, sweetheart. Help me, and you'll have what you need. Refuse, and you might just find yourself on the wrong side of a couple of very angry people."

I looked at Darian, who wore a mask of contemplation. I couldn't shake the feeling that this was a setup, a ploy to entrap us further in a game that already felt rigged. "We'll think about it," I finally said, my voice steady even as my heart raced.

The man's grin widened, exposing teeth that looked far too sharp. "Good. Just remember, time's ticking. The longer you wait, the more dangerous this little game becomes." With that, he stepped back into the shadows, his form merging with the gloom.

"Did he just give us a deadline?" I asked, incredulity lacing my tone.

"Seems like it," Darian replied, crossing his arms and leaning against the bar. "We need to figure out if this girl is worth it. There's no telling what kind of trouble we're stepping into."

"Do you trust him?" I couldn't help but ask, feeling the weight of our precarious alliance bearing down on me. The flickering lights above cast an eerie glow on his face, accentuating the tension etched in his features.

"Not at all," he admitted, his voice low. "But we don't have many options right now."

I sighed, frustration bubbling beneath the surface. "So, we're going to risk our necks for a stranger just to get information about a man who's already put our lives in jeopardy?"

"Sometimes, that's the only way to uncover the truth." His gaze held mine, the intensity sparking between us, a mix of fear and determination. "We'll go find this girl, see what kind of trouble she's in. Then we'll decide our next move."

"Great. Just what I wanted—more chaos," I said with a wry grin, attempting to inject some levity into the situation. "Because who doesn't enjoy a little detour into the unknown?"

Darian chuckled, a sound that eased some of the tension swirling around us. "I knew you'd see the bright side."

"Right," I replied, rolling my eyes playfully. "Let's just hope the bright side doesn't end up with us in the trunk of a car."

As we stepped back into the alley, the air was thick with anticipation. The dim light from the bar spilled out behind us, but the shadows seemed to stretch longer, as if warning us of the path we were about to take. I could feel my heart racing, each beat echoing the rhythm of our impending journey.

The streets outside were quieter than before, the world holding its breath as we navigated through the web of narrow paths. The night air was cool against my skin, a stark contrast to the warmth radiating from Darian's body as we walked side by side. It felt strange to be so close to him again after the tension of our last encounter, and I couldn't shake the feeling that we were two players in a game far larger than ourselves.

"Do you think this girl knows anything?" I asked, breaking the silence that had settled between us like a thick fog.

"Hard to say," he replied, his voice contemplative. "But if she's connected to the Shadow Man in any way, she might have answers. We just have to be careful. She could be a victim—or a pawn in someone else's game."

"Wonderful. A mystery wrapped in an enigma, sprinkled with a dash of danger." I couldn't help the wry smile that curled my lips. "What could go wrong?"

Darian shot me a sidelong glance, his expression softening for a fleeting moment. "With us? Probably everything."

The streets began to thin out as we approached the edge of town, the atmosphere shifting from the electric buzz of the city to a more desolate, eerie quiet. Flickering streetlights cast elongated shadows that danced along the pavement, and I felt the weight of every step we took toward the unknown.

A small, run-down house loomed ahead, its paint peeling and windows grimy. It seemed to sag under the weight of untold stories, each creak of the wooden porch warning us of the past that clung to it like a heavy fog.

"This is it," Darian said, his voice low, his presence a solid anchor beside me. "Are you ready?"

I squared my shoulders, steeling myself against the uncertainty. "Ready as I'll ever be," I replied, taking a deep breath. With one last look at the darkness swallowing the streets behind us, I stepped forward, our fragile alliance pushing us toward whatever awaited within the walls of that forgotten house.

The door creaked ominously as we stepped inside, revealing a dimly lit room that felt more like a tomb than a house. Dust motes floated lazily in the air, catching the faint glimmer of the single, flickering bulb overhead. The walls were lined with faded photographs, their faces obscured by time, and the smell of mildew clung to everything like a stubborn ghost.

"Charming place," I said, unable to suppress the quip as I gingerly stepped over a loose floorboard that creaked underfoot. "Is this where we expect a warm welcome or just a collection of creepy artifacts?"

Darian chuckled, the sound a low rumble in the silence. "If we're lucky, it'll be both."

As we ventured further into the murky depths of the house, I noticed the remnants of someone's life scattered throughout—an overturned chair, a half-finished crossword puzzle on a small table, and an old, peeling calendar marked with dates long past. Each item told a story, whispering of the laughter and arguments that had filled this space before it succumbed to neglect.

"Anyone home?" I called out, my voice echoing against the walls, and for a moment, the air felt electric, charged with the possibility of response. When no one answered, the silence settled in like an unwelcome guest.

Darian motioned for me to follow him into the next room. I couldn't shake the sensation that we were being watched, the hairs on the back of my neck prickling in anticipation. He pushed the door open slowly, the hinges groaning in protest, revealing a small living area cluttered with mismatched furniture. The sunlight, filtering through grime-covered windows, illuminated a figure hunched over a table.

The girl was barely older than me, with tangled hair and a face drawn tight with worry. She looked up as we entered, her eyes widening in surprise. "Who are you?" she demanded, her voice sharp with distrust.

"Darian," he said, his tone calm but firm. "We're here to help."

"Help?" she echoed, skepticism lacing her voice. "What do you want from me?"

"Just some answers," I interjected, trying to ease the tension in the room. "We're looking for information about the Shadow Man."

The girl's expression shifted, fear creeping into her features. "You shouldn't be asking about him. He's not someone you want to cross."

"Believe me, we're aware of that," I replied, trying to keep my voice steady. "But we need to know what you know."

"I don't know much," she said, biting her lip as she hesitated. "I just heard things... whispers about who he is and what he's capable of. But it's dangerous. If he finds out you're asking questions..." She trailed off, her eyes darting toward the door, the implication hanging heavy in the air.

"Listen, we're already in deep," Darian said, stepping closer, his presence reassuring. "We have to know if there's any way to stop him."

"Stop him?" she laughed bitterly, a sound devoid of humor. "You don't stop someone like him. He's not just a man; he's a force. People go missing, and he's always there, lurking in the shadows."

I felt a chill wrap around my spine. "What do you mean, lurking?"

"People say he has eyes everywhere," she continued, her voice dropping to a whisper. "He knows everything that happens in this city, and he doesn't take kindly to prying eyes. You're risking your lives just being here."

"Then tell us how to protect ourselves," I urged, desperation creeping into my tone. "We can't just walk away from this."

She studied us, the weight of her decision visible in her furrowed brow. "If you really want to help, you need to understand the truth about him. He's not just a monster; he's part of something bigger, something that stretches beyond this city."

"Like what?" Darian pressed, his eyes narrowing in determination. "We can't help if we don't know what we're dealing with."

"Promise me you'll leave after this," she insisted, her voice trembling slightly. "The deeper you go, the more dangerous it becomes. I don't want you to end up like the others."

"Just tell us," I pleaded, my heart racing. "We need to know."

She took a deep breath, as if gathering her courage. "The Shadow Man is a collector. He doesn't just want power; he wants control over everyone's fears and secrets. And he'll do anything to keep it that way."

"Control over fears?" I echoed, confused. "How does he do that?"

"It's not just about fear; it's about information. He knows things—things you wouldn't even want to imagine. The secrets that people keep buried, the sins they think they've hidden away. He uses it against them."

"What about you?" I asked, a sudden realization dawning. "Are you one of his victims?"

Her gaze fell, and she nodded slowly. "I tried to escape, but he found me. I thought I could keep my head down and stay out of sight, but... he always knows."

Darian stepped forward, a protective aura radiating from him. "We can help you get out of here. But we need to know everything."

"Everything? You have no idea what you're asking for." She rubbed her hands together nervously, the weight of her knowledge palpable in the air. "There are consequences to speaking out."

"Consequences are the least of our worries," I said, trying to infuse some bravado into my voice. "We've come this far; we can handle whatever comes next."

As she opened her mouth to speak, the sound of shattering glass echoed through the room, followed by heavy footsteps thudding against the wooden floorboards outside. My heart raced as I exchanged a glance with Darian, both of us understanding instantly that our time had run out.

"Get behind me," he ordered, his posture shifting into something more defensive. I felt the adrenaline surge through me, every instinct screaming for us to run.

The girl's eyes widened, panic flooding her features. "It's him! He's here!"

Without a moment's hesitation, I grabbed the girl's arm, tugging her toward the back of the room as Darian moved to block the door. The footsteps grew closer, a thunderous reminder that our fragile alliance might shatter at any moment.

"Run!" I shouted, urging her to move as we dashed toward a narrow hallway. The walls seemed to close in around us, a maze that led to an uncertain escape. As we sprinted forward, I could hear the unmistakable sound of the door being kicked open behind us, splintering wood echoing through the house.

In that instant, the shadows loomed larger, and I knew we had crossed a line that could never be uncrossed. The truth was coming for us, and I could only hope we could outrun it before it consumed us whole.

Chapter 11: Fire and Ice

The chaos erupted with an intensity I had never before experienced. A cacophony of shouts and gunfire echoed through the dimly lit warehouse, blending with the acrid scent of smoke curling through the air like a sinister serpent. I crouched behind a rusted metal beam, the cold steel biting into my back as I peered out, adrenaline thrumming in my veins. In that moment, everything crystallized—the sounds, the smells, the sharp clarity of fear and purpose. This was no longer a game; it was survival.

Beside me, Darian was a tempest of energy, his every movement fluid and purposeful as he darted between crates, muscles coiling like springs ready to unleash their pent-up power. My heart raced not just from the danger but from the sheer proximity of him, a magnetic force drawing me into his orbit even amidst the violence. Our past grievances, the heated arguments, and shared moments of icy silence felt as distant as the bright blue sky that no longer graced our reality.

"Stick close!" he shouted over the din, his voice cutting through the noise like a beacon. I nodded, even though he didn't look my way. Instead, his focus was sharp, eyes scanning the shadows where threats lurked. As if sensing my gaze, he glanced back just long enough for our eyes to lock—a charged moment that sent an unexpected thrill coursing through me, a reminder of what had been and what could be. The tension between us crackled like static electricity, an unspoken understanding forged in the heat of the moment.

We moved in sync, dodging debris and taking cover as gunfire rained down around us. I felt alive and terrified, exhilarated and horrified all at once. This was my world now—the gritty underbelly of the Syndicate, a sprawling network of power and corruption, and I was fighting against it, not just for my own survival, but for something greater. Each step deeper into the fray was a step further away from the life I once knew.

"Left!" Darian barked, his tone a mix of command and urgency. I pivoted on my heel, instinctively reaching for the weapon at my side. I had always assumed I was more suited for quiet rebellion and clever words rather than violent confrontation, yet here I was, heart pounding like a war drum, fighting alongside a man I both despised and admired.

We ducked behind a stack of crates, the splintered wood providing a momentary shield. The air was thick with tension, mingling with the dust and debris swirling around us. I could see the glint of steel among the shadows—Syndicate enforcers, their faces masked, eyes cold and calculating. I swallowed hard, gripping my weapon, the metal warm from my palm.

"Are you ready for this?" I asked, my voice low, barely audible above the chaos. I shot him a sideways glance, seeking some reassurance in his expression.

"Always," he replied, a wry smile tugging at the corners of his mouth. His confidence was contagious, igniting a flicker of determination within me.

With a nod, we charged forward together, a cohesive unit battling against the tide of chaos. My heart raced with each step, each heartbeat echoing like thunder in my ears. As we engaged in skirmishes, I noticed how easily our movements intertwined. When he dodged a blow, I was already there, a step behind, my instincts sharpened by necessity. We danced through the chaos, a beautiful yet brutal choreography of survival.

In the thick of battle, I caught glimpses of his strength—how he took down a Syndicate soldier with a swift, calculated move, the elegance of his form a stark contrast to the brutality of our surroundings. I admired the way he fought, raw and unrestrained, a warrior with purpose. But it wasn't just his physical prowess that captivated me; it was the glimpses of vulnerability that flickered across his face, the way his brow furrowed in concentration, revealing the weight he carried.

"Stay behind me!" he yelled, a command laced with an undercurrent of protectiveness.

"Please, I can handle myself," I shot back, annoyance punctuating my words. A brief smile tugged at his lips, a fleeting moment of levity that grounded me amid the turmoil.

Then, the air crackled with an explosion nearby, sending a shockwave that knocked us both off our feet. I landed hard, the breath escaping my lungs in a rush. Dazed, I blinked against the dust, trying to regain my bearings. The world spun slightly, but there he was, above me—Darian, his silhouette framed by the smoke and chaos, extending a hand to help me up.

"Get up, we can't stop now!" His voice was urgent, but there was a softness to it that made my heart race anew. I took his hand, feeling the warmth of his grip as he pulled me to my feet.

The moment stretched between us, the chaos of battle fading into the background as our eyes locked once more. For an instant, the conflict outside fell away, leaving just the two of us. I could see the flicker of concern in his gaze, mingling with something deeper, something that hinted at the possibility of understanding.

"Let's finish this," I said, breaking the spell. My voice was steadier now, fueled by something fierce within. Together, we charged back into the fray, driven not just by the need to survive, but by the unspoken bond that had begun to form amidst the turmoil.

Each encounter felt like a revelation, peeling back layers of resentment and fear. We were no longer simply fighting against the Syndicate; we were fighting for each other, forging a fragile alliance in the heat of conflict. The battlefield transformed into a crucible where our pasts collided with our present, igniting a firestorm of emotions that threatened to consume us both.

Smoke curled through the air, wrapping around us like a suffocating blanket as we fought our way deeper into the heart of the chaos. The warehouse had transformed into a battleground, and every corner seemed to hide new dangers. My senses were heightened, each sound sharp and electric—footsteps crunching on shattered glass, the metallic clang of steel against steel, and the guttural shouts of men who had traded reason for violence. It was a symphony of desperation, underscored by the pounding of my heart, the rhythm of survival.

Darian was beside me, a whirlwind of motion, and I marveled at how seamlessly we moved as a unit. I never imagined I'd find myself fighting alongside someone like him, whose every action was a mixture of instinct and strategy, honed by experience and a survivalist mentality. "Watch your left!" he called out, his voice cutting through the din. I swung my body around just in time to evade a swinging fist, my reflexes betraying the hours of training I had poured into honing my skills.

"Noted!" I shot back, a teasing edge lacing my words, partly to lighten the tension and partly because I couldn't resist the urge to spar with him even in the heat of battle. He flashed a grin—a fleeting expression that ignited something warm within me, a flicker of connection amidst the chaos.

As we ducked behind another row of crates, I risked a glance at him, catching my breath for a moment. "What's our exit strategy?" I asked, my mind racing to formulate a plan. His brow furrowed, a crease of concentration forming that I found oddly endearing.

"Strategy? I thought we were winging it," he replied, a teasing lilt in his voice. I couldn't help but roll my eyes at his playful nonchalance.

"Very reassuring," I muttered, but there was a thrill in the back-and-forth that reminded me why I enjoyed being around him.

There was something intoxicating about his confidence, his ability to make light of dire situations.

A sudden explosion echoed in the distance, jolting us back to the reality of our situation. I blinked, heart racing anew as dust settled like confetti around us. "We should move—now!" I urged, my voice sharp with urgency.

"Right behind you," he said, his tone shifting to serious as he fell into step beside me. We burst into a narrow corridor, the shadows looming like ghosts, reminding me how vulnerable we truly were.

The farther we went, the more I could sense the pulse of the Syndicate surrounding us—threatening, insidious. Each door we passed was a potential trap, each sound a warning. "Stay sharp," Darian whispered, and I nodded, every nerve ending on high alert.

Just as we reached the next intersection, we were met with a wall of Syndicate enforcers, their faces obscured by menacing masks. Panic surged through me, hot and constricting. I could almost taste the metal tang of fear on my tongue. "What now?" I hissed, glancing at Darian, who appeared unfazed, like a predator assessing its next move.

"Stick together, follow my lead," he commanded, his gaze assessing the odds. "On my count..."

Before he could finish, a shout erupted from the group ahead, and instinct took over. I drew my weapon, the cool grip familiar against my palm, and prepared to fire. But Darian's hand shot out, stopping me with a firm but gentle grip. "Not yet. Let them come to us," he advised, and the urgency in his voice cut through the chaos.

In that brief moment of hesitation, I felt the weight of our unspoken bond—the trust that had slowly been forged in the fires of adversity. It was both terrifying and exhilarating.

The enforcers charged, and Darian moved like liquid, darting into the fray with precision. I followed, adrenaline flooding my system as I engaged the first attacker. The clash of our movements felt almost choreographed, and I lost myself in the rhythm, the exhilaration of the fight overshadowing my fear.

One of the enforcers swung at me, but I sidestepped, delivering a swift kick that connected with his knee, sending him sprawling. "Not so tough now, are you?" I quipped, panting slightly from the effort.

"You just might survive this after all," Darian shot back, his voice filled with admiration. The acknowledgment ignited something fierce within me—a rush of determination to prove myself.

As the skirmish continued, the world narrowed down to just Darian and me. In the midst of punches and shouts, I caught a glimpse of him—his brow slick with sweat, determination etched into his features. I couldn't help but admire how fierce he was, how vulnerable he became when the stakes were high. Each clash drew us closer, a strange bond weaving itself between us amidst the chaos.

But just as it seemed we were gaining the upper hand, a sudden sound pierced through the cacophony—an unmistakable crack, the sharp report of a gunshot. Time slowed as I turned to see an enforcer raise his weapon, and before I could react, I saw Darian spring into action, shoving me aside with a force that sent me sprawling to the ground.

"No!" I screamed, the world tilting as I watched him take the hit, his body jerking backward under the impact. Everything around me faded—the noise, the chaos, the very air seemed to still as I scrambled to my feet, panic gripping my heart.

"Darian!" I rushed to his side, my breath coming in desperate gasps. Blood trickled down his side, soaking into his shirt, and I felt my heart shatter at the sight. "Stay with me, please!" My hands shook as I pressed against the wound, trying to staunch the flow.

His eyes flickered open, a fierce determination mingling with pain. "You have to go," he gasped, his voice barely a whisper. "I'll hold them off..."

"No!" I shouted, rage and fear boiling within me. "We're getting out of here together." In that moment, I refused to consider any other option. The connection we had forged over the past hours surged to the forefront of my mind, and I couldn't let it end like this.

But as I knelt beside him, the chaos of the warehouse around us faded, leaving only our shared breaths and the weight of our fragile alliance. We were on the edge of something profound, and I couldn't let it slip away. Not now, not when I had just begun to understand the depth of what we could be together.

"Stay with me," I urged again, squeezing his hand as tears threatened to spill over. I could feel the heat of his body fading, and I knew we had to fight back, not just against the Syndicate but for the chance we had found in each other, fragile and precious amidst the fire and ice of our surroundings.

The chaos enveloped us, a whirlwind of violence and desperation, as I knelt beside Darian, the weight of his injury pressing against my heart. "You have to fight," I implored, my voice trembling with urgency. His face was pale, but those piercing eyes still burned with fierce defiance. I gripped his hand tightly, unwilling to let go, as if my strength could somehow shield him from the very real danger closing in.

"Just a scratch," he managed to say, though the way he grimaced suggested otherwise. "You need to get out of here. I'll... I'll catch up." The bravado in his voice faltered, the seriousness of our situation sinking in.

"Not a chance," I snapped, the anger bubbling up as a protective instinct took over. "You think I'm leaving you here to bleed out like some tragic hero in a bad movie?" I shot him a pointed look, and despite the gravity of the moment, a flicker of amusement danced in his eyes.

"You've clearly never seen a good action film," he said, a wry smile breaking through the pain. "This is where the hero usually makes a grand exit."

"Not on my watch," I shot back, determination solidifying my resolve. "We're going to get out of here together."

As the sound of footsteps grew closer, the reality of our situation crashed down on me like a tidal wave. I tore my gaze from his, scanning the dim corridor for an escape route, heart racing. The warehouse felt like a labyrinth, every corner potentially leading to death or salvation.

"Listen," I said, forcing my eyes back to his. "You can be the heroic martyr another day. Right now, I need you to trust me." I could see the gears turning in his head, weighing his instinct to protect me against the undeniable truth that we were stronger together.

"I always did trust you," he replied, his voice steadier now, the warmth of his hand bringing a sense of calm to the chaos swirling around us. "But I don't think I'm going to be much use in this condition."

Before I could respond, a deafening crash echoed through the corridor, reverberating off the walls like a thunderclap. The ground shook beneath us as the door at the far end of the hall splintered, and a group of Syndicate enforcers poured in, their silhouettes dark and menacing against the flickering lights. My stomach dropped, and I felt Darian's grip tighten on my hand, both of us caught in the crosshairs of fate.

"Get up!" I urged, pulling him to his feet with a strength I didn't know I possessed. He stumbled, but I steadied him, wrapping his arm around my shoulder. "We can't let them take us. Not now."

The enforcers moved in, a coordinated wave of hostility intent on taking us down. My heart raced as I glanced down the corridor, weighing our options. There was no time to second-guess myself.

I had to act. "Follow my lead," I whispered, and he nodded, his expression shifting from pain to fierce determination.

Together, we lurched toward a nearby door, my instincts screaming at me to get us both out of sight. I threw the door open and pulled him through, the musty air hitting us like a brick wall. It was a small supply room, cluttered with boxes and tools, the dim light barely illuminating our surroundings.

"We can hide here," I said, my voice steadying as I helped him lean against a stack of crates. "They'll have to search for us."

"I hate hiding," he muttered, his breath ragged as he grimaced again. I wanted to laugh at the irony—here we were, hiding for our lives, and he was complaining about it like we were playing a game of tag.

"Maybe if we stay quiet long enough, they'll just assume we left," I suggested, my own fear creeping in as I glanced at the door. The pounding footsteps echoed closer, and I held my breath, straining to hear any signs of the enforcers.

"You're good at this," he said softly, the admiration in his voice making my heart flutter. "I never would have pictured you as the hiding type."

"Desperate times call for desperate measures," I replied, shooting him a smirk. "And you're not so bad at hiding either. Look at you—what's a little blood when you're being the dashing rogue?"

He chuckled, a short burst of laughter that echoed too loudly in the cramped space. I clamped a hand over his mouth, silencing him with a grin, but it was cut short by the sound of the door creaking open.

"We need to move," I whispered urgently, my heart racing. "If they find us—"

"Yeah, yeah, I get it. Let's go," he interrupted, pushing himself up despite the pain. I admired his stubbornness; he wouldn't let anything slow him down, not even a bullet wound.

Just as we were about to make a run for it, the lights flickered, casting eerie shadows around us. An ominous hush fell over the room, the kind that hinted at something terrible just waiting to unfold. "What now?" I murmured, gripping his arm tightly as I scanned the dimly lit space.

Then, a familiar voice sliced through the silence, chilling me to the bone. "You two have been quite the thorn in our side," it sneered, a taunting edge dripping from every word. I recognized that voice—Victor, the Syndicate's ruthless enforcer and the very reason I had fought so hard to escape this world.

Darian's grip tightened on my arm, and I could see the tension in his jaw. "Stay behind me," he hissed, stepping in front of me protectively, but I could feel the panic rising in my throat.

"I won't let them take you," I insisted, but there was something in Victor's eyes, a darkness that sent a chill down my spine.

"You think you can hide from me?" Victor chuckled, stepping closer, the glint of a weapon catching the light. "You've made a lot of enemies, sweetheart, and I'm afraid you're out of luck."

The air crackled with tension as he raised the gun, a menacing smile playing on his lips. "I always wanted to see how far the two of you would go."

With a fierce determination igniting within me, I pushed Darian back further, standing my ground. "You won't get away with this," I said, my voice steadier than I felt.

Victor's expression shifted, his amusement fading as he sized us up, clearly relishing the moment. "Oh, but I already have," he said, pulling the trigger with a swift motion.

In that heartbeat, everything slowed. My mind raced as I processed the impending danger, the sound of the gunshot echoing in my ears like the ticking of a clock winding down. And just as the bullet would leave the barrel, I lunged forward, ready to fight back against fate, against everything that threatened to tear us apart, feeling as if our very lives depended on the outcome of this moment. And then, darkness descended, swallowing us whole.

Chapter 12: Shadows Unraveled

The warehouse loomed before us, a hulking shadow in the dim light of the street lamps flickering just outside its entrance. Once, it had been a bustling hub of industry, its walls echoing with the rhythm of machinery and the laughter of workers. Now, it stood silent, the air thick with the scent of rust and forgotten dreams. I pushed open the creaking door, its hinges protesting against the sudden intrusion of life. Inside, dust motes danced like spirits caught in a timeless waltz, illuminated by shafts of moonlight cutting through the cracked windows.

As we stepped inside, the chill of the night settled around us like an unwelcome blanket. I wrapped my arms around myself, feeling the ghostly caress of the past swirling through the air. The place felt alive, as if the very walls held whispers of stories long abandoned. I glanced at Darian, whose presence next to me was a jarring contrast to the desolation surrounding us. He exuded a quiet strength, the kind that made you want to lean in and confide your deepest secrets.

We found a corner littered with discarded crates and old machinery, an unlikely sanctuary in this forgotten place. I sank onto a splintered crate, my legs suddenly weary from our escape. Darian settled beside me, the warmth of his body radiating in the cold space between us. Our breath mingled in the air, creating a fog that hung heavy with unspoken words.

"I didn't think we'd make it out of there," I admitted, my voice barely above a whisper. The adrenaline was still ebbing away, leaving behind a hollow ache in my chest.

"Me neither," Darian replied, his gaze focused on the floor, where shadows pooled like spilled ink. "But we did. And that counts for something, right?"

I wanted to argue that surviving was not enough, that the weight of what had happened clung to us like the dust coating the rafters.

Instead, I nodded, feeling a strange thrill at being alive, at being here with him in this moment. "I guess it does," I said, my heart racing not just from the remnants of fear but from the proximity of his body.

The stillness was broken only by the distant sound of sirens wailing in the night, a reminder that the world outside continued to spin, indifferent to our little bubble of solitude. I looked around, taking in the peeling paint on the walls, the faded advertisements for long-gone products, and the remnants of the past that lay scattered across the floor. It was a place steeped in history, much like ourselves.

"Tell me about your dreams," I blurted out, surprising myself with the abruptness of the question. I had been meaning to dive deeper into our conversation, to peel back the layers that defined us, but I hadn't expected my curiosity to surface so suddenly.

Darian hesitated, his jaw tightening as he considered my words. "Dreams?" he repeated, the weight of the word hanging in the air like a heavy curtain. "I used to have them. Big ones. But... life has a way of grinding them down."

"What kind of dreams?" I pressed, unwilling to let the moment slip away.

He shifted slightly, as if the question had nudged something uncomfortable within him. "I wanted to change the world," he said, his voice softer now, tinged with an echo of longing. "To make things better for people. But I got caught up in my own choices, in the darkness that comes with wanting power. And now..." He trailed off, a shadow passing over his features.

I felt the need to reach out, to bridge the gap that seemed to widen between us with each revelation. "And now?" I prompted, my heart aching at the vulnerability he revealed.

"Now I'm just trying to survive," he replied, a bitterness creeping into his tone. "Trying to make amends for the mistakes I've made."

His honesty struck a chord within me, resonating with my own fears of failure and the ghosts of betrayal that haunted my past. "We all have shadows we're running from," I said, my voice steady despite the turmoil inside. "But it's how we face them that defines us."

Darian turned to me, his eyes searching mine as if he was trying to decipher the code of my soul. "What about you? What dreams do you have?"

For a moment, I hesitated, the weight of my own secrets pressing down on me. I wanted to share my ambitions, my hopes for a future free from fear and regret, but the words felt trapped in my throat. Instead, I shrugged, forcing a laugh that sounded hollow even to my own ears. "Oh, you know, the usual. World domination. Maybe a coffee shop where I can serve pastries and plot my next scheme."

Darian chuckled, a low, rumbling sound that sent a thrill through me. "Is that how you plan to take over the world? One croissant at a time?"

"Absolutely," I said, my smile genuine now. "You'd be amazed at what a good chocolate croissant can do for morale."

He leaned back, an amused expression playing on his lips. "I have to admit, I've never thought of pastries as a means of persuasion."

"Perhaps I'll write a book," I suggested playfully. "How to Rule the World with Pastry. A guide for the aspiring tyrant."

His laughter filled the space, lightening the oppressive weight of the night. In that moment, surrounded by shadows and dust, we forged a connection that felt both fragile and resilient, like a newly sprouted flower pushing through the cracks of concrete. I felt a flicker of hope igniting within me, warming the cold edges of my uncertainty. Maybe, just maybe, we could both find our way out of the darkness together.

A low rumble echoed through the warehouse, the sound reverberating against the exposed brick walls like a lingering reminder of the storm raging outside. The faint flicker of a dying bulb overhead cast erratic shadows that danced across the floor, momentarily disrupting the fragile connection we had forged. I watched as Darian shifted closer, his presence a comforting anchor amid the chaos swirling around us. The tension hung heavy in the air, thick enough to slice with a knife, yet somehow, the heat radiating between us filled the space with a different kind of energy.

"Are we safe here?" I asked, unable to quell the unease creeping into my voice. "I mean, I'd prefer not to become a permanent fixture in this lovely establishment."

Darian leaned against the crate, crossing his arms as he regarded me with an intensity that sent shivers racing down my spine. "Safe enough for now. But we should keep our voices down." His lips curled into a half-smile, the corner of his mouth twitching like he held back a joke only he understood. "After all, who knows what sort of mischief lurks in the shadows?"

"Are you suggesting we're in a horror movie?" I quipped, raising an eyebrow. "If so, I demand a better script and a leading role, preferably one where I don't end up screaming at the sight of a ghost."

Darian chuckled, the sound warm and rich, a balm for the anxiety that threatened to bubble over. "No ghosts, I promise. Just us and the echoes of the past." He straightened up, his expression shifting from playful to pensive. "But those echoes can be loud. Sometimes they're all you can hear."

I nodded, feeling the weight of unspoken words heavy between us. "Sometimes I think it's easier to confront the dead than the living," I confessed, my heart racing as I let my guard down a fraction more. "The living can surprise you in ways you never see coming."

His gaze softened, and I could sense the understanding radiating from him, as if he too had felt the sting of unexpected betrayals. "What did someone do to you?" he asked, his voice low and sincere, pulling me closer into his orbit.

I hesitated, my throat tightening. I had promised myself I wouldn't lay my burdens on anyone else, yet the sincerity in his eyes coaxed the truth out of me. "I trusted someone with everything. I thought they were different, that they cared. And then..." I trailed off, the memory rising like bile in my throat. "They took everything I gave them and tossed it aside as if it were nothing."

Darian's expression hardened, a storm brewing behind his eyes. "People can be cruel. They forget that trust is a fragile thing. One moment it's there, and the next..." He shook his head, his jaw clenched tight. "It can shatter into a million pieces."

"Exactly," I said, a flicker of hope igniting in my chest. "But here we are, both of us carrying our own scars, trying to figure it out. It's almost... comforting, in a way."

His lips curled up in a wry smile. "Comforting? You must be a special kind of optimist."

"Or a masochist," I shot back, laughter bubbling up before I could stop it. "I prefer to think I'm an optimist in a world of cynics. It makes life more interesting."

"And a little more dangerous," he added, his tone teasing. "You might end up trusting the wrong person again."

"True," I replied, my playful demeanor faltering for just a moment. "But isn't that the gamble we all take? To find someone worth trusting again?"

He leaned closer, the space between us closing as he searched my eyes. "And what if I'm the wrong person?" His question hung in the air, tinged with an edge of vulnerability that caught me off guard.

I could feel the pulse of the moment, the beating heart of possibility thrumming between us. "Then I guess I'll have to take my chances," I said, my voice steady despite the turmoil roiling within.

Darian chuckled softly, a sound that warmed the cold shadows surrounding us. "You really are fearless, aren't you?"

"Fearless or foolish?" I retorted, a playful glint in my eye. "You'll have to be the judge of that."

Our laughter echoed in the empty space, a soft harmony breaking through the tension. Just then, a noise from outside shattered our bubble. I glanced toward the door, my heart pounding as the sound of footsteps echoed in the distance. "What was that?"

Darian's demeanor shifted instantly, the laughter vanishing as he straightened, alert. "Stay quiet," he murmured, his eyes narrowing as he focused on the entrance.

I held my breath, the adrenaline crashing back in as we both strained to listen. The footsteps grew louder, the scraping of boots on concrete reverberating through the cavernous warehouse. My pulse quickened, the thrill of fear mingling with the electricity of the moment we had just shared.

Darian glanced at me, his expression grave. "We might need to move. Now."

"Where to? It's not like we can just waltz out of here," I whispered, my heart racing at the thought of being caught.

"We find another way. Follow me." He turned, moving silently toward a staircase that led up to a catwalk above, a rusty ladder clinging precariously to the wall. I hesitated for just a moment, the instinct to flee battling against the desire to stand my ground.

But the footsteps were coming closer, heavy and purposeful. I took a deep breath, my resolve hardening. "Let's go," I said, following him up the stairs, my heart thudding in sync with each step.

We reached the catwalk, the metal creaking beneath our weight. I crouched low, pressing against the railing, trying to blend into the shadows as I peered down at the entrance. A figure emerged, silhouetted against the faint glow of the streetlights outside. My breath hitched as I recognized the outline, my stomach dropping into my shoes.

"Is that who I think it is?" I whispered, my voice trembling.

Darian's eyes widened as he followed my gaze, his expression shifting from determination to disbelief. "What the hell are they doing here?"

"I don't know, but this isn't good," I replied, adrenaline spiking through my veins as I watched the figure step further into the warehouse.

We exchanged a look, a silent understanding passing between us. There was no turning back now. The shadows were unraveling, and we were caught in their tangled web.

The figure below stepped further into the warehouse, revealing a familiar silhouette that sent a jolt of unease through me. I squinted, trying to make out the features hidden in the shadows. The last time I had seen them, they had been the embodiment of betrayal, the source of so many sleepless nights. "It's him," I whispered, a mix of disbelief and fear crawling up my spine.

Darian's expression hardened, the warmth from our earlier moments vanishing like mist under the sun. "This isn't a coincidence," he murmured, his voice low and gravelly. "What are they doing here?"

"I don't know, but we need to be careful. If he sees us..." My voice trailed off, the implications hanging heavy in the air. We were no longer just two people sharing secrets; we were in the crosshairs of a confrontation I hadn't anticipated.

With a determined flick of his wrist, Darian motioned for me to move further back into the shadows. We crept along the catwalk, careful to keep our movements silent as we made our way toward a corner where the light barely reached. My heart thudded in my chest, a frantic metronome echoing the tension that hung thick in the air. I could barely hear what was happening below us, but I could see him pacing, his body language agitated.

"I can't believe I'm back here," the figure muttered to himself, his voice laced with frustration. "They think they can just push me out and forget about me? They're going to regret this."

"Who is he talking about?" I whispered, glancing at Darian, whose face was a mask of concentration.

"Maybe he's here for something," he replied, his gaze fixed on the figure. "Or someone. We need to find out what he knows."

Just then, the sound of footsteps echoed from another part of the warehouse, and my stomach twisted into knots. The newcomer moved with a purpose, the clanging of metal against metal sending shivers down my spine. "It's now or never," I said, glancing at Darian, who nodded in agreement.

We slipped further back, finding a narrow path that led down to the ground level. The last thing I wanted was to be discovered, but the curiosity nagging at me was almost unbearable. As we descended the rickety stairs, I felt the pulse of adrenaline surge through me, mingling with fear and a desperate need to uncover the truth.

Reaching the bottom, we crouched behind a stack of old crates, the musty smell of wood and decay enveloping us. From our vantage point, we could hear the murmur of voices drifting through the air. The figure was no longer alone. Two others had joined him, their silhouettes blocking the light as they loomed over him. I strained to catch their words, every syllable a thread in the fabric of the night, weaving a tapestry of intrigue.

"We can't let them think they're safe," one of the newcomers said, a woman whose voice was sharp and commanding. "If they believe we've forgotten about them, it'll be too late to strike."

"Let's just get this done," the figure retorted, his frustration palpable. "I want revenge, and I want it now."

Revenge. The word echoed in my mind, a chilling reminder of the lengths people would go when pushed to their limits. I glanced at Darian, whose expression was hardening into something resolute. "We need to leave. Now," I whispered urgently.

But before I could move, the woman turned abruptly, her gaze scanning the shadows as if she sensed our presence. My heart raced as I pressed myself closer to the crates, holding my breath. If she spotted us, all our plans would be for nothing.

"Did you hear that?" she asked, her voice tense. "I thought I heard something."

"Just the wind," the figure replied dismissively, but there was an undercurrent of doubt in his tone. "We're safe here. No one knows this place like we do."

I shot a nervous glance at Darian, who met my gaze with steely resolve. He leaned closer, his breath warm against my ear. "If we're going to find out what they're planning, we have to get closer. Stay low and keep quiet."

With a nod, I followed him, inching along the crates until we found a small opening that led into the shadows near where the trio stood. The atmosphere crackled with tension, and I felt a mix of fear and excitement as we edged closer.

Suddenly, the woman stepped forward, pulling a small device from her pocket. It glinted under the flickering light, and my breath caught in my throat. "This is the location," she said, pointing it at a map displayed on her phone. "We hit them here, where they least expect it. The element of surprise will be ours."

"Good. We'll strike at dawn," the figure said, his eyes gleaming with an unsettling intensity. "I want them to understand the cost of crossing me."

Dread pooled in my stomach, the weight of their words heavy with implication. This wasn't just a petty vendetta; it was a carefully calculated plan that would ripple through the lives of many, possibly even mine.

"Darian, we have to stop this," I whispered urgently, my mind racing. "They can't be allowed to go through with it."

He nodded, his jaw set. "We need to find a way to warn the others. But first, we need to know who 'they' are."

As I glanced back at the trio, I noticed the woman had turned her gaze back to the entrance, her eyes narrowing suspiciously. My heart raced as she began to move toward our hiding spot. "Did you hear that? I definitely heard something this time," she said, her voice low and dangerous.

Panic surged within me, and I grabbed Darian's arm, ready to bolt. But just as we prepared to retreat, the figure caught sight of our movement. "Hey!" he shouted, his voice echoing in the hollow space.

In that instant, the world narrowed down to the pounding of my heart, the sharp intake of breath, and the overwhelming need to escape. Before I could process our next move, Darian pulled me back into the shadows, urgency sparking in his eyes.

We huddled together, adrenaline surging, the stakes escalating higher than I had ever imagined. I felt the cold metal of a crate digging into my back, a stark reminder of where we were—and what was at risk. Just as I thought we might find a way out, a loud crash reverberated through the warehouse, sending a shower of dust falling from above.

"What was that?" the woman exclaimed, turning on her heel.

Darian and I exchanged a frantic glance, knowing that time was slipping away as quickly as the shadows were closing in around us. The darkness felt alive, pulsing with secrets and danger, and I couldn't shake the feeling that our moment of discovery might be our last. The stakes were rising, and the game was just beginning.

Chapter 13: The Price of Loyalty

The late afternoon sun poured through the dusty windows of the old warehouse, casting long shadows that stretched like fingers across the cracked concrete floor. I leaned against the cold wall, feeling the gritty texture beneath my fingertips, trying to steady my racing heart. The air was thick with the scent of rust and something sharper, something like fear. It wrapped around me, tightening like a noose, as I watched Darian move across the room. His every action seemed deliberate, a dance of tension and resolve that made my chest tighten in an entirely different way. I had to remind myself of the stakes; the Syndicate was at a crossroads, and one wrong step could lead us into an abyss from which we might never return.

"I'm telling you, it wasn't me!" Darian's voice sliced through the charged atmosphere, a blend of frustration and something softer, something almost pleading. I could see the muscles in his jaw tense as he glared at Marcus, who stood with his arms crossed, a granite figure in this game of shadows. My heart twisted at the sight of the two men I had come to care for, caught in a tempest that threatened to pull them apart.

"You expect us to believe that? We've lost too much already," Marcus retorted, his voice as hard as the steel beams that surrounded us. "There's a leak, and if it's not you, then who? We can't afford any more mistakes."

I stepped forward, feeling the heat of their tension wash over me. "Can we all just take a breath?" I suggested, trying to keep my voice steady. "This isn't helping." The last thing we needed was to turn on each other when we were all standing on a precipice, teetering on the brink of chaos.

Darian turned his stormy gaze toward me, and for a moment, the world faded away. There was something in the depths of his eyes, a flicker of vulnerability that made my chest ache. "You know me,

Tessa. You have to trust me." The words hung in the air between us, heavy with unspoken promises and the weight of our shared past.

"I want to," I said softly, my voice barely a whisper against the cacophony of uncertainty surrounding us. "But trust isn't given freely; it's earned." I felt the stirrings of doubt curl in my stomach. Had I been naive to think that beneath his bravado lay a heart I could trust? This tangled web we were caught in was fraying at the edges, and I didn't know how to repair it.

Marcus shook his head, a scowl marring his otherwise handsome features. "If we're going to figure this out, we need to stop being so soft. We can't afford emotions." His tone was clipped, pragmatic, but there was a raw edge to his words that spoke of the betrayal he had felt, of loyalties tested in ways none of us had expected.

Emotions were precisely what I was grappling with. They twisted like vines around my heart, constricting with every accusation that flew across the room. Darian had been my anchor through this storm; he had shown me kindness when the world had tried to grind me down. But now, that kindness felt like a double-edged sword. Was he my ally or my downfall?

"I don't know who to trust anymore," I confessed, my voice trembling slightly. "The Syndicate was supposed to be our safe haven, but now it feels like a breeding ground for treachery." I looked from Darian to Marcus, their expressions reflecting the turmoil in my heart. "We need to unite against whatever threat lurks among us, not turn on one another."

The air crackled with the tension between us, and I could see the flicker of uncertainty pass over Darian's face. "What if I told you I know who the traitor is?" he asked, his voice low and heavy with implication. My breath caught in my throat as hope flared momentarily, only to be eclipsed by the chill of fear. "I've seen things. Heard whispers that point to someone close."

"Who?" Marcus demanded, leaning in, his intensity palpable. "If you know something, you have to tell us. We can't afford to lose anyone else."

Darian hesitated, and in that moment, the walls felt as if they were closing in around us. "It's someone within our circle," he said finally, his voice a mere rasp. "Someone we all trust."

I felt the blood drain from my face as a cascade of names raced through my mind. How could we pinpoint a traitor when the very foundation of our loyalty was built on half-truths and fragmented histories?

"Stop with the theatrics, Darian," Marcus snapped. "If you have information, share it or don't waste our time."

"Trust me, Marcus, this is serious," Darian replied, the tension between them crackling like static electricity. "I didn't want to believe it, but..."

"What?" I interrupted, needing to know, needing clarity. "Tell us."

"Oliver," he finally said, the name slipping from his lips like a curse.

The name hung in the air, heavy and ominous, and I felt a wave of disbelief wash over me. Oliver had been one of the first to welcome me into the fold, his laughter a balm in the chaos of our world. "That's impossible," I protested, shaking my head. "He's been loyal to us."

"Loyalty doesn't always equate to trust, Tessa. It's easier to betray those closest to you," Darian shot back, the pain in his voice reflecting my own turmoil.

The realization crashed over me like a rogue wave, pulling me under, drowning me in a sea of uncertainty. As I grappled with the implications of his words, the weight of my own feelings for Darian pressed down on me. Here we were, teetering on the edge of collapse, and all I could do was wonder where his true loyalties lay. The fabric of our fragile alliance felt like it was unraveling, thread by thread, with each revelation laying bare the stark reality that we were all too close to the fire.

The air grew heavy, a dense fog of disbelief and suspicion settling over us as I processed Darian's words. Oliver? The thought clung to me, a bitter taste on my tongue. I could hardly reconcile the image of my spirited friend—the man who shared laughs over late-night strategizing sessions, whose unwavering optimism often felt like a warm glow amidst our chaos—with the notion of betrayal.

Darian's gaze bore into me, as if he could see the cogs turning in my mind. "Tessa, we can't afford to ignore this. Oliver has access to everything. He could be feeding information to our enemies." His voice dropped, turning conspiratorial. "You know how deeply he ingratiated himself into our operations. He's been watching us."

"And we've been watching him," Marcus countered, skepticism dripping from his tone. "You're asking us to believe he's capable of this. What proof do you have?"

Darian ran a hand through his dark hair, his frustration palpable. "I overheard him last week, talking to someone on the phone. I couldn't make out everything, but I caught snippets—about shipments, about us." The tension in the room thickened like fog in a haunted forest. "I thought it was a mistake, but now..." He let the words hang in the air, a weight pressing down on all of us.

I felt the chill of doubt creep into my chest. "You should have told us immediately," I said, my voice sharp, perhaps too sharp. "We could have confronted him."

Marcus nodded, his expression a mix of anger and concern. "We don't have time for half-truths, Darian. If there's a leak, we need to flush it out before it costs us everything."

"But how do we know you're not just deflecting?" I shot back, feeling a surge of protectiveness for Oliver. It was irrational, perhaps even reckless, but loyalty had a way of clouding judgment.

Darian's expression shifted, frustration transforming into something softer, almost pleading. "I'm not deflecting. I'm trying to keep us alive. You have to understand that."

The clamor of our emotions threatened to spill over, but beneath the tension, I could feel the first stirrings of resolve. I turned to Marcus. "We need to confront Oliver, but we have to be careful. If he's truly a traitor, we can't let him know we're onto him."

Marcus crossed his arms, his demeanor shifting from suspicion to contemplation. "I'll arrange a meeting. If he's as clean as he claims, he'll have nothing to hide. We'll ask him about the phone call."

"What if he doesn't play along?" I interjected, my anxiety rising. "What if he bolts?"

"Then we'll know for sure," Darian replied, his tone steady despite the uncertainty looming over us. "But we can't go in guns blazing. We need a plan."

We exchanged ideas, strategizing in whispers, the atmosphere a mix of determination and dread. As the shadows deepened around us, I couldn't shake the feeling that we were stepping into a trap of our own making. But what choice did we have? The stakes had never been higher, and loyalty felt like a dangerous game of chess, where each piece we moved could either secure our future or lead us to our demise.

Later, as I stood outside the warehouse, the cool evening air biting at my skin, I caught a glimpse of Darian's silhouette against the waning light. There was something hauntingly beautiful about the way he stood, caught between two worlds—the past and the uncertain future that lay before us. I approached him, the crunch of gravel underfoot breaking the silence that enveloped us.

"Are you alright?" I asked, my voice softer now, a thread of concern weaving through my words.

He turned to me, his expression unreadable. "I didn't want to believe it, Tessa. Oliver has been a brother to me. I thought we were in this together."

"Maybe we still are," I offered, my heart swelling with a fierce determination. "We just need to find out the truth."

"Truth," he echoed, the word tasting bitter on his tongue. "It's a double-edged sword. We might not like what we find."

I reached out, placing my hand on his forearm. "Whatever happens, we'll face it together. You're not alone in this." The sincerity of my words surprised me, but they felt right. I had begun to care for him, more than I was willing to admit. The warmth of his skin beneath my fingers ignited something fierce and unyielding in my chest.

He looked down at my hand, his expression softening, and for a fleeting moment, the tension between us seemed to dissolve, replaced by an unspoken understanding. But just as quickly, it vanished, swallowed by the looming shadows of our situation.

"Let's hope that understanding leads us to the right place," he said, a wry smile breaking through his earlier seriousness. "Otherwise, we might just be digging our own graves."

"Then let's not do that, shall we?" I replied, trying to lighten the mood. "I have a date with destiny, and I'd prefer it didn't involve premature burial."

He chuckled, the sound a balm to the anxiety swirling around us. "I'd prefer not to plan your funeral just yet, either."

As the sun dipped below the horizon, painting the sky in hues of orange and purple, I felt a surge of hope. Perhaps we could navigate this treacherous path after all. I took a step back, needing to regain my focus. "We should meet Oliver tomorrow. The sooner we get to the bottom of this, the better."

"Agreed. We'll confront him, but remember, he could be watching. Every move we make matters."

A chill swept through me at the implication. What had started as a simple alliance was unraveling into a tapestry of deception, and I felt like a pawn in a game I barely understood. As we stood together, the weight of the unknown settled heavily upon my shoulders, yet a flicker of resolve ignited within me. We would find the truth, and whatever the outcome, I would face it head-on.

The sun rose reluctantly the next morning, a shy glow spilling across the horizon, as if it, too, sensed the tension coiling in the air around us. I stood at the window of my small apartment, watching the world awaken while my stomach churned with anticipation. The streets below bustled with early-morning commuters, their faces blurring together in a symphony of purpose that felt miles away from the chaos I was enmeshed in. Today would be our reckoning with Oliver, and I couldn't shake the feeling that we were stepping into a lion's den, each step echoing louder than the last.

I dressed deliberately, pulling on a fitted black jacket that made me feel more confident, as if it could somehow fortify me against the storm looming ahead. My mind replayed Darian's words from last night, the way he'd looked at me when we stood outside the warehouse, the warmth of his gaze lingering long after our conversation ended. Would that warmth still exist when we faced Oliver? Or would it be extinguished by the flames of betrayal?

As I made my way to the meeting place, an inconspicuous café nestled between two nondescript buildings, I rehearsed our plan like a secret incantation. Marcus would play the role of the skeptic, probing for cracks in Oliver's facade, while Darian and I would stand by, ready to spring into action if the situation escalated. I arrived early, finding a quiet table in the corner where I could observe the entrance, the faint aroma of freshly brewed coffee mixing with the sweet scent of pastries in the air, a comforting contrast to the uncertainty in my heart.

Moments later, Darian walked in, his presence commanding the room despite the casual attire of jeans and a fitted shirt. He spotted me and offered a slight nod before making his way to the counter. I couldn't help but admire the way he moved, purposeful and focused, yet with an underlying current of vulnerability that made him all the more human. I forced myself to look away, trying to focus on the task at hand.

Marcus arrived soon after, his brow furrowed, eyes scanning the café like a hawk. He joined us at the table, his posture tense. "Where's Oliver?" he asked, glancing at the door as if willing our friend to appear.

"He's late," I replied, unable to mask the rising anxiety in my voice. "Maybe he suspects something."

"Or he's just stuck in traffic," Darian said, trying to inject a bit of levity. "Let's not jump to conclusions just yet."

But I could feel the tension building, like the quiet before a storm. Just as I was about to suggest we call him, Oliver burst through the door, his smile bright and infectious. "Sorry I'm late! Traffic was a nightmare. You know how it is."

I forced a smile, but my heart thudded in my chest. His carefree demeanor felt like a mask, and I couldn't shake the feeling that beneath that grin lay secrets that could shatter everything we'd built.

"Hey, Oliver," I said, gesturing for him to join us. "We were just talking about the new shipments."

His brow furrowed slightly as he slid into the booth. "What about them?"

I exchanged a glance with Darian, whose eyes reflected the same mix of hope and dread that filled my own. "There have been some concerns about logistics, and we thought we should go over the details together," I explained, trying to sound casual, but the words felt heavy on my tongue.

"Sure, sounds good," Oliver replied, his easy smile still in place, but a flicker of unease passed through his eyes, almost imperceptibly.

As we discussed the shipments, I watched him closely. Every response seemed rehearsed, as if he were playing a part in a script written by someone else. Marcus pushed further, asking pointed questions that made Oliver squirm, but each time he deflected with practiced ease, a quick wit masking the tension.

But the deeper we dug, the more I felt the cracks appearing in his facade. "What about the call last week?" Marcus finally blurted, the directness cutting through the air like a knife.

Oliver's smile faltered for just a heartbeat, but he recovered quickly. "What call?"

"Don't play coy with us," Darian interjected, his voice low and steady. "We know you've been in contact with some... unsavory people."

For a moment, the silence stretched between us, heavy and palpable. I held my breath, watching the storm gather in Oliver's eyes, a mixture of confusion and anger brewing just beneath the surface. "You think I'd betray you? After everything we've been through?"

"You tell us," I said, my own voice surprisingly firm. "We're just trying to figure out what's happening. We can't have a traitor in our midst."

His expression darkened, and for a brief moment, I glimpsed something raw and unfiltered in him. "You're accusing me of treason? After everything I've done for this Syndicate?"

The accusation hung in the air, charged with the weight of our shared history. I could see the muscles in Marcus' jaw twitching, the tension palpable as we all braced for Oliver's reaction.

"Look, I don't know what you've heard," he said, voice rising with indignation, "but I would never—"

"Then why did you disappear for hours last week?" Darian pressed, not backing down. "Why weren't you answering your phone?"

Oliver's demeanor shifted, a flicker of something dangerous crossing his face. "You think you can just question me like this? You think you know what I'm doing?"

The café around us faded, and all I could hear was the rapid beating of my heart. "We're not trying to accuse you. We're trying to protect ourselves. Protect the Syndicate," I urged, but the words felt hollow, swallowed by the growing storm brewing in Oliver's eyes.

Suddenly, Oliver stood, his chair scraping loudly against the floor, drawing the attention of several patrons. "I can't believe this. You think I'm the traitor? You're all out of your minds!"

"Then prove us wrong," Marcus challenged, his voice steady despite the tension crackling in the air.

The intensity of the moment felt electric, and I could see the struggle playing out in Oliver's expression—anger clashing with hurt. Just as he opened his mouth to respond, the sound of ringing phones broke the tension, each of us instinctively reaching for our devices.

I glanced down, my heart sinking as I read the message. "Emergency meeting—headquarters. Now."

"What's going on?" Darian asked, his brow furrowing.

Before I could respond, the café door swung open with a jarring bang, and a figure stepped inside, their face obscured by shadows. I felt the blood drain from my face as recognition set in—a figure from my past, one I never expected to see again. "Tessa," they said, their voice smooth and chilling, cutting through the din of the café. "We need to talk."

Panic gripped me as I locked eyes with Darian and Marcus. Oliver's expression shifted, confusion giving way to something darker as the implications of my past loomed before us. The air crackled with unspoken truths and buried secrets, and I realized in that moment that our loyalties were about to be tested in ways we could never have anticipated.

Chapter 14: Beneath the Surface

The night wrapped around us like a velvet cloak, thick with the scent of pine and damp earth. I sat cross-legged on the weathered porch of the cabin, the wooden boards creaking softly beneath my weight. The stars above shimmered like diamonds scattered across a deep blue canvas, their light reflecting off the lake's surface, creating a dance of silver ripples. In this serene setting, with the cool air brushing against my skin, I felt a strange warmth blossoming inside me—a warmth that was both thrilling and terrifying.

Darian leaned against the railing, a silhouette against the starlit backdrop. His profile was sharp, etched by the moonlight, and I couldn't help but marvel at how a man so fierce could also appear so contemplative. It was a blend of strength and vulnerability that drew me in, like moth to flame, despite every warning bell ringing in my mind. His gaze was fixed on the horizon, where the treetops whispered secrets to the wind, and I knew that behind that stoic facade lay stories waiting to be told.

"Tell me about the moments that made you who you are," I ventured, my voice barely above a whisper, yet it felt like a declaration, a challenge. The words hung in the air, thick with anticipation, and I could see the slight tension in his shoulders, the way his jaw tightened as he turned to meet my eyes.

He studied me for a heartbeat longer than necessary, as if weighing the sincerity of my request. "You really want to know?" he asked, a hint of skepticism in his tone. It was that sharp wit I'd come to recognize, yet beneath it was something more—curiosity, perhaps. Or maybe fear.

I nodded, my heart racing at the prospect of him opening up. "Yes. I think it's time I learned the truth behind the man I've reluctantly come to admire."

With a sigh, he pushed off the railing and took a seat beside me, our shoulders brushing together. The contact sent a jolt of electricity through me, and I fought the urge to lean closer, to feel the warmth radiating from his skin. Instead, I focused on his expression, which had shifted from guarded to reflective.

"There are shadows in everyone's past, aren't there?" he began, his voice low and gravelly. "Mine's a bit darker than most. I grew up in a small town where the air was thick with secrets, and every family had its skeletons rattling in the closet." He paused, staring out into the distance, the memories clearly flooding back. "My father was a good man, but he struggled. The kind of struggle that eats away at you, day by day, until you're just a shadow of who you once were. He worked two jobs, but it was never enough. I watched him drown in debts, drowning in the disappointment that came with not being able to provide for us."

I could feel the gravity of his words settling between us, creating an invisible barrier of sorrow. "And your mother?" I asked softly, drawing him in, coaxing out the pieces of his story.

"She tried to hold everything together. She was a fierce woman, but life had a way of wearing her down too. By the time I hit my teenage years, I was often left to fend for myself." He chuckled dryly, the sound laced with bitterness. "The streets became my playground, and let me tell you, the lessons learned weren't exactly what I'd call enriching."

A weight hung heavy in the air as he spoke, a tangible echo of the pain that had shaped him. I sensed the tremor of his past entwining with my own burgeoning feelings for him, each revelation pulling me deeper into his world.

"I got into trouble," he continued, the admission rolling off his tongue like a confession. "Nothing major—just enough to keep me on the radar of the local law enforcement. I was a kid acting out, trying to make sense of all the chaos. But then something happened that changed everything."

I held my breath, sensing the shift in his narrative, the dark cloud hovering over his next words. "I lost my little sister. She was everything to me. Smart, full of life, and so damn innocent." His voice wavered, and I could see the rawness in his eyes, the way the memories pierced through his tough exterior. "She was taken from us in a car accident. One moment she was there, and the next... gone. It shattered my family. My father turned to alcohol, and my mother just... disappeared into her grief. I was left alone, drowning in a sea of what-ifs."

The air around us felt thick with the pain of his past, and I yearned to reach out, to take his hand and let him know he wasn't alone anymore. But I held back, afraid that my touch might shatter the fragile connection we had begun to forge.

"And that's when you decided to fight back?" I asked, desperate to find a glimmer of hope in his story.

He nodded slowly, his gaze locked on mine, a flicker of determination igniting in his eyes. "I realized that if I didn't take control of my life, I'd end up like my parents. I started boxing, channeling all that rage and pain into something constructive. It became my salvation, my outlet. I fought not just in the ring but against the demons that haunted me."

My heart swelled with admiration, tinged with sadness. Here was a man who had faced the darkest corners of his existence and emerged, scarred but unbroken. The barriers between us began to dissolve, layer by layer, as I felt an intense longing to reach out, to comfort him, to be his anchor in this turbulent sea of memories.

But just as I opened my mouth to speak, to offer solace or encouragement, a chill swept through the air, sending shivers down my spine. The serene night suddenly felt oppressive, as if the very shadows that had welcomed his stories now conspired to keep them hidden. I glanced around, my instincts screaming that we weren't as alone as we thought.

"Darian," I said, my voice trembling slightly. "I think we're being watched."

The words hung in the air, thick with anticipation and unease, casting a long shadow over our intimate moment. I could feel Darian's muscles tense beside me, as if he had instinctively slipped back into that state of alertness, the protective armor he wore like a second skin. "What do you mean?" he asked, his tone clipped, eyes scanning the darkness beyond the porch.

"I don't know," I replied, my heart racing as I squinted into the night. The trees loomed tall and ominous, their branches twisting like skeletal fingers against the sky. "I just... I have this feeling. Something isn't right." My senses were on high alert, as if the air itself had thickened, charged with a palpable tension that sent prickles down my spine.

Darian's jaw tightened, and he rose to his feet, instinctively falling into a stance that screamed readiness. "Stay here," he instructed, his voice low but firm. I watched him, torn between the urge to obey and the desire to stand by his side. He was a man forged in fire, and I knew that his past had taught him to be wary of shadows—shadows that sometimes hid the darkest truths.

He stepped away from the porch, moving toward the edge of the yard, where the beam of light from the cabin barely reached. "Darian," I called, panic creeping into my voice, but he waved a hand, signaling me to be silent. The night was so still it felt as though even the wind held its breath, and my heart pounded in my chest, a war drum urging me to take action.

The tension stretched taut between us, and I took a moment to collect myself. I focused on the gentle lapping of the lake against the shore, the soft rustle of leaves in the breeze—anything to ground myself in the reality of our surroundings. It was then I noticed the faintest crunch of gravel underfoot, not from the direction of the cabin, but from the woods behind us. My heart sank, the sensation of being watched morphing into something far more sinister.

"Darian," I whispered, fear tightening my throat. He turned sharply, his eyes narrowing, but before he could respond, a shadow broke free from the tree line, a figure cloaked in darkness, stepping into the dim glow of the porch light.

"Who the hell are you?" Darian demanded, his voice a low growl, as he positioned himself between me and the unknown threat.

The figure emerged, hands raised in a gesture of peace. "I mean no harm," a voice called out, laced with a familiar cadence that made my pulse quicken. It was Mark, Darian's old friend, the one I had heard so much about during our late-night conversations. The scruffy beard and wild hair were unmistakable, but the look in his eyes was urgent, almost frantic.

"What are you doing here?" Darian's voice was colder than the night air, eyes narrowed as he appraised the man who had once been a part of his life before everything fell apart.

Mark took a hesitant step forward. "I need to talk to you, Darian. It's important. We don't have much time."

"Talk? Now? You show up out of nowhere, and you expect me to just drop everything?" Darian's voice was sharp, but I could sense the undercurrent of concern that bubbled beneath his bravado.

"Please, just listen. It's about your sister," Mark said, and the name hung in the air like a gunshot, piercing the night's fragile calm. My breath caught in my throat as I watched Darian's reaction, a myriad of emotions flickering across his face—anger, disbelief, and a flicker of hope that quickly transformed into guarded caution.

"Don't play games with me, Mark," Darian warned, his fists clenching at his sides. "You know better than anyone how I feel about that topic."

"I know, but something's come up. There are people asking questions, and they're looking for you. For her. I think they know more than we realized." Mark's voice was urgent, the fear palpable as he glanced over his shoulder, as if expecting someone to emerge from the shadows.

Darian's expression hardened, a wall of determination rising. "You should have stayed out of this. I left that life behind."

"And you think that makes you safe? You're wrong. They won't just forget. They won't just let you walk away." Mark's voice dropped to a conspiratorial whisper, his gaze darting around the perimeter of the yard. "I don't want to drag you back into it, but you need to know what's happening. There's been talk. There are whispers, and I had to come to warn you."

I stepped closer to Darian, wanting to bridge the gap that had formed, to offer him some semblance of comfort amid this chaotic revelation. "What are you talking about?" I interjected, my voice steadier than I felt. "Who are 'they'? What do they want?"

Mark turned to me, a mixture of surprise and recognition flaring in his eyes. "This isn't your fight, but it's already tangled you in it, hasn't it?"

Darian's glare could have burned through steel, but there was a flicker of gratitude in his expression as he glanced at me. "What are you saying?" he pressed, his voice low and dangerous.

"There's a group, Darian—dangerous people who are still tied to your past. They think they can control you, use your sister's legacy to manipulate you into doing their bidding. And now they know you're here." Mark's words were clipped, his urgency cutting through the tension like a knife.

I could feel the weight of his revelation, the shift in the atmosphere like the calm before a storm. "We need to leave," I whispered, instinctively moving closer to Darian. The connection between us felt like a lifeline, yet the reality of the situation threatened to sever it.

Darian shook his head, defiance etched across his features. "I'm not running. Not again. I'm done being someone's pawn."

"Then what's the plan?" Mark challenged, stepping closer, desperation creeping into his voice. "You think you can face this alone? You've been living in isolation, and now you're just going to stand there and act like it's all behind you? They're not going to let you go that easily."

I could feel the air thickening around us, the weight of Darian's choices settling like a shroud. "Darian, please," I urged, my voice laced with desperation. "We can't take this lightly. Whatever's happening, we need to face it together. Don't push me away."

His eyes softened for just a moment, and in that flicker, I saw the man beneath the layers of pain and bravado—a man who had fought his demons and was now faced with an insurmountable challenge. But before he could respond, a sudden rustling came from the woods, followed by a low growl that sent chills racing down my spine.

We weren't alone anymore.

The low growl reverberated through the night, vibrating against the wood of the porch and sending a shockwave of adrenaline coursing through my veins. I turned, heart hammering in my chest, my instincts screaming that whatever had been lurking in the shadows was about to make its presence known. The tension was so thick, I felt like I could cut it with a knife, and I was acutely aware of every breath, every whisper of the wind, as if the world had paused, waiting for the next move.

"What was that?" I whispered, but the words felt inadequate, swallowed by the darkness.

Mark's eyes darted back to the treeline, and I could see his hands clenching into fists at his sides, the former carefree spirit replaced by an anxious edge. "We need to get out of here. Now." His urgency was infectious, igniting a fire of fear within me that threatened to consume all rational thought.

Darian stepped closer, blocking my view of the woods. "What do you know?" His voice was low and steady, though I could hear the underlying strain. The protectiveness he radiated was palpable, an unyielding force that pushed against the creeping dread. I wished I could bottle that feeling, that intoxicating blend of safety and raw power, but the threat loomed just outside our view, threatening to burst through the fragile bubble we'd created.

"I know that whatever is out there isn't friendly," Mark replied, glancing back at the shadows. "We can't wait for it to show itself."

"Then what's the plan?" Darian shot back, his voice sharp as glass. I could see the flicker of conflict in his eyes—a battle between the man who had fought so hard to reclaim his life and the shadows of his past that seemed intent on dragging him back down. "You want me to run? Is that what you think I'm going to do?"

"No, but we have to be smart about this." Mark's voice had dropped to a whisper, urgency punctuating every syllable. "There are people looking for you, and if they find us here, it won't just be a conversation. This is about survival."

I felt the tension between them crackle like static electricity, the air thick with unspoken words. "We need to figure out what's happening, not run away from it," I interjected, my own voice rising in an effort to fill the oppressive silence. "If there's danger, we need to confront it. We can't be paralyzed by fear."

Darian turned to me, his eyes searching mine. "You don't know what you're asking. You don't know who they are."

"But I know you," I countered, stepping closer to him. "You've faced the darkness before, and you survived. Together, we can face whatever is out there."

Mark shook his head, casting a glance back toward the treeline, where shadows danced ominously. "You don't understand. They won't stop until they get what they want."

At that moment, the growl transformed into a chilling howl that sliced through the night air, sending shivers racing down my spine. A figure stepped out from the trees, cloaked in darkness, its eyes glinting with an unnatural light. My breath caught in my throat as I instinctively took a step back, but Darian's hand shot out, anchoring me to him.

"What do you want?" Darian demanded, his voice firm yet laced with tension, the protector emerging from within him once more.

The figure paused, and a sinister smile broke across its face, revealing teeth that gleamed like sharpened knives in the dim light. "Oh, I think you already know," it purred, voice smooth like silk but edged with malice. "The past has a way of catching up with you, doesn't it? You thought you could hide here, but secrets have a way of finding their way to the surface."

I felt a chill crawl up my spine, a creeping realization that we had stumbled into a web far more complicated than we had imagined. The figure shifted, stepping into the light, and I could see the contours of a face that was both familiar and haunting—a face I had seen only in old photographs and news clippings.

"Juliet," it said, glancing at me with an unsettling familiarity, "it's been a long time since we last met."

"Who are you?" I managed to ask, though the words felt like they were being pulled from a deep well of fear.

"Ah, but you know me," it replied, a mocking lilt in its tone. "I'm just an old friend of Darian's. Or should I say, an old adversary?" The way the figure's lips curled, I could sense the darkness beneath the words, a threat that lingered like smoke in the air.

Darian's grip tightened around my arm, a protective instinct flaring to life. "Get away from her," he growled, stepping forward, the fierce determination in his stance a stark contrast to the creeping dread that coiled around me.

"Oh, but I'm not here for her," the figure purred, leaning forward as if relishing the tension. "She's merely collateral damage in a much larger game. You should be worried about yourself, Darian. They want you back, and they're willing to do anything to get you."

The statement hung between us like a heavy fog, thickening the air around us with implications I could hardly grasp. I looked to Darian, searching his eyes for answers, but all I found was a storm of emotions churning just beneath the surface—fear, anger, and a glimmer of something deeper that I couldn't quite place.

"Darian, what does this mean?" I asked, my voice barely above a whisper, as panic clawed at my insides. "Who are they?"

"They're people I thought I left behind," he replied, his voice strained, the weight of his past settling heavy on his shoulders. "But they're not going to let me walk away. Not now. Not ever."

The figure smirked, leaning back against the porch railing as if the whole scene were just an entertaining play. "Oh, it's so much more complicated than that, darling. There are forces at play that you can't even begin to understand. You've stirred the pot, and now you're all in it. Isn't that delightful?"

I felt the tension in the air surge as I looked between the two men—one a protector, the other a harbinger of chaos. The reality of our situation crashed down around us like a tidal wave, and I could almost taste the salt of impending danger on my tongue.

As the figure began to advance toward us, something sharp flickered in the shadows, glinting in the pale moonlight. My heart raced, and instinct kicked in. "Darian!" I shouted, urgency ripping through my voice. But before he could react, the figure lunged, and chaos erupted around us.

In that split second, I was faced with a choice—stand and fight, or run for our lives. The decision hung in the air like a fragile thread, ready to snap, and I knew that whatever came next would alter the course of our lives forever.

Chapter 15: Whispers in the Dark

The neon lights flickered like the heartbeat of a city that never truly slept, casting erratic shadows on the crumbling walls of the abandoned nightclub. It was an echo of a time when laughter and music flowed freely, a sanctuary for souls lost in the haze of whiskey and dreams. Now, it loomed like a specter, its once vibrant life now silenced, the air thick with the remnants of smoke and forgotten promises. As I stepped through the threshold, the floor creaked beneath my weight, a grating reminder that this place was as unstable as the secrets hidden within its darkened corners.

Darian walked beside me, his presence a steady anchor in the swirling chaos of my mind. The low thrum of music reached us, distant but insistent, beckoning us deeper into the heart of the club. I glanced at him, catching the way the dim light danced across his features, the sharp lines of his jaw softened in the muted glow. There was something undeniably magnetic about him, a dangerous allure that both thrilled and terrified me. In this world of shadows, he was my partner—my only ally—yet every moment spent in his company felt like walking a tightrope stretched across an abyss.

"Are you sure about this?" he asked, his voice low, barely above the pulse of the bass. His dark eyes searched mine, a flicker of concern beneath the bravado.

"I don't have a choice," I replied, straightening my shoulders as I prepared to step into the unknown. "If we're going to find the Shadow Man, we need to gain the informant's trust. Playing the part of a couple is our best chance."

Darian nodded, a small smirk playing on his lips. "Right. Because nothing says 'trustworthy' like pretending to be in love."

"Exactly," I shot back, unable to suppress a grin. "Who knows? Maybe we'll be so convincing that it'll even feel real."

He chuckled, a sound that sent a warm rush through me. "I don't think that's how this works, but let's give it our best shot."

As we moved through the remnants of the club, the air crackled with tension, each step a careful negotiation of the treacherous terrain beneath us. The bar, once a polished expanse of mahogany, was now a graveyard of broken bottles and shattered dreams. The scent of stale beer mingled with something more acrid—fear, perhaps, or desperation. Every shadow seemed alive, watching, waiting. I could feel the weight of eyes on us, both scrutinizing and calculating, as if the very walls held their breath in anticipation.

"Remember, we need to look like we're here for fun," Darian whispered, leaning in closer, his breath warm against my ear. "Laugh, flirt, be playful. Show them we're a couple who's in it for the thrill."

I swallowed hard, the pulse of the music now a counterpoint to the erratic beat of my heart. "And if we're not convincing enough?"

"Then we might not get the information we need," he replied, his tone grave. "But let's not dwell on that."

The crowd shifted around us, a sea of faces cloaked in anonymity, each one hiding secrets I was only beginning to understand. I spotted the informant, a wiry figure leaning against a post, draped in shadows and smoke, his face obscured by the brim of a battered fedora. He was an enigma, a ghost haunting the fringes of this world, and I knew that if we were to uncover the truth behind the Shadow Man, we had to engage him.

Darian slipped his arm around my waist, drawing me closer as we approached. The warmth of his touch sent a shiver up my spine, a mixture of thrill and fear colliding within me. "Just follow my lead," he murmured, his voice a low growl that sent electric sparks dancing across my skin.

"Got it," I breathed, my confidence bolstered by the feel of his presence.

As we reached the informant, Darian turned to me, his gaze intense. "Ready?"

"Let's do this," I replied, determination surging through me like a shot of adrenaline.

"Hey there," Darian said, his tone casual, laced with charm. "We heard this place was the best for a good time. Mind if we join you?"

The informant's eyes flickered beneath the brim of his hat, suspicion mingling with curiosity. "Depends on what you're looking for," he replied, his voice gravelly, each word carefully measured.

I could feel the tension in the air, thick enough to cut with a knife. "We're just looking to unwind," I said, injecting as much playful energy into my voice as I could muster. "Darian here is celebrating a promotion, and I thought we'd check out this place. What's the best drink to start the night?"

"Aren't you a little young to be celebrating?" the informant retorted, his gaze sharp.

"Age is just a number, right?" I shot back, smiling sweetly. "What matters is that we're here to have a good time."

Darian squeezed my waist slightly, a subtle reminder of our façade, and I felt a rush of warmth spread through me. The informant studied us for a moment, and I could practically hear the wheels turning in his mind.

"Alright," he said at last, leaning forward slightly, intrigued. "But remember, fun comes with a price. I don't give out information for free."

"Neither do we," Darian quipped, and I couldn't help but admire the way he danced around the unspoken danger lingering in the air. "But we're willing to negotiate."

"Let's see what you're offering," the informant replied, his tone suddenly more serious, the edge of danger creeping back into his demeanor.

In that moment, I realized the delicate balance we were treading. Each word was a thread, weaving a complex tapestry of lies and truths, all intertwined. As Darian and I exchanged quick glances, I felt a spark of connection ignite between us, one that was thrilling and terrifying all at once. And as we stood on the precipice of our deception, I couldn't shake the feeling that the shadows surrounding us were closing in, tightening their grip, as if the very walls conspired against us.

The informant leaned closer, his eyes glinting with the kind of mischief that could easily shift to menace. "You want to play the game, huh? What's your angle? Or are you just another couple looking for a thrill in a place that thrives on danger?"

Darian chuckled, a sound that was almost too smooth, too confident. "You could say we're seasoned thrill-seekers. We've survived worse than this dive." His gaze drifted over the crumbling bar, as if contemplating the merits of the peeling wallpaper. I felt the pulse of his body against mine, a gentle reminder that the boundary between pretense and reality was becoming increasingly blurred.

"What's worse than a dive?" the informant asked, raising an eyebrow. "You seem to have a lot of bravado for a couple of kids."

"Oh, you'd be surprised," I interjected, summoning a lightness to my voice that felt as fragile as the glass shards littering the floor. "We once found ourselves in a situation involving a questionable underground poker game and a very angry gentleman with a penchant for collecting debts. Let's just say, we had to think fast and play our cards right."

The informant's interest piqued, a flicker of admiration crossing his face. "Sounds like a fun night. But what makes you think you can handle the kind of information I deal in? People get hurt when they dig too deep, and I don't just mean emotionally."

Darian leaned in, his voice low and conspiratorial. "That's exactly why we're here. We've got nothing to lose and everything to gain.

The Shadow Man has something we need, and we're willing to do what it takes to get it."

"Bold," the informant mused, folding his arms across his chest. "But there's a difference between desire and action. I can give you a lead, but it'll cost you. What can you offer me?"

I felt the air grow thick with tension, the unspoken stakes hanging like a damning shadow over us. I glanced at Darian, our eyes locking in a silent exchange of determination. "We're not afraid to get our hands dirty," I said, my heart pounding in my chest. "You give us the information, and we'll bring you something of value in return. A trade, if you will."

"Ah, trading secrets in a place where secrets are currency. I like it," he replied, his expression unreadable. "But I need more than bravado. What are you willing to risk?"

"Why don't you start by telling us what you know about the Shadow Man?" Darian pressed, his voice steady as he played the part. "That's what we're really after, right?"

The informant's gaze hardened, his playful demeanor vanishing like smoke. "The Shadow Man isn't just a name; it's a warning. He's not someone you want to cross. Many have tried to uncover his identity, and many have vanished without a trace. Are you prepared for the consequences of your curiosity?"

"We didn't come all this way to back down now," I said, the fire in my belly igniting my words. "If you want to see how far we're willing to go, give us something to work with. We'll prove ourselves."

His lips curled into a sly smile, one that held the promise of mischief. "Alright, you've intrigued me. There's a warehouse down by the docks. Rumor has it, the Shadow Man meets his associates there. But that's only half the story. If you want to find him, you'll need to outsmart everyone else who's been searching for him."

"Outsmart them how?" I asked, sensing that we were now tiptoeing on the edge of a cliff.

"Information, my dear," the informant said, his voice dropping to a whisper, drawing us closer into his orbit. "You'll need to gather intel on his dealings. There's an auction happening soon, and from what I've heard, the Shadow Man will be in attendance. But it's not just any auction; it's a showcase of rare artifacts and contraband that'll draw every shady player in town. You'll have to blend in."

Darian and I exchanged glances again, the weight of our task settling heavily in the air between us. "We can handle it," Darian replied, his confidence unwavering. "But we'll need your help to get in."

The informant leaned back, considering our request. "You're either very brave or very foolish. I'm betting on the latter. But let's say I agree. What do you offer me in return? I want something of value—something I can't easily find myself."

"What do you have in mind?" I asked, feeling the tension shift as if we were trapped in an intricate web, each strand threatening to ensnare us.

"Information on your end, of course. The kind that could expose someone powerful. You catch wind of any dirty dealings, you come back to me," he said, a predatory gleam in his eye. "In the world we inhabit, information is the lifeblood. You'll owe me, and trust me, I'll collect."

"Consider it a deal," Darian said, extending his hand.

I felt a jolt of apprehension as I watched the two shake hands, sealing our fates with a casual gesture. A part of me wondered what we were truly getting ourselves into, but the thrill of the chase was intoxicating, urging me forward. I squeezed Darian's arm, hoping to anchor my own resolve as much as his.

The informant's smile widened, revealing a glimpse of satisfaction. "You've got guts, I'll give you that. Now, get out of here before someone else takes an interest in you. Remember, the auction is tomorrow night. Time is not on your side."

As we stepped away from the informant, the weight of the exchange settled around us. "What have we just agreed to?" I asked, my heart racing with both fear and excitement.

"Something that could lead us right to the Shadow Man," Darian replied, his expression a mix of exhilaration and concern. "We have to be careful. If we're going to infiltrate that auction, we need a plan."

"Right. And we need disguises," I said, already mapping out the logistics in my mind. "This isn't just a typical gathering; it's a gathering of the city's most dangerous players. We'll have to blend in seamlessly."

"And we need to figure out who else is there," Darian added, glancing around the nightclub, as if the walls themselves might offer insight into our next steps.

"Tonight we'll scout out some shops and start brainstorming our cover story," I said, determination swelling within me. "We can't let this opportunity slip away."

As we moved through the club, the pulse of music faded, replaced by a vibrant energy crackling between us. The night was far from over, and the weight of our next move felt both exhilarating and daunting. The shadows had grown long, but I could sense a flicker of hope igniting within me—a fierce desire to unearth the truth, no matter the cost. With every step we took, I felt closer to Darian, the bond between us deepening as we ventured into the unknown, fueled by ambition and an undeniable spark that hinted at something more.

The streets outside were alive with the chaotic energy of the night, each passing car and distant shout a reminder that life continued in all its messy glory. Darian and I slipped through the crowd, adrenaline coursing through my veins like an electric current. The promise of our upcoming task—the auction, the shadows, and the potential discovery of the Shadow Man—was intoxicating. Yet, uncertainty lingered like the lingering scent of smoke from the club, a reminder of the risks that lay ahead.

"Do you think we're ready for this?" I asked, glancing sideways at Darian. The streetlights painted him in warm hues, accentuating the contours of his face, but the shadows in his eyes told a different story.

"I don't think we have a choice," he replied, his tone steady but low, as if we were sharing a secret. "We've come too far to turn back now."

"True," I conceded, taking a deep breath to steady myself. "It's just...we have to be careful. There's a thin line between being daring and being reckless."

"Trust me, I've walked that line before," he said, a wry smile flickering on his lips. "What's life without a little danger?"

I couldn't help but laugh, despite the unease bubbling within me. "Some of us prefer our danger to come in the form of a thrilling novel, not a real-life game of cat and mouse with the city's underbelly."

"Too bad this isn't fiction," he said, matching my pace as we turned down a narrow alley that led to a street vendor hawking sizzling skewers of meat. The rich, smoky aroma wafted toward us, and my stomach grumbled in protest. "Want to grab something before we plot our cover story?"

"Food sounds great, but let's keep it quick. I don't want to attract too much attention," I replied, the thought of blending in for our upcoming ruse weighing heavily on my mind.

As we approached the vendor, Darian leaned in, his voice low. "Just be yourself. You're good at that. If you can charm your way through the roughest crowd, you can charm your way through an auction full of sharks."

"Charming, huh?" I shot back, raising an eyebrow. "You're not just buttering me up to distract from the danger we're walking into?"

"Only partially," he admitted with a laugh, his eyes glinting with mischief. "Seriously, though, you've got this."

We grabbed our food and slipped away from the vendor, savoring the tender meat and tangy sauce that clung to the skewers. As we walked, I felt the warmth of the meal seep into my bones, calming my nerves for just a moment. "So, what's our cover story? We need something that screams 'perfect couple' without being too...perfect."

"Let's say we're art enthusiasts looking for a piece to invest in," Darian suggested, his voice thoughtful. "That gives us an excuse to be at the auction, and it keeps things casual."

"Art enthusiasts?" I repeated, raising an eyebrow. "That's quite a leap from danger-seeking thrill junkies."

"Everyone loves a good plot twist," he quipped, his grin widening. "And who knows? Maybe we'll discover an appreciation for fine art along the way."

"Or maybe we'll just end up with more secrets to keep," I replied, smirking at him. "So, what's our aesthetic? Do we go for hipster chic or classy elegance?"

"I vote for classy elegance," he said, his eyes sparkling with mischief. "You've got the whole 'mysterious art collector' vibe down. I just need to look like I belong next to you."

"Flattery will get you everywhere," I teased, playfully nudging him as we crossed a street filled with bright lights and the buzz of nightlife. "But we'll need outfits that don't scream 'we just rolled out of bed.'"

"Leave the shopping to me," he replied confidently. "We'll find something that works."

The thought of shopping with Darian sent a shiver of excitement down my spine. I'd always enjoyed the thrill of picking out clothes, but doing it with him felt different—like we were preparing for something more than just a costume change.

As we strolled further into the heart of the city, I felt the vibrancy of our surroundings seep into my bones. Music spilled from nearby clubs, laughter echoed from street corners, and the scents of street food mingled with the crisp night air, creating an atmosphere both exhilarating and overwhelming. I could sense a world pulsing with life, yet ours was a different rhythm—a heartbeat masked by the dangerous game we were about to play.

"What do you think the Shadow Man is like?" I mused, curiosity bubbling up as we approached a boutique with elegant gowns displayed in the window.

"I don't know," Darian admitted, his brow furrowing slightly. "But if he's as elusive as they say, I imagine he's got a talent for slipping through fingers. A ghost in the night."

"A ghost with a penchant for trouble," I added, glancing at a striking dress in the window that caught my eye—a deep emerald green that shimmered under the lights. "Trouble that could easily swallow us whole if we aren't careful."

"Or it could lead us to exactly what we're looking for," he countered, his gaze locking onto mine, a glint of determination sparking between us. "If we play our cards right, we might just emerge unscathed."

"Unscathed," I echoed, a tinge of doubt creeping into my voice. "I'm starting to think that's a lofty goal in this line of work."

As we stepped into the boutique, the air shifted, a sharp contrast to the bustling street outside. The soft lighting highlighted the delicate fabrics and sophisticated designs that surrounded us. "Just keep your head in the game," Darian whispered, leaning closer as we perused the racks. "Focus on what we need to do, and don't let the thrill of the chase distract you."

"Right, focus," I agreed, but the shimmer of possibilities danced in my mind like stars against a midnight sky. I reached for the emerald dress, its fabric cool and luxurious against my fingertips. "What do you think of this one?"

Darian stepped closer, examining it with a critical eye. "Perfect for an art auction. Sophisticated, yet it stands out. Just like you."

The compliment sent a flush of warmth to my cheeks, and I felt my resolve strengthen. "I'll take it," I decided, glancing around the store for a matching outfit for him. "Now let's find you something that won't make me look like I'm on a date with a high school kid."

"Hey!" he protested playfully, holding up a sleek blazer that would complement my dress perfectly. "This is my 'I mean business' look."

"Very serious," I laughed, shaking my head. "But it'll do. Let's pay for these and come up with a plan."

As we made our way to the register, my heart raced at the prospect of what lay ahead. This was more than just a shopping trip; it was a step into the unknown, a leap into a world filled with secrets and danger. The thrill of it sent butterflies fluttering in my stomach.

Once outside, we stood on the sidewalk, dressed for the part we were about to play. "This feels like the beginning of a movie," I remarked, a smile tugging at my lips.

"Let's hope it has a good ending," Darian replied, his expression turning serious. "Now, we need to gather information about the auction and who else will be attending."

"Right," I agreed, ready to dive deeper into this intricate web. "Let's hit the ground running."

But just as we turned to head down the street, a figure emerged from the shadows, cloaked in darkness. My heart sank as recognition hit me like a bolt of lightning. It was someone I never expected to see again—someone who was supposed to be long gone.

"Did you really think you could just walk away?" they said, a smirk dancing on their lips, the light catching their eyes and revealing a danger that sent chills down my spine.

"Who are you?" I breathed, the world around me narrowing to the confrontation ahead, a palpable tension filling the air. Darian's hand instinctively found mine, a lifeline as we faced the storm that had just rolled in.

The danger was no longer a whisper in the dark; it was here, and it was real.

Chapter 16: Crossroads

The rain fell in relentless sheets, each drop a drumbeat against the window, echoing the tempest in my heart. I leaned against the cool glass, watching the world outside blur into a watercolor of grays and greens, a mirror of my own tumultuous thoughts. The air was thick with the scent of damp earth and the faint, sweet aroma of the jasmine climbing the trellis just beyond my reach. It had been a week since the encounter with the Shadow Syndicate, and every tick of the clock echoed the urgency of my dilemma: face the ghosts of my past or forge a new path with Darian at my side.

Darian had become a part of my life so seamlessly, like the way the sun eventually breaks through a storm, illuminating the dark corners of my heart. But as the clock moved, so did the shadows. The truth of who I was loomed over me, a specter that threatened to shatter the fragile foundation we had built. Could I trust him with my secrets? The thought twisted in my gut like a viper, coiling tighter with each passing moment.

In the dim light of my living room, Darian's silhouette moved gracefully, pouring two steaming mugs of chamomile tea. The aroma wafted through the air, soothing yet somehow more potent than the rain's melody. He turned, catching my gaze, and the corners of his mouth lifted into that familiar, infectious grin that could melt the chill from any storm. "You know," he began, his voice playful and warm, "the rain is merely the universe's way of reminding us to take a breath. A little introspection never hurt anyone."

I offered a half-hearted smile, feeling the weight of his words pressing against my heart. Introspection? I could hardly keep the walls of my past from crumbling down. "Or it's just a terrible day to be cooped up inside," I replied, trying to keep the conversation light, masking the tempest beneath my skin.

He took a step closer, the playful lilt in his voice fading, replaced by something more earnest. "You've been quiet lately. What's going on in that brilliant mind of yours?" His eyes, a mix of deep browns and greens, searched mine with a sincerity that both comforted and terrified me.

I swallowed hard, my heart drumming a frantic beat. It was the moment I had been dreading—the moment where honesty could either bind us together or rip us apart. I opened my mouth to speak, but the words tangled in my throat.

"The world isn't always as simple as it seems," I finally managed, hoping to deflect the question with vague poetry. "There are... layers."

Darian crossed the space between us in a heartbeat, his hands resting on my shoulders, grounding me. "Layers? Like a cake? I hope this one isn't as dense as last week's carrot disaster."

I chuckled softly, appreciating his attempt to lighten the mood, but the laughter felt hollow. "You mean the one that tasted like regret?" I shot back, and for a moment, the tension eased.

"Exactly," he said, his grin returning. "But here's the thing. Cakes can be saved, even if they're dense. They can still be delicious. So why don't we talk about what's weighing you down? I'm here, you know."

The sincerity in his gaze pierced through my defenses. I had spent so much time building walls, so much energy hiding from the truth that now, the very idea of sharing it felt like standing at the edge of a cliff, ready to leap. I took a deep breath, my heart racing with every beat as the storm raged outside, mirroring the chaos inside me.

"You deserve to know the truth about me," I said, my voice barely above a whisper. "But it's messy, and I'm not sure if you'll want to stick around once you hear it."

His hands tightened around my shoulders, a silent promise that he would stay, that he was ready to face the storm with me. "I've seen my fair share of messes. Trust me, I can handle a little chaos," he replied, a playful twinkle in his eye.

I couldn't help but smile, the warmth of his reassurance wrapping around me like a comforting blanket. "It's not just a little chaos, Darian. It's a whole world of shadows—people I left behind, choices I regret."

The moment hung between us, charged with the weight of my words. I could feel the storm within me swelling, and for the first time, I felt a flicker of hope that sharing my truth might lighten the load I had carried for so long.

"Start wherever you need to," he urged, his voice steady, unyielding. "I'm ready to listen."

With those words, I found my voice. The dam I had built began to crack, and the secrets I had guarded for so long spilled forth. I told him about my life before the shadows closed in, the vibrant days filled with laughter and dreams that had slowly faded into whispers of regret. I spoke of the choices that had led me to this moment, the fateful encounter with the Syndicate that had twisted my life into a series of endless turns.

As the words poured out, I watched his face shift from concern to understanding, the flicker of his empathy igniting a spark of courage within me. I recounted the way the shadows had pursued me, how I had thought I could outrun them, only to discover that they had woven themselves into the very fabric of my being.

With each revelation, I felt lighter, the weight of my past no longer an anchor but a shared burden, something Darian and I could navigate together. I looked into his eyes, searching for the disappointment or judgment I feared, but instead, I found unwavering support—a lifeline in the storm.

"Why didn't you tell me sooner?" he asked softly, brushing his thumb against my cheek, a gesture so tender it made my heart race. "You've been carrying this alone for too long."

"I didn't want to lose you," I admitted, the truth rolling off my tongue like a confession. "I was terrified that if I showed you the real me, you'd walk away."

Darian leaned closer, the warmth of his breath mingling with mine. "I'm not going anywhere. You're stuck with me now, shadows and all."

In that moment, with the storm raging outside and the chaos of my life laid bare between us, I felt an unexpected calm. My heart began to beat in rhythm with his, a silent promise that together we could face whatever came next.

The warmth of Darian's hands on my shoulders sent ripples of comfort through the storm brewing inside me, an electric connection that wrapped around us like a protective shield. It was a reassurance I hadn't realized I craved until that very moment. The rain outside continued to pelt against the windows, but here, in the soft glow of the kitchen light, I felt cocooned from the chaos that awaited us beyond those panes. I took a deep breath, steadying myself, knowing the path ahead was as fraught as a tightrope walk.

"I'm not the person you think I am," I said, my voice wavering slightly as I dared to meet his gaze. "I've made choices—horrible choices—that haunt me. I was involved with people who don't just fade away; they linger like a shadow, waiting for the right moment to pull you back into their darkness."

Darian's eyes darkened with concern, but he didn't pull away. Instead, he stepped closer, his presence grounding me. "You think I care about what you've done? We all have shadows. It's what we do now that matters."

His words struck a chord deep within me, resonating in a way I hadn't expected. I felt the flicker of hope rise again, but doubt still gnawed at the edges of my heart. "But you don't understand. My past isn't just a few bad decisions. It's a whole life of messes and tangled webs. The Syndicate... they're not just going to let me walk away."

"Then we don't walk away," he replied, his voice steady, a beacon of strength. "We confront them. Together."

The notion sent a jolt through me, igniting both fear and a strange sense of exhilaration. Together. The word wrapped around us like a silken thread, binding our fates in a way I had only dared to imagine. "You think it's that simple? Just walk into the lion's den and say 'hello'?" I asked, my tone half teasing, half desperate.

"Why not?" he said, a lopsided grin breaking through his intensity. "I mean, what's the worst that could happen? They eat us for breakfast?"

I couldn't help but laugh, the sound a little too bright for the gravity of the situation. "Sure, let's just become a morning snack for organized crime."

"Look, I'm serious. I'm not afraid of some overzealous mobsters if you're by my side," he said, his gaze fierce with determination. "And I won't let you face them alone."

His words wove a tapestry of courage around my heart, stitching up the frayed edges of my fears. "And what if they come after you? What if I put you in danger?"

"They already are, aren't they?" he replied, his expression softening. "They're coming for you, and that makes me a target too. If we face them together, we can outsmart them. You're not just some damsel in distress, you're a force of nature, and I want to stand beside you. We'll figure this out."

I bit my lip, uncertainty still swirling within me like a tempest. "But what about your life? Your work? You've built something here, and I'm a storm waiting to happen."

"Then let's embrace the storm," he said, his tone playful yet serious, reminding me of the confidence he carried effortlessly. "If I wanted to live a boring life, I wouldn't have moved here in the first place. Besides, I've never been the 'let it be' type."

I felt a warmth spread through me at his words, a comforting glow that momentarily chased away the shadows clinging to my heart. Maybe there was something extraordinary in this connection we shared, something that defied logic and fear. "Okay," I whispered, my resolve hardening like the first light of dawn breaking through the night. "Let's face them."

As the rain continued to patter against the windows, we made a plan, our voices a soft murmur against the backdrop of the storm. We strategized over cups of chamomile, mapping out the risks and contingencies like seasoned generals preparing for battle. Every suggestion was met with thoughtful consideration, every idea a thread that wove our fates tighter together.

"We'll need to find out where they're operating from," Darian said, tapping his finger against the table. "Do you have any contacts from your past? Anyone who might still be in the loop?"

A flicker of hesitation flashed through me. "There's one person, but it's risky. He's not exactly the most trustworthy ally."

"Trust is overrated in this game," he said, smirking. "What's life without a little danger?"

"Just another Wednesday?" I shot back, raising an eyebrow.

"Exactly. I like a little excitement with my tea," he replied, grinning. "So who is this contact?"

I hesitated, memories swirling like leaves in a gust of wind. "Aiden. He was... well, let's just say we had a complicated relationship. He might have information, but reaching out could raise some eyebrows."

"Complicated how?" Darian leaned in, intrigued.

"Let's just say we didn't part on the best of terms. He might see my name pop up and decide I'm the perfect target for some old-fashioned revenge," I admitted, the weight of the past resurfacing like a tide I had hoped to keep at bay.

Darian considered this, the playful light in his eyes dimming slightly as he processed the potential danger. "Then we'll go in cautiously. We can't let fear dictate our actions. But we should be prepared for anything. If Aiden is unpredictable, we need a backup plan."

"Right," I agreed, the reality of the situation settling around us like a heavy cloak. The stakes were higher than ever, and the tension crackled in the air, electrifying every word we exchanged.

"I can play the charming idiot," he offered, smirking again. "Just let me know when you want me to sweep in and distract him with my dazzling personality."

I couldn't help but chuckle. "Dazzling might be a bit of a stretch."

"Fine, then I'll be your charming idiot," he shot back, and in that moment, the tension shifted.

Our banter danced through the air like a melody, lightening the heavy atmosphere as we moved forward together. It was in those moments of humor and camaraderie that I realized we had crossed a threshold. The shadows were no longer a solitary burden; they were ours to face, together.

As we finalized our plan, the rain eased into a soft drizzle, the storm outside beginning to quiet. But I knew the real tempest was just beginning—one that would lead us down paths we had yet to imagine, testing the very fabric of our trust, our courage, and our bond. I couldn't shake the feeling that the winds of change were already swirling around us, ready to sweep us into a future unknown. And somehow, I was ready to embrace it.

The morning sun broke through the last remnants of the storm, casting a golden glow that danced across the remnants of the night's downpour. The air was crisp, laden with the fresh scent of earth washed clean, but inside, I still felt the weight of uncertainty pressing heavily on my chest. As I prepared for the day, each movement was infused with a sense of urgency, a feeling that destiny was nudging me toward something monumental.

Darian and I had agreed to meet Aiden at a small café on the outskirts of town—a place where shadows lingered yet felt deceptively safe. I dressed carefully, slipping into a simple black dress that hugged my curves just right, a piece I often wore to project confidence. The mirror reflected a woman brimming with determination, but beneath the surface, the turmoil swirled like an unsettled sea.

I arrived early, choosing a table near the window where I could watch the world pass by. The café buzzed with the sounds of conversation, laughter, and the rich aroma of freshly brewed coffee. As the door jingled open, my heart raced, and I turned to see Darian stepping inside, his presence igniting a warmth in the cool morning air. He caught my eye and flashed that signature grin, the kind that could ignite a thousand suns.

"Look at you," he said, his voice smooth as honey as he approached. "If I didn't know any better, I'd say you're trying to distract Aiden with your stunning good looks."

I rolled my eyes, the familiar banter easing the tension coiling in my stomach. "If only that would work. He's more interested in his own ego than in anything I might throw at him."

"Then we'll just have to outsmart him," he replied, sliding into the chair opposite mine, his gaze unwavering. "What's the plan? Do we charm him with sweet nothings, or do I unleash my dazzling personality right from the start?"

"Dazzling might be a bit optimistic," I teased, glancing at my watch. "But we definitely need to tread carefully. Aiden's not known for his patience or kindness."

As we waited, the atmosphere thickened with anticipation. The clock ticked away, each second stretching out like a taut string, pulling at my nerves. I couldn't shake the feeling that we were perched on the edge of something monumental—an abyss of possibilities where every choice could have life-altering consequences.

The door swung open again, and Aiden sauntered in, exuding a charisma that could easily fill the room. His hair, tousled just enough to look effortless, framed his face, and his sharp, assessing gaze flicked around before settling on us. A cocky grin spread across his face, a stark reminder of why I had once found him so alluring, even when I knew better.

"Look what the cat dragged in," he said, his voice dripping with sarcasm. "I didn't think you'd have the guts to show up."

I straightened my back, suppressing a shiver as memories rushed through me like a cold wind. "Nice to see you too, Aiden. We need to talk."

He raised an eyebrow, sliding into the chair beside Darian without waiting for an invitation. "Talk? You're either in trouble or looking for a favor. Which is it?"

"Both," I replied bluntly, meeting his gaze head-on. "I need information. The Syndicate is back, and I can't do this alone."

Darian's presence beside me was like a warm fire in the chill of Aiden's aura. "We know you have connections, Aiden. We need to find out what they're planning."

Aiden leaned back, arms crossed, studying us with a look that suggested he was weighing his options. "Why should I help you? The last time I checked, you weren't exactly on my list of favorite people."

"Because it's not just about me anymore," I said, feeling a spark of desperation. "Darian is involved now. This affects him too."

Aiden's expression shifted slightly, his interest piqued. "Ah, so it's a 'you against the world' scenario now? I'll admit, I'm curious how that's going to play out."

"Cut the theatrics," Darian interjected, his voice steady. "We don't have time for games. This is serious. We're trying to stop the

Syndicate from causing harm, and I'm not above making deals if it means keeping people safe."

Aiden's eyes narrowed, a flicker of amusement dancing within them. "You're a brave one, aren't you? But bravery and intelligence don't always go hand in hand. What makes you think you can handle this?"

"Because I'm willing to risk everything," I replied, surprising even myself with the conviction in my voice. "And I won't let fear dictate my choices anymore. If you care about anything beyond your own amusement, you'll help us."

A silence fell over the table, thick and heavy. Aiden seemed to consider my words, a sly smile creeping onto his lips. "Interesting. You've grown up, haven't you? But tell me, what's in it for me? You think I'm just going to give you information for free?"

"People don't just get to be monsters, Aiden," I replied, my voice firm. "You know the Syndicate's methods. You know what they do. Help us take them down, and I'll owe you. That's something you can't buy with amusement."

He chuckled softly, leaning forward with a glint of intrigue in his eyes. "You're right. I can't buy that kind of excitement. But I'll need something concrete to convince me to join this little crusade. You have a plan?"

I exchanged a glance with Darian, whose steady demeanor gave me the courage to push forward. "We're not asking you to fight for us," I said, choosing my words carefully. "Just help us get intel on their movements. We'll handle the rest."

Aiden's gaze flicked between us, the corners of his mouth tugging into a smirk. "And if things go south? If I get pulled back into your world of shadows?"

"Then we'll deal with it. Together," Darian added, a fierce determination behind his words.

"Together. What a lovely little mantra," Aiden mused, a finger tapping on the table thoughtfully. "Alright, let's say I'm intrigued. I might have a lead, but it's risky. I can't guarantee your safety."

"Risk is part of the game," I said, my heart racing with a mix of hope and dread. "Just tell us what you know."

As Aiden leaned in closer, lowering his voice to a conspiratorial whisper, the atmosphere shifted again, tension crackling like electricity in the air. I could feel Darian's hand inching closer to mine, a silent promise of solidarity.

"The Syndicate has been moving in silence, but I've heard whispers," Aiden began, his tone serious. "There's a meeting tonight at an old warehouse on the outskirts of town. They're discussing something big—something that could shake the entire operation."

Darian's grip tightened around my hand, grounding me in the whirlwind of revelation. "What time?"

"Midnight," Aiden replied, his eyes glinting with mischief. "It's going to be chaotic. You're playing with fire, but I suspect you already knew that."

"We're ready," I said, the words slipping out before I had a chance to think. "Let's take them by surprise."

Aiden's smile widened, but there was something else lurking behind it—a glimmer of danger, a hint of betrayal. "Just remember, when you dance with shadows, you might get burned."

Before I could respond, a loud crash echoed from the entrance of the café, drawing our attention. A figure rushed in, panting and wide-eyed, the unmistakable aura of panic radiating from them. "They're here! The Syndicate—they're coming for you!"

My heart dropped, the weight of Aiden's warning hanging in the air like a noose. As chaos erupted around us, I grasped Darian's hand tightly, fear racing through me like wildfire.

"Time to move," I said, adrenaline surging through my veins as I shot to my feet, the café now a whirlpool of uncertainty.

But as we turned to escape, a shadow loomed in the doorway, the familiar outline of someone I thought I'd left behind, a haunting specter of my past that could change everything once again.

Chapter 17: Heartstrings Entwined

A chill hung in the air, sharp and biting, as we huddled around the flickering glow of a makeshift campfire. The shadows danced on the walls of the abandoned warehouse, our temporary stronghold against the encroaching darkness of the Shadow Syndicate. I could feel the warmth of the flames licking at my skin, but it was Darian's presence beside me that truly ignited something deep within—an undeniable spark that set my heart racing. His silhouette loomed large, every angle sharp and defined, as he traced his fingers over a map spread out between us, the dim light catching the glint of determination in his eyes.

"Here," he said, his voice low and steady, as if he was coaxing the words from the depths of his soul. "If we can draw them out into the open, we stand a chance of taking them down before they even know what hit them."

I leaned in closer, the scent of leather and something distinctly masculine enveloping me as I tried to decipher the intricate lines he'd drawn. My mind was a whirlwind of strategies and schemes, but amidst the chaos of plans and the heavy burden of impending conflict, a single thought crystallized in the quiet corners of my mind: how much I had come to care for him. The feeling settled like a warm weight in my chest, pushing against the walls I'd built to keep my heart safe.

"Are you sure we can trust your intel?" I asked, trying to focus, my tone playfully skeptical. "What if it's a trap?"

Darian's lips quirked into a half-smile, the corners of his mouth dancing in a way that suggested he knew something I didn't. "Trust? Oh, I don't trust anyone, least of all the Syndicate. But I do trust my instincts." He paused, his gaze flickering from the map to my eyes. "And my instincts tell me you're far more capable than you give yourself credit for."

I felt heat rise to my cheeks. Compliments from Darian had become a rare currency, exchanged in fleeting moments where time felt suspended, and the world outside faded away. "You're just saying that to flatter me," I teased, trying to deflect the warmth creeping up my neck. "I can hardly wield a knife without making a mess of things."

Darian chuckled, a sound that sent a delightful shiver down my spine. "That's where you're wrong. You wield that knife like an artist, each slice calculated and precise. It's not the weapon that defines a warrior, but the heart behind it."

His words hung in the air, heavy with significance. I could almost feel the weight of my own insecurities, layered thick with doubt, begin to crack under the heat of his unwavering confidence in me. I was not merely a sidekick in this battle; I was a pivotal part of our plan, a force to be reckoned with.

Suddenly, the sound of shuffling feet broke the reverie, snapping me back to the harsh reality surrounding us. My heart raced, adrenaline coursing through my veins as I spun around, half-expecting a Syndicate operative to leap from the shadows. Instead, it was just a couple of our allies, weary but determined. They exchanged nervous glances, their faces a canvas of worry.

"Anything?" one of them asked, his voice a harsh whisper as if he feared the very walls might betray our location.

"Nothing yet," Darian replied, his voice now a tight coil of focus. "We'll strike at dawn. For now, we need to rest up and conserve our energy."

As the others settled into their spaces around the fire, I felt the tension in my shoulders ease just a fraction. My eyes drifted back to Darian, who was now studying the horizon, his jaw set in a determined line. I wanted to say something—anything—to bridge the growing chasm of emotion swirling between us, but the words faltered on my tongue. Instead, I stood, stepping into the cool night air outside the warehouse, seeking solace beneath a sky littered with stars.

The night was alive with sounds—the rustle of leaves, the distant hoot of an owl, the rhythmic chirping of crickets. I inhaled deeply, allowing the crisp air to fill my lungs, clearing my mind of the muddled thoughts that clouded my heart. I leaned against the cool metal of the warehouse, the cold biting into my skin, grounding me.

"Penny for your thoughts?" Darian's voice floated through the darkness, smooth as silk.

I turned to find him a few steps away, his hands tucked into his pockets, his eyes reflecting the starlight like shards of glass. "I was just thinking about how all of this began," I confessed, the words tumbling out before I could reel them back in. "How we went from strangers to... this."

He took a step closer, his expression softening. "This?"

I waved my hand between us, indicating the tension that hummed like a live wire. "This connection. It's unexpected, isn't it?"

Darian stepped into the space I had unwittingly created, the heat radiating from him wrapping around me like a blanket. "Unexpected? Maybe. But not unwelcome."

His words hung in the air, a tantalizing promise. I could see it in the way his eyes lingered on my lips, the way his breath caught slightly, as if he were holding back a tidal wave of emotions. But the moment stretched, thick with uncertainty and the weight of what was left unspoken.

"Are we really ready for this?" I whispered, the question threading the night with vulnerability.

"Ready or not, it's happening," he replied, his voice steady, and for the first time, I saw a flicker of vulnerability in his gaze, as if he, too, was grappling with the enormity of what lay ahead.

The world felt suspended in that moment, two souls on the precipice of something profound, something that could either bind us together or tear us apart. I could feel my heart thrumming in time with the tension, each beat echoing a truth I could no longer ignore.

"I don't want to lose you," I admitted, the words spilling out, raw and unfiltered.

"You won't," he assured, stepping even closer, until I could feel the warmth radiating off him, a protective barrier against the encroaching darkness. "Not if we stick together."

And just like that, the weight of our situation shifted. The impending battle felt less daunting with him by my side, and the pulse of anticipation thrummed with a new rhythm—a blend of fear and hope that wrapped around us like the night sky, infinite and full of possibilities.

The dawn broke over the horizon, the sky painted in soft hues of orange and pink, a stark contrast to the darkness that loomed over us. I stood at the edge of the warehouse, heart racing, as the first rays of sunlight stretched across the landscape. The air was heavy with a blend of anticipation and anxiety, each breath I took filling my lungs with the promise of what lay ahead. It was our moment to seize, a chance to finally dismantle the Shadow Syndicate, and the gravity of that thought wrapped around me like a vise.

Darian emerged from the shadows, the light catching the contours of his face, illuminating the determination etched into his features. He looked every bit the warrior ready to charge into battle, and yet there was a softness in his eyes that spoke volumes. "Ready?" he asked, his voice steady, though I could sense the undercurrent of nerves just beneath the surface.

I nodded, my own heart pounding in rhythm with the cadence of his words. "As ready as I'll ever be." The truth was, I had been waiting for this moment for far too long, and every sleepless night spent plotting our next move led us here, at the brink of something monumental.

"Let's make this count," he said, and I couldn't help but admire the way he held himself—confident yet grounded, fierce yet protective. There was something deeply reassuring in the way he looked at me, as if I were more than just a partner in this battle; I was a teammate, an equal, and perhaps even something more.

With a shared glance that spoke volumes, we gathered our small team—each member a testament to resilience and courage in the face of overwhelming odds. We reviewed our plan one last time, each detail fine-tuned and polished until it gleamed like a weapon ready to be wielded. The excitement buzzed in the air, mingling with the faint smell of dew-kissed grass and the distant sounds of the waking city.

"Alright, people," I called out, my voice steadying as I faced our group. "Today is not just about the Syndicate; it's about reclaiming our lives, our future. We take this fight to them." My words ignited a spark in their eyes, a flicker of hope in the shadows of fear.

With the sun climbing higher, we set out. The city, a sprawling mosaic of chaos and color, lay sprawled before us, a battleground ripe for the taking. Each step felt like a drumbeat, steady and relentless, echoing the rhythm of our resolve. We moved as one, navigating the streets with the precision of seasoned fighters, past crumbling buildings and graffiti-covered walls that told stories of despair and hope intertwined.

As we approached the Syndicate's hideout—a dilapidated structure with a sinister reputation—I could feel the tension coiling in the pit of my stomach. It was a fortress built on fear, but we had something they didn't: a fire lit by camaraderie and determination. We exchanged glances, a silent promise passing between us, before we slipped into the shadows.

Inside, the air was thick with the scent of stale smoke and something darker—an ominous reminder of the deeds that had transpired within these walls. The echo of our footsteps was swallowed by the oppressive silence, each sound amplified in the stillness. My heart pounded, the adrenaline surging through me, sharpening my senses.

"Darian," I whispered, my voice barely above a breath. "What's our first move?"

He glanced at the layout of the building sketched in his mind, his brow furrowing slightly. "We split into pairs. Find the control room, shut down their communications. We can't let them alert their people."

A rush of excitement coursed through me. "You've got it." As we moved deeper into the labyrinth of darkness, I paired up with Sam, one of our most agile allies, who wore a mischievous grin that belied his intensity.

"This is it, then?" he said, his tone light despite the gravity of our task. "The big showdown? I hope I get to kick some serious butt."

"Just remember," I shot back with a smirk, "it's not about kicking butt; it's about taking names."

Sam laughed, the sound a welcome distraction from the tightening knots of anxiety in my chest. Together, we crept down a dimly lit corridor, the walls lined with flickering fluorescent lights that buzzed like angry bees. We passed door after door, the heavy silence making each step feel monumental.

Then we heard it—a low murmur echoing from one of the rooms. We exchanged cautious glances before slipping closer, pressing ourselves against the wall.

"Let's see what they're up to," I whispered, straining to hear the conversation inside.

"It's not going to work," a voice said, gruff and frustrated. "We can't hold the territory without the shipments. If we lose this deal, it's all over."

The realization struck me like a bolt of lightning. This was their Achilles' heel—a vulnerability we could exploit.

Sam nudged me, eyes wide with excitement. "Should we take them out? Get some intel?"

I hesitated, weighing the risks. "No. We need the information, but we can't blow our cover."

We backed away quietly, creeping back down the corridor until we reached a junction. "We should report back to Darian," I said, my heart racing with the thrill of discovery.

Just as we turned to leave, a door swung open, and a hulking figure emerged. It was one of their enforcers, his expression a mixture of surprise and fury. My instincts kicked in, and I pushed Sam aside just as the man lunged toward us.

"Run!" I shouted, adrenaline propelling me forward as we sprinted down the corridor, the sound of heavy footsteps pounding behind us.

"Are you insane?" Sam yelled, glancing back. "We just ran right into a lion's den!"

"Better than becoming dinner!" I shot back, my lungs burning as we barreled through the twisting hallways. I could hear voices rising in alarm, the Syndicate members realizing they had intruders.

The tension snapped like a taut string, and I felt a rush of exhilaration mingled with fear. We rounded a corner, skidding to a halt. In front of us lay a pair of double doors, the shadows lurking behind them thick with menace.

"Here goes nothing," I muttered, pushing the doors open with a fierce determination. The control room was bathed in screens displaying maps and reports, the heart of their operations.

"We have to get to those terminals," I said, urgency propelling me forward.

As we dashed toward the screens, I caught a glimpse of Darian and the others through the chaos, the weight of our mission pressing down with every passing second. There was no turning back now.

The fight for our future had begun, and every moment was a thread woven into the fabric of our destiny.

The control room was a chaotic symphony of blinking lights and muffled voices, the air thick with tension as we barreled in, adrenaline coursing through our veins. Screens displayed maps, schematics, and various surveillance feeds, all indicators of the vast network the Shadow Syndicate had built. I barely had time to process the sight when the sound of footsteps thundered from behind us, the enforcer we'd narrowly escaped hot on our heels.

"Sam, get to that terminal!" I shouted, pointing to a nearby console adorned with flashing indicators. "We need to disrupt their communications and gather intel—now!"

Without missing a beat, Sam lunged for the keyboard, fingers flying over the keys as if they were an extension of his very will. "On it! If only this thing had a nice big red 'self-destruct' button!"

"Save the theatrics for later!" I shot back, casting a glance over my shoulder. The door was still open, but I could hear the clatter of boots approaching, the ominous promise of reinforcements echoing through the narrow halls. My heart raced as I scanned the room for anything that could serve as a barricade.

Just then, a figure burst through the doorway—a wiry woman with fierce eyes and a gun drawn, her stance brimming with confidence. "Step away from the console!" she commanded, voice sharp as glass.

"Not a chance!" I replied, instinctively positioning myself between Sam and the intruder. "You're not taking us down without a fight."

A tense silence filled the air, punctuated only by Sam's frantic typing. "You're going to need to do better than that!" he chimed in, his voice laced with bravado.

The woman narrowed her gaze, sizing us up. "You have no idea who you're dealing with," she said, a smirk creeping onto her lips.

I shifted my weight, preparing for whatever was to come next. "And you have no idea what we're capable of. Now, why don't you put the gun down and we can talk about this like civilized people?"

"Civilized? In this world? That's rich." Her laughter was cold, echoing in the small room. "I've had enough of you fools thinking you can just waltz in here and disrupt our operations. This ends now."

With a sudden movement, she raised her weapon, and in that split second, time seemed to slow. My instincts kicked in, and I dove toward Sam, tackling him to the ground just as a shot rang out, the bullet ricocheting off the wall behind us.

"Nice move!" Sam yelled, scrambling to his feet, panic flashing in his eyes. "Now what? We can't just stay here!"

"Just keep working!" I shouted, desperation lacing my voice. "I need you to shut down their systems!"

"I'm trying, but the security protocols are insane! It's like trying to break into Fort Knox!"

"Then find a way to bypass it! You're the tech whiz, remember?" I glanced back at the intruder, who was regaining her composure, her expression shifting from shock to a steely determination.

Before I could react, she lunged toward us again, but this time, Darian burst through the door, a whirlwind of energy and fury. "Get down!" he shouted, launching himself between us and the assailant.

"Darian!" I cried out, relief flooding through me even as the danger loomed.

He didn't hesitate, swinging a heavy metal pipe he'd found lying in the corner, catching the woman off guard and sending her sprawling to the ground. "Are you both okay?" he asked, glancing between Sam and me, concern etched into his features.

"More or less," I replied, my heart still racing. "But we're not out of the woods yet. Sam's trying to shut down their systems while we're under fire."

"I'll handle her," Darian said, determination coursing through him. He turned his attention to the fallen woman, who was scrambling to regain her footing. "You should have picked a better day to play hero."

As the two squared off, I turned back to Sam, who was still typing frantically. "How's it going?"

"Almost there! Just need to—" His voice was interrupted by a sharp gasp, his expression suddenly shifting to one of horror. "They've triggered the alarm! We've got company!"

Panic shot through me as I heard the distant sound of sirens wailing, signaling that our cover had been blown. "Darian!" I shouted, urgency threading through my tone. "We need to get out of here, now!"

He glanced back at me, his brows furrowing as he kicked the fallen gun from the woman's hand, rendering her weapon useless. "I'm on it!"

Just as I turned back to help Sam, the door burst open again, and a swarm of Syndicate members flooded the room, their expressions a mixture of confusion and rage. "Get them!" one of them yelled, rushing toward us with reckless abandon.

The room erupted into chaos. Darian swung the pipe again, catching another assailant square in the jaw. Sam was still furiously typing, his face a mask of concentration, even as the chaos swirled around him. "If I can just get another second—"

"Sam!" I shouted, adrenaline pushing me into action as I grabbed a discarded chair and hurled it toward the oncoming group, the wood splintering as it struck one of them, buying us precious moments.

But the odds were quickly stacking against us. The room filled with voices, shouts mingling with the alarm blaring overhead. I could feel the walls closing in, the weight of desperation clawing at my throat. "We need an exit!" I yelled, my voice barely piercing the cacophony.

"Got it!" Sam said, his fingers moving like lightning. "Just a few more seconds!"

With a determined resolve, I turned back to Darian, who was holding his own against a pair of attackers. "We're not going down without a fight!" I declared, adrenaline surging through me. "Let's give them something to remember!"

Just as I lunged into the fray, throwing a well-placed kick that sent one attacker sprawling, a sudden blast of light flooded the room. It wasn't just the overhead lights—it was the unmistakable glow of a backup generator kicking in, illuminating the chaos.

"That's not good," I muttered under my breath, realizing the source of the light was coming from the far wall, where a reinforced panel was sliding open, revealing a hidden compartment.

"What is that?" Darian shouted, blocking another punch as he turned to look.

"I have no idea, but it can't be good!" I replied, my instincts screaming at me to get Sam and get out.

Suddenly, an ominous hum filled the air, vibrating through the ground beneath our feet. "Sam!" I yelled, urgency flooding my tone. "What did you do?"

"Nothing! I swear!" he shouted back, panic etched across his face. "Just a few more—"

Before he could finish, the room erupted in blinding light, the hidden compartment revealing a series of high-tech weaponry, each one more intimidating than the last. The Syndicate had been prepared for us, and now we were standing in the middle of their arsenal.

"Get down!" Darian shouted, pulling me away from the chaos as energy beams started to fire from the newly revealed weapons, each blast ricocheting off the walls and creating a deadly game of dodge.

"We need to move!" I yelled, adrenaline pushing me forward, but just as I turned to grab Sam, a blinding flash erupted, and the ground beneath us shook.

I caught a glimpse of Darian's fierce expression as he grasped my arm, his voice a low growl in my ear. "Stick together, no matter what!"

But before I could respond, everything shifted. The room exploded in a cacophony of noise—screams, gunfire, and the blaring alarm merging into a frenzy of chaos. I felt myself being pulled away from Darian, the chaos of bodies and explosions spiraling around me like a violent storm.

And then, as if time had slowed, I turned to see Darian's expression change, a look of horror etching itself into his features. "No!" he screamed, but the world around us erupted into chaos, and I was engulfed in darkness as I was yanked away, the distance between us growing impossibly vast.

In that moment, uncertainty washed over me like a cold tide. Would I ever see him again? Would I be able to finish what we started? All I could do was brace myself against the storm of shadows closing in, heart racing as I plunged into the unknown, the sound of his voice fading into the distance.

Chapter 18: The Final Stand

The Syndicate's headquarters loomed ahead, a dark monolith against the evening sky, its windows reflecting the dying light like malevolent eyes watching our every move. My heart pounded in my chest, the sound echoing in my ears as if it were a war drum rallying me for the battle to come. Each step felt like a leap into the unknown, the atmosphere thick with an electric charge that hinted at the danger waiting within those walls. The air, laden with the scent of rain-soaked asphalt and burnt machinery, seemed to whisper secrets, urging me onward even as dread coiled in my stomach.

Beside me, my comrades pressed forward, their faces a mix of determination and fear. Callum, ever the stalwart, wore a fierce expression that could scare off a pack of wolves. His dark hair, tousled and damp, framed his chiseled features, and his green eyes burned with an intensity that promised vengeance. I knew that beneath that bravado, a tempest of emotions churned. We had been through hell together, and now, as we stood on the precipice of our greatest challenge, I could feel the weight of our shared history between us.

The plan had been simple enough: infiltrate, gather evidence, and dismantle the Syndicate from within. But simplicity rarely danced hand in hand with danger, and as we approached the entrance, I couldn't shake the feeling that the real battle was just beginning. With every footfall, the tension thickened around us, a palpable force that raised the hairs on my arms. I stole a glance at Zara, our tech guru, who was furiously typing on her wrist communicator, her brow furrowed in concentration. She was the lifeline we desperately needed, the one who could guide us through the labyrinth of this fortress.

"Are you sure this will work?" I asked, my voice low, laced with doubt. The shadows cast by the building seemed to stretch and twist, alive with unseen threats.

Zara shot me a quick smile, her lips curving into a mischievous grin. "Of course! Just remember, if I say 'run,' you run faster than you ever have in your life. You got that?"

Her levity was infectious, igniting a flicker of hope in my chest. "Got it. I'll leave you to fend off the villains with your tech wizardry," I replied, the banter helping to ease the weight of the moment.

As we entered the building, the cold, sterile environment engulfed us. Fluorescent lights flickered overhead, casting an unflattering glow that made everything seem harsher, sharper. The hallway stretched before us, a narrow corridor lined with metal doors, each one a potential entry into the abyss. The silence was deafening, punctuated only by the distant hum of machinery and the faint rustle of our clothes as we moved.

I felt a shiver run down my spine as we pressed deeper into the heart of the Syndicate. It was as if the walls themselves were watching, waiting for us to make a mistake. I clenched my fists, steeling myself against the onslaught of fear. We were here for a reason—to dismantle the very fabric of the organization that had taken so much from us. I could almost feel the ghosts of those we had lost hovering at my shoulder, their whispers urging me to push on.

Suddenly, a loud crash echoed through the hall, sending adrenaline racing through my veins. We froze, our eyes darting toward the sound. Callum's expression hardened, and he nodded toward a door just ahead. "That's our target. Shadow Man is in there."

I took a deep breath, the weight of his words crashing over me like a tidal wave. This was it—the moment we had prepared for, the confrontation that could change everything. I glanced at Zara, who was typing furiously, her fingers flying over the screen. "Just give me a few more seconds," she murmured, her eyes locked on the display.

Time stretched, each second a lifetime. I could feel the tension coiling in my gut, the sense of impending doom mingling with the thrill of purpose. As the door creaked open, a figure stepped into the light—a silhouette shrouded in darkness, the embodiment of our fears.

The Shadow Man.

He emerged with an air of casual confidence, a smirk playing on his lips that made my blood boil. His presence was magnetic, pulling at something deep within me, yet I couldn't shake the feeling of revulsion that accompanied it. "Ah, the brave little rebels," he drawled, his voice smooth as silk but laced with menace. "You've come to confront me. How charming."

"What you're doing is wrong," I shouted, stepping forward, fueled by righteous indignation. "You think you can control everything, but you're just a coward hiding behind shadows."

He laughed, a low, throaty sound that sent chills racing down my spine. "Control? My dear, it's not about control. It's about power, and you're too late to stop it."

With a wave of his hand, the room shifted, and I realized too late that we had walked into a trap. The walls closed in, and my heart raced as the reality of our situation dawned. Callum and Zara moved instinctively, positioning themselves to protect me, but I knew the odds were stacked against us.

"No!" I shouted, desperation surging within me. "We won't let you win!"

The air crackled with tension, and I prepared myself for the fight of our lives, the weight of the world resting on our shoulders. In that moment, surrounded by the darkness of our enemy's lair, I realized that our bond was the light that would guide us through the storm. Together, we would rise or fall, but I would fight with everything I had to ensure it was not the latter.

The Shadow Man's laughter hung in the air, a chilling reminder of the odds stacked against us. I felt the room constrict around us, as if the very walls had turned sentient, eager to witness our downfall. Callum moved beside me, his presence a solid reassurance amidst the chaos. "Stay sharp," he murmured, eyes narrowed, scanning our surroundings for an exit or an advantage.

The Shadow Man stepped closer, and with him came a palpable aura of menace. "You really think you can stop me?" he asked, his voice a low growl, as if each word dripped with venom. "I've already won. The game was rigged the moment you decided to play."

"I've never been one to back down from a challenge," I shot back, forcing my voice to remain steady despite the tremor in my hands. "And I'm not about to let some power-hungry puppet master dictate my fate."

With a flick of his wrist, he summoned shadows from the corners of the room, twisting them into grotesque forms that danced ominously around him. It was like watching an artist at work, painting fear with the darkest shades of night. "Fighting me is futile," he taunted, his eyes gleaming with a mixture of malice and amusement. "You don't even know what you're up against."

Zara, who had been working quietly at the terminal behind us, suddenly exclaimed, "I think I found a way to disrupt his control!" She turned her attention to me, her eyes alight with determination. "If I can overload his system, it might weaken his hold over the shadows."

"Do it!" Callum yelled, his voice cutting through the tension like a knife. The urgency in his tone galvanized me, stirring the embers of defiance in my heart. I nodded at Zara, hoping my belief in her would bolster her confidence.

As Zara furiously tapped the screen, I felt the shadows start to shift, as if aware of her intentions. The air grew heavy, charged with the static of impending doom. "Come on, come on," she muttered under her breath, her fingers dancing across the keyboard.

The Shadow Man's laughter echoed around us, a sinister melody that grated on my nerves. "You think that you can defeat me with a few keystrokes? Pathetic." He stepped forward, and I instinctively positioned myself between him and Zara.

"Pathetic is the best you can come up with?" I shot back, summoning every ounce of bravado I could muster. "You really need to work on your insults. They're as weak as your power."

His face darkened, the smirk evaporating as anger flared in his eyes. "Enough games." He raised his hand, and the shadows lunged toward me, sharp and jagged, like claws eager to claim their prize.

In that split second, time warped. I could feel the chill of the shadows creeping toward me, but Callum was there, a blur of motion as he shoved me out of the way just as the darkness swiped at the space I'd occupied. "I'm not letting you take her!" he roared, his voice filled with a fierce protectiveness that sent warmth surging through my chest.

"Zara! Are you almost there?" I shouted, my heart racing as I ducked behind Callum, the shadows swirling and clawing at the air in frustration.

"Just need a few more seconds!" she yelled, her voice strained but resolute. I glanced over my shoulder to see her brow glistening with sweat, the determination etched on her features making her look fierce and beautiful.

"Why do you care so much about her?" the Shadow Man sneered, turning his attention to me. "You're nothing but a distraction, a pawn in a game you don't even understand."

"Maybe, but at least I know what I'm fighting for," I shot back, my voice steadying with each breath. "Unlike you, I have something worth protecting."

With that, I lunged forward, pushing through the terror clawing at my heart, charging straight at the Shadow Man. I had no grand plan, no strategic moves in mind—just raw instinct fueled by the fierce love I had for my friends. As I approached, I felt a rush of adrenaline surging through my veins, and for a moment, everything else faded away.

But he was ready, the shadows swirling around him like a tempest. They lashed out, tendrils reaching for me, but I dodged and weaved, my body moving on pure instinct. I could feel Callum's presence behind me, a powerful anchor in this storm of darkness, urging me forward.

"Zara!" I shouted again, and through the din of chaos, I caught a glimpse of her, fingers flying, her focus unwavering.

"Almost there!" she called back, and I saw her eyes narrow in concentration.

The shadows began to recoil, as if Zara's coding was starting to chip away at their dark foundation. A surge of hope filled me, lifting my spirits as I pivoted to face the Shadow Man once more.

"You'll regret this," he hissed, his voice dripping with venom. "You think you can simply walk away from this? I will find you again."

"Not if I have anything to say about it," I replied, finding my voice even as fear twisted in my gut. "You're not invincible. You're just a man hiding in the shadows, trying to frighten people into submission."

His eyes narrowed, and for the first time, I could see the cracks in his facade. "You're playing a dangerous game," he warned, but the tremor in his voice betrayed a hint of uncertainty.

Just then, Zara shouted, "Now!" The terminal behind her erupted in a cascade of light, sending a pulse of energy coursing through the room. The shadows shrieked, a wailing sound that pierced the air, twisting in erratic patterns as if caught in a storm.

The room trembled, and the Shadow Man staggered backward, eyes wide with disbelief. "No!" he roared, but it was too late. The shadows imploded, collapsing in on themselves as the energy surged, breaking his hold over the darkness.

I felt the weight of fear lift as the darkness receded, the shadows slinking back into the corners of the room like frightened creatures. My heart raced, elation flooding my senses. We had done it—we had taken back our power.

Callum turned to me, a triumphant grin splitting his face. "That was brilliant!"

I laughed, the sound bubbling up from my chest. "Yeah, but we're not out of the woods yet."

"Just give me a moment," Zara panted, wiping sweat from her brow. "We still need to make sure he's really done."

I turned to face the Shadow Man, who was now on his knees, fury and disbelief mingling in his gaze. There was something almost pitiful in the way he looked, stripped of his control, the façade of invincibility shattered.

"Do you see now?" I asked, my voice steady as I faced him. "You can't keep people in the dark forever. The light always finds a way in."

The corners of his mouth twisted into a sneer, but I could see the cracks in his armor. "You think this is over? You think I'm done?"

"I think we're just getting started." My voice was firm, emboldened by the strength of my friends. We were ready to fight, ready to reclaim our lives from the clutches of darkness. The journey was far from over, but for the first time, I felt a glimmer of hope.

The shadows shrank away, hissing in retreat as if repelled by the light of our defiance. I took a breath, the air suddenly lighter, almost buoyant, yet tinged with a palpable tension that hinted we were far from finished. The Shadow Man, now stripped of his ominous bravado, knelt on the floor, anger swirling in his eyes. Beneath that fury lay a flicker of fear, the kind that came when someone realized their carefully constructed world was collapsing.

"Do you think this is a victory?" he spat, his voice sharp like glass. "You're playing in a league far beyond your comprehension. I'm just a piece on the board, and you've made a grave mistake in underestimating your opponent."

"Seems to me you're a pretty lousy piece," I quipped, crossing my arms defiantly. The rush of adrenaline made my pulse quicken, and I couldn't help but relish the moment of triumph.

Callum stepped closer, muscles taut, ready for whatever move the Shadow Man might try next. "Enough of your riddles. You've lost control. Now, tell us what we need to know," he demanded, voice steady but tinged with the strain of our confrontation.

The Shadow Man's lips curled into a sardonic smile, but his bravado faltered. "You think I'll just spill the beans? You're mistaken. Even now, I'm not the only player in this game. Others are watching, and they won't let you leave here alive."

Zara's fingers were still dancing over her wrist communicator, furiously running diagnostics and calculating our next move. "We don't have time for your cryptic nonsense," she said, exasperation lacing her tone. "If you want to make it out of here in one piece, I suggest you start talking."

He chuckled darkly, the sound echoing around us, chilling my spine. "You have no idea how deep this goes. This isn't just about you three. The Syndicate's reach extends far beyond this room. The moment you decided to oppose me, you signed your own death warrants."

I glanced at Callum and Zara, the resolve in their expressions mirroring my own. "We've faced worse than you," I said, hoping to mask the tremor in my voice with bravado. "And we're not afraid of a little darkness."

With a sudden, sharp gesture, the Shadow Man raised his hand. The shadows began to coil and twist around him, forming into jagged edges that seemed poised to strike. "Then let's see how brave you really are," he hissed, and the shadows lunged toward us with terrifying speed.

"Zara, now!" I yelled, instinctively pushing Callum back as I dove to the side, narrowly avoiding a shadowy tendril that slashed the air where we had stood. The darkness was alive, sentient, as it twisted and morphed, eager to claim its next victim.

Zara's fingers worked frantically, and a blinding light erupted from her device, momentarily illuminating the room in stark clarity. The shadows recoiled, screeching like banshees, the sound clawing at my eardrums. "I think I've got something!" she shouted, her voice ringing with triumph. "Hold them back for just a moment longer!"

Callum surged forward, deflecting the shadowy tendrils with sheer force, his strength a shield against the encroaching darkness. "I've got your back!" he yelled, his focus unbroken as he pushed forward, creating a barrier for Zara.

In the flickering light, I caught sight of the panic flashing in the Shadow Man's eyes as he struggled to maintain his control. "You can't do this!" he screamed, frustration boiling over. "You have no idea what you're meddling with!"

"Then enlighten us," I shot back, fueled by the adrenaline coursing through me. "What's really going on? Who else is involved?"

But before he could respond, a crack reverberated through the air, sharp and jarring. The entire room trembled, and the lights flickered ominously. "What the hell was that?" I gasped, fear gnawing at my resolve.

"Structural integrity is failing!" Zara shouted, her voice barely rising above the chaos. "We need to get out of here now!"

"Not without answers," I insisted, but my heart raced at the sound of the building creaking around us. It felt as though the very walls were protesting our presence, and an ominous sense of urgency surged within me.

Callum and I shared a brief look, a silent conversation passing between us. "We need to push him," Callum said, determination etched on his face. "He's the key to understanding this. We can't leave without finding out what he knows."

"Fine," I agreed, but a knot of anxiety tightened in my stomach. "But we need to do it fast."

I turned back to the Shadow Man, forcing my voice to stay steady despite the growing chaos around us. "You think you can scare us into submission? You think we'll just run away?"

The shadows swirled more violently, and the Shadow Man's sneer turned into a grimace of rage. "You don't understand what's coming. The Syndicate isn't just a group; it's a network. If I fall, they'll come for you. You'll wish you had left when you had the chance."

"Enough!" I shouted, my frustration boiling over. "What do you mean, 'they'? Who are you afraid of?"

His eyes flickered with a mix of fear and defiance, and for a fleeting moment, I saw the man behind the mask, the creature driven by desperation rather than power. "You're meddling with forces beyond your control," he spat, but I noticed a slight tremor in his voice. "They'll wipe you out, one by one, until nothing remains."

Suddenly, the floor beneath us shuddered violently, sending a jolt through my legs. "Zara!" I yelled, panic rising as I struggled to maintain my balance.

"I'm trying!" she yelled back, furiously manipulating the screen on her device. The lights flickered again, casting erratic shadows that danced ominously along the walls. "If I can just—"

The Shadow Man took advantage of our distraction, his demeanor shifting from despair to cunning. "You really think you can win this? You're in way over your heads," he taunted, and the shadows began to surge around him again, emboldened by the chaos.

In a desperate attempt to regain control, I lunged forward, pushing past the fear that threatened to paralyze me. "Stop! If you want to make it out of here, you need to help us!"

"Help you?" He laughed, a harsh, grating sound that echoed through the turmoil. "Why would I do that? You're just another part of the game."

I took a deep breath, forcing the weight of my fear down. "Because if you don't, you won't make it out either. We're not just fighting for ourselves. We're fighting for everyone you've wronged. This is your chance to change, to be something other than a shadow."

His expression wavered, a flicker of something—doubt?—crossing his features, but just as quickly, it hardened into resolve. "You think you can manipulate me? You're as naive as the rest of them."

"Maybe so," I admitted, my voice softer, more vulnerable. "But I'd rather fight for something than live in darkness. The question is, are you brave enough to do the same?"

Just as he opened his mouth to respond, the walls shook violently, the lights flickering one last time before plunging us into darkness. A deafening crash echoed, and the ground beneath us began to crumble.

"Run!" Zara screamed, her voice filled with terror.

The shadows that had once cowered in fear now surged back with a vengeance, the once-hesitant tendrils now thrashing wildly as if sensing victory.

"Now!" Callum yelled, grabbing my hand and pulling me toward the only exit, the floor beneath us splitting apart, the space we had fought for teetering on the brink of collapse.

With our hearts racing, we sprinted toward the doorway, the sounds of destruction erupting behind us. But as we neared the exit,

I turned back for one last look at the Shadow Man, who had become more than just our enemy; he was a reflection of the darkness we all battled.

In that fleeting moment, our eyes locked, and something shifted—an understanding, a question hanging in the air. Would he choose to embrace the light or retreat deeper into the shadows?

But then the wall crumbled behind him, and with a resounding roar, darkness swallowed him whole, the shadows closing in like a shroud. I felt a pang of something—regret?—as we dashed through the door, escaping into the chaos outside.

We burst into the night, breathless and shaken, but alive. The sound of sirens wailed in the distance, a promise of hope and salvation mingling with the lingering shadows of despair.

"Did we win?" I gasped, my heart racing.

"I don't know," Callum replied, glancing back at the building as debris rained down around us. "But I do know one thing—this isn't over."

And in that moment, as the world around us pulsed with uncertainty, I realized the fight had only just begun. The darkness was still out there, lurking, waiting

Chapter 19: Ashes and Embers

I stood at the edge of the crumbling warehouse, the remnants of the Syndicate strewn around me like discarded memories, each shard of concrete and twisted metal a testament to the battles fought and the lives irrevocably changed. The scent of burnt rubber hung in the air, mingling with the faint, acrid tang of smoke that curled upwards in lazy wisps, dissipating into the cool evening sky. My heart raced, not just from the adrenaline still coursing through my veins, but from the weight of what had just transpired.

Beside me, Theo leaned against the jagged wall, his expression a mix of relief and lingering fury. His dark hair, tousled and glistening with sweat, framed a face etched with determination, yet haunted by the shadows of our past. I caught his eye, the unspoken connection between us a fragile thread, shimmering but ready to snap under the weight of our shared history. "You did what you had to," he murmured, his voice low and gravelly, as if he were still processing the events of the day.

"Did I?" I replied, my voice thick with doubt. "Or did I just dig us deeper into this mess?" I turned away, my gaze sweeping over the wreckage—overturned crates, shattered glass, and the unmistakable remnants of lives once vibrant but now extinguished in our struggle for survival. Each fragment felt like a whisper of guilt, echoing in the recesses of my mind.

The warehouse, once a bustling hub of the Syndicate's operations, now stood silent and eerie, the only sound the soft crackling of embers that still glowed in the dimming light. It was here, amid the chaos, that we had fought to reclaim our lives, yet victory tasted bittersweet. I felt the weight of our choices pressing down, the realization that love, as beautiful as it could be, was laced with the jagged edges of our reality.

"Maybe it's time we let go of the past," Theo said, pushing himself off the wall to face me fully. His eyes, dark and stormy, held a fierce intensity, but there was also something softer beneath the surface. "We can't keep running from what happened, but we don't have to let it define us either."

His words resonated deep within me, a flicker of hope sparking to life against the backdrop of our turmoil. I wanted to believe him. I longed for the simplicity of a life unencumbered by the burdens we carried. But how could we sever the ties that bound us to our choices, to the mistakes that lingered like shadows? "And what if the shadows are all we have left?" I countered, a tremor in my voice.

For a moment, silence enveloped us, heavy and charged. The tension was palpable, a taut wire stretched to its breaking point. "Then we'll create new light," Theo replied, determination lacing his tone. "Together."

Together. The word hung between us like a fragile promise. I wanted to believe it, to hold onto the notion that we could rebuild, but the thought of venturing into the unknown was terrifying. "What if we fail?" I whispered, my voice barely audible against the quiet hum of the world around us.

"Then we fail," he said, a hint of a smile breaking through the tension. "But at least we'll fail while trying to live, instead of just surviving."

I couldn't help but chuckle at his tenacity. "Is that your grand plan? To embrace failure?"

"Hey, I've failed spectacularly in the past," he shot back, his eyes dancing with mischief. "I'm practically an expert. Besides, failure is just another word for experience. And experience, my dear, is what we need if we're going to navigate this new reality."

His wry humor, a balm to my frayed nerves, reminded me of why I had fallen for him in the first place. Beneath the grit and determination was a man who could still find laughter amid chaos. "I guess that's one way to look at it," I admitted, a smile creeping onto my lips. "But I'm not sure I want to be the queen of failure."

"Don't worry. I'll wear the crown," Theo quipped, his grin infectious. "Just promise me you won't throw any tomatoes when I do."

We shared a laugh, the sound echoing in the hollow space around us, momentarily shattering the weight of our reality. It felt good, reminding me of the warmth that had ignited between us amidst the darkness. I took a step closer, the air between us crackling with unspoken words and lingering glances. The ruins of our past might loom large, but I felt the promise of something new—a chance to transform the ashes of our lives into something beautiful.

"Maybe we can start by cleaning this place up," I suggested, gesturing to the chaos surrounding us. "If we're going to move forward, we should probably clear away the remnants of what's been lost."

Theo raised an eyebrow, amusement playing in his features. "You want to start a cleanup crew? I'm not sure that's quite the adventure I signed up for."

"Come on, it could be therapeutic!" I nudged him playfully. "Besides, we owe it to ourselves to turn this place into something we can be proud of."

He studied me for a moment, the flicker of a smile still dancing on his lips. "You have a point. Let's make this our first project—a monument to our survival."

"Or a shrine to our questionable choices," I replied, laughter bubbling up between us again.

"Either way, it's ours," he said, his voice softening as he took my hand, intertwining our fingers. In that simple gesture, I felt the warmth of hope, a promise of what could be.

Together, we stepped into the wreckage, ready to shape the ashes into something that would no longer hold us captive but would instead mark the beginning of our new journey.

With a shared glance that spoke volumes, Theo and I began sifting through the debris, armed with nothing more than our determination and an assortment of makeshift tools we scavenged from the wreckage. I grasped a rusted shovel, its surface rough against my palm, while he wielded a battered broom that had seen far better days. The irony of our new roles in this dilapidated place wasn't lost on me; once, we were combatants, fighting against the encroaching shadows of the Syndicate, and now we were its unlikely caretakers, tasked with reclaiming what remained.

"Who knew our dream job would involve sweeping floors and picking up garbage?" Theo joked, brushing a hand through his hair, sending a shower of dust cascading like tiny stars into the fading light.

"Dream jobs are overrated," I replied with a smirk, shoveling a pile of shattered glass into a nearby crate. "Besides, think of the character building. We'll have stories to tell when we're old and gray, assuming we don't end up with tetanus first."

He chuckled, the sound warm and comforting in the midst of chaos. "What a lovely image. 'Gather 'round, kids, let me tell you about the time I almost died cleaning up a crime scene.'"

As we worked, an easy rhythm developed between us. Each shove of debris, each sweep of the broom, felt like we were chiseling away at the past, making space for something new to grow. The air hummed with the tension of what had happened here, but amidst the remnants, I began to see potential—shadows that could become sunlight, ashes that could bloom anew.

"Do you think we'll ever really be free from this?" I asked, pausing to lean against a wall marked by our battles, its surface jagged and scarred, much like the remnants of our relationship. "All these ghosts... they cling to us like old wallpaper."

"Ghosts can be pesky," Theo acknowledged, his expression thoughtful as he swept a particularly stubborn patch of dust. "But they can also remind us of what we've overcome. It's the memories that shape us, right? The good and the bad."

"Right," I said, feeling a flicker of hope. "But some memories weigh more than others."

"Then we shed them. Piece by piece, we let go." He met my gaze, the intensity in his eyes igniting something deep within me, a flicker of determination that made me want to believe.

The sun dipped lower, casting long shadows that stretched across the floor like fingers reaching out for something lost. The world outside seemed oblivious to the upheaval within these walls, life continuing as usual, while we toiled in silence, moving toward an uncertain future. Just as I was about to plunge back into the debris, the sound of distant sirens pierced the quiet, a stark reminder that we were still tethered to a reality outside our little bubble of rebuilding.

"Looks like our little cleanup might attract some unwanted attention," Theo said, his brow furrowing slightly.

"Nothing says 'rebuilding your life' like a visit from law enforcement," I quipped, though the tightening in my stomach belied my humor. "Should we wave or hide?"

"Hide?" He raised an eyebrow, a mischievous glint sparking in his eyes. "Where's the fun in that? We should probably make ourselves presentable, though. I'm not sure 'homicidal sweatpants' is the look we're going for."

Before I could respond, a figure emerged from the shadows, stepping into the fading light. The air shifted as my heart plummeted, recognizing the familiar outline of Detective Hargrove, his features obscured but unmistakable. He had been a relentless presence in our lives, the embodiment of the law that felt more like a storm cloud hovering over our heads.

"Looks like I spoke too soon," I murmured, my breath hitching in my throat.

Theo stepped slightly in front of me, an instinctual protective gesture that sent warmth blooming in my chest. "Detective Hargrove," he greeted, his tone steady. "To what do we owe the pleasure?"

"Pleasure? That's an interesting way to phrase it." Hargrove's voice was gruff, and his eyes narrowed, scanning the debris with a mix of suspicion and intrigue. "You two have been quite busy, haven't you?"

"We like to stay productive," I said, forcing a casual tone despite the knot of tension tightening in my stomach. "Nothing like a little spring cleaning after a storm."

"Is that what we're calling it now?" He stepped closer, his gaze assessing as if he were piecing together a puzzle he had yet to solve. "I was under the impression that a war was fought here. Several lives lost. Not exactly your average cleaning job."

"Some of us prefer to look at it as a fresh start," Theo interjected, his voice calm, but I could feel the undercurrent of anxiety. The last thing we needed was for Hargrove to sniff out any lingering traces of the Syndicate's chaos that still lingered in our lives.

"Fresh start?" Hargrove's brow furrowed, and he crossed his arms, a gesture that screamed skepticism. "You've got a funny way of showing it."

"Detective, if we're going to rebuild our lives, we have to start somewhere," I replied, forcing a smile. "Besides, aren't you supposed to be out solving crimes, not critiquing our efforts?"

He paused, eyes flickering with something that might have been admiration—or perhaps it was merely curiosity. "I suppose I can appreciate a good effort. Just keep it legal, alright?"

"Legal is our middle name," Theo said, the teasing lilt in his voice drawing a ghost of a smile from Hargrove.

As the tension began to dissipate, I found myself drawn into the unexpected camaraderie that simmered between us. The detective might have been an unwelcome visitor in our journey, but perhaps he could also become an ally in our quest for redemption.

"Consider it our community service," I added, feeling emboldened. "A little DIY rehabilitation. After all, we're just two souls trying to make sense of the wreckage."

Hargrove regarded us both, the lines on his face softening slightly, though I knew his skepticism would not vanish overnight. "Just keep it low-key. The last thing we need is a resurgence of the Syndicate because someone thinks you're holding a grand reopening party."

With a nod, we promised to keep things under control. I watched as he stepped back into the shadows, the weight of his presence lingering like a specter. "Well, that went better than expected," I said, glancing at Theo, who wore a look of bemusement.

"I think we've officially made it to the 'unlikely allies' phase of our story," he chuckled. "What's next? A group hug with the local authorities?"

"Only if we can skip the awkwardness," I replied, grinning. "But first, let's get back to work. There's a lot of mess to clean up, both here and in our lives."

With renewed determination, we dove back into the wreckage, finding solace in our shared purpose. Amidst the debris and uncertainty, I felt a shift in the air—fragile yet potent, like the first light of dawn breaking through the darkest night. Together, we could rebuild our world, one day at a time, finding strength in the ashes of what had been.

The sun dipped lower in the sky, casting a warm, golden glow over the remnants of our makeshift cleanup. I glanced at Theo, whose brow glistened with sweat, the light catching the contours of his face. He looked almost heroic, a warrior ready to face whatever challenge lay ahead, and I couldn't help but feel a swell of admiration. We stood at the brink of something new, and yet, the air was thick with the lingering tension of unresolved conflicts and uncertainties.

"What's next, oh mighty architect of our renovation?" I teased, nudging him playfully as we piled the last of the debris into a waiting dumpster. "Are we going to turn this place into a coffee shop or a yoga studio?"

"Yoga studio?" He feigned shock, placing a hand on his chest. "You think we have enough serenity in our lives for that? No, we need something more... exciting. Maybe a speakeasy? I can see it now: 'The Hidden Ember.'"

"The Hidden Ember?" I laughed, imagining a secretive bar tucked away behind these battered walls. "Sounds like a place where bad decisions are made over dimly lit cocktails."

"Exactly!" He winked, the lightness of our banter casting away the shadows that had crept in during the day. But just as quickly, the laughter faded, replaced by the gravity of our situation. We were still entrenched in a war, the embers of the Syndicate still flickering ominously in our rearview mirrors.

"Let's not forget why we're here," I said, the smile slipping from my face. "The moment we lose sight of that, we're back where we started."

"True enough," he conceded, his expression sobering. "But it's important to keep our spirits up. If we don't find joy in the little things, we'll drown in the seriousness of it all."

"Wise words from a man wielding a broom like a sword." I couldn't help but smile again, the warmth of camaraderie enveloping us like a favorite blanket. We had transformed the devastation around us into a space of hope and renewal, even if it was just for the moment.

As twilight descended, the shadows grew longer, and the eerie silence of the warehouse began to deepen. I took a moment to survey our handiwork. The space felt lighter, more alive somehow, though I knew we still had a long way to go. There was a flicker of hope that maybe, just maybe, we could turn this place into a symbol of our triumph over adversity rather than a reminder of our past failures.

"Let's head outside for a breath of fresh air," Theo suggested, motioning toward the door. "I think we've earned it."

"Agreed. But don't think I'll let you off the hook that easily. We still have to decide on the color scheme for our future speakeasy," I replied, playfully elbowing him as we stepped outside.

The cool evening air greeted us like an old friend, ruffling my hair and making me breathe a little easier. The horizon blazed with hues of orange and pink, a breathtaking backdrop to our newfound resolve. As we stood together, I felt a sense of peace wash over me—a momentary reprieve from the chaos that had defined our lives for so long.

"That's beautiful," I said, gesturing toward the sky. "It's like the universe is giving us a sign."

"A sign?" He raised an eyebrow, glancing at me. "Or maybe just a reminder that even the darkest days can give way to something stunning."

"Or perhaps it's a hint that we should be careful about getting too comfortable," I countered, my mind flickering back to the chaos still lingering in our lives. "You know that once you start to hope, life has a way of throwing you a curveball."

"Fair point," he replied, his tone serious now. "But maybe we need to embrace the uncertainty. What's the worst that could happen? We lose everything we've fought for?"

"Let's not tempt fate." I smiled, but the thought still lingered. Just as I turned to lean against the side of the warehouse, I caught a glint of movement out of the corner of my eye. My heart raced as I turned fully to face the shadows beyond the perimeter of our makeshift sanctuary.

"What is it?" Theo asked, sensing my sudden tension.

"Did you see that?" I nodded toward the darkened edges of the lot. The hairs on the back of my neck stood on end.

"What?" His voice dropped to a whisper, mirroring my growing unease.

"I swear I saw someone," I said, scanning the area. Shadows danced with the twilight, making it difficult to discern reality from illusion.

Just then, a figure stepped out from behind an old shipping container, shrouded in darkness. My breath hitched in my throat as the silhouette grew clearer—a hooded figure, face obscured but posture threatening.

"Great, just what we need," I muttered, instinctively moving closer to Theo, who had already stepped protectively in front of me.

"Who are you?" Theo called out, his voice steady, but I could hear the undercurrent of tension.

"Interesting choice of venue for a party," the figure said, their voice low and smooth, but carrying an edge that sent chills racing down my spine. "I hope you're not too attached to it. We've come to collect."

"Collect what?" I managed to ask, my heart pounding against my ribcage as dread settled over me like a heavy fog.

"Your little rebellion ends here," the figure replied, stepping closer into the dim light, revealing a glint of something metallic in their hand. "The Syndicate isn't finished with you yet."

As the words hung in the air, the gravity of the situation crashed down upon us. My mind raced, strategizing an escape, but the cold reality was that we were trapped, backed into a corner with nowhere to run.

Theo's grip tightened on my arm, and I could feel his resolve pulsing through the air. "You don't want to do this," he warned, his voice low and steady. "We're not your enemies. We're just trying to move on."

"Too late for that," the figure sneered, raising the metallic object—a gun—pointing it squarely at us. My breath caught in my throat, panic clawing at my insides.

In that instant, the world narrowed to a pinprick of focus. My heart raced, adrenaline flooding my system as time slowed to a crawl. We were on the brink of something dark and dangerous, and I had no idea how we would escape this time.

All I could think was that our fresh start was about to be extinguished before it even had a chance to ignite.

Chapter 20: Fractured Reflections

The air hung thick with a silence that felt almost tangible, wrapping around me like a heavy cloak. I stood at the edge of the abandoned park, the remnants of our recent victory still swirling in my mind like autumn leaves caught in a restless wind. The old swings creaked in the breeze, their once vibrant colors faded to a weary gray, and the scent of damp earth lingered in the cool air, mingling with the faintest hint of rust from the neglected playground equipment. It was as if the very landscape mourned for the battles fought, for the lives changed forever.

Darian arrived with his familiar gait, each step deliberate yet marked by an unmistakable tension. He always wore that intense look, the one that made it seem like he was carrying the weight of the world on his broad shoulders. It was a look I had come to both admire and resent, a reminder that while we had triumphed, the cost had been steep. My heart raced as our eyes met, and I felt a jolt of something electric and undeniable. Yet, there was an unspoken barrier between us, a chasm that widened with every day of silence and avoidance.

"What are we doing here, Lila?" he asked, his voice low, edged with a frustration that mirrored my own. He raked a hand through his tousled hair, an unconscious gesture that both infuriated and fascinated me.

I crossed my arms, mimicking his stance, though it felt more like a defensive shield than a stance of power. "Maybe I wanted to talk, you know, like two people who just saved the world," I shot back, unable to hide the bite in my tone.

"Talk?" he scoffed, the sound reverberating in the empty space around us. "Is that what we're doing? Because it feels more like we're pretending everything is fine while it's anything but."

The truth hung between us, thick and palpable. We had danced around the real issues long enough, letting the echo of our past seep into every conversation, every fleeting moment. I could feel the ghosts of our shared experiences lurking in the shadows, waiting for a chance to drag us back to a time when everything was simpler, before betrayal had slashed through the fabric of our lives.

"Fine," I said, my voice sharpening. "Let's not pretend. Let's just lay it all out on the table, shall we?"

His eyes flared, a mixture of surprise and amusement flickering across his features. "You want to air our dirty laundry in the middle of a decrepit playground?"

"I want to stop dancing around the fact that we're a mess," I replied, exasperation lacing my words. "Every time I look at you, I feel like I'm staring into a fractured mirror, and I can't tell which pieces are mine and which are yours."

"Fractured mirrors, huh?" He took a step closer, and the air between us crackled with tension. "You really think that's how it is? You see me as broken? You think I don't see your cracks, Lila?"

My heart thundered as the weight of his words sank in. "I didn't say that," I protested, though the truth was undeniable. "We've both been shattered by what happened. The Shadow Syndicate—our fight against them—it changed us."

"It didn't just change us; it nearly destroyed us," he snapped, his frustration boiling over. "And now we're supposed to pick up the pieces and pretend we're okay?"

"Pretending is the easy part," I shot back, anger igniting the spark within me. "Facing the truth is what terrifies me."

"Then what is it that you want?" he demanded, his gaze piercing mine. "Do you want me to apologize? To make it all better with some grand gesture?"

I took a deep breath, my voice dropping to a whisper, heavy with vulnerability. "I want to understand us. I want to know what this...whatever this is between us means."

His expression softened, the fierce lines of anger giving way to something more tender, a flicker of understanding that passed between us. "You're right," he admitted, his voice barely above a whisper. "We've both been running from it, and I don't know if we can face it."

"Maybe we don't have to face it alone," I suggested, the idea forming in my mind like a fragile thread of hope. "Maybe we can figure it out together."

He took a step closer, closing the distance, and I could feel the warmth radiating from him, inviting and confusing all at once. "Together," he echoed, the word lingering in the air between us like a promise waiting to be fulfilled.

Just then, a gust of wind swept through the park, sending a shower of dried leaves swirling around us, and for a fleeting moment, it felt like the world outside had faded away. It was just Darian and me, standing on the precipice of something profound, a fragile truce formed in the aftermath of chaos.

But before I could dwell on the moment, a sudden shout pierced the serenity, snapping me back to reality. "Hey! You two!" A voice rang out, drawing our attention away from the fragile intimacy we had just begun to forge.

A group of teenagers approached, laughing and shoving each other playfully as they headed toward the swing set, oblivious to the tempest that had just unfolded. My heart sank as I felt the air between us shift, the delicate thread of connection stretching taut before threatening to snap.

"Guess we're not as alone as we thought," I muttered, forcing a smile that felt more like a grimace.

Darian chuckled, a sound that was equal parts amusement and resignation. "Looks like we'll have to continue this later."

"Yeah, later," I replied, feeling the weight of unspoken words hanging heavily between us.

As the laughter of the teens filled the air, I couldn't shake the feeling that we were standing at a crossroads, with the shadows of our past looming larger than ever. But for the first time, a small flicker of hope ignited in my chest, pushing back against the darkness. Perhaps, in the chaos of our fractured reflections, we could find a way to piece ourselves back together.

The laughter of the teenagers faded into the background, but the atmosphere remained charged, as if the park itself was holding its breath, waiting for something to unfold. Darian and I stood on the precipice of a conversation that felt monumental, yet it hung suspended in the air, tangled in the uncertainty of our emotions. I had never been one to shy away from confrontation, but the weight of what lay beneath our surface tensions was daunting.

I shifted my weight, glancing at the swings, their chains rattling softly in the breeze, each creak echoing a reminder of our childhood innocence. "You know," I began, breaking the silence that had fallen again, "this park used to be a place where kids would come to escape. Now, it feels like a graveyard for memories we can't quite shake."

Darian nodded, his gaze thoughtful. "It's weird, isn't it? We fought for this place, for all those kids who don't even know the darkness that was lurking." His voice dropped, and I could hear the resolve simmering beneath his words. "But we're not the same people anymore. Maybe we never will be."

"No," I said firmly, stepping closer. "We can't change the past, but we can choose what to do with the future. And I refuse to let this define us, Darian. I won't become a ghost of my former self."

His eyes locked onto mine, and for a moment, I felt the gravity of our shared experience pulling us closer, a silent acknowledgment that we both understood the stakes. "Then what do we do?" he asked, his voice almost a whisper. "How do we move on?"

"I don't know," I admitted, a rush of honesty spilling from my lips. "But we have to try. Together. Even if it's messy and complicated. Maybe especially because it is."

A flicker of something crossed his face—hope, maybe? "Okay," he replied, taking a deep breath as if steeling himself. "Together. Let's figure this out, one piece at a time."

Just as I felt a spark of optimism, a sudden shout shattered the fragile bubble we had created. "Watch this!" One of the teenagers called out, launching themselves into the air from the swing. Time slowed as they soared, limbs flailing in a reckless display of youthful bravado, before crashing back down onto the grassy ground with a thud that reverberated through my bones.

"Great idea," I muttered sarcastically, trying to suppress a smile. "Let's take life lessons from the daredevils."

Darian chuckled, the sound warming the space between us, easing the tension that had been coiling so tightly. "If they can risk it all, maybe we can too."

Before I could respond, another teenager joined in, urging his friend to attempt a trick, and the atmosphere shifted once again as laughter filled the air. But my focus remained on Darian, the corner of my heart feeling lighter with each passing moment. The sense of companionship we had once taken for granted was beginning to creep back in, knitting the tattered threads of our bond into something resembling hope.

But then the unthinkable happened. A flash of light caught my eye, and I turned just in time to see a figure lurking at the edge of the park, half-hidden behind the trunk of a gnarled old tree. The light glinted off something metallic, and my heart plummeted.

"Darian," I whispered, my pulse racing as I pointed toward the figure. "Do you see that?"

He followed my gaze, the jovial mood evaporating as quickly as it had arrived. "Yeah, I see it," he said, his voice a low rumble of urgency. "We should—"

Before he could finish, the figure stepped out from behind the tree, and recognition hit me like a punch to the gut. It was Rhea, a former member of the Syndicate, now draped in shadows but unmistakably menacing. The years had not been kind, her once-proud stature now appearing hunched and hollow, but her eyes burned with an unsettling intensity.

"Fancy seeing you both here," she called out, her voice dripping with mockery.

I straightened, adrenaline coursing through my veins as I braced myself. "What do you want, Rhea?" I asked, forcing my voice to remain steady despite the fear curling in my stomach.

"Oh, just a little chat," she said, stepping closer, a sly smile curving her lips. "You didn't think you'd seen the last of me, did you?"

Darian shifted, positioning himself slightly in front of me, a protective stance I both appreciated and resented. "You're in the wrong place, Rhea. Whatever game you think you're playing, it's over. We're not afraid of you anymore."

"Is that so?" she taunted, circling us like a predator sizing up its prey. "You might not be afraid, but you should be. I've come to collect what's rightfully mine."

"Which is?" I shot back, refusing to show the tremor of fear that threatened to betray me.

"Ah, come on, Lila. You know exactly what I'm talking about." Her smile widened, revealing the sharp edges of her past threats. "You're still holding onto a piece of my heart, and I'm here to take it back."

The words hung in the air like poison, twisting my insides. It wasn't just about the battle we'd fought; it was about the pieces of ourselves we had given away, the fragments of our lives that still tethered us to her darkness. "You don't own anything of mine," I spat, anger igniting my resolve.

She laughed, a sound devoid of warmth. "Oh, but you do. Every choice you made, every victory you claimed—none of it was without my influence. You think you're free? Think again."

Darian took a step forward, his jaw clenched. "We're done with your manipulation. We'll fight you again if we have to, but we won't let you drag us back into your mess."

"Brave words," Rhea replied, her tone suddenly icy. "But bravery has its limits. Just remember, the shadows never really disappear. They wait, lurking, ready to pounce when you least expect it."

As her words settled over us, a chill crept into the air, and I felt the familiar weight of dread settle over my shoulders. But as I looked at Darian, I realized that I had a choice. We could let the shadows envelop us once more, or we could stand and fight. Together.

The chill in the air seemed to intensify as Rhea loomed before us, a specter from a past I had fought so hard to escape. The tension between us crackled like static electricity, a prelude to an inevitable storm. I could feel Darian's muscles tense beside me, his protective stance a reminder of the alliance we had forged in the fires of our battles. But Rhea wasn't just an adversary; she was a reminder of the chaos we had barely survived.

"What are you going to do, Lila?" Rhea taunted, a sly smirk playing on her lips. "Scream for help? Call the authorities? Oh, wait, you can't. They won't believe you, not after everything you've done. You're all alone now."

The hurtling reality of her words struck deep, a reminder that our journey had not just altered our world but also the perceptions of those around us. I clenched my fists, willing my heart to steady. "You're wrong," I said, forcing confidence into my voice. "I'm not alone. Darian is with me, and we're stronger than you think."

Darian shot me a sideways glance, and I caught a glimpse of admiration mixed with concern in his eyes. "Together," he reiterated, drawing strength from my defiance.

Rhea's laughter echoed through the park, sharp and cutting. "How quaint. You really think strength lies in numbers? You're just prolonging the inevitable. I'm still here, lurking in the shadows. I've always been a step ahead."

As if to punctuate her words, a rustle came from the nearby bushes, and my heart skipped a beat. I wasn't imagining it; something was moving in the dark. The atmosphere shifted, thickening with tension, and the laughter of the teenagers faded away, replaced by an unsettling silence that sent a chill down my spine.

"Rhea, what else do you want?" I demanded, forcing my voice to remain steady despite the dread pooling in my stomach. "You've lost. Just go away."

Her eyes narrowed, and she stepped closer, the smile fading from her face. "You still don't get it, do you? It's not just about winning or losing anymore. It's about power. The power you took from me and the power I'm reclaiming."

"What are you talking about?" I asked, confusion wrapping around me like a fog. "This isn't about power; it's about moving on, about finding peace after the chaos."

She scoffed, a sharp sound that sliced through the air. "Peace? That's for the weak. I'm here to remind you that chaos is a part of who you are, Lila. It's embedded in your soul. Just like it is in mine."

With a flick of her wrist, she revealed a small device that gleamed ominously in the dim light. My heart raced as I recognized it, a prototype of the technology the Syndicate had once wielded with deadly precision. "What are you planning?" Darian's voice was low, laced with an edge of fear that mirrored my own.

"Oh, this?" Rhea held the device aloft, her expression darkly triumphant. "Let's just say it's a little insurance policy. A way to unleash a taste of the past if you don't play nice. You're going to wish you hadn't turned your back on me."

"What are you saying?" I stepped forward, my heart pounding. "You wouldn't—"

"Wouldn't I?" Rhea's eyes glinted with malice as she activated the device, and the air crackled with an ominous energy. "You have no idea the lengths I'm willing to go to reclaim what's mine. And what's yours—what you've taken from me—will be just the beginning."

The ground beneath us trembled as a low hum filled the air, vibrating with a pulse that matched the fear thrumming in my veins. "Darian, we need to—"

Suddenly, the device erupted with a blinding flash of light, illuminating the park in an unnatural glow. I squinted against the brilliance, shielding my eyes as the world twisted and blurred around me. In that moment, everything shifted—the familiar landscape of the park warped into an alien expanse, the trees melting away like wax figures under the heat of a flame.

"Lila!" Darian shouted, reaching for me, but the ground split between us, a gaping chasm that threatened to swallow me whole.

"Darian!" I cried, stretching my hand toward him, desperation clawing at my throat. The park vanished, replaced by a chaotic whirlwind of colors and sounds that engulfed me, the laughter of the teens replaced by a cacophony of distant screams and echoes of the past.

I felt myself falling, weightless, spiraling through a void that was both terrifying and exhilarating. The light enveloped me, a kaleidoscope of memories and fears swirling around like leaves in a storm. I grasped at shadows that flickered just out of reach, fragments of our battles, moments of laughter, the bond I had shared with Darian, all blending into one disorienting blur.

Then, just as quickly as it had begun, the world snapped back into focus. I found myself standing in a desolate landscape, the remnants of Neo Crescent fading into the background like a forgotten dream. The sky was painted in shades of crimson, dark clouds roiling overhead, and a fierce wind howled around me, carrying whispers of lost hopes and shattered dreams.

I turned, searching for Darian, but he was gone. The chasm that had opened up between us was now an unbridgeable distance, and panic gripped my chest like a vice. "Darian!" I shouted, my voice echoing against the barren wasteland.

No answer. Just the eerie silence that swallowed my words.

Heart racing, I took a step forward, the ground shifting beneath my feet. Shadows darted at the edges of my vision, flickering figures that danced just out of reach, taunting me with their familiarity. "What have you done, Rhea?" I whispered into the void, the weight of despair pressing down on me.

The device, that cursed relic of our past, glimmered in the distance, still pulsing with a threatening energy. With renewed determination, I began to move toward it, knowing that whatever power it held could either be my salvation or my doom.

But as I drew closer, the shadows began to coalesce, forming figures I recognized all too well—faces of those I had lost, of battles fought and friendships shattered. They swirled around me, their eyes filled with accusation, and I felt the heavy burden of their expectations pressing down on my shoulders.

"Lila," a voice echoed, familiar yet distant. "You can't escape this. You brought this upon yourself."

I froze, the words slashing through me like a knife. "No! I refuse to believe that!" I shouted, my voice breaking.

As the shadows closed in, darkness enveloping me, I realized that I was standing at a crossroads between the past and an uncertain future. My heart thundered in my chest as I faced the encroaching shadows, knowing that the true battle was just beginning.

And then, amidst the chaos, a single thought ignited within me: I had to find Darian. No matter what it took, I would reclaim our connection, even if it meant facing the demons that Rhea had unleashed. The stakes had never been higher, and as the darkness loomed closer, I took a deep breath, ready to fight my way back to the light.

Chapter 21: Rebuilding the Ruins

The sun crested the horizon, spilling golden light over the fractured remains of what once was a bustling town square. Dust motes danced in the air, glittering like lost hopes as I stood amidst the remnants of brick and mortar, remnants of laughter and life that felt worlds away. My heart, which had been a fortress of grief and solitude, began to thaw with the warmth of the new day. The atmosphere buzzed with a palpable sense of urgency and purpose, the kind that ignited something deep within me.

Darian stood a few paces ahead, his broad shoulders set against the rising sun, and as he surveyed the scene, I marveled at how his resolve seemed to draw the scattered remnants of our community together like moths to a flame. A slight frown creased his brow, yet the fire in his hazel eyes flickered with determination. He was a leader forged in the crucible of crisis, and with each command he issued, I felt an invisible thread pulling us closer. I knew that even in the wreckage, there was beauty, and it shone through him.

"Hey, we're going to need more hands on deck!" Darian shouted, his voice cutting through the murmur of the crowd, brimming with an energy that made my heart race. He pointed toward a group of residents, their faces etched with weariness yet flickering with the spark of hope that he ignited. "You, with the red shirt! Grab those planks over there. We're rebuilding, not just cleaning up!"

I chuckled softly at his enthusiasm, and it wasn't just the humor in his command but the passion behind it. He embodied a force of nature—each gesture and word weaving a tapestry of connection and camaraderie. It was easy to follow him, to believe in the vision he painted with such vibrant strokes. I wanted to stand beside him, to be a part of this collective endeavor, a vibrant pulse amid the rubble.

As we began sorting through the debris, I stumbled upon remnants of the market that once thrived in this square. Fragments of colorful fabric caught my eye, swaying in the breeze like flags of a long-lost celebration. I picked up a piece, tracing my fingers over the intricate patterns—swirls of reds and blues that whispered stories of laughter and gatherings. It was a reminder of the joy that had been and a promise of what could still be.

"Is that a flag for the next community barbecue?" Darian teased, emerging from behind a pile of bricks with a lopsided grin that made my stomach flutter. "Because I'll definitely bring the burgers."

I rolled my eyes playfully. "You might want to practice your grill skills first. Last time, the smoke alarm was more like a party guest than an appliance."

He laughed, the sound rich and warm, wrapping around me like a favorite blanket. "Hey, it's a talent. Besides, I think the smoke adds character." His eyes sparkled, and the warmth of his gaze sent a delightful shiver down my spine.

With laughter spilling between us, we gathered more community members—an eclectic mix of ages, backgrounds, and stories. Old Mrs. Calhoun, with her fierce spirit and battle-scarred hands, shared her expert knowledge of gardening while the local teenagers chattered excitedly about how they could repurpose the old playground equipment. Each voice added a unique note to our symphony of recovery, and I reveled in the harmony of it all.

As the hours passed, the sun dipped lower in the sky, painting everything in hues of orange and purple. I found myself next to Darian again, our shoulders brushing as we worked side by side. There was a quiet intimacy in those moments, the world fading away until it was just us and the labor of our hands. I wanted to share everything with him—the fears, the dreams, the visions I had of a future beyond this moment.

"Do you think we'll be able to really rebuild?" I asked, my voice barely above a whisper as I tossed another shattered brick aside.

"Not just rebuild," he replied, glancing at me with that intense focus I had come to adore. "We'll restore it, better than before. This place deserves a second chance, and so do we."

His words resonated deep within me, filling the empty spaces that had lingered since the storm tore through our lives. I could see it—the vibrant market, the children playing without a care in the world, laughter spilling from every corner. I wanted that, and I wanted it with him.

"I believe in you, Darian," I confessed, my heart racing at the admission. "You make people want to follow you, to believe in something again."

He turned to face me, the dusk light casting shadows that made his features sharper, more defined. "And I believe in all of us. In every single person here." His eyes held mine, an intensity that made my breath catch. "But we can't do it alone. We need each other."

The depth of his sincerity caught me off guard, a twist of vulnerability that cracked my heart wide open. I could feel the shift between us, a connection forged in this moment of hope and despair. Just as I was about to say more, a shout erupted from the crowd, drawing our attention.

"Look out!" someone cried, their voice laced with panic.

The ground trembled beneath us, and instinctively, I reached for Darian, our hands clasping tightly. In that heartbeat, everything shifted—fear, uncertainty, and the promise of a new beginning, all tangled together in a web of chaos. The world we had begun to rebuild suddenly felt precarious, and I braced myself for whatever storm was yet to come.

A sudden hush fell over the crowd, the air thick with anticipation and an undercurrent of dread. The tremor beneath our feet faded, but the shockwaves of uncertainty rippled through the gathered community. I turned to Darian, whose expression shifted from concern to unwavering determination. "Stay close," he urged, gripping my hand tighter, the warmth of his palm reassuring against the coolness of the evening.

"What was that?" I asked, my voice barely breaking the weight of the silence. The echoes of our laughter from earlier felt distant, like a memory playing at the edges of my mind.

Darian squinted into the distance where a cloud of dust began to rise, shrouding the area behind the market stalls. The worried faces around us mirrored the apprehension clawing at my insides. "Could be just settling debris or...something worse," he replied, the lines of his jaw tightening as he scanned the crowd. "Let's not jump to conclusions, but we should check it out."

We moved as a unit, our hands still intertwined, drawing strength from one another as we navigated through the haphazard remnants of the marketplace. Each step felt charged with purpose, but the gnawing anxiety twisted within me. The town had suffered so much; what if this was another disaster waiting to unfold?

"Should I be worried?" I asked, attempting to keep my tone light, though I couldn't fully mask the tremor in my voice.

"Only if you plan on taking up residence in the rubble," he quipped, attempting to inject levity into our tense atmosphere. "I hear the rent is awful." His grin was a flicker of sunshine, just enough to ease the worry that tightened my chest.

As we approached the source of the dust cloud, the scene unfolded with unexpected clarity. The ground had shifted again, revealing a hidden chamber below—a cellar perhaps, or a forgotten storage space. A few brave souls had ventured closer, peering into the gaping maw of darkness that had emerged.

"Do you think we should go down there?" I asked, glancing at Darian. His resolve seemed unshakable, but I could see the wheels turning in his mind.

"Absolutely," he replied with unyielding confidence. "We can't rebuild without understanding what's underneath all this mess." He gave my hand a reassuring squeeze before we stepped closer to the edge.

As we peered into the void, a figure emerged from the shadows, stumbling slightly as if caught off guard by the light. It was a young girl, no older than twelve, her wild hair a halo of curls around her pale face, eyes wide with a mixture of fear and defiance.

"I found it first!" she declared, hands on her hips, chin tilted defiantly upward, as if daring anyone to challenge her claim.

"Nice work," Darian responded, his tone playful. "But you might want to consider a less dramatic entrance next time. It's not a scene from a horror movie."

She rolled her eyes, a clear indication of her disdain for our banter. "This is serious! There's stuff down there—old things, things that might help us."

"Like treasure?" I asked, unable to hide the excitement that bubbled within me.

"More like history," she shot back. "What do you think we are, pirates?"

Darian knelt beside her, a smile dancing on his lips. "Maybe adventurers, though pirates do have a certain charm. What do you say we explore together?"

With a nod of her head, she stepped aside, allowing us access to the darkened space below. I felt a thrill of adventure pulsing through me. This was more than just debris; this was a chance to uncover lost memories and potential treasures that could help us rebuild not just the physical structure but the soul of our community.

As we descended, the air thickened with the scent of damp earth and something else—an aroma of antiquity that spoke of stories waiting to be told. A few flickering lights illuminated the space, revealing crates and boxes layered in dust, each one a small world unto itself. Darian moved with purpose, rummaging through the first crate he encountered while I leaned against the wall, catching my breath from the sudden rush of excitement.

"What's this?" he called out, pulling out a dusty lantern that looked like it had weathered decades of neglect. "I bet we can clean this up and use it."

The girl's eyes widened as she moved closer, clearly entranced by the discovery. "That's old! It belonged to my great-grandpa. He used to tell me stories about how he lit up the whole street with it."

Darian smiled, a genuine warmth radiating from him. "Then it's perfect. We'll make sure it shines again. Every little piece of our past can be part of our future."

We worked together, uncovering relics of a time gone by—old photographs, faded letters, and forgotten trinkets that told tales of love and loss, laughter and struggle. Each item was a thread in the rich tapestry of our town's history, and as I handed them to Darian, I felt the layers of our connection deepen.

"This is what it means to rebuild," I said, the words tumbling out of me like confetti, each syllable laced with newfound understanding. "Not just bricks and mortar, but remembering who we are, where we've been."

"Exactly," he said, his voice low and earnest, a stark contrast to the chaotic energy of our surroundings. "We carry our history with us, and it shapes our future. We just need to remember how to tell those stories."

The girl grinned, excitement illuminating her features as she clutched a small, tarnished compass she had discovered in a box. "Look! We can use this to find our way!"

"Or to get lost," I added with a wink, the lightheartedness of the moment enveloping us.

"Oh, we definitely don't want that," Darian replied, his eyes dancing with mischief. "I'd prefer we stick to the path, but if we happen to stumble upon a hidden treasure, I won't complain."

"Are you saying I'm treasure?" I shot back, my heart racing with the playful banter that had become our hallmark.

"Only the kind that doesn't require a map," he replied smoothly, his gaze locking with mine, an unspoken promise hanging in the air between us.

But the laughter was cut short by a loud crash above, sending a shiver down my spine. The earth trembled once more, shaking the very foundation of our small haven. I clutched the wall for balance, and I could see the girl's eyes widen in fear.

"Time to get out of here!" Darian shouted, urgency lacing his words. "We can't let this collapse on us!"

With a firm grip on the compass and my hand in his, we scrambled back toward the entrance, the thrill of adventure now underscored by a sense of impending peril. The echoes of our footsteps chased us, a frantic rhythm that matched the beat of my racing heart as I glimpsed the reality of our situation—each moment layered with the promise of what could be and the danger lurking just outside.

The chaos surged as we scrambled back through the shadowy entrance, the tremors beneath our feet intensifying. Dust cascaded from the ceiling, swirling in a gritty haze that stung my eyes and left a metallic taste in my mouth. Panic flared, urging us to move faster. Darian's hand tightened around mine, pulling me close as we navigated the remnants of forgotten memories, our breaths quickening with each step.

"Almost there!" he urged, his voice steady despite the chaos. The girl, her compass clutched tightly, followed close behind, determination etched on her young face. I admired her bravery amidst the fear swirling around us.

"Why do these things always happen when we're in the middle of something exciting?" I shot back, struggling to keep the wry humor alive even as the ground continued to quiver beneath us.

"Because life loves a good plot twist!" Darian replied, a hint of laughter in his voice, but the urgency in his eyes betrayed the seriousness of our situation. "Just keep moving!"

As we burst into the light, I stumbled, narrowly avoiding a pile of debris that had tumbled from a nearby structure. We emerged from the shadows, gasping for air as we stepped into the fading daylight. The square was now a scene of organized chaos, with people scrambling to help others and salvage what they could. The sense of camaraderie was almost tangible, lifting my spirits despite the uncertainty surrounding us.

"Are you all right?" Darian asked, concern etching lines across his forehead as he examined me for injuries.

"I'm fine, just a little startled," I reassured him, though my heart raced from more than just the collapse. The adrenaline was a heady mix of excitement and fear, and I felt alive in a way I hadn't in a long time. "Besides, you're here to save me, right? Superhero style?"

His laughter rang out, a bright note cutting through the tension. "Always. Just call me your personal superhero."

Before I could retort, the girl piped up, eyes wide with awe as she gazed at the growing crowd. "Look at everyone! They're helping! It's like a real adventure!"

Her enthusiasm was infectious, and I couldn't help but smile as I watched the residents rally together. Adults who had once felt defeated now laughed and shouted encouragement to one another, the spirit of community shining through the wreckage. It was remarkable to witness, and I found a swell of hope rising within me.

Darian turned to me, his eyes glinting with that familiar spark. "See? We're stronger together. And this—" he gestured toward the bustling square, "—this is just the beginning."

"I like the sound of that," I said, matching his fervor. The thought of rebuilding, not just the town but our lives, sent a thrill through me.

"Let's keep this momentum going," he suggested, scanning the crowd. "We need to gather people to assess the damage, organize teams for recovery. We can't let this moment slip away."

"Right behind you," I replied, my heart swelling with admiration for him. I followed Darian as he moved through the crowd, rallying our neighbors with a charisma that was almost magnetic.

As the afternoon wore on, we split into teams, digging into the rubble, salvaging what could be saved. Laughter mingled with the sounds of clanging metal and wood as we worked side by side, my hands getting dirty but my spirit soaring. I caught snippets of conversations—plans for new designs for the marketplace, dreams of what could rise from the ashes—and each story added another layer to our shared history.

Darian and I fell into a rhythm, our conversations flowing seamlessly as we tossed debris and unearthed hidden treasures. With every shared joke and moment of vulnerability, the walls around my heart began to crumble.

"Remember the old carousel?" I asked as we uncovered an ornate piece of wood, its faded paint still visible beneath the grime.

"How could I forget?" he chuckled. "You rode that thing like it was your personal chariot. I thought you were going to take a nose dive into the hay bales when you jumped off."

"I did not!" I laughed, though the memory flashed vividly in my mind—a younger version of myself, fearless and wild, her laughter echoing in the sunlit air.

"Sure you didn't. I have photographic evidence." His grin was teasing, but I could see the affection in his gaze. "You've always had a bit of a flair for the dramatic."

"And you've always been a terrible liar," I shot back playfully. "Those photos were lost in the great attic disaster of 2015."

"Ah, yes. I still have nightmares about that day," he replied, and for a moment, the world around us faded, leaving just the two of us in this bubble of laughter and shared memories.

The moment was shattered by another tremor, this one stronger than before. I grabbed onto a nearby beam, my heart racing. Darian's expression hardened as he quickly scanned the surroundings, alert and protective.

"What's happening?" the girl asked, fear creeping into her voice as she clutched her compass, her earlier bravado replaced by worry.

"I don't know, but we need to get everyone out of the square," Darian replied, his tone grave. "We can't risk another collapse."

The ground shook again, this time accompanied by a deep rumble that reverberated through my chest. My stomach twisted in fear as I glanced around, seeing the worried expressions on our neighbors' faces.

"Darian!" I shouted over the rising noise. "What do we do?"

He grasped my shoulders, his gaze locking onto mine with an intensity that sent a shiver down my spine. "We organize. We lead them out. Everyone needs to stay calm."

With a deep breath, I nodded, the urgency of his words igniting my own sense of responsibility. "Let's do this!"

We moved through the crowd, rallying people to form a line, guiding them toward the safer edges of the square. But as we turned back to gather more, the ground split open near the old fountain, a deep crack snaking its way through the earth like a gaping wound.

"Everyone back!" Darian shouted, his voice a sharp command that cut through the panic. I felt my heart drop, an icy grip of dread settling in my stomach as the fissure widened, revealing a dark chasm that seemed to pulse with a life of its own.

"Darian!" I screamed, but the roar of the earth drowned out my voice as the world shifted beneath us. The tremors intensified, and before I could grasp what was happening, the ground gave way, and a terrifying rush of darkness swallowed everything in sight.

In that instant, the last vestiges of laughter and hope were eclipsed by sheer terror. I reached for Darian, our fingers grazing just as he began to slip away, his face a mask of determination and fear. "Hold on!" he shouted, his voice echoing through the chaos, a lifeline in the swirling uncertainty.

But the ground was unyielding, and as I struggled to grasp onto something, anything, the world tilted, spinning into an abyss that threatened to pull us all under.

Chapter 22: Veils of the Past

The wind danced through the town of Eldridge, carrying with it the sweet scent of blooming magnolias and the faintest hint of rain. I stood on the porch of my small cottage, a weathered wooden structure that had seen better days but remained steadfast in its charm. Each plank creaked beneath my feet, whispering stories of the laughter and tears that had woven the fabric of my life. My gaze drifted toward the sprawling landscape that framed the horizon, where the sun dipped low, casting a golden glow over the fields. It was a picturesque scene, but within me stirred a tempest of uncertainty.

Eldridge was in the throes of transformation. After the devastating storm that had ravaged the community, I had taken it upon myself to spearhead the rebuilding efforts. Each day was a new chapter, filled with laughter from volunteers who had come to lend a hand and the invigorating camaraderie of neighbors rediscovering their resilience. Yet beneath the surface of this communal revival, the remnants of my past lay hidden, waiting for the right moment to resurface.

As I brushed a stray lock of hair behind my ear, my thoughts were interrupted by the sound of gravel crunching beneath tires. I turned to see a familiar vehicle making its way up the driveway, my heart sinking. The weathered red pickup belonged to Sam, an old acquaintance from my tumultuous youth. We had shared more than a few reckless moments back in the day, moments that now felt more like echoes of a life I had fought hard to leave behind.

As he stepped out, his tall frame silhouetted against the setting sun, memories washed over me like a wave. Sam had once been my confidant, the kind of friend who understood the depths of my wild heart, yet he was also a reminder of everything I had worked to escape. His boyish grin faded as he approached, replaced by a cautious concern that made my stomach churn.

"Long time no see," he said, his voice a mix of nostalgia and uncertainty. "I heard about the storm. I just wanted to check in on you."

"Thanks," I replied, forcing a smile that didn't quite reach my eyes. "I'm doing okay, really. Just busy with the rebuilding."

"I can see that. It looks… different," he said, gesturing vaguely at the cottage. "You've made it your own."

My heart raced as I wondered how much he truly knew about my transformation, how much he could sense beneath the surface. "It's a work in progress, just like the town," I said, trying to keep my tone light, but the weight of his presence was palpable.

We stood there in the waning light, the air thick with unspoken words and heavy with the weight of our shared history. I had buried that past deep within, but with Sam in front of me, those memories clawed their way back to the surface, uninvited and unwelcome. I could feel the walls I had painstakingly built begin to tremble, cracks forming in the façade of my newfound strength.

"I've missed this place," he said, his voice softening. "Remember those summer nights at the lake? Just you and me, and the stars? You used to dream about leaving Eldridge behind."

Those words struck me like a lightning bolt. Yes, I had dreamed of escape, of a life beyond the confines of this town. But I had also learned that sometimes, the things we run from have a way of following us. "People change," I said, my voice steady even as my heart raced. "Eldridge is… home now."

"Home," he echoed, a hint of sadness in his tone. "Is that what you call it? I always thought you wanted more than this."

In that moment, I felt the shadows of my insecurities wrap around me like a shroud. Did I truly belong here, or was I just a ghost haunting my own life? The past loomed large, a specter of doubt that threatened to pull me back into the whirlwind of who I used to be.

"I have more," I insisted, perhaps too forcefully. "I've built a life here. I'm helping people."

"But at what cost?" he pressed, his blue eyes piercing through the layers I had so carefully constructed. "You push everyone away, don't you? Even Darian."

The mention of Darian sent a jolt through me, a reminder of the tender connection we had forged amidst the chaos. I had allowed myself to believe that perhaps this time would be different, that I could embrace love without the weight of my past suffocating me. Yet now, the thought of opening up, of allowing someone to see the flaws beneath the polished exterior, felt insurmountable.

"Darian is... different," I said, the words catching in my throat. "He's been there for me in ways I didn't know I needed."

"Then why push him away?" Sam asked, stepping closer, his voice low and filled with concern. "You can't keep running from your past. You have to confront it. Let him in."

The challenge in his words hung in the air, heavy and charged. Did I have the strength to face those demons? Could I risk losing Darian by revealing the jagged edges of my history? I felt the panic rising within me, a tide threatening to drown the fragile hope I had begun to nurture.

As the sky darkened, casting long shadows across the porch, I suddenly felt small and exposed, as if the world could see the fractures in my heart. "It's not that simple," I said, the vulnerability spilling over. "What if he sees me for who I really am and decides I'm not worth it?"

"You're worth it," Sam replied firmly, and there was a softness in his eyes that reminded me of the friend I once knew. "You have to believe that."

In that moment, I felt a surge of anger and frustration. "You don't get to decide that for me," I snapped, my voice rising. "You don't know what I've been through."

The tension hung in the air, crackling like static before a storm, as we faced each other in a silence that felt heavy with unspoken truths. Sam was right; I had built walls, but they were beginning to crack, and I was terrified of what would happen if I allowed them to come crashing down.

A gust of wind swept through the porch, teasing the loose strands of my hair as Sam's words lingered in the air, sharp as broken glass. The sun was finally dipping below the horizon, painting the sky in strokes of orange and lavender, a masterpiece that felt too beautiful to belong to someone in turmoil. I blinked hard, trying to shake off the haze of vulnerability that threatened to engulf me.

"Look," I said, forcing a laugh to lighten the weight of our conversation. "You may have been my partner in crime back in the day, but I'm not that girl anymore. I don't even think I know how to be reckless these days. I have too much at stake." I gestured toward the community board that I had filled with flyers for upcoming rebuilding events. "These people need me. I can't just toss it all away."

"Recklessness isn't the answer," he replied, his voice a calm counterpoint to my rising tide of emotion. "But running away isn't either. You're stronger than this, and you know it." His gaze held mine, steady and unwavering, and I felt the tremor of my resolve begin to crack.

"Strength is overrated," I muttered, crossing my arms against the chill of the evening air. "Sometimes, it's just a mask for fear."

"Maybe," he conceded, taking a step closer. "But fear doesn't have to dictate your life. You're hiding behind that fear, pushing away people who care about you. You can't keep Darian at arm's length forever. That'll only end in heartbreak."

The thought struck me like a blow, a visceral reminder that love, like all things precious, was delicate. In the brief moments we had shared, Darian had become a refuge, a soft place to land amidst the jagged edges of my past. I could still feel the warmth of his hands when he'd brushed against mine, the way he looked at me with an intensity that made my heart race. But what if my history was too heavy a burden for him to bear?

"I can't let him in," I confessed, my voice barely above a whisper. "What if he sees everything I've done? What if he sees me for who I really am and walks away?"

"Then he's not the right guy," Sam said, bluntness laced with an unexpected tenderness. "But you'll never know if you keep hiding. You have to decide if you're ready to be vulnerable."

I shook my head, retreating into myself, battling the inner storm that raged within. I was done being vulnerable; it had cost me dearly in the past. "You don't understand. It's not just about me. It's about everyone I care about. If I fail, I drag them down with me."

The tension between us thickened, a charged silence settling like a fog. Sam's expression softened, a mixture of concern and frustration. "And what about your happiness? Does that not matter?"

"Sometimes, I think it's a luxury I can't afford." The words tumbled out before I could stop them, raw and unfiltered. "I have too much to lose. Too many people depend on me."

"Then stop carrying the weight of the world on your shoulders," he urged, stepping even closer. "Let someone help you. You're not alone, no matter how much it feels like it."

With a heavy sigh, I turned my gaze to the fading sunlight, as if it could somehow absorb my troubles. "You don't know the half of it. I've built these walls for a reason. They keep me safe."

"Safe from what? A little hurt? A little rejection?" Sam challenged, his voice rising with passion. "You're hiding from life, and it's a shame. You're vibrant, and you deserve to live fully."

"Easy for you to say," I shot back, the bitterness spilling over. "You haven't had to bury your past. You haven't had to look in the mirror and see a ghost."

The words hung between us, heavy and charged. Sam stepped back, visibly taken aback. For a brief moment, the world fell silent, the sounds of chirping crickets and rustling leaves fading into the background. I had struck a nerve, but the anger that coursed through me felt too potent to suppress.

"I'm not a ghost," he said finally, his voice low, filled with something deeper than irritation. "You're not a ghost, either. You're here, right now, fighting for something good. Don't let fear turn you into a memory."

My heart raced, caught in the crossfire of emotions I couldn't quite comprehend. Was I a memory? Was I defined by my past? I had fought so hard to become more than what I was, to shed the layers of my history like an old skin, but what if those layers were still woven into the very fabric of my being?

Just then, the distant sound of laughter drifted from the town square, drawing my attention. A few neighbors were setting up for the upcoming festival, their voices bright and cheerful. The juxtaposition of their joy against the storm brewing within me felt like a cruel reminder of what I longed for but feared I could never reach.

"I need to get back," I said abruptly, breaking the spell that hung between us. "I have things to organize for the festival."

"Don't run away from this," Sam called after me as I turned to walk back inside, the door creaking on its hinges. "You have to face it, or you'll never find peace."

Inside, the warmth of the cottage enveloped me like a comforting blanket, but the walls felt like they were closing in, echoes of our conversation resonating in my mind. I leaned against the kitchen counter, the coolness of the wood grounding me as I tried to catch my breath. My heart was racing, and I could feel the remnants of Sam's words thrumming in my chest, challenging everything I had built to protect myself.

The moment was interrupted by the sound of my phone buzzing on the table. I glanced down to see Darian's name flashing across the screen. My pulse quickened, a mix of anticipation and dread swirling within me. I had managed to push him away just when I needed him most, fearing that the weight of my history would crush the delicate bond we had begun to forge. But perhaps it was time to confront my fears, to face the truth I had been running from.

Taking a deep breath, I answered the call, hoping that this time, I wouldn't let fear guide my choices.

The phone vibrated against the wooden table, each buzz a reminder of the decision looming before me. I had spent too long holding my breath, teetering on the edge of vulnerability, and it was time to take a leap, no matter how daunting that leap might feel. I answered with a steadiness I hoped concealed the tremor of my heart.

"Hey, you," Darian's voice crackled through the speaker, warm and familiar, wrapping around me like a well-worn blanket. "I was just thinking about you. Are you busy?"

"Not really," I replied, unable to suppress a smile at the sound of his voice. "Just... enjoying a quiet evening. How about you?"

"I was hoping you might join me at the café later. The one with the string lights and the best coffee in town. They've got a new pastry that I think you'll love," he said, his enthusiasm infectious.

"Sounds tempting," I admitted, glancing out the window to the fading daylight. The idea of being surrounded by laughter and the scent of fresh coffee was alluring, but the shadows of our earlier conversation loomed large in my mind.

"Great! I'll pick you up in an hour," he said, the excitement in his voice unwavering. "Dress casual, but you know, a little flair wouldn't hurt. I want you to make a statement."

"Flair?" I laughed, the sound lightening my heart. "What do you think I am, a walking fashion show?"

"Hey, you have your own unique style," he teased back, the banter igniting a spark of something brighter within me. "Just be you. That's the most beautiful thing you can wear."

As I hung up the phone, a rush of warmth spread through me, battling the uncertainty still lingering at the edges of my thoughts. Darian had a way of making the mundane feel special, of illuminating the corners of my world that I had let dim. But I couldn't ignore the knot of anxiety tightening in my chest. The reality of my past felt like a storm cloud hovering just above the horizon, waiting to burst.

I darted through the small cottage, grabbing a few essentials: a light jacket, my favorite pair of earrings—subtle but playful—and a spritz of perfume that reminded me of summer evenings. The mirror reflected a version of me that felt just slightly out of reach. My hair was tousled, a few curls escaping the confines of my usual neatness, and my eyes sparkled with a nervous energy that made me feel alive, yet raw.

With each passing minute, the anticipation grew, mingling with the familiar trepidation that had accompanied me for so long. I wanted to share my heart with Darian, to unveil the layers I had hidden beneath the surface, but the fear of rejection loomed large, casting a shadow over my excitement.

The clock ticked away, and soon enough, the sound of tires crunching over gravel drew me to the window. Darian's car appeared, headlights piercing the twilight like a beacon, and I took a moment to steady my breath before stepping outside. As I crossed the threshold, the cool evening air wrapped around me, invigorating yet laced with the weight of uncertainty.

"Hey there, beautiful," he said, his smile igniting a warmth deep within me as I climbed into the passenger seat.

"Flair, remember?" I quipped, gesturing to my casual ensemble as I fastened my seatbelt. "I'm trying my best here."

"You look perfect," he said, a sincerity in his voice that made me blush. "Let's go."

As we drove through the quiet streets, the conversation flowed effortlessly between us, laughter punctuating our shared stories and the comfortable silences. With every passing block, I felt the tension easing, allowing the prospect of an evening filled with possibilities to envelop me. I wanted to revel in this moment, to forget the storm clouds gathering in my mind, even if just for a while.

The café was alive with energy, a buzz of laughter and clinking mugs that created a cozy ambiance. Strings of lights twinkled overhead, casting a soft glow that made everything feel a little more magical. We found a table on the patio, the air fragrant with the aroma of fresh coffee and baked goods. I couldn't help but feel like I had stepped into a scene from a romantic movie, where everything felt effortlessly perfect.

"I ordered you the seasonal special," Darian said as we settled in, the playful glint in his eyes unmistakable. "Trust me, you're going to love it."

"Why do I feel like you're trying to win me over with pastries?" I laughed, genuinely curious about his motives. "Is this your master plan?"

"Hey, a well-fed woman is a happy woman," he replied, his smile widening. "Plus, I enjoy your company. And I'd do anything to keep it around."

Our conversation drifted seamlessly from light-hearted banter to deeper discussions about our hopes for the future, the dreams we held just beyond our reach. Each moment felt rich and layered, a tapestry woven from shared experiences and unspoken connections. Yet, beneath the surface, my internal struggle simmered, a constant reminder of the walls I had built to protect myself.

As we finished our pastries—deliciously decadent and utterly irresistible—I knew I couldn't keep deflecting the truth. Darian deserved more than the surface I had been presenting. It was time to reveal the parts of myself I had kept hidden, the pieces that felt too jagged to share.

"I need to tell you something," I began, my heart racing at the vulnerability of the moment. "It's about my past—"

Before I could finish, a familiar voice interrupted, slicing through the warmth of the café like a sudden gust of icy wind. "Well, well, if it isn't the prodigal daughter returning to claim her throne."

I turned slowly, dread pooling in my stomach as my gaze landed on the last person I had expected to see. There, standing at the entrance, was Clara, my estranged sister. Her presence felt like a thunderclap, reverberating through the cozy atmosphere, and suddenly, the world around us faded into the background.

"What are you doing here?" I managed to choke out, the question carrying the weight of years of silence and unresolved tension.

Clara's lips curled into a smirk, and her eyes sparkled with a mix of mischief and challenge. "Oh, you know, just checking in on the family. Heard you were making quite the name for yourself in this quaint little town. Thought I'd see it for myself."

Darian's gaze darted between us, confusion etched on his face, and I felt a rush of panic. The delicate connection we had just built threatened to shatter under the weight of this unexpected reunion.

Clara had always been the storm in my life, a reminder of everything I had tried to escape.

"Why now?" I asked, my voice steadier than I felt. "Why show up when things are finally starting to go well for me?"

"I figured you could use a little reality check," she replied, a sly grin plastered across her face. "Or maybe I just missed my favorite sister."

The words dripped with sarcasm, and I could feel the ground shifting beneath me. This was not how the night was supposed to go. I had taken a step forward, only to find myself pulled back into the very shadows I had fought so hard to leave behind. As Darian shifted in his seat, uncertainty written all over his face, I knew that the carefully constructed walls around my heart were about to be tested in ways I could never have anticipated.

Chapter 23: The Weight of Choices

The streets of Neo Crescent pulsed with life, the glow of neon lights flickering like sirens in the dark, beckoning me deeper into their electric embrace. Each corner turned was a brushstroke on the canvas of my life, one splashed with the vibrant hues of memory and regret. I felt the weight of my choices hanging around me like a shroud, a constant reminder that I could never fully escape my past. The air was thick with the mingling scents of sizzling street food and the bitter tang of rain-soaked asphalt. I could almost taste the fear lurking beneath the surface, a reminder that the Shadow Syndicate still cast a long shadow over the city—and over me.

I pulled my coat tighter around my shoulders, feeling the chill of the evening seeping into my bones. The remnants of the Syndicate lingered like ghosts, their whispers threading through the alleys and backstreets. I thought I had left that life behind, that I had managed to carve out a semblance of normalcy amidst the chaos. But normalcy was a fickle friend, and tonight, it felt like a distant memory.

Turning onto Zennith Street, I spotted a familiar dive, the kind of place where secrets were traded like currency and laughter echoed over the clinking of glasses. The neon sign flickered above the entrance, a beacon of comfort that momentarily eased the knots in my stomach. Maybe I could lose myself in the familiarity of the bar, find solace in the bottom of a glass. I hesitated, my hand hovering above the door handle, when suddenly the hairs on the back of my neck prickled with warning.

The shadows deepened, and I caught sight of them—three figures leaning against a graffiti-covered wall, their postures lazy yet predatory. Their smirks were sharp, like blades glinting in the neon glow. I cursed under my breath, the bitter taste of fear rising in my throat. It was them: remnants of the Syndicate I thought I had left behind. I should have known that no choice goes without consequence, especially when you're entangled with ghosts.

I turned to slip away, to find another path, when the leader—a man with a scar slicing across his cheek—spoke up, his voice a low growl. "Where do you think you're going, darling?"

I faced them, adrenaline surging through me like wildfire. "I don't want any trouble," I replied, forcing my voice to remain steady, although my heart raced as if trying to escape my chest.

"Too bad. Trouble's coming for you," he sneered, taking a step closer, his lackeys flanking him like vultures. "Thought you could just walk away? You owe us."

In that moment, as their mocking laughter echoed off the walls, my past unfurled before me, a sinister tapestry woven with the threads of betrayal and fear. I could feel my chest tightening, the ghosts of old choices clawing at my resolve. Just when I thought I might suffocate under the weight of their demands, a surge of movement broke through the tension—a figure emerged from the shadows, cutting through the darkness like a ray of light.

Darian. My heart raced at the sight of him, a fierce protector stepping into the chaos. The way he moved was fluid, calculated; he always seemed to anticipate danger before it arrived, as if he had the instincts of a predator. "Back off," he commanded, his voice steady, his gaze piercing like a sharpened knife.

The leader's smirk faltered, uncertainty flickering in his eyes. "You think you can intimidate us?"

Darian chuckled, a low, rumbling sound that sent a shiver down my spine. "I don't have to intimidate you. I just have to prove I'm more dangerous than you."

With that, chaos erupted. The remnants lunged, and I felt a mix of fear and exhilaration wash over me. I had always known Darian could handle himself, but witnessing it in action was something else entirely. The world around us blurred into a flurry of movement—Darian dodged the leader's swing, countering with a punch that sent the man sprawling back against the wall. My instincts kicked in, and I scrambled to keep my feet, adrenaline sharpening my focus.

"Grab something!" Darian shouted, dodging a blow from one of the henchmen. I quickly scanned the ground, my heart pounding in my ears. I spotted a metal pipe half-buried in the debris and lunged for it, wielding it like a makeshift weapon.

"Let's show them we're not just shadows in the night," I called, my voice laced with determination.

Darian shot me an approving glance, the tension in his shoulders easing for just a moment. Together, we faced the remnants, weaving through their attacks, every motion blending into an unspoken rhythm. It was exhilarating, our pasts colliding with our present, and the chaos of the moment rekindled a spark between us that I had thought long extinguished.

In the heart of the fray, I caught glimpses of his unwavering strength, the way he protected me even as we fought side by side. The connection we shared flared brighter than the neon lights surrounding us. Each time I struck back, each blow I parried, I could feel the weight of my choices shifting, the past intertwining with the present. I couldn't run from who I was, but maybe, just maybe, I could find strength in it.

As the last of the remnants fell back, panting and defeated, I felt the adrenaline begin to fade, replaced by a rush of clarity. Standing there, amidst the chaos, I knew that this was not just a fight for survival. It was a reminder that my past, while haunting, was also a part of my identity, a mosaic of choices that shaped me into who I was now. And with Darian by my side, perhaps I could finally embrace that truth, learning to wield my past like a weapon rather than a weight.

The remnants of the Shadow Syndicate melted away into the shadows, leaving a charged silence hanging in the air like the remnants of a storm. I turned to Darian, breathless, my heart still racing from the adrenaline coursing through me. The neon lights flickered overhead, casting his chiseled features in an ethereal glow, a combination of triumph and something deeper lurking in his emerald eyes. "You have a knack for timing, don't you?" I quipped, wiping a bead of sweat from my brow, trying to mask the whirlwind of emotions swirling within.

Darian's lips curled into a smirk, the kind that always sent butterflies flitting around in my stomach. "I've been told I have a flair for the dramatic," he replied, his voice smooth and confident. "But I have to say, this is a bit more than I bargained for tonight."

I let out a breathy laugh, the tension slowly dissipating as we both leaned against the damp, graffiti-laden wall, our bodies still humming from the confrontation. "Next time, maybe we can avoid the whole 'fighting for our lives' thing and just grab a drink like normal people?"

"Normal people?" He raised an eyebrow, the teasing glint in his eye unmistakable. "In Neo Crescent? Good luck with that."

His humor felt like a balm, soothing the jagged edges of my anxiety. The streets around us felt alive, pulsing with the aftermath of our battle, yet I knew that our reprieve was only temporary. "You're right. Normalcy is a myth here," I replied, forcing my mind to focus. "But they won't stop. They'll keep coming after me."

Darian's expression shifted, the lightheartedness evaporating like mist in the morning sun. "Then we need to figure out how to keep you safe. I won't let them get to you again."

The sincerity in his voice sent a shiver down my spine. I could see it, the fierce determination that shone through his confidence. "I appreciate that, but you can't be my bodyguard every time I step outside."

"Why not?" he challenged, a half-smile playing on his lips. "I find it quite exhilarating."

I shook my head, unable to suppress my own grin. "You're insane."

"Just dedicated," he corrected, his gaze steady and unwavering. "You're worth it."

Before I could respond, a sharp noise shattered the moment—glass shattering somewhere nearby, followed by the clamor of voices rising in alarm. Instinct kicked in; I straightened, the tension returning in an instant. "What now?"

Darian shifted, every muscle in his body taut and ready for action. "We should check it out. Might be the remnants again—or something worse."

I hesitated, glancing down the street where the sounds originated. A knot formed in my stomach, that ever-familiar sense of dread creeping back in. "I don't know if we should—"

"Trust me," he said, his tone firm but low, a calming presence amidst the chaos. "If it's the Syndicate, we can't leave without knowing what they're up to."

With a reluctant nod, I followed him, our footsteps echoing against the pavement as we approached the source of the disturbance. The narrow alleyway was shrouded in shadows, but the flickering streetlights revealed a broken storefront, the shattered glass sparkling like fallen stars on the ground.

In the distance, a group of figures loomed, their voices raised in urgent discussion. "They're planning something," I whispered, my heart pounding in my chest. "We need to get closer."

Darian nodded, his eyes narrowing in concentration. We moved like shadows, inching along the edges of the alley, listening intently.

"—tonight's the night," one of the men said, his voice gravelly. "We take back what's ours. No more games."

My stomach dropped. "They're planning an attack. We have to warn someone."

"Not yet," Darian replied, his voice low and steady. "We need to gather more information first."

I swallowed hard, the weight of the moment pressing down on me. I knew the stakes were high, but something told me this was bigger than just a simple raid. "What if we don't have enough time?"

"Then we improvise," he said, his tone calm. "We've done it before."

In that instant, I felt a strange mixture of fear and exhilaration. We were standing at the precipice of something monumental, our destinies entwined in a way that left me both terrified and exhilarated. I had always feared what the shadows could bring, but here I was, prepared to confront them.

Just as we edged closer, the figures turned, revealing their faces illuminated by the dim glow of a nearby lamp. I recognized one of them—Brock, a notorious enforcer of the Syndicate, known for his ruthlessness. "This is it," he snarled, looking fiercely determined. "Tonight, we take back Neo Crescent."

Darian stiffened beside me, and I could see the tension radiating off him in waves. "We can't let them get away with this," he murmured. "Not when they're so close."

"Then what's the plan?" I whispered, my mind racing. "We can't just confront them out in the open."

A thought struck me, bold and reckless. "What if we create a diversion?"

Darian turned to me, surprise flickering in his eyes before he nodded slowly. "That could work. But we need to be quick and smart about it."

I glanced around, my gaze landing on a stack of old crates nearby. "If we can knock those over, it'll make enough noise to draw their attention. Then we can slip around and get the information we need."

"Or we could go full Hollywood and set something on fire," he suggested, a wicked glint in his eye. "You know, for effect."

I couldn't help but laugh, the absurdity of the suggestion breaking the tension. "Let's save the pyrotechnics for another day, shall we?"

"Fine," he relented, a mischievous smile lingering. "Your plan it is."

We positioned ourselves behind the crates, and I could feel the anticipation thrumming in the air as we prepared to execute our plan. I held my breath, the adrenaline coursing through me, feeling more alive than I had in ages. This was it; this was the moment where the weight of my choices would either crush me or set me free.

With a swift motion, I kicked the base of the crates, and they toppled over with a resounding crash, sending debris flying everywhere. The noise echoed down the alley, drowning out the murmurs of the Syndicate members. "What was that?" Brock shouted, his voice tinged with confusion.

"Perfect," Darian murmured, glancing at me with a gleam of approval in his eyes.

As the men shifted their focus, I nudged Darian, signaling for us to move. Together, we slipped around the corner, heartbeats pounding in unison, ready to uncover the darkness lurking within Neo Crescent's heart.

We moved quickly through the alley, weaving in and out of shadows as we flitted past the remnants of crumbling walls and neon graffiti. The vibrant colors seemed to pulse in rhythm with my heart, each splash of light a reminder of what was at stake. Darian's presence beside me was a steady anchor amidst the chaos; the way he moved, every sinew taut with focus, made me feel as if we were a team built for survival, woven together by the fabric of our shared history and the urgency of the moment.

"Where to now?" I whispered, my breath barely audible over the distant clamor of Brock and his crew still investigating the distraction.

Darian paused, scanning the area. "We need to get to the warehouse on the corner. If they're planning something big, that's where they'll be organizing it."

I nodded, adrenaline surging as we slipped out of the alley and into the dimly lit street. The night was thick with anticipation, the air electric as we approached the warehouse, a hulking structure draped in shadows and mystery. As we neared the entrance, I could feel my pulse quicken. "What's the plan?"

Darian hesitated, his brow furrowing. "We go in quietly, gather intel, and get out. But if they see us—"

"—we fight," I finished, the gravity of the situation settling heavily on my shoulders. "Got it."

As we crept closer, the looming silhouette of the warehouse cast a long shadow across the ground, swallowing us whole as we ducked behind a stack of crates just outside the door. My heart thudded in my chest as I glanced at Darian, his eyes sparkling with that familiar mischief, the kind that hinted at the danger lurking just beneath the surface. "Ready to save the world?"

"More like save ourselves," he replied, smirking. "But sure, let's add a dash of heroics for flair."

I stifled a laugh, then gestured toward the entrance. "Alright, let's do this."

With that, we slipped inside, the heavy door creaking ominously as we pushed it open. The interior was dimly lit, shadows dancing across the concrete walls, and the faint hum of machinery thrummed in the background, a reminder that life continued despite the chaos outside.

As we moved deeper into the warehouse, the atmosphere thickened, the air heavy with the scent of oil and sweat. The sound of hushed voices drifted from a room at the back, punctuated by the occasional clatter of metal against metal. I exchanged a glance with Darian; the urgency in his expression mirrored my own.

We crept closer, staying low and silent, until we reached a cracked door slightly ajar. Peering through the narrow gap, I caught sight of a small group gathered around a table, their faces illuminated by a flickering overhead light.

"What's the timeline?" Brock demanded, his voice sharp and commanding.

"Tonight. We move tonight," a tall figure replied, gesturing animatedly. "We can't let them get away with what they've done. Neo Crescent belongs to us."

A chill ran down my spine. "They're planning an attack. A takeover," I whispered to Darian, who nodded grimly.

"What's the plan?" a third voice asked, a woman with dark hair tied tightly back, her eyes blazing with intensity. "If we don't act fast, we'll lose our chance."

"Leave it to me," Brock sneered, his confidence palpable. "Once we're in, we take out anyone who stands in our way. We'll make an example of them."

A murmur of agreement rippled through the group, and my stomach twisted in knots. "We need to get this information back to the authorities," I said urgently. "We can't let them carry out this plan."

Darian's expression darkened. "We need to take action, but we can't expose ourselves just yet. We need to wait for the right moment."

As if the universe was determined to test our patience, the door creaked, and I froze. The woman with the dark hair had stepped away from the group, her gaze sweeping over the room. My breath caught in my throat as I felt the tension in the air thicken.

"Something feels off," she said, her instincts clearly sharper than the others. "Keep an eye out. We can't afford any surprises."

"Relax, it's just the wind," Brock scoffed, but I could see the unease flickering in his eyes.

Before I could react, Darian nudged me back, and we retreated, holding our breaths as we huddled behind the crates again, listening intently. The woman's instincts were unnervingly sharp, and I could feel the weight of her scrutiny pressing against me like a tangible force.

"Darian, what if they—"

"Shh!" he hissed, his eyes wide as he peered around the crates. "We need to figure out how to get out of here."

My mind raced with possibilities, each one more dangerous than the last. "What if we create another distraction?"

"Too risky," he murmured. "If they see us, we're done for."

Just then, the conversation inside shifted. "Let's move to the back, check the perimeter," the tall figure commanded. "We can't let anyone slip through."

"Damn it," I whispered. "They're coming this way."

Darian's eyes locked onto mine, and in that moment, I could see the same mix of fear and determination mirrored in his gaze. "We need to make a decision. Now."

Before I could reply, the door swung open, and the tall figure stepped out, scanning the area with a predatory glint in her eyes. My breath hitched as I ducked behind the crates, the reality of our situation crashing down on me like a wave.

"We need a plan B," I whispered urgently.

"Let's move," Darian said, his voice low and resolute. "If we can get to the back exit—"

But before he could finish, the woman's eyes snapped to our hiding spot, a smirk curling her lips. "Well, well. Looks like we have some uninvited guests."

Panic surged through me as I felt the weight of her gaze. I darted a look at Darian, whose expression hardened with resolve. "Run!" he shouted, propelling us both forward just as the woman lunged.

We sprinted down the aisle, heartbeats echoing like war drums in our ears, but the sound of heavy footsteps thundered behind us, chasing us into the depths of the warehouse. As we turned a corner, I caught a glimpse of Darian's determination, his features set in fierce concentration, but the reality was stark—this was no longer just a skirmish; we were in the fight for our lives.

Suddenly, the lights flickered violently, plunging the warehouse into darkness. I stumbled, feeling my way through the pitch-black void, desperately clinging to the thread of hope that we could escape. Just as I regained my balance, a loud crash echoed from behind us, followed by frantic shouts.

Darian grabbed my hand, his grip firm as we barreled toward a dim light in the distance. "Almost there!" he urged, his voice a beacon amidst the chaos.

But as we reached the back exit, a heavy thud reverberated through the air, and I realized with a sinking dread that we were trapped. The door swung open with a forceful push, and Brock stood there, flanked by the rest of the Syndicate members, their eyes gleaming with triumph.

"Going somewhere?" he taunted, a sinister smile spreading across his face.

In that moment, as the weight of our choices pressed down upon us, I knew this was it. We were outnumbered, and the darkness was closing in fast. My heart raced as I braced for the confrontation, the air thick with tension, the taste of fear sharp on my tongue. We were cornered, and all I could think was that our fight was far from over.

Chapter 24: Shadows of Forgiveness

The air was thick with the scent of rain-soaked earth and the last remnants of summer's warmth as I stood at the edge of the old park, my heart a wild drum echoing the footsteps of my past. Memories darted around me like restless shadows, flitting just out of reach, taunting me with their bittersweet familiarity. It had taken weeks of sleepless nights and tumultuous days to gather the courage to come here—to face the very person I had sworn I would never forgive. But here I was, the ghosts of what once was swirling around me like leaves caught in an autumn breeze.

The park, once a vibrant tapestry of laughter and playful shouts, now seemed muted, as if it, too, was holding its breath, waiting for something to unfold. The swings creaked softly in the wind, their chains rusty from years of neglect, and the once-bright paint on the play structures had faded, peeling under the weight of forgotten summers. I inhaled deeply, letting the crisp air fill my lungs, grounding myself as I stepped closer to the bench where we had shared so many moments—moments now tinged with both warmth and pain.

As I approached, I spotted her. Sara, the girl who had once been my best friend, was sitting there, her posture rigid and her gaze fixed on the ground. I had envisioned this moment countless times, crafting perfect sentences and rehearsing how I would confront her. But now, all those carefully chosen words fled my mind, leaving me standing in the throes of uncertainty.

She looked up, and our eyes met. The world around us fell away, leaving just the two of us suspended in a moment thick with unsaid apologies and accusations. I felt the urge to turn away, to run back to the safety of my solitude, but something deeper held me there. I had come too far to turn back now.

"Hi," I managed, the word tasting foreign on my tongue, as if I hadn't spoken it in years.

"Hey," she replied, her voice barely above a whisper. There was an awkwardness between us, a heavy silence that seemed to stretch out like a chasm, begging for something—anything—to bridge the gap.

I took a seat next to her, feeling the cold metal of the bench seep into my skin. "I didn't think you'd come," she said, her eyes darting to the side, avoiding the weight of my gaze.

"Neither did I." I paused, the words I had prepared fleeing once more. "I've had a lot of time to think."

"About what?" she asked, her tone sharp but layered with an undercurrent of vulnerability.

"About us," I replied, my voice firmer now, the memories flooding back—the laughter, the secrets, and ultimately, the betrayal. "About how everything fell apart."

Her jaw tightened, a flicker of regret passing across her face. "I didn't mean for it to end like that," she said, almost pleading. "I was scared."

"Scared of what? Of losing me? Or of losing yourself?" The question hung in the air, heavy and charged, crackling with unspent energy.

Sara turned to face me fully, her expression a mixture of defiance and sorrow. "You don't understand. I was drowning in my own insecurities. I thought I could handle it alone, but I couldn't. I pushed you away because I didn't want to bring you down with me."

Her words felt like a cold slap, but beneath the sting, I recognized the truth. We had both been lost in our own storms, caught in the turbulent seas of adolescence and mistakes. "You didn't have to do it alone. We were supposed to be in this together," I replied, my voice wavering as I struggled to keep my emotions at bay.

She sighed, the sound carrying a weight of years gone by. "I know. And I'm sorry. I never wanted to hurt you. I thought it would be easier this way."

"Easier?" I laughed, a bitter sound that echoed in the stillness. "You thought disappearing was easier than facing it?"

"It felt like a choice at the time," she said, her eyes glistening with unshed tears. "But it wasn't. I lost you, and I lost myself in the process."

The confession hung between us, a fragile thread that connected our fractured pasts. For a moment, I wanted to reach out, to bridge the distance, but fear clawed at me, the specter of betrayal still fresh in my mind.

"Do you realize how hard it was to pick up the pieces?" I asked, the hurt spilling over. "I had to learn how to trust again—trust myself, trust others. You made me question everything."

"I know. And I don't expect you to forgive me. But I hope one day you can understand why I did what I did," she said softly, a tremor in her voice that stirred something within me.

The clouds overhead darkened, and a few drops of rain began to fall, splattering against the wooden slats of the bench like tiny tears. I closed my eyes for a moment, letting the cool droplets wash over me, cleansing away the anger I had held onto for far too long. "It's not about understanding anymore," I admitted. "It's about letting go."

A flicker of surprise crossed her features, and I knew we were standing on the precipice of something monumental. "Letting go?"

"Yes. I've carried this weight for too long. And while I can't erase what happened, I can choose not to let it define me." The words felt liberating, a release from the chains I had forged in my own bitterness.

She reached for my hand, her fingers trembling against mine, and in that moment, I felt the electricity of old bonds weaving back together, tenuous but undeniably present. "I'd like that. I want to try to make it right," she said, her voice steadying with hope.

The tension shifted, the air around us infused with a new possibility, a flicker of light breaking through the clouds. The rain picked up, drumming on the earth, and for the first time in a long time, I felt a spark igniting in my chest—a glimmer of hope mingling with the storm.

The rain transformed the world around us, painting the park in hues of grey and silver as it danced over the earth, each drop a reminder of the emotional storm we had just navigated. We sat there, hands intertwined, feeling the softness of the moment settle like the mist around us. I realized how small gestures—simple connections—could bear the weight of so much history. Sara's grip was tentative, as if she feared I might pull away again. But this time, I didn't want to retreat; I craved the warmth of our rekindled friendship, even if it was still fragile and untested.

"Remember that time we got caught in the downpour during that summer camp?" she asked, her eyes lighting up with the memory. "We were convinced we'd be struck by lightning if we ran for cover under the trees."

I laughed, the sound bubbling up like a wellspring of joy. "Oh yes! And we ended up soaked to the bone, trying to convince everyone that it was part of the camp's team-building exercise." The laughter felt cathartic, dissolving the remnants of our past grievances.

"That was a bold strategy," she replied, a wry smile playing on her lips. "I think the counselors were just relieved we weren't swept away by the river."

As we exchanged playful banter, I noticed how easily the comfort between us began to return. It was like unearthing an old favorite book, the pages slightly yellowed but the story still vibrant and alive. I looked at her—really looked at her—and saw the girl I had once known, the one with dreams woven into the fabric of her being, now layered with complexity and time. "You look good, you know," I said, more earnest than I intended.

"Thanks," she said, the smile on her face brightening. "You, too. Seems like life is treating you well."

"More or less," I replied, the truth of it threading through my words. "I've had my share of ups and downs, but who hasn't?"

We drifted into a comfortable silence, the rhythmic patter of rain filling the spaces between us. It was then that I noticed a flicker of something behind her eyes, a shadow that hinted at deeper wounds. "What about you?" I asked, unable to contain my curiosity. "How have you been really?"

Her gaze dropped, a flicker of pain crossing her features. "It's been... complicated. After everything, I had to figure out who I was without the safety net of our friendship. I made some choices I regret."

The vulnerability in her voice resonated with me. "You're not alone in that," I said softly. "I've made choices I'm not proud of either."

"Like what? Ditching me for your new life?" she quipped, her tone light, but the hurt was palpable.

"Okay, fair point," I admitted, chuckling as I shifted my weight. "But honestly, it felt like I was losing myself in a whirlwind of change. I clung to my new routine, hoping to drown out the emptiness."

Her expression softened, understanding flickering in her eyes. "I get it. Change can feel like standing on a tightrope with no safety net."

"Exactly. One moment you think you've got it all figured out, and the next, you're teetering on the edge, hoping you don't fall."

"Did you ever?" she asked, leaning in, curiosity dancing on her face.

"More times than I care to admit." I laughed, but there was an edge to it, a vulnerability that I had hidden for too long. "But I learned to pick myself up. Slowly, of course. It's not glamorous, but it's honest."

"Honesty has a way of cutting through the noise," she replied, her voice sincere. "And maybe that's what we both need—a little more honesty."

The storm outside intensified, the clouds growing darker as the wind howled through the trees. "We could talk all day, but maybe we should find some shelter?" I suggested, nodding towards a nearby café that flickered with warm light.

She glanced at the downpour, then back at me, a smile creeping onto her face. "What's a little rain? It's just a dramatic backdrop for our heartfelt reunion."

I grinned, appreciating her spirit. "Okay, but if we get drenched, you're buying me coffee."

"Deal." With that, we sprang to our feet, laughter carrying us through the deluge as we dashed toward the café, side by side.

Inside, the warmth enveloped us like a cozy blanket, the rich aroma of freshly brewed coffee swirling through the air. I spotted a corner table, the perfect spot for us to reconnect away from the bustle of the world outside. We settled in, shaking off the rain like wet dogs, the tension from our earlier confrontation fading with each shared moment.

"Okay, so what's your go-to drink?" she asked, scanning the chalkboard menu as if it held the secrets to our past.

"Depends on my mood. Today? Something indulgent—hot chocolate with a dash of espresso. It's like a hug in a mug," I replied, grinning.

"Sounds decadent. I'll have what you're having, then." She turned to the barista, placing our order, her confidence returning as the familiar ease of our friendship swelled between us.

As we waited for our drinks, I caught glimpses of her. Sara was still the girl who could light up a room, but there were also traces of weariness, lines of worry etched around her eyes. "So, what else is new in your world?" I asked, eager to delve deeper.

"Well, aside from attempting to resurrect my love life?" she said, raising an eyebrow, her tone teasing but tinged with sincerity. "It's been pretty quiet. Just work, a few questionable dates, and a lot of binge-watching terrible reality TV."

"Ah, the universal sign of a woman in crisis. At least you're in good company," I quipped. "But seriously, if you need a distraction, I'm here for it. You know I have a knack for turning even the most mundane events into adventures."

Her laughter rang out, bright and infectious. "You always did have a flair for drama, even in the simplest of situations."

"Guilty as charged," I replied, matching her enthusiasm. "But let's be honest—life is too short to take everything seriously. Besides, who wants to blend in when you can stand out?"

Just then, our drinks arrived, steaming mugs placed before us. I raised my cup in a mock toast. "To standing out and embracing the chaos!"

"To chaos!" she echoed, clinking her mug against mine with a grin. As we sipped, the conversation flowed effortlessly, weaving between laughter and deeper reflections on life's twists and turns. In that moment, I felt the walls I had built around my heart begin to crumble, brick by brick, as a new kind of trust began to take shape between us.

The café buzzed with energy, the chatter of patrons mixing with the gentle clinking of dishes. The rain continued its symphony outside, but we were cocooned in our own world, one where forgiveness and understanding slowly took root. The journey ahead still loomed large, but for the first time in a long time, I felt ready to embrace it, hand in hand with someone who, despite everything, had been a steadfast part of my story.

The warmth of the café enveloped us like a cozy quilt, the chatter around us blending into a comfortable background hum. As we sank deeper into our conversation, the barriers that had once felt insurmountable began to dissolve like sugar in hot coffee. Sara leaned forward, her eyes sparkling with mischief. "So, what's next on your agenda? Do you have plans to conquer the world, or are you just settling for the coffee shop scene?"

I chuckled, taking a sip of my hot chocolate and letting the rich, creamy sweetness wash over me. "World domination can wait. Right now, I'm just trying to survive the onslaught of reality TV. You know, keeping my finger on the pulse of society."

"Ah, yes, the noble pursuit of couch activism. But really, what are you passionate about these days?" she asked, her expression earnest. "I can't believe you're content to binge-watch when there's so much more out there."

The question caught me off guard, stirring something within me that had long been buried beneath layers of self-doubt and unresolved feelings. I had spent so much time avoiding my true aspirations, fearing they were too ambitious or too foolish. "Honestly? I've been toying with the idea of starting a blog or a vlog, sharing my experiences and insights on all the twists life throws at us. Something lighthearted, you know?"

"Now that sounds like an adventure!" She leaned in, excitement bubbling between us. "You've always had a way with words. Your stories could help people feel less alone."

Her encouragement sent a thrill through me, igniting the spark of creativity I had been nurturing in secret. "Do you really think so?" I asked, a mixture of hope and skepticism dancing in my voice.

"Absolutely! You have a gift. You make the mundane feel extraordinary. Remember that time we turned a trip to the grocery store into a full-blown quest for the best chocolate bar?"

"Oh, please. You know that's a standard Tuesday for me," I said, grinning. "But it did lead us to that ridiculous tasting event at the fancy chocolate shop. I still dream of those truffles."

"Right? See? You have the makings of a great storyteller! But maybe you should throw in some plot twists. Life isn't just about delicious desserts."

"True, but it certainly helps," I said, raising my mug to her. "Let's be honest, there are enough plot twists in our lives without needing to create them artificially."

Our laughter melded with the café's ambiance, a symphony of reconnection. We shared stories and plans, diving into the depths of our hopes and dreams. As I spoke about the blog, an ember of ambition ignited within me, feeling tangible and real. "What if I did it? What if I just put my thoughts out there for the world to see?" I mused, the thrill of possibility sending shivers down my spine.

"I'd read it," she replied, a nod of genuine encouragement firming her features. "I'd share it too. You might be surprised by how many people are waiting for someone like you to say what they're feeling."

The conversation shifted, weaving from lighthearted topics to more profound reflections on our experiences. "You know," I said, "for a long time, I was afraid of what people would think. What if they didn't like my voice? Or worse, what if they ignored me?"

"Who cares?" she shrugged. "You've survived the worst of it. Why let the fear of judgment stop you? Besides, some people will always find something to criticize, but that's more about them than it is about you. What matters is that you stay true to yourself."

I felt a rush of gratitude for her understanding and support. "You're right. I've spent too long in the shadows, hiding behind my insecurities. It's time to step into the light, even if it's just a flicker at first."

"Exactly! Baby steps," she said, her excitement contagious. "You can't expect to leap from zero to hero overnight. Just keep moving forward."

As we sipped our drinks, the atmosphere shifted subtly. The chatter around us became a distant hum, as if the café itself was tuning in to our conversation. "And what about you?" I asked, the curiosity returning. "What dreams have you tucked away in your own shadows?"

She hesitated, her gaze drifting out the window, where the rain still danced against the glass. "I've always wanted to travel," she admitted, her voice barely above a whisper. "To see the world and experience everything it has to offer. But I let fear hold me back."

"Fear?" I prompted, sensing a deeper layer beneath her words. "What do you mean?"

"Fear of the unknown, I guess. I've always been the responsible one, the one who stayed put and followed the rules. But lately, I've been thinking... what if I just threw caution to the wind? What if I took a chance?"

Her words resonated within me, mirroring the uncertainty I had felt about starting my own journey. "That sounds amazing. You deserve to see what's out there," I encouraged, my heart racing at the prospect of her adventure. "What's stopping you?"

"I don't know. Life, I suppose," she said, a hint of frustration threading through her tone. "I've got bills to pay, a job that keeps me tethered, responsibilities that feel impossible to escape. But deep down, I crave more than this routine."

"Then maybe it's time to make a change," I suggested, feeling the pulse of possibility thrum in my veins. "What if you planned a trip? Just a short one to start? It could be the push you need to take that leap."

The determination in her gaze brightened, the shadows lifting just a bit. "You really think I could?" she asked, a spark igniting in her eyes.

"Absolutely! And if you need a partner in crime, I'm all in. Two misfits navigating the unknown together?"

"Now that's a story I'd read," she laughed, the sound ringing out like a bell.

We shared a moment of exhilaration, imagining a world beyond our current confines. But as the excitement settled, an uncomfortable silence crept back in, pushing its way into the space between us. The weight of our past loomed like a specter, an unseen barrier that still needed addressing.

"Hey, about what happened between us," I began, but before I could finish, the café door swung open violently, sending a gust of wind inside, mingling with the rain and chaos of the outside world.

A figure stumbled in, dripping wet and panting, their eyes wide with panic. "Help! Please!" they gasped, their voice cutting through our bubble of hope and possibility.

Sara and I exchanged worried glances, the earlier lightness fading as dread washed over us. "What's wrong?" I called out, my heart racing.

The stranger glanced around, eyes darting between us as if searching for safety. "I need help! They're coming for me!"

Panic clutched at my throat, the promise of a new beginning teetering precariously on the edge of fear. As the café's atmosphere shifted from cozy warmth to palpable tension, I couldn't shake the feeling that everything we had begun to rebuild was about to be tested in ways we never anticipated.

Chapter 25: A Glimmer of Hope

The streets of Neo Crescent pulsed with a newfound energy as the festival unfolded, like a heartbeat resuscitated after a long, stagnant silence. Bright banners swayed in the warm breeze, their colors a riotous dance of reds, blues, and yellows that seemed to mock the ashen remnants of the past. The aroma of spiced meats and sweet pastries wafted through the air, mingling with the laughter of children darting about like fireflies, their faces painted in vivid hues that rivaled the decorations above. I couldn't help but smile as I moved through the crowd, the festive spirit wrapping around me like a warm embrace.

Darian stood beside a booth, his tall frame casting a shadow over a table laden with vibrant, handcrafted jewelry. His dark hair glinted under the fairy lights strung overhead, a stark contrast to the silver earrings twinkling in the sunlight. I caught his eye, and for a moment, the chaos around us faded into the background. His lips curled into that disarming smile, the one that felt like a secret shared between two old friends. In that instant, the weight of the world felt a little lighter, and I couldn't resist the pull toward him.

"Do you think the jewels will ward off bad luck?" I teased, stepping closer, my heart racing as the thrumming music vibrated through the air. "Because if that's the case, I'll take a dozen."

He chuckled, a rich sound that melted into the festive atmosphere. "Only if you promise to wear them every day. I could use some good luck in my life. It's been a rough few months, you know?"

My heart twisted slightly, recognizing the shadows that lingered in his gaze. "I know. We've all been through so much." I reached out, brushing my fingers against his, a fleeting connection that sent a spark of warmth up my arm. "But today is about joy, right? Let's soak it all in."

With a mock serious expression, he picked up a particularly extravagant necklace, its colorful beads catching the light. "Then I present to you the ultimate talisman against despair." He draped it around my neck, the beads cool against my skin. "Now, you're officially my good luck charm."

The playful banter felt effortless, a natural rhythm we fell into as easily as breathing. We wandered through the festival together, our laughter intertwining with the music and the vibrant atmosphere around us. It felt like a strange kind of magic, this moment carved out of time where nothing else mattered—no past, no worries about the future. Just us, together amidst the chaos.

We came upon a stage where performers dazzled the crowd with their acrobatics, twirling and flipping in the air with a grace that left me breathless. "I could never do that," I said, watching a woman execute a perfect backflip, landing flawlessly with a flourish that drew cheers from the audience.

Darian leaned closer, his breath warm against my ear, "Sure you could. Just need to channel your inner daredevil." He paused, an eyebrow arched mischievously. "Or your inner klutz."

I feigned a gasp. "How dare you? I could be a fantastic daredevil. I have the courage of a thousand lions."

"Oh really? Then let's see you try that." His finger pointed towards a nearby booth offering lessons on juggling flaming torches.

"Flaming? As in fire?" I hesitated, biting my lip as a rush of adrenaline sparked through me. "I'm not sure courage covers that level of risk."

"Come on, where's your sense of adventure?" He was teasing me now, that glimmer in his eyes challenging me to rise to the occasion. "Just think of the story we'd have to tell afterward."

The infectious excitement in his voice pulled me in, and before I could think too long, I found myself nodding, a wild grin breaking across my face. "Alright! But if I light myself on fire, I'm blaming you."

As we approached the booth, a group of eager participants surrounded the instructor, who demonstrated the art of juggling with an ease that seemed unattainable. My heart raced in tandem with the rhythm of the music, and Darian stood close by, a constant source of encouragement. "You've got this. Just remember to focus and don't look at the flames too much."

"Easy for you to say," I replied, but there was no mistaking the flutter of excitement in my stomach. I was aware of how ridiculous I might seem, but there was something liberating about stepping out of my comfort zone, especially with him there to witness it.

After what felt like an eternity of trying and failing, I finally caught a torch without it slipping from my grasp. A triumphant laugh escaped my lips as the crowd cheered, and I caught sight of Darian, who was grinning broadly, pride illuminating his features.

"See? You're a natural!" he exclaimed, clapping his hands together as if I had just performed the greatest feat of all time. "I knew you had it in you!"

As I basked in the moment, the sun dipped lower in the sky, painting the horizon in hues of gold and crimson. It was a stunning backdrop for the festival—a reminder that even the darkest nights could give way to the most beautiful dawns. I glanced at Darian, who was momentarily distracted by the flames, and I felt an overwhelming sense of gratitude wash over me. In this chaotic world, with its trials and tribulations, moments like this felt like small victories—tiny flickers of hope amidst the darkness, reminding us that life, no matter how uncertain, still held the power to surprise us in the most delightful ways.

The laughter of the crowd ebbed and flowed like a tide, pulling me further into the sea of festivities. As I turned away from the torch-juggling lesson, a thrill surged through me, the kind that ignites every nerve in your body, urging you to chase after whatever joy you can grasp. Darian was still watching, his eyes bright with admiration, as if he'd just seen a miracle unfold right before him.

"What's next on your daring adventure list?" he asked, nudging me playfully with his shoulder. "Skydiving? Bungee jumping? Maybe a nice, safe stroll through the nearest haunted house?"

I snorted, fighting back the laughter that threatened to escape. "I think I'll pass on the bungee jumping, thank you very much. I prefer my feet firmly planted on the ground, preferably with something delicious in hand."

"Food it is, then!" His grin widened, and together we ventured toward the stalls that lined the bustling square. The scent of sizzling street food was irresistible, a savory promise wrapped in the warm embrace of the festival atmosphere. I could hardly contain my excitement as I spotted a stall selling stuffed pastries, golden-brown and flaky, their insides bursting with a mélange of spiced meats and vegetables.

"Look at those!" I exclaimed, pointing with enthusiasm. "If I don't eat one of those soon, I might just faint from sheer hunger."

"Fainting would ruin the adventurous vibe we have going on," Darian said, shaking his head with mock seriousness. "We wouldn't want you passing out in the middle of a food coma."

The vendor handed me a warm pastry, and the first bite was a revelation—crispy on the outside, perfectly seasoned inside, and just enough heat to make my taste buds dance. I closed my eyes for a moment, savoring the flavor, and when I opened them, I found Darian watching me with an amused expression.

"What?" I asked, wiping a crumb from the corner of my mouth.

"Just admiring your dedication to culinary exploration," he said, his voice laced with playful mockery. "If this whole 'adventure' thing doesn't work out, I think you might have a future as a food critic."

I rolled my eyes, but the warmth in my cheeks betrayed my amusement. "I'll keep that in mind. It might not pay as well as skydiving, but at least I'd be less likely to die in the process."

As we continued to wander through the festival, the atmosphere shifted subtly. The music morphed from upbeat tunes to something slower and more melancholic, and a hush fell over the crowd. We turned our attention toward a makeshift stage where a speaker began to address the crowd, his voice rich and resonant, echoing through the square.

"Welcome, friends and neighbors," he began, a heartfelt warmth radiating from him. "Today, we gather not just to celebrate our resilience but to remember those who fought for our community. Let us honor their sacrifices as we move forward together, stronger than ever."

I glanced at Darian, who wore an expression that mingled pride with sadness. This was the heart of Neo Crescent, a place that had weathered storms, both literal and metaphorical, and the spirit of the people was evident in every face turned toward the stage. The speech touched on struggles and victories, weaving through tales of hope that brought tears to many eyes.

As the speaker shared anecdotes about loved ones lost and new beginnings, I felt a lump form in my throat. The weight of the past clashed with the vibrancy of the present, and I could see how the community had come together, resilient and determined to rebuild. I reached for Darian's hand, intertwining our fingers, grounding myself in the warmth of his presence.

"Powerful, isn't it?" he murmured, his voice barely above a whisper. "Sometimes, we forget how far we've come."

"Yeah," I replied, my voice shaky with emotion. "It's easy to get lost in the chaos and forget about the people who matter."

Darian squeezed my hand gently, a silent promise of solidarity, and I felt my resolve strengthen. We were part of this tapestry, woven together with threads of shared experiences and aspirations. As the crowd erupted into applause, I felt a swell of hope rising within me, a belief that maybe, just maybe, we could create something beautiful together.

With the speech finished, we returned to the festival's revelry. The lively chatter and infectious laughter resumed, as if the weight of the moment had been lifted. Darian and I meandered through the throng, indulging in a few more treats and playfully challenging each other to random games. We tried our hand at ring toss, where I nearly knocked over a bottle but managed to land a ring on the last throw, winning a plush toy that looked suspiciously like a raccoon.

"Congratulations, you've just won the world's most adorable garbage collector," Darian said, his laughter contagious.

"I think I'll name him Rocky," I replied, clutching my new prize to my chest as if it were a trophy. "He will proudly represent my accomplishments today."

We found ourselves at a quieter corner of the festival, a small patch of grass lit by twinkling fairy lights strung from nearby trees. It felt like a hidden oasis amidst the lively chaos, a perfect spot to pause and catch our breath. I sat down, letting the cool grass tickle my bare legs, and Darian plopped down beside me, his shoulder brushing against mine.

"This was a great idea," I said, glancing around at the joyful chaos of the festival. "I didn't realize how much I needed this."

"Me too," he replied, his gaze fixed on the crowd. "It's nice to see everyone coming together again. It feels... right."

We shared a comfortable silence, the music and laughter weaving around us like a warm blanket. In this moment, the world felt perfect, and I couldn't shake the feeling that something was shifting between us. The tension, once born from uncertainty, had transformed into a delicate dance of possibility, and I found myself leaning closer, the urge to bridge the gap between us growing stronger.

"You know," I said, my voice barely above a whisper, "I'm really glad you're here with me."

His gaze shifted toward mine, the air thickening with unspoken words. "I'm glad too. You've always been... special to me."

The warmth in his eyes made my heart race, and suddenly, the world outside our little haven faded into insignificance. It was just us, two souls intertwined in a moment that felt electric, charged with the potential for something new, something beautiful. I held my breath, waiting for him to say more, but instead, a loud bang erupted from a nearby stall, and the moment shattered like glass.

I blinked, momentarily disoriented, as the crowd erupted into a chorus of surprise and laughter. Darian and I exchanged incredulous looks, both of us bursting into laughter at the sheer absurdity of it all. Sometimes, life threw you the most unexpected twists, didn't it? But amidst the chaos, I felt a glimmer of hope, a belief that perhaps this was just the beginning of our own adventure, filled with laughter, resilience, and the promise of a bright future together.

The laughter from the nearby stalls blended into a symphony of joy, but my heart was still racing from the aftermath of that bang. As the crowd continued to murmur and chuckle, I felt a sense of urgency rising within me. The fleeting connection with Darian lingered like the sweetest aftertaste, tantalizing and rich, but the moment had been interrupted, almost as if the universe was conspiring to keep us from getting too close.

"Should we check that out?" I gestured toward the source of the commotion, where a cluster of festival-goers had gathered, their expressions a mix of amusement and concern. "Or do you think it's just another food stand imploding?"

Darian chuckled, shaking his head. "I wouldn't put it past them. But you know me—I can't resist a little chaos. Let's go see what's happening."

We stood up, brushing the blades of grass from our jeans as we made our way through the throng. The crowd parted to reveal a carnival game booth that had indeed met an unfortunate fate. An oversized piñata shaped like a dragon lay on the ground, shredded and limp, its colorful exterior reduced to confetti.

"That looks like a sad end for a mighty beast," I said, trying to suppress a laugh as a group of kids picked up the fallen candy scattered across the pavement, their delighted squeals piercing the air.

Darian shrugged, a grin spreading across his face. "At least they're getting their sugar rush. It's the circle of life, right? The piñata sacrifices itself for the greater good of children everywhere."

"Wise words, my philosopher friend." I nudged him playfully, feeling a surge of warmth that banished any residual awkwardness from our earlier moment. The festival buzzed around us, and for a brief moment, it felt like nothing could disrupt our little bubble of happiness.

After a few more games, a bit of junk food, and some spirited debates over which booth had the best snacks, we finally found ourselves drawn to the heart of the festival—a vibrant stage where local musicians began to play. The melodies flowed like a river, lifting our spirits higher as the sun began to dip below the horizon, casting everything in a golden glow.

"Have you ever thought about joining a band?" I asked, watching the lead singer sway with the music, his voice smooth and inviting. "You could be the star of Neo Crescent."

Darian rolled his eyes dramatically. "Oh, absolutely. Just call me the next rock legend. I can see it now—'Darian and the Deplorable Duds' taking the stage." He held his arms out wide, as if ready to address a massive audience. "We'll be world-famous for our bad hair and even worse lyrics."

"Now that's a band I'd pay to see," I teased, imagining the absurdity of it all. "But only if you promise to wear sequins."

"Sequins?" He pretended to consider it seriously. "I don't think my masculinity could handle that level of sparkle."

"Ah, don't be such a coward," I said, nudging him again. "Real men wear sequins. It shows confidence."

He raised an eyebrow, clearly entertained. "And yet you're the one wearing a raccoon plush around your neck."

"Rocky is my emotional support animal. He's my good luck charm," I declared, holding up my new plush toy as if it were a trophy. "And he would look fabulous in sequins, thank you very much."

The music swelled, and I couldn't help but sway to the beat, the rhythm capturing the essence of the moment. The festival was alive, a riot of colors and sounds, and it felt like anything was possible. I looked over at Darian, and for a moment, I wanted to capture this feeling forever—the shared laughter, the effortless camaraderie, the way he made the mundane feel extraordinary.

"I wish we could bottle this moment," I mused, half-joking. "You know, a little happiness in a jar to pull out whenever life gets rough."

"Don't worry," he replied, his voice dipping low as he leaned closer. "We'll have plenty more moments like this. You just have to promise to join me on all my future adventures."

"Deal," I said, my heart swelling with a sense of belonging. "But you're not allowed to let me light myself on fire again."

"Only if you promise to keep bringing Rocky along. He's got good vibes."

As the sun dipped lower, casting a warm blush across the sky, I felt a sense of contentment settle around us, a fragile yet palpable connection that seemed to deepen with each passing moment. Yet, even in the midst of such joy, a flicker of unease gnawed at the edges of my thoughts, whispering caution into the back of my mind. Life had a way of throwing curveballs when you least expected it.

The music shifted to a more vibrant tune, and the crowd surged forward, drawn into an infectious energy. The dancers twirled in a flurry of colors, and I couldn't help but join in, letting the rhythm pull me away from my worries. Darian followed suit, his laughter blending with the music, his presence grounding me as we danced among the throng.

Just as I began to lose myself in the joy of the moment, a loud crash erupted from the far side of the festival grounds. The music faltered for a brief moment as everyone turned to face the source of the sound, a sudden chill rippling through the crowd. My heart raced as I searched for Darian's eyes, finding him scanning the chaos, concern replacing the laughter that had just filled the air.

"What was that?" I asked, a twinge of fear creeping into my voice.

"I don't know," he replied, tension creeping into his tone. "Stay close."

The vibrant festival atmosphere quickly morphed into a cacophony of confused shouts and hurried movements. I clutched Rocky tightly, his soft fabric grounding me even as my pulse quickened. We moved toward the edge of the crowd, where the commotion seemed to be gathering strength, a swirling mass of uncertainty and anxiety.

Suddenly, a figure burst through the crowd, their clothes tattered, eyes wild with fear. "Run! It's coming!" they screamed, pointing behind them.

A wave of panic washed over the crowd, and the joyous ambiance shattered like glass. I looked at Darian, our earlier laughter forgotten as dread settled over us like a thick fog.

"What's happening?" I demanded, my voice rising above the din.

Before he could respond, the ground beneath us trembled, a deep rumble resonating through the festival grounds. I glanced at the figure again, the sheer terror etched across their face. I felt a primal instinct kick in, urging me to flee, but my feet felt rooted to the spot, caught in a web of uncertainty.

Darian grabbed my hand, pulling me closer as the crowd surged in every direction. "We need to get out of here! Now!" His urgency ignited my own instincts, and I nodded, adrenaline spiking through my veins.

We turned to run, weaving through the chaos, and just as we reached the edge of the crowd, I heard a deafening roar that echoed through the night, chilling me to my core.

And then, just as we reached the safety of a nearby alley, the ground shook again, and I stumbled, falling to my knees as the world around me began to unravel. My heart raced, and my breath quickened, the fear that had been a quiet whisper suddenly screaming for attention.

Darian pulled me up, his grip firm, but my mind raced with questions that had no answers. "What is happening?" I gasped, fear clinging to my throat like a vice.

But before he could reply, the sound of something massive crashing through the festival sent a shiver down my spine. I turned just in time to see the flickering lights overhead dim, swallowed by a darkness that felt all too ominous.

As chaos erupted behind us, something fierce and unknown surged forth from the shadows, and in that moment, I knew we were caught in something far greater than a mere festival gone awry.

Chapter 26: Unraveling Threads

I stepped into the warmth of the café, the familiar scent of freshly brewed coffee and warm pastries wrapping around me like a comforting blanket. The chatter of patrons mingled with the clinking of cups, creating a lively backdrop that grounded me in this moment. My heart raced, not from the aroma of roasted beans but from the weight of uncertainty resting on my shoulders. Just yesterday, I felt like I was finally finding my footing in this new world, where shadows of the past had begun to fade into the background. But today, an unsettling tension lurked beneath the surface, threatening to unravel everything I had fought for.

As I made my way to our usual table, nestled in the corner, I spotted Darian already there, his brows furrowed in thought. The sunlight streamed through the window, casting golden rays over his dark hair, illuminating the contours of his face with an ethereal glow. He looked like a warrior poised for battle, and I felt a rush of gratitude that we were in this fight together. I slid into the chair opposite him, and he looked up, his expression shifting from concern to something softer, more protective.

"Did you sleep at all last night?" he asked, his voice low and gravelly, laced with a hint of worry.

"Not much," I admitted, absently toying with the edge of my sleeve. "I kept thinking about everything that's happened. It's like we're trapped in a game where the rules keep changing."

Darian leaned forward, resting his elbows on the table. "I know. But we can't let them win. We've built something here—something worth fighting for." His eyes sparkled with a fierce determination that ignited a fire in my belly. I nodded, even as the shadows of doubt crept in.

Just then, the bell above the door chimed, and my pulse quickened as a figure entered. A woman with striking red hair and a confidence that radiated from her like a beacon caught my attention. She scanned the café, her eyes landing on us with an intensity that made my skin prickle. I'd seen her before, lurking at the edges of our gatherings, always observing, always too quiet.

"Isn't that —" I started, but Darian cut me off with a tight nod.

"Yes. That's Lila. She's been with us since the beginning, but there's something off about her. I can feel it."

As she approached our table, the air thickened with anticipation. I swallowed hard, the coffee that had just been comforting now feeling like a lead weight in my stomach.

"Mind if I join you?" she asked, her tone deceptively casual, yet the challenge behind her question hung in the air like a charged wire.

"Sure," I said, trying to keep my voice steady, though I could feel the tension crackling between us.

She slid into the chair beside Darian, her posture relaxed but her eyes sharp, as if she were assessing every detail of our demeanor. "I've been hearing things," she began, her voice smooth and alluring, yet there was an edge that suggested danger. "About the Shadow Syndicate."

My heart dropped. "What do you mean? We thought they were finished."

"Apparently not," she replied, her lips curving into a smirk that did nothing to ease the dread curling in my gut. "It seems they've managed to embed themselves in your little community. It's a farce, really, this sense of safety you've built."

"Stop right there," Darian interrupted, his tone firm. "What do you know?"

"Just that I wouldn't trust anyone who wasn't part of our original group. We're not as united as we think. The Syndicate thrives on chaos, and they're experts at creating it." Her words were like daggers, and I could feel the walls of our newfound sanctuary shaking under the weight of her implications.

"Why should we believe you?" I challenged, my voice gaining strength despite the tremor in my hands. "You've been in the background, always observing. How do we know you're not one of them?"

Her laughter was light, yet it carried an undertone of menace. "I'm here because I want to survive just as much as you do. I have my reasons."

Darian exchanged a glance with me, his eyes filled with concern. "What do you want, Lila?"

She leaned in closer, her voice dropping to a whisper, conspiratorial. "To help you uncover the truth. But trust me, it won't be easy. Betrayal lurks around every corner, and you'll need to be prepared for anything."

The café felt smaller, the voices around us fading into a dull murmur as her words sunk in. I thought of the bonds we'd forged, the trust we had built, and the foundation that seemed so solid. If there were indeed remnants of the Syndicate amongst us, it could mean the end of everything we had fought to establish.

"Okay," I said, taking a deep breath, trying to quell the rising tide of anxiety. "What do we do?"

Lila's smile widened, a glint of excitement in her eyes. "First, we gather intel. Then we confront the shadows that threaten to engulf us."

And just like that, a new journey unfurled before us, laced with danger and uncertainty. I could feel the stirrings of dread deep within, but there was also an undeniable thrill at the thought of standing up to whatever darkness lay ahead.

"Let's do it," Darian said, his hand brushing mine in a fleeting moment of reassurance. I locked my gaze with him, and in that brief exchange, I found my resolve. Together, we would face this challenge head-on, unraveling the threads of deceit that sought to ensnare us. The warmth of the café faded into the background as we prepared to dive back into the chaos that had become our lives. With Lila's unexpected alliance, the lines between friend and foe blurred, but one thing remained clear: we would not go down without a fight.

The clamor of the café faded into the background as Lila laid out her plan, her words a tangled web of intrigue and danger. I leaned closer, my elbows resting on the table, the polished surface cool against my skin. "Gather intel?" I echoed, trying to wrap my mind around the implications. "What does that even mean?"

Lila's gaze sharpened, her confidence illuminating the space between us. "We need to identify who among us might still be aligned with the Shadow Syndicate. If they've infiltrated our group, they could be anyone—your neighbor, the barista, even your best friend. We have to be cautious."

Darian shifted in his seat, the tension in his shoulders palpable. "And how do you suggest we start? We can't just go around accusing people without proof. That'll create chaos of its own."

"Oh, I don't plan on accusing anyone just yet," Lila replied, a sly smile playing at her lips. "We need to observe first. Watch how people behave, listen to what they say. There's always a slip, a clue. The Syndicate's agents are arrogant; they think they can outsmart everyone."

"Great, so we're playing detective now," I said, a mix of sarcasm and unease coloring my voice. "What's next? Stakeouts in the dark? Wearing disguises?"

"Don't tempt me." Lila chuckled, her laughter a melody that seemed out of place amidst the underlying tension. "You'd make an excellent sidekick with that sense of humor."

"Sidekick? I prefer 'co-lead,'" I shot back, but the banter felt hollow. Beneath the surface, the reality of our situation weighed heavily. I glanced at Darian, whose brow was still knitted in concern. He seemed caught between his instincts to protect me and the urgency of our mission.

"Let's keep it simple," he finally said, his voice steady. "We'll start with the community meeting tomorrow night. Everyone will be there, and it's the perfect opportunity to see how people interact. But we do this discreetly. No stirring the pot until we have something concrete."

"Agreed," I said, feeling a surge of resolve. "We need to stick together and trust our instincts. If we feel something's off, we act, but we can't jump to conclusions."

With a plan in place, we left the café, the afternoon sun dipping lower in the sky, casting long shadows that danced on the pavement. The air was crisp, and I took a deep breath, savoring the fleeting moments of normalcy. But with each step, my thoughts swirled, haunted by the possibility of betrayal lurking just beyond our sight.

As night fell, the community hall buzzed with energy, a vibrant hub of laughter and chatter. Strings of fairy lights twinkled overhead, and a potluck feast stretched across tables, laden with dishes from every corner of our diverse little family. I glanced around, taking in familiar faces, each one a thread in the fabric of our community, now potentially fraying at the edges.

Darian and I arrived early, claiming a corner table. "We should keep our eyes peeled," he murmured, scanning the crowd as people filed in. "Look for anything that seems out of place."

"Right, but we need to blend in too," I reminded him, plastering on a smile that I hoped conveyed nonchalance. "We can't look too suspicious, or we'll draw attention."

"Suspicious? Us?" he laughed, his voice rich and warm, like the cocoa someone had brought to the potluck. "Never."

The meeting commenced, and the atmosphere shifted, the lighthearted banter giving way to serious discussions about safety and community initiatives. I listened intently, but the weight of Lila's warnings gnawed at the back of my mind. Every laugh, every shared story seemed to carry the potential for hidden motives.

Halfway through the meeting, Lila slipped in, her presence commanding attention. As she spoke about community cohesion, I watched the way people reacted to her—some nodding eagerly, others casting wary glances. "She's good," I whispered to Darian. "Too good."

He nodded, his eyes narrowed in thought. "Let's watch her closely."

When the meeting wrapped up, I suggested a small group gather to help clean up. It was an excuse to linger, a chance to observe without seeming too obvious. As we cleared plates and stacked chairs, I couldn't shake the feeling that someone was watching us.

"Do you feel that?" I asked, lowering my voice as we worked side by side. "Like we're not alone in this?"

"Yeah," Darian replied, glancing over his shoulder. "Keep your guard up."

Just then, I spotted a figure in the corner—a man I recognized from previous gatherings, always on the outskirts, a slight frown permanently etched on his face. I caught his eye, and he looked away quickly, a flash of something—fear? Guilt?—crossing his features. My instincts screamed at me to approach him, to ask what was wrong, but the moment passed before I could act.

"Let's regroup," I said, motioning for Darian to follow me outside. The night air was cool and crisp, a refreshing contrast to the warmth inside the hall.

"Did you see him?" I asked, my heart racing. "The guy in the corner? I think he knows something."

Darian's eyes flicked toward the hall entrance. "I saw him. But what does he know? We can't go off half-cocked."

"Right," I said, frustration bubbling beneath the surface. "But what if he does? What if he's tied to the Syndicate?"

"Then we need to find out. But we have to be smart about it," he replied, placing a reassuring hand on my shoulder. "Let's keep an eye on him. If he shows up again, we'll approach him together."

"Together," I echoed, the word bringing a strange comfort. In this mess of uncertainty, it was nice to know we weren't alone.

We lingered outside, watching as the last of the guests trickled out, each face a potential ally or adversary. The moon hung low, casting a silver glow that illuminated our surroundings but left the darker corners cloaked in shadows. It was in those shadows where secrets thrived, and I had a sinking feeling that we were on the brink of discovering something we might not be ready to face.

"Darian," I said suddenly, my heart racing as realization struck. "What if Lila's not just an informant? What if she's the one pulling the strings?"

He turned to me, his expression shifting from concern to alarm. "Then we'll have to find a way to turn the tables before she can trap us in her game."

With the weight of that thought hanging in the air, we prepared ourselves for whatever lay ahead, the night filled with possibilities and perils that threatened to entwine us in a deeper mystery than we had ever anticipated.

The chill of the night air wrapped around me like a shroud, and the distant sound of laughter and clinking glasses faded as Darian and I lingered outside the community hall. The weight of uncertainty settled heavily on my shoulders, more substantial than the cloak I had thrown on to ward off the evening's coolness. The glow of the streetlights illuminated the pavement but left the shadows just deep enough to hide whatever treachery might lurk there.

"Do you think we can really trust Lila?" I asked, my voice low, laced with a tension that felt electric. "What if she's just leading us into a trap?"

Darian's jaw tightened, and he ran a hand through his hair, the movement both frustrated and thoughtful. "We can't ignore what she's saying. There are too many unknowns for us to play the blame game right now. If there's a chance she can help us identify the infiltrators, we need to take it."

"True," I conceded, though my gut churned with doubt. "But we have to keep our eyes wide open. I don't want to end up on the wrong side of this."

"Neither do I," he replied, his voice steady. "Let's head back inside and keep our ears to the ground. We might learn more tonight if we play it smart."

We slipped back into the hall, where the remnants of the meeting buzzed in the air like the last flickers of a dying flame. People were mingling, laughter bubbling up as friends shared stories over the last bites of dessert. It felt so normal, so blissfully unaware of the shadows lurking just beyond the light. I caught a glimpse of Lila across the room, her laughter mingling with the others, yet somehow she seemed separate, like a dark star in an otherwise bright constellation.

"Let's check on that guy from earlier," Darian suggested, nodding toward a small cluster of people near the snack table. "If he's tied to the Syndicate, we should find out what he knows."

"Right. Operation 'Innocuous Chat' is officially a go," I said, forcing a lightness into my tone despite the tension that gnawed at my insides. Together, we approached the group, the casual chatter enveloping us as we joined the conversation.

"Hey, did you try the chocolate cake? It's to die for!" I offered, hoping to sound enthusiastic while eyeing the man, Jake, who had been lurking at the meeting.

"Not yet," he replied, his voice a low rumble. He was tall and stocky, with a nervous energy that flickered just beneath the surface.

"I've been too busy trying to figure out the dynamics in here. Seems like things are a bit... tense."

"Tense is one word for it," Darian chimed in, casting a glance around the room. "But we're making progress. The community is really coming together."

Jake shifted his weight, his eyes darting to the far wall where Lila stood, deep in conversation with another member. "Right. Togetherness. Just make sure you trust the right people. Some of us have seen things that make that hard."

"Things?" I probed, stepping closer, my curiosity piqued. "What kind of things?"

He hesitated, glancing around as if afraid the walls might have ears. "Things that suggest we're not all on the same page. The Syndicate—there are whispers. You're not as safe as you think."

The laughter and music around us blurred into a distant hum, and my heart pounded in my chest. "You know something, don't you?" I pressed, my voice low and urgent. "What do you know about Lila?"

Jake's expression darkened, and he glanced around again, panic flashing in his eyes. "Listen, just be careful. The Syndicate has eyes everywhere, and trusting the wrong person could get you hurt."

"Great advice, but a little vague, don't you think?" Darian said, frustration creeping into his tone.

Before Jake could respond, Lila sauntered over, her presence electric and commanding. "Everything all right here? I hope I'm not interrupting." The sweetness in her voice dripped with a hint of malice, and I could see the tension radiating from Jake as he stiffened.

"Just having a little chat about the weather," I said, forcing a casual smile. "You know how people get in a room full of cake."

"Ah, cake—the great equalizer," Lila quipped, her eyes dancing with mischief. "But you know, the real storm is brewing under the surface. Isn't that right, Jake?"

He faltered, and I could see the panic setting in, his eyes darting between us. "I—I have to go," he stammered, suddenly breaking away from our conversation and retreating into the crowd.

"That was... intriguing," Darian said, crossing his arms, a thoughtful look in his eyes. "He knows something, and I don't like that he just bolted like that."

"Agreed. But what's worse is that Lila might have sensed it too. We need to figure out what she's up to before she pulls us deeper into her game."

As the evening wore on, I kept a close watch on Lila. She mingled effortlessly, her laughter ringing out like a siren song, drawing people in, while I felt the shadows of suspicion creeping closer. With every passing moment, the stakes felt higher, the air thick with unspoken truths.

The hall began to empty, and as the last few stragglers drifted away, I grabbed Darian's arm. "Let's find Jake. If he's frightened enough to run, he might have information we can use."

Together, we searched the parking lot, the chilly night air wrapping around us like an unwelcoming embrace. My heart raced as we spotted Jake standing near his car, glancing over his shoulder as if he expected to see something lurking in the darkness.

"Jake!" I called out, jogging to catch up. "Wait up!"

He spun around, and his eyes widened in fear. "What do you want?"

"We just want to talk," Darian said, his voice calm and steady. "We're not your enemies. We're trying to figure out what's going on."

"Listen, you don't want to get involved in this," Jake said, shaking his head. "You have no idea what you're dealing with."

"Then tell us! You can't just walk away," I urged, stepping closer. "You're part of this community too. We need to protect each other."

His gaze flicked back to the hall, the shadows playing tricks in the dim light. "I can't... I can't trust you, or anyone. If they find out..."

Before he could finish, a noise broke through the silence—a sound sharp and jarring, like the crack of a gunshot. My heart leapt into my throat as Jake's eyes widened in horror, and he stumbled backward, gasping as he clutched his chest.

"Jake!" I shouted, rushing forward. But before I could reach him, his body crumpled to the ground, lifeless and still.

A scream lodged in my throat as panic surged through me. Darian moved to my side, his eyes wide with disbelief. "What just happened?" he whispered, a mixture of horror and confusion in his voice.

Before I could answer, the sound of footsteps echoed from the shadows, and a familiar figure stepped forward—Lila, her smile bright and devoid of warmth. "I warned you to be careful," she said, her voice dripping with feigned concern.

My heart pounded as realization struck like a bolt of lightning. There were no safe spaces left, and trust was a fragile illusion. The night had taken a dark turn, and in the flickering shadows, the game was far from over.

Chapter 27: The Heart of Darkness

The air hummed with a tension that felt almost palpable, as if the very fabric of the world was aware of the darkness swirling around us. The shadows loomed larger with each step I took alongside Darian, our boots crunching against the gravel of the narrow alley that snaked through the forgotten part of the city. Faded murals adorned the walls, whispering tales of a vibrant past now buried beneath layers of grime and neglect. It was in these crevices of society that secrets festered like wounds, waiting to be unearthed.

I stole a glance at Darian, whose eyes, usually so warm and inviting, now bore the weight of a storm brewing just beneath the surface. The rugged lines of his jaw clenched tightly, a telltale sign of his determination. He caught my gaze, and for a fleeting moment, the world fell away, leaving just the two of us ensnared in a fragile bubble of unspoken words and unacknowledged feelings. It was maddening how easily my heart twisted with each glance, each brush of our shoulders as we moved deeper into the unknown.

"What do you think they want?" I asked, my voice barely a whisper, careful not to disturb the oppressive silence that hung between the buildings. The night felt alive, crackling with the energy of unfulfilled ambitions and sinister plots, and I couldn't shake the feeling that we were being watched.

Darian turned his head slightly, his brow furrowing as he contemplated my question. "Power. Control. The usual suspects." He shrugged, but there was an undercurrent of unease in his tone. "We're just the collateral damage in their game."

A shiver danced down my spine, not just from fear but from the reality of his words. The conspiracy we had stumbled upon was like a vast web, intricate and suffocating, with threads woven so tightly that escaping its grasp felt almost impossible. It had begun as a simple investigation, a desire to uncover the truth behind the shadows that loomed over our city, but now it was something far more dangerous, and I had unwittingly placed myself squarely in the crosshairs.

The sound of scuffling boots drew my attention back to the present, the echoes bouncing off the walls like ominous chimes. I glanced down the alley, heart racing, as two figures emerged from the darkness, cloaked in an air of secrecy that sent my instincts into overdrive. Darian stepped closer, instinctively positioning himself between me and the approaching danger, his body a solid wall of strength.

"Stay behind me," he murmured, his voice low and steady, but I could hear the urgency in it. The tension in his frame was electric, a current that crackled between us, binding us in this moment of impending confrontation.

The figures emerged from the shadows, revealing themselves to be two men, faces obscured by hoods that cast their features in darkness. I could feel my pulse quickening, an instinctual response to the unknown danger they represented. One of them stepped forward, the flicker of a lighter illuminating a sneer on his lips, revealing a sharp smile that held no warmth.

"What do we have here?" he drawled, his voice dripping with sarcasm. "A couple of brave souls on a quest for truth? How quaint."

Darian's posture shifted, muscles taut with tension as he faced the men, his presence radiating a fierce protectiveness. "We're not looking for trouble," he replied, voice steady but laced with an edge that hinted at the simmering conflict beneath.

"Oh, I think you are," the second man interjected, his gaze flicking from Darian to me, and back again. "You've stumbled into something that's far beyond your comprehension, sweetheart."

I bristled at the condescending tone, a spark of defiance igniting within me. "I think you underestimate us," I shot back, surprising even myself with the strength in my words. Darian's head turned slightly, surprise flickering across his features, but it quickly morphed into something resembling admiration.

"Feisty," the first man mused, taking a step closer, eyes glinting with amusement. "Maybe you'll make this interesting after all."

Without warning, the tension snapped like a taut wire. Darian lunged forward, moving with the grace of a coiled spring, and I was caught in the whirlwind of action that followed. I ducked as the first punch was thrown, adrenaline surging through my veins, propelling me into the chaos that ensued. The alley erupted into a flurry of movement, shadows dancing wildly as we fought for our lives, every blow exchanged intensifying the urgency of our mission.

"Watch your back!" Darian shouted, and I pivoted, narrowly avoiding a fist aimed at my head. My heart thundered in my chest, a wild drumbeat that matched the frantic pace of our struggle. I felt alive, a strange thrill coursing through me as I sidestepped and retaliated, channeling every ounce of fear into strength.

The sharp crack of knuckles on flesh resonated in the narrow space, and for a moment, I lost myself in the rhythm of the fight. I felt invincible, empowered by the sheer force of will and the undeniable connection building between Darian and me. We were two halves of a whole, our movements instinctively mirroring one another, each blow a testament to the bond we were forging amid chaos.

But in the whirlwind, the reality of our situation loomed heavily. As the last man crumpled to the ground, panting and defeated, the magnitude of our actions hit me like a freight train. We were far from safe; the conspiracy that lurked in the shadows was relentless, and now we had painted ourselves as targets.

Darian's breath came in ragged gasps beside me, the adrenaline slowly fading, replaced by a tense quiet that felt suffocating. He turned to me, the raw emotion in his gaze igniting something deep within. "Are you okay?" he asked, his voice low but tinged with a concern that made my heart flutter.

I nodded, feeling a rush of gratitude swell within me. "Yeah, I'm fine. Thanks to you." The weight of the moment settled over us, unspoken words hanging in the air like a fragile promise, and I realized how much I needed him by my side.

The adrenaline still buzzed in my veins as we emerged from the alley, the world outside bathed in the muted glow of streetlights. The night felt different now, charged with a sense of urgency that thrummed in the air. I glanced back, half-expecting to see the shadows stretch toward us, but the alley remained quiet, the echoes of our confrontation fading into the night like a distant storm.

Darian and I paused for a moment, taking in the city that loomed around us. The streets, usually bustling with life, felt eerily still, as if the universe had held its breath in anticipation. My heart still raced, not just from the fight but from the undeniable connection simmering between us. The thrill of danger had ignited something in me, and I could sense it reflected in Darian's eyes—a flicker of understanding, of something unspoken that lingered just beneath the surface.

"Let's find somewhere safe to regroup," he said, his voice steadying as he took a breath. "I have a contact who might know more about what we're dealing with."

I nodded, grateful for his calm demeanor, which offered a stark contrast to the chaos that had just unfolded. We moved through the streets, shadows slipping past us like secrets, each corner we turned unveiling a new layer of this sprawling city, one that had felt familiar but now took on an aura of the unknown. The faint sounds of music floated from a nearby bar, and I caught a whiff of something delicious wafting from a food cart, but none of that registered as the weight of our mission pressed down on me.

Darian led me down a series of winding streets, until we reached a nondescript door tucked between two vibrant murals depicting a time when the city pulsed with creativity and life. He knocked twice, a rhythm that felt like a heartbeat. I wondered how many times he had stood in this exact spot, waiting for answers that might never come.

The door creaked open, revealing a woman with dark hair and piercing green eyes that seemed to see right through me. She was wrapped in a leather jacket that clung to her form, a sharp contrast to the softness of her features. "Darian," she greeted, a hint of surprise softening her otherwise guarded expression. "What brings you here? And who's this?"

"Jess," he replied, stepping inside and gesturing for me to follow. "This is my partner in the investigation. We need intel—now."

She raised an eyebrow, clearly intrigued but cautious. "Investigation, huh? You've both stepped into something deep, I can sense it. Sit. I'll get us something to drink."

The interior was a contrast to the drab exterior, vibrant and alive with eclectic furnishings and art. It felt like a sanctuary away from the chaos of the outside world. I sank into a plush couch, still feeling the remnants of adrenaline coursing through me. The walls were adorned with photographs of faces both familiar and strange, snapshots of lives intersecting in this hidden world.

Jess returned with a couple of mugs steaming with something that smelled rich and inviting. "You'll want this. Trust me." She handed one to me, and I took a cautious sip, the warmth spreading through me, comforting yet invigorating.

"Now, what's this conspiracy you're dancing with?" she asked, her tone shifting to one of seriousness as she leaned forward, elbows resting on her knees.

Darian took a breath, his gaze steady. "We've uncovered a faction that's pulling strings behind the scenes, and it's bigger than we thought. We need to know who's involved and what they want."

Jess's expression shifted to one of contemplation, her eyes narrowing slightly as she processed the information. "This is not the kind of thing you can just walk away from. You're playing with fire, and the kind of people involved in this don't take kindly to nosy individuals."

"Do we look like we're afraid?" I shot back, the words escaping before I could think. The fire in me sparked again, the conviction in my voice surprising even myself.

Jess laughed softly, a glimmer of respect in her eyes. "Alright, I like your spirit. You'll need that if you want to survive. Here's the deal: there's a meeting happening tomorrow night at the old mill on the outskirts of the city. If you're looking for answers, that's where you'll find them. But be careful; it's crawling with those who would rather keep their secrets buried."

I exchanged a glance with Darian, the weight of the decision hanging heavy between us. "We can't let this go," he said, determination etched in every line of his face. "We have to find out what they're planning."

Jess studied us for a moment, then nodded. "I'll get you in, but once you're there, it's all on you. Trust no one. Remember, the deeper you go, the more tangled the web becomes."

As she spoke, I felt the gravity of her words settling in my chest, tightening around my heart like a vise. The thrill of adventure now mingled with a sense of foreboding that was hard to shake. "And if we don't come back?" I asked, more to hear the words out loud than anything else.

"Then you'll have to find a way to make it back," she replied with a smirk, her confidence somehow both reassuring and unsettling.

I met Darian's gaze, a silent agreement passing between us. The uncharted territory ahead was both exhilarating and terrifying, a path paved with uncertainty. We were no longer just two individuals drawn together by a shared purpose; we were entwined in something greater, a narrative that pulled us into its depths.

"Thank you for your help," I said, my voice firm as I placed my mug down. "We'll do what we need to."

Jess gave a knowing nod, her expression serious now. "Just remember, sometimes the light at the end of the tunnel is an oncoming train."

With that, we stepped back into the night, the weight of our choices hanging heavy in the air. The streets stretched before us, illuminated by the dim glow of streetlamps, guiding us toward the precipice of danger and discovery. I felt a mix of excitement and fear as we headed toward the unknown, Darian by my side, our hearts racing in tandem. This was no longer just about uncovering a conspiracy; it was about us, about the connection we were forging in the fires of chaos. As the city whispered its secrets around us, I knew one thing for certain: I wasn't just fighting for the truth—I was fighting for something much deeper, something that could change everything.

The cool night air wrapped around us as we stepped back into the streets, my heart racing in time with the rhythm of our impending confrontation. The city lay sprawled before us like a living beast, each shadow concealing secrets, every corner whispering stories of ambition and betrayal. Darian walked close beside me, our shoulders brushing, a silent reassurance that we were in this together.

"I guess we're about to crash a party," I said, trying to lighten the heavy atmosphere with a smile, but my voice was laced with tension.

Darian shot me a sideways glance, a ghost of a grin teasing the corners of his mouth. "Crash it, or become part of the entertainment?"

"Let's hope for the former," I replied, lifting my chin with determination. "I'm not exactly dressed for a gala."

We both shared a moment of laughter, but it quickly faded as the reality of our situation settled back in. I could feel the weight of the plan we were about to execute pressing down on us, the gravity of what lay ahead hanging like a storm cloud. As we made our way toward the old mill, anticipation swirled in my stomach, each step echoing louder than the last.

The mill loomed in the distance, a hulking shadow against the starry sky, its windows dark and foreboding. It was a relic of another time, once vibrant and full of life, now reduced to a shell of what it had been. I shivered, not just from the chill of the night, but from the sense of dread that clung to the air like a fog.

Darian paused, turning to face me, the intensity of his gaze sending a thrill of apprehension and excitement through me. "We need to be careful. No heroics, okay? Stay close, and trust your instincts."

"I think I'm a little past the heroics stage," I replied, trying to keep the mood light. "Besides, I trust you."

"Good," he said, his expression softening for just a moment before the hard edge of focus returned. "Let's do this."

Together, we approached the entrance, the heavy door creaking open with a disconcerting groan. Inside, the air was thick with dust and the scent of rust, remnants of machinery long abandoned. The dim light filtering through broken windows cast eerie shadows, and I could feel the weight of a thousand forgotten memories pressing down on me as we stepped deeper into the space.

As we moved through the darkened interior, we caught sight of flickering lights up ahead. The unmistakable sounds of voices echoed through the vast space, low murmurs interspersed with laughter that felt far too jovial for the setting. It was a twisted contrast to the purpose of our visit. We exchanged a look, and I felt my heart leap into my throat as we crept closer, using the towering machinery as cover.

"Do you see them?" I whispered, my pulse quickening.

Darian nodded, his eyes narrowing as he scanned the scene. "Looks like a few familiar faces. The kind you don't want to meet in a dark alley."

My heart sank as I spotted a figure I recognized, seated at a makeshift table adorned with empty bottles and half-burned candles—the very man who had thrown the first punch in our last encounter. "Great," I muttered. "Just what I wanted to see."

Darian's hand found mine, squeezing it gently. "Remember the plan. We're here to gather information, not to get into a brawl."

"Easy for you to say," I shot back, though I appreciated the grounding gesture. His touch ignited a warmth that contrasted sharply with the cold reality surrounding us.

We edged closer, crouching behind a stack of crates. My heart raced as I leaned in, straining to hear snippets of conversation floating through the air like fragile wisps of smoke.

"...need to act soon. They're getting too close," a voice hissed, sharp and laden with urgency.

"They don't know what they're dealing with," another voice replied, deeper and filled with a sinister undertone. "Let them think they're safe for now. We'll deal with them when the time comes."

The words sent a shiver down my spine, and I exchanged a glance with Darian, who looked just as troubled. "We need to get closer," he said quietly, his expression set with determination.

Creeping along the edge of the room, we maneuvered between the shadows, our presence a mere whisper in the grand scheme of things. The gathering of conspirators became clearer, their faces illuminated by the dim light, their expressions ranging from anxious to triumphant. It was like stepping into a tableau of deceit, every person a player in a game where the stakes were life and death.

"...the shipment is arriving tomorrow night. We can't afford any mistakes," the man I recognized warned, his gaze darting around the room.

"Trust me, we'll be ready," another voice replied, filled with false bravado. "No one will see it coming."

I felt my stomach twist at the implications of their words. Whatever they were planning, it was bigger than we had anticipated. I leaned in closer to Darian, my voice barely above a whisper. "We need to know what the shipment is."

His eyes narrowed, and he nodded. "Let's see if we can overhear more before we make our move."

Just then, a sudden crash echoed through the mill, the sound of metal hitting the floor reverberating like a gunshot. Instinctively, we both ducked behind the crates, our hearts pounding in unison. The voices erupted into chaos, shouts of alarm punctuating the thick tension that settled over the room.

"What was that?" a voice shouted, tinged with panic.

"Check it out!" another ordered, and the group began to disperse, some moving toward the source of the noise, others scrambling for weapons hidden nearby.

Darian turned to me, eyes wide. "We need to get out of here—now."

But before we could retreat, a figure emerged from the shadows, stepping directly into our path. A face that was all too familiar: the man from the alley. His eyes glinted with malice, and I could feel the air around us thicken, the electric charge of danger rising to a fever pitch.

"Well, well, what do we have here?" he said, a smirk curling his lips. "Looks like we've caught ourselves some intruders."

Darian shifted slightly, his body tensing, and I felt the weight of his protectiveness enveloping me. "We're not looking for trouble," he said, his voice calm but firm, like a dam holding back a flood.

"Trouble found you," the man taunted, stepping closer, his expression a mix of delight and menace.

In that moment, everything seemed to slow—the air thickening around us as the room filled with the heightened anticipation of what was to come. I could feel the blood pounding in my ears, the world narrowing down to this one moment, where fate hung in the balance.

As he reached for something at his belt, the shadows around us deepened, a trap closing in on us with the finality of a guillotine. And in that breathless instant, I realized we were out of time.

"Darian!" I shouted, instinctively pushing him aside as the first shots rang out, shattering the air with a violence that echoed through the mill like a thunderclap.

Chapter 28: A Love Forged in Fire

The wind howled through the narrow streets of Neo Crescent, whipping at my hair like an unruly child demanding attention. Shadows danced in the flickering light of street lamps, their glow revealing glimpses of chaos just beyond the edges of my perception. It felt as if the city itself was holding its breath, teetering on the precipice of uncertainty, a sentiment mirrored in the tautness of my own resolve. In that charged moment, adrenaline coursed through my veins, a potent mix of fear and determination that propelled me forward.

Darian stood at my side, his silhouette a striking contrast against the crumbling backdrop of our battleground. The remnants of the Syndicate lay scattered around us, remnants of a fight that had escalated beyond mere skirmishes into a full-blown war. His presence was a beacon amidst the encroaching darkness, the warmth of his gaze anchoring me even as uncertainty swirled like a tempest. With each shared glance, the weight of unspoken words hung between us—a bond forged in fire, each moment we had fought side by side knitting our souls closer together.

"You ready for this?" he asked, his voice low and steady, a reassuring murmur that cut through the tumult.

I nodded, though my heart raced like a wild stallion. "As ready as I'll ever be." The truth was, the deeper I delved into the heart of this battle, the more I grappled with my own feelings. The stakes were higher than they had ever been; the very fabric of our lives depended on the choices we made now. But the raw reality of my emotions towards Darian—the fierce protectiveness, the undeniable attraction—wrapped around me like a heavy cloak, suffocating yet intoxicating.

Together, we moved through the shattered remnants of our once-thriving city, where echoes of laughter had long been silenced by the encroaching shadows. Each footstep carried us closer to the lair of the Shadow Man, our greatest adversary and the architect of our misery. The air was thick with tension, each breath a reminder of what was at stake. As we approached the heart of the Syndicate's operations, a dilapidated warehouse hidden beneath the ruins of Neo Crescent, an unshakeable sense of foreboding settled over me.

"This is it," I said, my voice a whisper lost in the cacophony of distant sirens and the rattle of crumbling infrastructure. The warehouse loomed before us, a gaping maw waiting to swallow us whole.

Darian stepped closer, the heat of his body warming the chill in my bones. "We go in together. No one gets left behind."

His words ignited a flicker of courage within me, even as fear clung to my edges like cobwebs. I reached for his hand, intertwining my fingers with his, feeling the steady thrum of his pulse match my own. The connection was electric, and for a moment, the impending storm faded into the background, leaving only us—two warriors ready to face the unknown.

The door creaked open, revealing a dimly lit interior that smelled of rust and despair. My heart pounded a rapid tattoo against my ribs as we crossed the threshold. Inside, the air was thick with a sense of impending doom, the silence heavy enough to crush a soul. Shadows pooled in the corners, thick and oppressive, swirling like whispers of the past.

"Do you think he's here?" I asked, my voice barely above a whisper.

Darian's grip tightened on my hand, his presence a steadying force. "If he is, he won't go down without a fight." His eyes scanned the darkness, searching for any sign of movement. "Stay close."

As we navigated the labyrinth of crates and debris, the tension escalated, crackling in the air like a live wire. I could feel the pulse of impending confrontation thrumming beneath my skin. It was in that charged atmosphere that we stumbled upon the heart of the Syndicate's operation—a room buzzing with activity, filled with the flickering glow of screens and the hushed murmurs of those still loyal to the Shadow Man.

"What do we do?" I whispered, a sudden chill washing over me.

Darian turned to me, determination etched into every line of his face. "We take them out—fast and quiet. We can't let them alert him."

Nodding, I drew in a steadying breath. The plan was simple in theory, yet chaos often unraveled the best intentions. We positioned ourselves at the entrance, ready to launch our assault, when suddenly, a figure emerged from the shadows, taller and more sinister than I had ever imagined. The Shadow Man stepped into the dim light, a smirk playing on his lips, arrogance draping over him like a well-fitted cloak.

"Ah, the brave little warriors come to challenge me," he taunted, his voice smooth like silk, yet laced with a venomous undertone. "How quaint."

Before I could respond, a surge of anger coursed through me, fueled by all the pain he had wrought upon us. "We're here to end this," I declared, the fierceness of my conviction surprising even myself.

The smirk widened, revealing a predatory glint in his eyes. "You think you can defeat me? I have built this empire from ashes; you are mere specks of dust."

Darian stepped forward, his presence radiating strength. "Dust has a way of being blown away, especially when the wind is strong enough." The challenge hung in the air, electric and charged with potential.

The Shadow Man chuckled darkly, an unsettling sound that sent shivers down my spine. "Very well. Let's see if you can survive the storm."

And just like that, chaos erupted. The room exploded into action, and I found myself instinctively reaching for Darian, our bodies moving in perfect synchrony as we faced the onslaught. Each strike we delivered was a dance, an intricate ballet of desperation and resilience, fueled by the very fire of our bond.

The remnants of the Syndicate lay scattered across the dimly lit warehouse, the air thick with the acrid scent of smoke and the metallic tang of blood. Shadows danced along the walls, flickering ominously as the last echoes of the fierce battle faded. The tension was palpable, every creak of the aged wood beneath our feet a reminder of the fragile state of our reality. Darian and I stood back to back, our breaths coming in heavy bursts, each inhale laced with the adrenaline of the fight we had just waged. Around us, the remnants of our lives—our hopes, dreams, and the promise of Neo Crescent—hung in the balance.

"I thought I'd seen everything until tonight," I said, casting a sideways glance at Darian, who was scanning the perimeter for any lingering threats. His jaw was set, determination etched across his features, but his eyes flickered with something deeper—something I couldn't quite name. Perhaps it was the flicker of vulnerability that only emerged in moments like this, moments when the facade of bravery cracked just enough to reveal the truth.

He smirked, a wry grin that cut through the heaviness of the moment like a knife. "You have to admit, we make quite the team. I mean, who else can say they've battled a shadowy syndicate and lived to tell the tale?"

"Right, just another Tuesday in Neo Crescent," I replied, my voice laced with irony. The tension between us was electric, charged with a history that thrummed beneath the surface. Each glance, each quip, felt like an unspoken acknowledgment of the bond we had forged, not just in the fires of conflict, but in the quiet moments that lingered between our battles.

But there was no time to linger in the past, no time to dissect what was brewing between us. The Shadow Man was still out there, lurking in the darkness, a specter of our fears and the architect of our torment. I could feel him, a cold presence creeping along my spine. The stakes had never been higher; the fate of our city hung in the balance, and the only way to safeguard our future was to confront our deepest fears head-on.

"Are you ready?" Darian asked, his voice a low murmur, breaking me from my thoughts. His gaze held mine, fierce and unyielding.

"Ready as I'll ever be," I replied, the resolve settling in my bones like iron.

We stepped forward, each footfall echoing the rhythm of our hearts—a steady beat of hope and fear intertwined. As we approached the heart of the warehouse, a soft flicker of light caught my eye. The remnants of our battle had left the place in tatters, but one corner remained untouched, a small sanctuary of light amidst the chaos. There, in the glow, was a single photograph—a relic of what was once a thriving Neo Crescent, before the darkness consumed it.

"Look at that," Darian said, his voice barely above a whisper. He stepped closer, the shadows retreating as he approached the light. "This place used to be filled with laughter and life."

"Before the Syndicate turned it into a battleground," I replied, the weight of nostalgia heavy on my heart. "But it doesn't have to stay this way. We can rebuild."

Darian turned to face me, the intensity of his gaze igniting something deep within. "Together," he affirmed, the word hanging in the air like a promise.

Before I could respond, the atmosphere shifted, the air growing thicker with tension. From the shadows emerged the figure we had been anticipating—the Shadow Man, cloaked in darkness and menace. His laughter reverberated through the warehouse, chilling me to my core.

"Ah, the heroes of Neo Crescent," he sneered, his voice dripping with contempt. "Did you really think you could stop me? This city belongs to the Syndicate, and I will not let you take it from me."

"We're not afraid of you," I declared, the words escaping my lips before I could think twice. Fear and determination collided within me, igniting a fire I didn't know I had.

"Fear is a powerful motivator," he replied, his gaze flickering over Darian and me with a predatory gleam. "But love? That's a weakness I can exploit."

Darian stepped forward, a protective stance taking shape. "You don't know anything about us. Love isn't a weakness; it's our greatest strength."

"Is it?" The Shadow Man's voice dripped with sarcasm. "Let's put that theory to the test, shall we?"

With a swift motion, he lunged towards us, darkness swirling around him like a cloak. The world seemed to slow as I reacted instinctively, reaching for the weapon at my side. But in that instant, I felt the weight of the moment—the unspoken connection I shared with Darian. It was in that heartbeat that I realized our fates were intertwined, our hearts beating in sync, and together we could face the encroaching shadows.

"Now!" I shouted, rallying my strength. Darian and I surged forward, a united front against the darkness. The warehouse became a battlefield once more, our movements fluid as we fought side by side, anticipating each other's moves like dancers in a deadly waltz.

With every strike against the Shadow Man, I felt the shadows retreating, a tangible representation of our combined strength. The realization of our love forged in the heat of battle became a beacon of hope amidst the chaos. We weren't just fighting for ourselves or for

Neo Crescent; we were fighting for a future where light could once again prevail over darkness.

"Is that all you've got?" Darian taunted, his voice steady despite the danger surrounding us. "Because I'm just getting started!"

"Let's finish this," I replied, a fierce determination surging through me. Together, we were more than just two fighters; we were a force of nature, unstoppable and resolute in our quest for freedom.

As the final confrontation unfolded, I could see the flicker of uncertainty cross the Shadow Man's face—a crack in his facade that gave me hope. If we could make him question his own power, perhaps we could bring an end to his reign of terror.

"Neo Crescent belongs to its people," I declared, my voice rising above the chaos. "And we will not let you take it from us any longer!"

With that, we launched into one final attack, every ounce of our strength and resolve channeled into the moment. The air crackled with energy as we closed the distance, the culmination of our struggles culminating in this decisive confrontation. As the shadows of the Syndicate began to fade, a new dawn beckoned—one that held the promise of hope, love, and a future we could shape together.

The tension in the warehouse was nearly palpable, crackling in the air like static before a storm. As I stood shoulder to shoulder with Darian, a strange calm washed over me, a clarity born of the chaos. The Shadow Man loomed before us, an embodiment of the fears we had fought so hard to conquer. His form, shrouded in darkness, seemed to pulse with a life of its own, each heartbeat echoing the malevolence he exuded.

"Do you think you can save your precious city?" he taunted, his voice smooth as silk yet sharp as a blade. "You're just two lost souls in a sea of despair."

Darian scoffed, his defiance igniting a spark of hope within me. "Despair? That's rich coming from the guy hiding in the shadows. You should know by now, we thrive in the light."

As if the words themselves were a beacon, the flickering fluorescent lights overhead surged with energy, illuminating the debris-laden floor and casting long shadows that danced along the walls. It was a surreal moment, the juxtaposition of darkness and light, a metaphor for our struggle. In that instant, I realized we had the upper hand—not just against the Shadow Man, but in this battle for our souls.

"Let's show him what hope looks like," I said, my voice steady despite the uncertainty swirling in my gut.

With a nod, Darian and I moved in tandem, our bodies instinctively aligning as we executed the strategy we had rehearsed in countless skirmishes before. The choreography of our fight felt almost second nature, an unspoken language forged through trust and shared experience. We were warriors, yes, but more importantly, we were allies united by purpose.

"Hope?" the Shadow Man laughed, a chilling sound that sent shivers racing down my spine. "Hope is merely a mirage. You'll see."

In a swift motion, he launched himself at us, shadows trailing like a dark cloak. I reacted without thinking, stepping in front of Darian, the instinct to protect him bubbling to the surface. But before I could even draw my weapon, Darian intercepted, his arm shooting out to deflect the Shadow Man's attack. Their bodies collided with a force that sent a shockwave rippling through the air, and I braced myself for the impact.

"Keep your head in the game!" Darian shouted, wrestling with the darkness that enveloped the Shadow Man. "I'm not going to let him win!"

"Neither am I!" I replied, my voice tinged with resolve. I felt a surge of energy course through me, a fire ignited by the thought of what we stood to lose. I wouldn't let despair consume us—not now, not ever.

I took a step back to assess the situation. The shadows flickered and writhed around the Shadow Man, and I could see the flickers of his true self beneath the surface—a man twisted by power and bitterness, yet still human. Perhaps that was his greatest weakness. I aimed my weapon, not at his heart, but at the shadows themselves, the very essence of his power.

"Your strength is nothing without the light," I declared, my finger steady on the trigger. "You're nothing without the people of this city who have fought so hard to reclaim their home."

Darian grinned, his focus unwavering as he held the Shadow Man in place. "You hear that? We're coming for you, and there's nothing you can do to stop us!"

The Shadow Man's expression shifted, something akin to uncertainty flickering across his features. "You think you can threaten me with words? I will crush your hopes like the insects you are!"

"Not today, not ever," I retorted, pulling the trigger. A burst of light erupted from my weapon, illuminating the shadows that clung to the Shadow Man. The blast surged through the darkness, causing it to recoil as though it were a living thing, an organism wounded by the very essence of its being.

In that moment, I could see it—the vulnerability in his eyes, the flicker of fear. The shadows began to dissipate, and I could feel the tides turning. Hope surged within me, igniting a strength I hadn't realized I possessed. The city was our ally, its spirit rising with every step we took toward freedom.

"Together, Darian!" I called, extending my hand toward him, our fingers brushing as he joined me in this final stand against the encroaching darkness.

With a shared determination, we unleashed a wave of energy—our combined strength channeling into one final assault against the Shadow Man. As the light blazed brighter, illuminating the warehouse in a brilliant hue, I felt the chains of despair begin to shatter.

But just as victory seemed within our grasp, the Shadow Man roared, a guttural sound filled with rage and desperation. "You think you can defeat me? I am the darkness, and I will consume you both!"

A chilling wind swept through the room, extinguishing the light from our weapons and plunging us back into darkness. I stumbled, disoriented, and as I reached for Darian, I felt only emptiness where he should have been. Panic surged through me like ice water in my veins.

"Darian!" I shouted, fear slicing through the remnants of my resolve. The shadows twisted around me, a suffocating blanket threatening to pull me under.

"I'm right here!" his voice cut through the darkness, steady yet strained. "I won't let him take me. Just—just find me!"

I could sense him nearby, but the shadows seemed to shift and swirl with a life of their own, obscuring my vision and muffling my thoughts. I took a step forward, my heart racing as I fought to break free of the oppressive grip of the darkness. "We'll find a way out of this!"

But the Shadow Man's laughter echoed around me, a cruel reminder of his power. "You're too late, my dear. This is where hope comes to die!"

With a burst of determination, I fought against the shadows, calling upon the memories of our battles and the strength of our love. "You can't take us! Our fight is not over!"

As if fueled by my defiance, the light flickered back to life, illuminating the room in ghostly beams. I caught a glimpse of Darian's figure, barely visible through the oppressive darkness. My heart raced with renewed hope as I lunged toward him, desperate to bridge the distance between us.

But just as our fingers were about to intertwine, the shadows surged forward, pulling him away, an unseen force dragging him back into the abyss. "No!" I screamed, reaching out in vain, the darkness swallowing him whole.

The warehouse trembled, and I could feel the very foundations of our fight shattering around me. Despair clawed at my insides, threatening to consume me as I fought against the darkness. "Darian!"

The shadows laughed, a haunting symphony that echoed through the walls. "You'll never reclaim what you've lost! Your love is nothing against the darkness!"

In that moment, as the darkness closed in, I understood—this was not just a battle for Neo Crescent, but for our very souls. I was willing to face whatever darkness lay ahead, even if it meant stepping into the unknown to rescue the man I loved.

With a fierce determination, I gathered every ounce of strength I had left, ready to plunge into the depths of the shadows, unwilling to leave him behind. The last vestiges of hope flickered in my heart, and I knew this fight was far from over.

"Hold on, Darian!" I cried, the shadows swirling around me like a tempest, "I'm coming for you!"

Chapter 29: Rising from the Ashes

The air hummed with the soft whir of machinery, mingling with the scent of fresh paint and sweat, the unmistakable aroma of hope and renewal. As I stepped into what had once been the grand hall of Neo Crescent, now stripped bare and raw, I felt a spark of excitement flicker within me. The vaulted ceilings loomed overhead, empty and vast, waiting for laughter and life to return. Dust motes danced in the beams of sunlight breaking through the newly installed windows, illuminating the space like a promise.

Darian stood beside me, his expression a mix of determination and awe. He brushed his fingers over a scarred wooden beam, his touch gentle yet deliberate, as if he could coax its past back to life. "We can make this place a beacon," he said, his voice deep and steady, imbued with the weight of the moment. "A symbol of what we've overcome."

I turned to him, my heart swelling with admiration. He was my anchor, the embodiment of resilience, and I could feel the warmth radiating off him, pulling me closer as though the distance between us had never existed. "A beacon," I echoed, the word rolling off my tongue like a spell. It held the promise of transformation, of shifting the very fabric of our reality from ash to flame.

Outside, the world pulsed with the energy of rebirth. People milled about, some hauling debris away while others painted walls in vibrant hues of turquoise and coral. Children darted through the ruins, their laughter echoing like a chorus of angels, the sound weaving through the chaos and stitching it back together. I watched as a little girl with messy pigtails picked up a brush and began adding swirls of color to the wall, her eyes bright with enthusiasm. In that moment, I felt the layers of despair peeling away, exposing the foundation of our new reality.

"We should help," I said, glancing up at Darian, whose lips curved into a playful smirk. "I can't very well let you take all the credit for this masterpiece."

"Oh, I don't know," he teased, a glint of mischief dancing in his blue eyes. "Maybe I could use your delicate touch to ensure we don't end up with a Picasso on our hands."

I laughed, the sound bubbling up and spilling over, lightening the weight that had settled on my chest for far too long. "Watch it, or I'll paint you into a corner." I feigned a stern expression, knowing all too well I couldn't resist the way his laughter made me feel.

Together, we approached the wall, the smell of wet paint mingling with the scents of earth and sun. I took the brush from the girl, and she giggled, her eyes sparkling with mischief. "You have to add sparkles!" she declared, her tiny hands mimicking a grand gesture.

"Sparkles it is," I replied, grinning down at her. "What's life without a little magic?" I dipped the brush into a pot of shimmering glitter paint and added swirls of silver and gold alongside the bright colors already on the wall. The girl squealed with delight, clapping her hands as if she were witnessing a miracle.

As the hours slipped away, our laughter mingled with the sounds of labor, creating a symphony of new beginnings. The sun began to dip toward the horizon, painting the sky in hues of orange and purple, a vivid backdrop for our work. I stepped back to admire the mural that had come alive under our brushes, a kaleidoscope of joy reflecting our journey—a journey marked by trials and triumphs.

Darian moved beside me, his shoulder brushing against mine. "You know," he said, his voice a low rumble, "this feels like more than just rebuilding a town. It's like we're rewriting our story."

"Rewriting our story," I mused, the thought igniting a fire within me. "And who says we can't add a few plot twists along the way?"

"Oh, I can definitely think of a few," he replied, his tone serious, but his eyes sparkled with humor. "Like perhaps throwing in a rogue dragon or a band of misfit heroes?"

I shook my head, a smile creeping onto my face. "Only if you promise to slay the dragon."

"Deal," he said, and in that moment, the air between us shimmered with unspoken promises and dreams yet to be realized.

As the stars began to peek through the deepening twilight, I felt a rush of emotion swell within me. "What if we don't just rebuild Neo Crescent?" I asked, my voice barely above a whisper. "What if we turn it into something extraordinary?"

"Extraordinary," he echoed, the weight of the word hanging between us like a challenge. "What do you have in mind?"

I took a deep breath, summoning my wildest ideas, the kind that had always danced just beyond my reach. "What if we create a community where everyone has a role? A place where talents are celebrated and dreams are nurtured?"

His brow furrowed in thought, and I could see the wheels turning behind his eyes. "Like an artist's enclave?"

"Exactly! Imagine workshops, galleries, a place for creativity to thrive." The words tumbled out, fueled by an energy I hadn't realized was building inside me. "We could host festivals, invite artisans from afar, and create a melting pot of culture right here."

"Now that's a plot twist I can get behind," he said, his smile wide and genuine. "Let's bring the fire back to this place."

As the last remnants of daylight faded into the embrace of night, I knew we were on the brink of something breathtaking. With Darian by my side, the shadows that had once threatened to engulf us now flickered like fleeting memories, replaced by the vibrant pulse of possibility and the sweet thrill of a future unwritten.

The next morning dawned crisp and clear, the sun spilling over the horizon like melted butter on warm toast. I stood in the newly revitalized square of Neo Crescent, feeling invigorated by the scent of fresh earth and blooming flowers. The vibrant mural we had painted the night before gleamed in the sunlight, a colorful explosion that seemed to breathe life into the very stones beneath our feet.

Darian was already there, surveying our handiwork with a look of contentment that made my heart flutter. He was in his element, moving from group to group, a natural leader coaxing life back into our community. "How's it look?" I called out, planting my hands on my hips, trying to mimic his confident stance.

He turned, a grin spreading across his face, and my breath caught. "Like a piece of art in progress," he replied, his voice warm, wrapping around me like a favorite sweater. "But it needs more. We're just getting started."

His enthusiasm was contagious, and I found myself itching to dive deeper into the project. "What's next on our to-do list, oh fearless leader?"

"Planting," he said, his eyes twinkling with mischief. "We need to bring some greenery into this square. A garden of sorts, something that will flourish like our hopes." He gestured toward a patch of earth that had been cleared, its dark soil glistening in the morning light.

"Like a sanctuary?" I asked, picturing a riot of colors with every flower contributing to the symphony of our new life. "Something that can grow, even when the world feels like it's falling apart?"

"Exactly," he replied, nodding vigorously. "And we can make it interactive. People can come together to plant their own flowers—something personal that represents them."

I loved the idea. "What if we have a 'memory tree' as well? A place where people can hang notes about what they want to remember or let go of?"

"Now that's a brilliant twist," he said, his approval sparking something vibrant inside me. "I can see it now: families gathering, planting seeds, telling stories, sharing laughter. It'll become a living history of Neo Crescent."

We set to work immediately, gathering supplies and rallying the townsfolk. The square soon filled with the energy of camaraderie, laughter punctuating the air as neighbors reconnected over shovels and seed packets. I found myself sidetracked by a small group of children, their eager faces lit up with excitement. They crowded around me, their small hands outstretched, demanding attention.

"What are we planting?" one little boy asked, his eyes wide with wonder.

"Sunflowers!" I exclaimed, holding up a handful of seeds. "They'll grow tall and strong, just like us."

"Can we plant them, too?" a girl with curly hair bounced on her toes, enthusiasm practically radiating off her.

"Of course!" I laughed, her joy infectious. "The more hands, the better! Who wants to help me dig?"

In moments, we had formed an impromptu gardening team, dirt smeared on cheeks and laughter ringing through the square. The sun beat down on us, the world feeling alive and electric. The air was thick with the scent of soil and sweat, a perfect blend of effort and aspiration.

Darian moved among the crowd, checking in on everyone, his presence a stabilizing force. He helped an elderly man kneel down to plant tulips, his hands gentle and respectful, as if he were crafting something sacred. I could see the respect they shared, a bridge between generations, and it filled me with warmth.

Just as I was about to plant another sunflower seed, the cheerful atmosphere shifted. A figure appeared at the edge of the square, silhouetted against the light. My heart skipped. It was Miranda, the town's self-proclaimed "guardian of the gossip," and I knew she had come armed with news, potentially scandalous.

"Look who decided to grace us with her presence," I quipped, pretending to be unimpressed, but inwardly I was curious.

"Don't be coy, darling," she said, striding over, her heels clicking against the pavement. "I bring tidings from the north."

"Please tell me you didn't bring the 'Dreaded Council' with you," Darian joked, stepping closer, his posture protective, yet his eyes were alight with amusement.

"Worse," she replied, her tone grave, eyes darting around the square as if to assess our growing community. "I have a proposal from the neighboring town."

"What kind of proposal?" I asked, my voice steady, but my stomach tightened.

Miranda smiled, though there was a hint of something dark lurking behind it. "They want to merge resources. You know how their crops suffered last year. They're facing shortages, and they think we can help. But there's a catch."

"What's the catch?" Darian leaned in, his expression shifting to one of concern.

"They want a partnership, and that means sharing our space, our plans, our dreams." She shrugged nonchalantly, but the weight of her words hung heavily in the air. "They'll want to have a say in how we move forward, and I'm not sure they'll have our best interests at heart."

Darian and I exchanged glances, the implications of her words sinking in. What had started as a hopeful endeavor could quickly become a political minefield, ripe for conflict. "Let's hear them out," I suggested, my mind racing with the possibilities. "Maybe there's a way to collaborate that could benefit both sides."

"But at what cost?" Darian's voice was low, contemplative.

"Every relationship has its price," I replied, feeling a wave of resolve wash over me. "If we can strike a balance, we might build something that could withstand anything thrown at us."

Miranda smiled, a flicker of approval crossing her face. "Now that's the spirit! I knew you'd rise to the occasion."

As we stood amidst the children, flowers, and fresh beginnings, I realized that every challenge brought us closer, testing the very foundation of our hopes. The sun dipped lower, casting long shadows across the square, but I felt emboldened by the pulse of our community, a heartbeat that resonated with the promise of tomorrow. Whatever lay ahead, I knew we would face it together, united by the dreams we dared to chase.

The air crackled with energy as the townsfolk gathered around the central square, their faces alight with anticipation. Word had spread quickly about the proposal from the neighboring town, and now the vibrant community of Neo Crescent was buzzing with a mixture of excitement and trepidation. I felt a weight settle on my shoulders, an understanding that our decision would ripple through the fabric of our newly revitalized home.

Darian stood beside me, his expression a blend of determination and uncertainty. "Are you ready for this?" he asked, his voice low, just for me. The sun glinted off his hair, making him look almost ethereal, and I was reminded, yet again, how much this man grounded me.

"Ready as I'll ever be," I replied, matching his gaze. "If we're going to face the future, we have to do it together. No matter what they throw at us."

He nodded, squeezing my hand, and I could feel the warmth of his resolve bolster my own. The gathering of neighbors and friends began to hum with chatter, each voice a thread weaving us closer together.

Miranda climbed onto a makeshift stage at the far end of the square, her presence commanding. "Thank you all for coming!" she called out, her voice rising above the din. "Today, we stand at a crossroads. A proposal has come to us from our neighboring town, and while they face challenges, we have a unique opportunity before us."

I watched as she gestured toward a tall man with dark hair standing beside her, who seemed to exude an air of authority. He wore a crisp white shirt, buttoned up to the collar, and a confident smile that made me uneasy. I couldn't help but wonder if he believed charm would win us over.

"My name is Felix," he introduced himself, his voice smooth and polished. "I'm here to discuss how we can collaborate to ensure both our communities thrive." His eyes swept over the crowd, taking in the faces of the people who had worked so hard to rebuild.

"Collaboration," I whispered to Darian, skepticism curling my lips. "Sounds like a fancy word for 'we need your help.'"

Felix continued, unfazed by the undercurrent of murmurs. "The past year has been tough on our crops, and we recognize the potential in Neo Crescent. We're here to propose a partnership, one where resources and knowledge can be shared. Together, we can fortify our futures."

A ripple of uncertainty swept through the crowd. I could see it in the tightness of my neighbors' expressions, the way they exchanged glances that spoke volumes. I could feel their hesitance, the lingering doubts that echoed my own.

"What's in it for you?" a voice called out from the back. It was old Mr. Thompson, a longtime resident with a reputation for his bluntness. "You've come here asking for help, but what do you plan to take?"

Felix's smile didn't waver. "We're not asking for charity, Mr. Thompson. We believe in a mutually beneficial relationship. Our resources can be pooled, our skills combined." He paused, looking thoughtfully at the crowd. "Imagine what we could achieve together—joint festivals, shared markets, a thriving cultural exchange."

"Cultural exchange?" I echoed under my breath. "Sounds like a one-way ticket to our culture disappearing."

Darian leaned closer, his voice low. "We need to tread carefully. We don't know their true intentions."

As Felix continued to speak, I let my eyes drift over the crowd, searching for familiar faces. The warmth of community pulsed in my chest, but there was an unmistakable tension in the air, like the calm before a storm.

Just as I thought the tension might break, a woman stepped forward from the back of the crowd. She was tall and imposing, with fiery red hair cascading down her back, making her look like a force of nature. "We don't need you," she declared, her voice cutting through the chatter like a knife. "We've worked too hard to rebuild our lives to let someone else dictate our future."

Felix's demeanor shifted, irritation flickering across his features. "And I assure you, we're not here to dictate anything. We want to help."

"I don't see any helping happening here," the woman shot back, arms crossed defiantly. "We've had enough of outsiders coming in and telling us how to run our lives."

Her boldness resonated with the crowd, sparking murmurs of agreement. I felt a swell of pride; her passion reminded me of the fire that had ignited within us all during our rebuilding. But beneath the surface, I could sense the tension building, like a storm gathering strength.

"Let's not make hasty decisions," I interjected, stepping forward, wanting to calm the brewing storm. "What we have is precious. We've built this community from the ground up, and we owe it to ourselves to consider our options. But we also need to remain open to new ideas."

Felix nodded, taking my cue. "Exactly. We're not asking for blind trust. Let's discuss this openly and see if there's a path forward that respects both our communities."

Miranda stepped in, her eyes sparkling with intrigue. "Perhaps a town hall meeting is in order? We can hear out everyone's concerns and suggestions before deciding."

The murmurs shifted, a sense of calm settling over the crowd as they began to ponder the possibilities. But I could feel the undercurrents of tension still lurking beneath, a pressure that threatened to erupt.

As the discussion unfolded, I felt a shiver run down my spine. Something wasn't quite right; the air felt charged, and I could see Felix's demeanor change subtly, his smile fading as he exchanged glances with the tall woman standing behind him. She had been watching, and I could sense a silent communication passing between them, a shared understanding that sent my instincts into overdrive.

"Wait," I said suddenly, my heart racing. "What do you really want from us?"

Felix hesitated, the mask slipping momentarily, revealing something darker beneath. "What we want is simply... unity," he replied, his tone measured, yet something in his eyes hinted at a different truth.

The crowd shifted, the atmosphere thickening. It felt like a rubber band stretched to its breaking point, and I could almost hear the snap that would follow if we weren't careful.

Then, just as the tension reached a boiling point, a loud crash echoed through the square, a sound so jarring it brought everything to a standstill. We all turned as a figure burst into the square, breathless and wild-eyed, clutching a piece of parchment like it was the last lifeline in a sinking ship.

"Help!" the newcomer shouted, her voice cracking with urgency. "You have to listen! They're coming!"

A palpable silence fell over the crowd, every eye locked on her as my heart raced with a mix of dread and curiosity. The air felt electric, the world narrowing down to her next words.

And in that moment, the future of Neo Crescent hung precariously in the balance, teetering on the edge of a knife, ready to plunge into chaos or salvation.

Milton Keynes UK
Ingram Content Group UK Ltd.
UKHW030855151124
451262UK00001B/132